THE LANTERN-LIT CITY

SOVEREIGNS OF THE DEAD: BOOK ONE

VISTA MCDOWALL

Library of Congress Control Number: 2020906923

ISBN: 0-9795113-4-8
ISBN-13: 978-0-9795113-4-9

For Dad, who always told me I'd be a better writer than an actress.

You were right.

PART ONE

CHAPTER ONE
Cara

ULTON THE COOK lay dead on the table. No scars nor wounds traced his pale corpse, yet the unmistakable air of murder clenched to him.

Around him, the manor home lay silent and still. On a normal night, Ulton would be cleaning his kitchens with the help of a scullery maid while the steward readied the stock lists for the following day. As the lady of the house prepared for bed, the watchman and his apprentice would check the manor's perimeter walls.

But this night, the lady of the house had vanished into the void, and Ulton lay dead on the large oak table in the great hall, seeming peacefully asleep. Havershim the steward, Merick the watchman, and Cara his apprentice stared at the corpse. Merick grunted and leaned back, his hand held tightly to a rag on his stomach. Blood soaked through it, stinking strangely of decay.

"I'll get you another one," Cara mumbled. She staggered to her feet and left the room to pull an armful of blankets from the chest at the end of the hall. For just a moment, she leaned her forehead against the wall and dragged in a long breath. Her lungs still felt full of that overwhelming stench...

Merick pulled at the chain around the gate, satisfied. In the darkness beyond, Cara could see the silhouettes of trees and shrubs lining the road to the village. She followed her master along the wall, somewhat bored with the routine. As she breathed deeply of the warm late-summer air, Cara gagged. She took another breath, and found not sweet pine in her nose, but old eggs and feces mixed with a sickly sweet odor.

The ground shook, throwing Cara and Merick off their feet. As they struggled up, a purplish hue spread out from the manor house, struck through with veins of deepest black. A low whine buzzed in their ears, and the stench crept into their mouths and throats, choking them.

Cara shook her head to dispel the memory. She swallowed and found that her throat opened up again. She wouldn't focus on those thoughts, wouldn't awaken the monster inside her that rose at such pain. *Build the walls*, she reminded herself. *Keep the beast below.* Back in the great hall, she saw that Merick had lain down on the bench, one eye cracked open.

Merick took a blanket and pressed it to his stomach. He asked, "Is the girl back yet?"

"No," Cara said. "It shouldn't be long now." The scullery maid, upon seeing Merick's injury, had bravely resisted fainting and went to fetch the local healer.

They sat in silence, each trying to understand the night's occurrences. The Nellestere Manor, which ran the fief in and around the village of Kell, had always been peaceful and quiet. Markets occupied the town square once a quinn in summer and once a deshe in winter – every five and ten days, respectively – and the manor's lord held harvest and spring festivals on the estate each year. Mountains surrounded the large valley, summers brought ample sunshine for crops, spring rains were cool and plentiful, and bountiful harvests came each autumn.

Nothing strange nor unexplained had ever happened in the Nellestere fief.

Cara ran through the dim light toward the house, her breath ragged. Each step fought against the power of an ocean wave, the purple light trying to pull her feet out from under her. Normal evening sounds were lost in a cloud of otherworldly silence. A journey that should only have taken a few minutes seemed to last twice as long as Cara and Merick swam through the darkness.

4

Cara rolled her shoulders. Her limbs ached from the effort of that journey, her legs trembling under the table. Deep within the dark places of her belly, the beast stirred. She clenched a fist over it, urging it to stay down. *Not tonight*, she prayed. *I can't deal with you tonight.*

"What's going on?"

The three survivors jerked their heads up. The new stablehand, Sandu, stood at the door. He cautiously stepped forward, looking between them and the corpse on the table. His clothes smelled of horse and dirt speckled his face. "Good gods, what happened here?"

"Maid Nellestere is gone," Havershim gritted out. "Someone took her."

"Some magical bastard," said Merick. "Ulton were the only one in the room when it happened. He were already dead when we ran in. We saw...there were a..." Words weren't enough, so he stopped trying.

A void, blacker than black, as tall as a stained glass window and twice as wide, hung in the air of the great hall, the purplish light emanating from it. Black tentacles burst from the void, and, between them stood a hooded figure in dark robes, a shining light emanating from his hand. Cara froze on the threshold, transfixed. Her friend and lady, Renna Nellestere, stood tall in the center of the room, her long blonde hair rising around her in a crackling halo. Ulton was dead on the floor in front of her. The hooded man held out his free hand, and, as if in a trance, Renna stepped forward.

Merick shouted and ran at the figure, drawing his sword. With barely a glance at Merick, the stranger waved his hand. A black tentacle lashed out, striking Merick's torso and sending him sprawling across the floor toward Cara. She knelt beside him, and when she looked back up, the man and Renna had vanished into the void.

A lump formed in Cara's throat. She swallowed past it and blinked away tears. She had failed her lady, her only friend. Who knew what dark rituals the hooded man had in store for poor Renna?

"Gods." Sandu sank onto the bench. "Ulton doesn't even look hurt. Like he could be sleeping."

"Black magic," Merick said darkly. "No other explanation for it."

The scullery maid appeared just outside the great hall. An older woman with flyaway hair pushed her way past the maid, carrying a large bag that smelled of herbs and spices and clinked as she walked. The woman paused, taking in the scene, then hurried into the room.

Havershim sent the maid away. "Go home and try to get some sleep, there's a good girl. I'll send for you in the morning. But not a word to anyone else, understand? Not until we know what's going on."

The scullery maid hurried away. Cara made room on the bench for the healer and asked, "Is he badly hurt?"

The healer, Madame Freebane, peeled off the blanket and lifted Merick's shirt. Tutting to herself, she rummaged through her leather bag. "He'll live, I should think. Needs rest, though, for a few days at least. And a poultice changed every few candles. The cut isn't deep enough to require stitching, but the edges–"

"Just the poultice," Merick grunted. "And some o' your special potion as makes the pain go away."

"I haven't any sweet-milk on hand," Freebane said. "But the poultice will help. So Ulton's really dead. I hadn't quite believed poor Ella. Where's Maid Nellestere?"

"We don't know," Cara said. "There's been dark magic here tonight."

"Clearly. See the edges of Merick's wound? They're black and hard. This isn't the work of a blade or bludgeon. Were you struck by the magic?" Freebane asked. Merick nodded.

"Mm. Then we must pray the poultice is effective against such things." Madame Freebane quickly packed the cut, then wrapped a bandage around Merick's torso. Cara merely watched, tiredness settling on her. Part of her wished she had been the one to rush forward, to take the magical blow...maybe then she wouldn't have been so useless.

For almost as long as she could remember, Cara had been apprenticed under Merick. He was an ex-mercenary, and though he balked at teaching a girl how to fight, he agreed after seeing the sack of gold her mother offered him. Cara, only five years old at the time, cried and clung to her mother at the sight of Merick's cragged cheeks, partly-missing nose, and roped scars. He had leaned over her, breath smelling of beer, and tousled her hair. She remembered his callused hands being incongruously gentle. That first night, he told a story in his gruff voice of a warrior who rescued a child from a witch. It became her favorite, and she begged him to tell it for many years. But as she grew older, stories turned into explanations of battles and fighting, small lectures on survival or teamwork. Lessons turned into practical applications of sword and shield, then into daily sparring. When he was hired as the watchman of the Nellestere house, he brought Cara with him and assigned her to protect the lord's daughter, Renna. By that time, she no longer thought of his scars as frightening: they told their own story.

He had also taught her to be brave, in those dark moments when the beast overcame her and she couldn't control the rage and fear that welled up with it. He lent her his courage. Cara vowed that her fits, as she called them, wouldn't interfere with her duty to Renna.

But Cara hadn't stopped Renna's kidnapping. She hadn't leapt forward as Merick had. All those years of sparring, training, and patrolling, yet when Renna needed her most, she did nothing.

"We have to tell Earl Stonetree," Havershim said. Madame Freebane closed her bag, but did not leave.

"And who'll go?" Merick asked. "You?"

"Well," Havershim blustered, "I'm not sure travel would be good for me. Bad humors, and all that. You and Cara should go."

"Merick's not fit for the road," Freebane said.

"Then just Cara," Havershim said. "She's got her sword, hasn't she? And she's young enough, the trip won't be hardly a bother."

"No chance in the nine hells am I send'n Cara off on her own," Merick grunted.

"I'm perfectly capable–" Cara started, but Sandu interrupted her.

"Earl Stonetree won't be at his keep," Sandu said.

"Why not?" Havershim asked.

"Because of the Masque. All the earls and nobles will be in Riverfen by now for the month of parties before the festival."

"Mott is on the way," Cara said, latching onto the idea. "If anyone would know anything about magic and sorcery, it would be the scholars there. They might be able to tell us who could possess such powers."

"'We'? Who's this 'we'?" Havershim protested. "Merick and I should stay here, and Sandu knows nothing about Renna – no offense meant, lad, but you see–"

"I know the roads to Riverfen and Mott," Sandu interjected. "I used to peddle goods all along these mountains. Merick doesn't want Cara to go alone, so I'll go with her."

"Why would you bother? You're not a proper member of this household," Havershim said.

"I'm not send'n Cara off alone, nor with a stablehand," Merick said. "If'n she leaves this house, I'm goin' with her."

"Not with an injury like that!" Madame Freebane said.

"Try and bloody well stop me, woman!"

"I still think that Stonetree is the best place–"

"What good would that do if'n the earl ain't even there?"

Havershim, Merick, and Madame Freebane yelled over each other.

"Well, the earl may not have left yet! And it's our duty to report to him the goings-on of this household."

"And what if'n Maid Nellestere is killed afore we can get to her? Would the *duty* of tell'n the earl have helped her at all?"

"You can't help anyone if you die on the road, Merick!"

The table quieted for a moment, the air hanging with seething anger. The three glared at each other, and Cara caught Sandu's eye. He quirked a brow, a silent question. Before any of them could start shouting again, before she could second-guess herself, Cara said, "Renna is my mistress, and I vowed to protect her. I'm going to Mott, and then on to Riverfen. Sandu knows the roads; I don't. He'll come with me, and we'll bring Renna's horse in case we find her. Havershim should send a messenger with a letter to Stonetree in case the earl hasn't left yet, and then wait here: tell the staff what they need to know, arrange a burial for Ulton, and keep the house running until we return." For a second, everyone was speechless, taken aback by her confidence. A confidence Cara felt was plainly false. Freebane sank slowly into her seat as Havershim and Merick awkwardly looked away from each other. In that moment, Cara could plainly see their fatigue.

"And what about me?" Merick asked.

Not meeting Freebane's eye, Cara said, "I can't force you to do anything you don't want to do. If you feel well enough, I think you should come with me. If not–"

"I'm well enough."

"Hmph," Madame Freebane snorted. "And what if that wound doesn't close properly?"

"Then I'll find another healer. You're not the only one in the damn country."

"We can take some of your salves and potions," Cara said quickly as Freebane's nostrils flared. "You've shown me well enough how to pack and bandage a wound."

Madame Freebane sniffed, but nodded. She pulled out more bandages, two vials, and a handful of moss. Giving the lot to Cara, she said, "Use the moss to pack in the salve, which is the blue ointment. There should be enough bandages to last two or three changes, but you'll have to buy more after that. The green liquid is a few mouthfuls of jirriloe. A few drops at a time can be a powerful sedative, but too much will kill."

"Thank you." Cara laid the bandages and moss on the table, then placed the vials in the pouch she kept on her belt. She looked to the rest of the group. "We'll leave in the morning. Sandu, can you prepare our horses and Renna's gelding for the trip? Merick, you should rest tonight. I'll make sure we have rations and full water bladders."

To Cara's surprise, none of the others argued. They all looked *vecking* tired. After covering Ulton's body with a blanket, Havershim went upstairs, his steps dragging. Madame Freebane wished them good luck before departing. Merick clapped a hand to Cara's shoulder, and asked in a low voice, "Are you sure you've got the humors for this, Cari?" He didn't need to ask aloud, but Cara knew he referred to her fits, those times when the beast rose from its hiding place. *If I had the time, I could conquer them...but I don't. Renna doesn't.* Cara nodded to Merick, and he squeezed her affectionately, then left. Cara listened as he went up the stairs, the sounds pausing every other step. *He hurts*, she thought, wishing she could do more.

Soon, only Cara and Sandu remained in the great hall with poor Ulton.

"Why do *you* want to go to Riverfen?" Cara asked. "It can't just be for Renna's sake."

Sandu shrugged. "Assuming we don't find your mistress, then I'll be needing a new job. Riverfen's the place for that now, what with the Masque and all. If we do somehow get lucky and find her, then I've had a bit of an adventure."

"That's not how most people would see it."

"I get bored easily."

Cara gave him a funny look. "Aren't you afraid of the man who took Renna? He killed Ulton."

"Not really. I'm a coward – if there's any fighting, I'll just run away 'til it's over." Sandu stood up, stretched, and said, "I better go now. Goodnight. I'll see you bright and early."

Cara watched him leave. She had often dreamt of grand adventures and shining knights. When she and Renna were little, Renna would play the damsel while Cara pretended to be a brave knight come to her rescue. But their games had never included the stink of death or the cold body left over after the fight.

If all went as planned, their travels would take them to Mott, the ancient city of scholars with its enormous libraries where countless secrets lay hidden in stacks and tomes. And then they would go to Riverfen, the city of lights, where every night thousands of lanterns of all colors were lit and strung over the streets and canals. *Like the land of the faeries*, Cara's mother had said when Cara was very young. *A land where magic is real and good always wins in the end.*

Even once the fire had gone out, Cara stayed up for a long time. She didn't know why, but being alone with Ulton's corpse didn't frighten her. Squeezing his cold hand, she said, "I'll find Renna and bring her home. I promise you, your death will not have been for nothing." Having no idea what else to say, Cara said no more, and went up to bed. Sleep evaded her, and as morning came bright and clear, she wondered what the journey ahead would bring. The heroes from the old ballads always succeeded in their noble quests. *But this isn't an old ballad, and we're not the heroes. Merick has no shining armor, Sandu's a stablehand, and I'm a girl. Who's ever heard of a girl saving the fair lady?*

CHAPTER TWO
Sandu

MONTHS BEFORE he found the Nellestere manor stricken with dark magic, Sandu had been a peddler. One night, ill luck caused him to sleep in the stables of an inn. Though the spring winds blew hard outside, here at least he was warm. A lantern shone with comfortable light, giving a soft glow to an otherwise dull scene. The hay on the floor had been replaced only that day and smelled sweetly. His horse, Galen, stood sleeping to one side, her tack piled haphazardly on the floor, her chin resting on the partition between stalls. If she were to unexpectedly stamp her hoof, it might land on Sandu's foot as he lay sprawled across the straw, propped up by the saddle he bought with his reward money. It wasn't quality, by any means, and had to have its leather straps and buckles replaced soon after he bought it, but it was his. All he owned in the world, in fact, had been carelessly strewn around this stall.

A man of the world – so he liked to think of himself – Sandu Crin often had no place to sleep *but* the natural world. This warm stable, sheltered from late snows, was a luxury he couldn't often afford. Most things, really, were luxuries he couldn't afford. His horse was a gift from another peddler, his gear bought second-hand and amassed slowly over the years. He couldn't remember the last time he had worn a new, perfectly clean shirt. Even his beard, which he preferred to keep trim, had grown unruly during his long journey through the mountains.

Tonight, Sandu had gambled away his money for a room. Since the stable had already been paid for, it was here that he would sleep. Galen wouldn't mind, as she was quite used to him sleeping near her.

I have to stop playing cards, Sandu chastised himself.

Sleep eluded him, and a nagging sense of responsibility finally pushed him to take a worn piece of parchment from the smallest pocket of his knapsack. He knew this list well: he had carried it for years as part of his duties for the Peddler's Guild. The first quinn he held it, he nearly threw it into the fire when a name crossed itself out and another one was added as if with an invisible hand. When he'd asked his master at the Guild, the master laughed and said, "Of course it's magic, dolt. How else are the peddlers supposed to keep track of marks if we don't have a way to communicate all over D'Ehsen?" Eventually, Sandu crossed names and jobs off, knowing that peddlers all over would see that he had completed the task.

Only after he had become a full Guild member did they trust him with the list. Peddlers, being known by most people and rarely questioned, had duties for the Guild beyond selling and buying wares: finding a missing person, collecting a debt or stolen item, delivering a sensitive message. Some jobs were more difficult than those, requiring months of spying and subterfuge. They paid the best reward, but...

But nothing. Sandu shook his head. *Money is money.*

Perusing the list, he noted the tasks still open, and the rewards. Good jobs. Simple ones, too. One name kept floating above the others. Sandu devoted a full second to it, then looked away, up at Galen, then back, holding the name as he would a stare. With an effort, he took out his quill, dipped it in nearly-gone ink, and crossed out the words 'Fauste's Shiv - Notably Jagger Cross.' *If only I didn't have to. If only I had said 'no' to that money. Jagger might still be alive.* Jagger was dead, not personally by Sandu's hands, but by his words. One report to the right soldiers, and an entire keep of people had been wiped out. Few of them innocent, it was true, for Fauste's Shiv had hired out criminals for various misdeeds ranging from larceny to murder. Yet how many lives had been ended too early? How many–

Stop it. Look to the next job, Sandu chided himself. *You made that choice, you have to live with it.*

As he scanned the list, Sandu saw a name that hadn't been there just the night before: 'Maid Caralyn Gellder. Reward of five marks for delivering to High Peddler Laris Stanthorpe.' Sandu chewed his lip. A reward offered by the high peddler himself! If Stanthorpe set a target...almost every peddler would be after it. But five whole marks. That could buy a good saddle, food for months, beds in decent inns, new clothes, a fine wool cloak...and possibly his father's freedom.

After pricking the back of his hand with the quill, Sandu slowly wrote his name in his own blood, marking his intention to find Maid Gellder.

The weather took a turn for the worse as Sandu traveled down from Skålland into Dotschar. Hail pounded the summer leaves to the ground before autumn had a chance at them. A blanket around his head provided Sandu's only protection, though it was a thin ratty thing. His brown hair turned black with the moisture. Poor Galen had nothing against the hail. She plodded onward, his stalwart steed, her coat desperately in need of brushing and her mane and tail tangled.

From village to village, Sandu made his slow way over the mountains toward Kell. After he circled the name, more information had been transcribed to his bit of paper: *Maid Gellder is a young woman, about twenty, dark hair, Dotsch-Gall. Known to be working at the Nellestere Manor in Kell. To be delivered alive to Stanthorpe at the Guild's property in Riverfen.*

For the most part, Sandu stayed on the larger roads, sleeping beneath wayfarer pines or in barns, though he left before the farmers woke up. A full two deshes after starting, he finally reached Kell. He paid for a drink at the inn (his purse nearly empty now), and listened to the talk of the town. From what he gathered, Maid Nellestere's father had recently died of the White Plague, leaving her a ward of Earl Stonetree. The lady and her household still lived in Kell, though she would be taken to Stonetree by the end of the summer.

What interested Sandu most, though, was the news that the manor's stable hand had also perished, leaving a position open.

As he rode alongside Cara and Merick, Sandu couldn't help but feel horribly under-armed. Each of them carried a sword and a dagger while he only had a small knife. Cara rode straight and tall, her hips flowing with the horse's gait, while Merick slumped in his saddle, one hand held tight around his stomach. Sandu noticed Cara's inquiring touch and Merick shaking his head. *Curious. I wonder if he'll actually change his poultice as often as the healer ordered.*

Only a deshe after Sandu came to the manor, Maid Nellestere went missing. He had only eaten dinner around Cara a few times in that span, as she often ate with the lady, and he hadn't tried getting to know Merick. Both of them paid him little attention. It was all for the best that the lady had been taken, otherwise Sandu hadn't known how he would extract Cara from the manor.

Late the first morning – after two candles of near silence – Sandu spoke up, "How long have you worked for the Nellesteres?"

"Must be abou' ten years, eh, Cari?" said Merick. As the morning progressed, he gradually straightened in his saddle, only wincing now and then as his horse corrected a misstep.

"Almost thirteen," Cara corrected him. "We started there when I was seven."

"Damn, that long?" Merick chuckled, then coughed. He waved away Cara's concern.

Cara turned to Sandu. "Merick and I stayed in a bunkhouse in the lowlands when I first apprenticed with him. But, my mother's coin ran out, and he had to take a position in order to keep me. That's when he became watchman for the Nellesteres."

"What are you apprenticing for?" Sandu asked. "I've watched you training in the yard each day, so I thought maybe you were to become the watchman after him. But then I wondered why Merick wouldn't take up a boy instead as his apprentice."

"My mother paid him–" Cara started, but Merick said over her, "Shoulda asked for more coin! You've been more hassle than you're worth."

Rolling her eyes at him and smiling, Cara continued, "Merick used to be a mercenary, and Mother had him take me on. She wanted me taught to use a sword, as well as how to wear armor and lay out strategies for battle. Merick becoming a watchman was only to pay for our food and lodging."

"So...you're a soldier, then?"

"Of a sort. It's not as if any knights would take me on as a page, so this seemed the best course in Mother's opinion."

"But *why*?" Sandu had never heard of a female soldier, much less a woman taking up arms as a knight. True, there were stories and ballads of old that spoke of Skallish shieldmaidens, and he knew that faraway places like the Eadrion Empire conscripted women as well as men for their armies, but he had never seen or heard of it in Dotschar. "Why not smithing, or tailoring, or any other Guild trades? Why *fighting*? You've not exactly got a warrior's build."

"You'd have to ask Mother," Cara said. She looked sideways at Merick. "Whenever I ask him, he just tells me to shut up and keep running through my forms."

"Cause your forms are shoddy and your arms are weak," Merick grunted. Beneath his gruffness, though, Sandu thought he saw the hint of a smile.

"Your mother has strange opinions," Sandu said. "What does *she* do, then? Your apprenticeship must have cost a fortune."

"I've no clue. She's not very talkative about her life, even on the rare occasion I see her. She could be an heiress or the mistress of a grand lord for all I know. She also paid a scholar from Mott to stay with us and teach me to read and write, as well as basic mathematics and Dotsch history."

Sandu whistled. "Most noble ladies don't receive an education like that."

"No," Cara said simply. "I'm grateful for what Mother's done for me. And Merick, for that matter, despite his constant whinging."

"I don't whinge," Merick said. "Whingin's for women. I grumble."

"Where are you from?" Cara asked Sandu.

"Barrowfort originally. I've not had roots anywhere for a few years, though." Despite himself, Sandu enjoyed the easy conversation. He knew he couldn't afford to befriend this girl, and that the watchman would prove an obstacle, but he had never been one for stoic silence.

They passed the rest of that day chatting about light subjects. When evening came, Merick found them a place to camp. Sandu built up a fire and watched Merick bark out numbers as Cara went through her forms, first without a sword and then with it. She turned gracefully, her muscles fluid under her tunic. Unlike many other rustic women, she wore breeches under her simple dress. Her skirts were open at the sides, allowing her legs free movement.

Even with her unusual education, Sandu couldn't fathom why Stanthorpe wanted Cara Gellder. Her looks, while pretty, were common enough: she had pale yet ruddy skin and long, dark, curly hair in a single braid down her back. Her hands had calluses on them, and all of her dresses were torn, dirtied, or otherwise unkempt. People on the road barely looked at her or Sandu. If anything, Sandu would have expected Merick, the ex-mercenary with a checkered past, to be the target.

Why would anyone pay five marks for a rustic girl?

"Aren't you two going to spar?" Sandu asked when Merick and Cara unpacked their haversacks.

Cara looked to Merick. He shook his head. "Not quite up to it yet. Give me a few days an' I'll be fresh as grass."

The next three days passed in much the same manner: slightly before dawn, Merick had Cara go through her forms, then they'd all pack up and leave their camp not half a candle later and ride until noon. Once they'd eaten and their horses rested, they'd ride again until a candle before dark. Merick went off to change his poultice, refusing help from the others. When Sandu lit the fire to cook each night, Cara practiced. Their conversations never strayed beyond polite acquaintanceship.

The fifth evening, Merick called back, "There's a journeyer's tower up ahead. We can stay there tonight."

Saddle-sore and irritable – it rained on them nearly the whole day – the trio tied their four horses on the leeward side of the tower before stumbling inside. The tower had two levels, one below with a fire pit and room for blankets, and one above with yet more sleeping space. The ceiling of the second level was made of old wooden beams and covered in stale straw which had holes throughout. The creaking door didn't quite close properly, and windows on both floors had shutters hanging from their hinges. Merick lit his lantern to look around.

"Lord Hardenel isn' takin' care of this place," Merick commented. "Years ago, when his father ran this fief, this tower had logs piled up and fresh straw on the roof every deshe." He pointed to a wooden trapdoor near the fireplace. "They'd stock vegetables and dried meats in the cellar, too. No reason to check it now, though. I doubt there's enough for a mouse."

As they unrolled their blankets, Sandu paused. He strained, listening. Outside, the horses snuffled to each other and the wind blew softly against the door. But he heard something else, too: a scraping sound and low, guttural growls. Sandu crept toward the fire pit.

"What are you doing?" Cara asked. Sandu shushed her, putting a finger to his lips. Merick straightened, frowning. Stepping as quietly as he could, Sandu moved to the trapdoor and put his ear against it.

Nothing.

Feeling foolish, Sandu sat back on his haunches. He opened his mouth to apologize when a piercing cry from below stabbed the still air. Sandu scrambled back from the trapdoor and mouthed, *Prowlers.* The cry sounded again, joined by two more, both human and demonic.

Shit. Vecking shit.

Sandu hadn't encountered prowlers since he was a small boy, when they had come upon his Valadi caravan during the night. Smarter than beasts and faster than men, they had rampaged across the country for years. No one knew where they came from, but scholars made guesses on how the monsters reproduced: they poisoned humans and elves and turned them from rational to blood-hungry. Few had seen one and lived to tell of it. Some said they heard the beasts communicating to each other, but many more whispered that the prowlers were nothing more than animals. Sandu didn't know what he believed, just that he didn't want to find out.

Cara and Merick quickly gathered their blankets as Sandu grabbed his haversack. He wrenched open the door and peered out into the darkness. He saw nothing but moonlight and shadowy trees.

The trapdoor crashed open. Sandu whirled around, his knife held up. Merick drew his sword, and Cara stood riveted to the floor. An earthy scent mingled with rot and blood drifted into the room as the prowlers scrambled up from the cellar.

Light from Merick's lantern reflected in the prowlers' red eyes, which had lost any trace of the humanity they once possessed. Long teeth poked from their lips, and their noses twitched. Rough ridges of skin crested their brows where worry lines might be, their sunken cheeks sucking in and out as they breathed. Their claws scraped across the stone floor. Horrid scars crisscrossed their skin, which was pale, corpse-like, and covered with dried blood, dirt, ashes, and unspeakable fluids which crusted into the beasts' hair and ragged clothes. The prowlers snarled, creeping closer.

"Get out," Merick said quickly, edging in front of Cara and Sandu. "I'll follow."

Fear urging him, Sandu grasped Cara's hand and pulled her out the door. They ran to the horses and cut the pickets. From behind, Sandu heard Merick shouting.

"Get your horse saddled!" Sandu yelled. Cara stared at him a second, something strange reflected in her hazel eyes, before throwing her saddle and lead onto her horse and grabbing the spare gelding's lead. Sandu quickly strapped Galen's saddle and reins onto her, then ran to Merick's black charger. The charger reared back, snorting, and Sandu raised a hand to quiet it.

A cry of anger sounded by the tower, then the door slammed. Cara huddled by her horse as Sandu tightened Merick's saddle, peering into the darkness. Merick emerged from the gloom, breathing hard, his sword bloodied. Sandu helped him into his saddle.

"We've got to move," Merick gritted out. "The door won' hold 'em for long."

Sandu leapt onto Galen and turned her head to the road, pushing her to a gallop. Merick's horse had already sprinted ahead, Merick leaning low over its neck. Cara rode beside Sandu, her expression tight. As they rode, Sandu glanced back. *Shit.* The prowlers raced after them, their red eyes flashing in the moonlight.

"Give me your sword!" Sandu shouted at Cara. She looked at him as if he had two heads.

"What?"

"Just give it to me!" Galen ran right up to Cara's horse, and Sandu tore her sword from its scabbard. He let Galen slow, the spare horse catching up to them. He rode side-by-side with the gelding now. Its eyes rolled in terror. *I'm sorry*, he thought as he swung Cara's sharp blade down across the back of the horse's legs. The sword cut a jagged slice into its muscle. The animal dropped, its momentum carrying it forward a few feet in the dust. Cara's mount reared and she quickly cut the lead, releasing her horse from the downed animal. Both she and Sandu surged forward as the gelding struggled to rise, its back legs failing it. The prowlers fell upon it, ripping at its hide. The horse screamed – a loud horrible sound that hit Sandu to his bones –

until the prowlers tore open its throat.

Damn shame. That was a fine animal. But with a meal in their bellies, the prowlers might not pursue them any farther.

"Good think'n, lad," Merick said when they paused to rest half a candle later. Their horses, foaming and lathered, drank deeply from a puddle next to the road. "Veck, those things were horrible."

Sandu nodded, too out-of-breath to say anything. From the corner of his eye, he noticed Cara's whistling breath, her heaving shoulders. Merick leaned over to her, and she shook her head.

Merick turned to Sandu. "She needs to rest."

Sandu peered back at the road, sure he'd see glowing red eyes. "No, we should keep moving. They've hunted men for miles from what I've heard."

Another wordless exchange between the other two. *What's wrong with her?*

After a moment, Merick nodded. "Alright. We keep movin'."

They're hiding something from me, Sandu thought, watching them. *Something that may have to do with why Stanthorpe wants her.*

CHAPTER THREE
Cara

CARA'S HANDS SHOOK, her knees weak from squeezing the horse's sides. It was over a candle's time after the prowler attack. She thought she should be fine again, that her heart should slow, her trembling gone. But each time it felt like the panic receded, she remembered the prowlers' red eyes, their blood-blackened fangs, the shrieks as they flew over the ground toward her. Each time, she descended back into that awful place where it felt like the fit would overpower her and release the beast.

She thought, too, of the fits of years past. Spasms that shook her whole body, sharp nails raking her own skin, dark terror taking over her limbs and invading her head, the beast in all its foul glory reveling in her distress. She had screamed for Merick every time, shaking as he held her, begging for it to stop. He'd hold her until the nightmare retreated from her arms and legs, the beast coiling itself in the bottom of her belly, waiting to emerge until she was too weak, angry, or frightened to stop it.

Cara hugged herself and stared out into the night. Memory after memory bored into her head: crimson eyes; blood staining her clothes; Freebane forcing calming draughts between her teeth; screaming in the dark–

A cool hand touched hers. Cara jumped, her eyes darting back and forth, expecting to see a red gleam in the darkness. It was only Merick with his familiar calloused fingers. Cara took a deep breath and focused on his touch. She didn't look out at the dark forest again, for the prowlers lurked within its depths, and she didn't know if she could hold back her inner beast all night.

"You're doin' fine, Cari," Merick said, his grumbling voice soothing and warm. "Jus' keep breathin'. Don' worry 'bout nothin' else. Remember what Freebane told you? Breathe."

Breathe in for the count of five, Freebane had said one sunny afternoon three years before. She held Cara's arms while she shook and raged. *Hold it for the count of three, and then breathe out for the count of five. Imagine stamping the beast down where it belongs. Bury it in your stomach, build a wall to keep it in.*

For five eternal seconds, Cara breathed in through her nose, filling her lungs with sweet night air. She held it, then released out her mouth. She anchored her mind to Merick's hand. With the movement of her breath, she forced the beast down and down, picturing herself stomping on its head and stacking bricks to keep it away. Though it retreated, the beast left a hot, burning trail down her throat as it went.

The beast was both her and not her. When it came, Cara could still see, think, and move, but as if through a thick pane of distorted glass, all her intentions funneled through the beast's hunger.

Calmer now, Cara said to Merick, "When I saw the prowlers, the beast woke. It was worse than ever before; I only resisted because I didn't want Sandu to see." She twisted around in her saddle, but thankfully the stablehand slept on his horse, head bobbing on his chest.

"Aye, lass. You did a fine job, too."

A shriek sounded in the far distance, a prowler's high-pitched cry. Cara's throat felt dry as she swiveled, peering into the darkness. No glowing red eyes manifested in the woods. She swallowed her fear and prayed that the beast would leave her be.

Another candle passed, then another. Merick didn't let them stop or sleep, and Cara felt grateful for the hard pace. As the night grew darker before the tint of dawn brushed the sky, she calmed. Ride, pause, drink, ride again: the beast was driven down by her overwhelming fatigue. A soreness gathered behind her eyes, and the aches and pains of the previous day came to haunt her.

As the blue-black of night gave way to pale tendrils of day, Cara thought of Renna. How many days was it now since she'd seen her friend and mistress? Three? Four? In the limbo between waking and sleeping, as her body cried out for rest, she couldn't recall. *I was useless when Renna was taken, and then against the prowlers. I did nothing while Merick saved me. How can I hope to rescue Renna from the Hooded Man when I can't even rescue myself from the beast?*

For the first time, Cara wondered if she should have stayed home in Kell and let the Realm's Protectors find her friend. A lump rose in her throat, and she knew she would have gone mad if she had done so. She remembered the only time Renna had ever left the fief without her, for a deshe trip to meet her future husband. The days had passed slowly, each filled with worry. Cara did her chores without complaint, but she looked at the manor's gate every candle, hoping to see Renna. When her friend did finally come home, Cara had clung to her for candles, drinking in every word that fell from Renna's lips and savoring her lady's beautiful features.

This separation was far, far worse, for Cara had no notion when it might come to an end.

"What's on your mind, Cari?" Merick asked. He slouched over his horse's mane, tired and grey-faced. One hand clutched the bandaged wound on his stomach, but his eyes were attentive.

"Renna," Cara said. In the early light, she thought that Merick looked so *old* now. When had he aged? "I miss her."

"Me too, Cari."

"When I wake up, sometimes I think I'm still back in Kell, and that I'll hear her singing before breakfast. And then I see she'd enjoy, like a stand of flowers or a bird's song, but when I turn to tell her about it...she's not there. Do you remember the first time we danced at the harvest feast, and how lovely she looked with a crown of leaves in her hair? I think of that sometimes, and I become afraid that we won't find her in time for this year's harvest." Cara's words bled from her heart. "What if we're not strong enough? My fits aren't going to go away, or they may get worse. If I can't fight the prowlers, how can I defeat the Hooded Man?"

"We're strong, we'll get her back." He spoke confidently, but she doubted his words. She was a girl prone to strange fits, and he was a wounded mercenary who should have long since retired. Not to mention Sandu, a cowardly stablehand who fled the tower at the first sign of trouble. *Be kinder to him,* Cara chastised herself. *He saved you all by killing the gelding.*

Merick frowned. "A lot goin' on in that head, eh Cari? Once was a time you'd tell me everythin'."

That was before all this. "I know." She changed the subject. "Your wound hurting you?"

"Aye. I think it came open. And all Freebane's potions are gone."

"Not the jirriloe."

"I'm not risk'n my life for a few drops of that stuff."

Sandu's horse rode between theirs, its rider now awake and alert. "There's a healer in the next village, a bloke named Kirri. We shouldn't be too far now."

As he spoke, the trees around them parted to reveal a decent-sized town. The road changed from dirt to cobbled stone as they rode closer. Chimney smoke drifted into the air along with the scent of freshly-baked bread. In the center of the town, a grassy space opened up between the buildings. Around the square were various shops and homes, along with a steepled novum and a two-story inn with a weathered sign hanging above its door. The novum here was smaller than Kell's, and would host only a clothman as its religious leader. In the cities and high lords' estates, the novums might belong to a curate. The Grand Novum in Con Salur was the home of the predicants and the Exalt, the greatest men of Dotschar's religion. In recent years, Cara had entertained the notion of traveling all the way to the Novum to be healed by the Exalt himself, for the holy man must be able to cure her fits.

"The novum's quiet this morning," Sandu said, frowning. "No dawn bell?"

In the square, townspeople gathered dressed in drab colors. They faced the novum's closed doors as if waiting for them to open.

"Is it Deshem Day?" Cara asked.

"No," Sandu said. "Something's not right here." From the inn's doorstep, they could see the crowd and novum. In the middle of the square was a raised dais with an upright pole and wood stacked all around it: a pyre.

More and more villagers gathered, their expressions grim. Mothers held tightly to their children while men gripped farm tools or daggers. All stared at the closed novum, silent but not still. They pressed together, fingers taut on their meager weapons, straining toward the door though none of them broke for it. An angry murmur started somewhere in the throng, building into hoarse whispers and grunts. As she watched, Cara's hands sweated, her pulse raging through her skull. The beast in her belly woke, delighted by the tension, and crawled slowly up her windpipe.

"Get inside," Merick grunted, his eyes darting over the people. "We don' want to be mixed up in this." They all dismounted, and Sandu took their horse's reins to lead them to the stables around the back. But Cara couldn't tear her eyes from the expectant villagers.

"Cari?" Merick asked. She stood stiffly, nostrils flaring. The beast filled her throat, choking her with its presence.

One of the village men shouted, "Bring her out, Paol! We're done waiting!"

The crowd's noise rose to a swelling wave. They pushed and pulled at each other. Just before their fury reached a breaking point, the novum doors opened. The clothman edged out, his red robes stark against the pine-wood doors. At his presence, the swarm fell back, still seething, bottled lightning that churned in its container.

"My children, return to your homes," the clothman pleaded, his hands raised in supplication. "Let there be no deaths here today. Haven't the prowlers made us suffer enough? Let there be an end to it."

"It's all her fault!" someone yelled.

"My boy's dead because of her!"

Their cries poured into the air. The clothman shrank back against the novum. Cara's beast tittered in delight, and she gritted her teeth, not letting it take over her head. Her hands clenched in front of her.

Sandu came running back up to them, the horses secured away. "Come on!" he urged, waving at the inn's door. "Where are the Realm's Protectors? Shouldn't they be doing something?"

"Four or five Protectors agains' a mob? Not bloody likely," Merick said as he grasped Cara's arm. "We're goin' inside afore–"

The mob surged forward and flung the clothman away from the door. He cried out, but his words were lost amid the uproar. The forerunners tore open the novum's doors, bursting inside. Merick and Sandu hauled Cara into the inn and slammed the door behind them. A wisp of a woman stood at one of the windows, wringing her hands.

"Oh, poor Marta," the woman said, sparing only a glance for her guests. "They'll burn her for sure."

Away from the crowd, the beast seemed louder, more insistent, drilling at Cara's resistance. With an effort, she gripped Merick's hand, tight enough that his skin turned white. His eyes asked a silent question, and she shook her head in reply. *It's not going away.*

"We need a bath," Merick said to the innkeeper.

"I'd readied one for myself, but then I heard..." The innkeeper drew away from the window. As she did, Sandu peered out of the cloudy glass. The woman's voice was timid and small. "The water must be cold by now."

"It'll do. C'mon, Cari, let's get that road grime washed off." Taking Cara by the waist, Merick steered her to follow the woman, his steady hand a welcome relief. They came to a small room on the second floor with a full tub. A window looked out on the square, with a mirror on the left-hand wall. Merick said in a low voice as the innkeeper bustled about, "Take yer time. I'll get our room an' the bags sorted." He seemed as if he were about to say more, but he cast his eyes down and left abruptly.

"D'you need help, Maid?" the innkeeper asked. "Or...?"

"You can go," Cara managed. Once the woman left, she leaned her sword against the wall, stripped off her clothes, and quickly got into the bath. The water was cool, but it felt like a balm on her hot skin. She ducked her head under, surfacing only when she absolutely needed to breathe.

A wailing scream greeted Cara as her ears drained of water. A scream, and cheers. Unable to stop herself, Cara clambered from the tub and went dripping to the window. She crouched at it, only her head peeking over the sill, and watched the pandemonium below.

Two men held tightly to a struggling woman's arms as they dragged her through the throng to the pyre. The woman screeched, her hair flying about her face. Townsfolk pelted her with vegetables and rotted meat. Cara watched in horror. She imagined the feel of their rough hands on her arms.

When they reached the pyre, the men forced the woman toward the pole. They raised her arms above her head and tied her hands to the pole, then wound a rope around her writhing body – Cara had felt that once, rough rope biting into her skin as she thrashed in her fits. She pressed one hand over her lips as hot tears poured over her fingers, yet she couldn't tear her gaze away. The woman's mouth moved, praying or begging. One of the men poured oil over the woman's head, and she spluttered. Cara wanted to cry out, to help the woman, but what could she do? Terror pinned her to the window, and she was but one woman against many.

The beast quivered in Cara's belly, and she sensed a new emotion from it: fright.

A strong-looking man stepped from the mob, bearing a torch aloft. He walked around the pyre, lighting it in multiple places until the whole thing blazed. Within the flames, the desperate woman thrashed, her cries of pain piercing Cara to the marrow. The beast overcame Cara in a single, horrible moment, and she spasmed as she clung to the windowsill.

Cara's nails elongated into claws. The woman on the pyre screamed again, then fell silent. Cara's vision changed, becoming sharper. Below, the raucous shouts sounded not victorious, but dreadful. The beast squirmed in Cara's head, urging her to go down, to fight these people, to save the burning woman—

But it was too late. The woman fell silent, her charred remains consumed by the red flame and black smoke.

The beast roared in her head, and Cara cried out. She beat at her head, too knotted up to breathe, too contorted with the sight of that poor woman to imagine her beast behind a stone wall. One hand scratched at her own cheek, almost piercing her skin.

In that moment, Cara saw herself in the mirror. She screeched and tripped over the tub. Water splashed over the wooden floors.

It was not herself she saw. Her own forehead was ridged, her teeth fangs. Her cheekbones shadowed her gaunt face. Red tinged her eyes. A prowler's eyes.

Cara scrambled forward, examining herself in the mirror again. Yes, it was her, but a prowler version of herself. Was this the beast's doing? Did a monster lurk in her very blood and taint her soul? Was *this* truly the cause of her fits?

As she questioned, the beast fed her indignation. Freebane knew, *Merick* knew, yet they told her nothing! All those candles of agony, of fear, yet they never told her what she became. They had spoken to Cara's mother in whispers, but never Cara herself.

Then Cara thought of Renna. Gods, what would her lady think, to have employed such a monster? Was Cara any better than the Hooded Man?

Of all of them, Renna was the most innocent. She had never seen Cara's fits, never been told of them. Cara tried to picture her monstrous self standing next to beautiful, golden-haired Renna, but the image seemed all too wrong. What lady would want a corrupted watchwoman, one who felt the urges of evil when confronted with danger? There was only one way to be worthy of her: Cara had to rid herself of the beast.

But first, Cara had to find Merick. She wanted to slap him and hug him, to demand answers yet be soothed by his gruff voice. She could almost hear the beast saying, *Yes, demand answers from him. Make him pay for his deception.* Cara shook her head. Her anger was righteous, but the beast's was not. It would have to slumber while she confronted her master.

After some minutes of breathing and imagining, the beast slunk back to its hiding place, and Cara's features transformed back to normal. She checked to make sure before she dressed, strapped on her sword, and left the room.

Voices drifted up from the inn's common room, and Cara went slowly down the stairs, expecting Sandu and Merick. Instead, she saw the innkeeper and clothman, heads bent together in close conversation.

"...nothing I could do," the clothman was saying. "I'm so sorry, Elise. I tried to stop them."

The innkeeper sobbed, and he brought her head to his shoulder, murmuring comforting words. Awkwardly, Cara lingered at the bottom of the stairs. Her righteous temper was momentarily set aside at the sight of the mourning woman.

A moment later, the clothman saw her. His brow crinkled at her weapon, but then he smiled. "We're not alone, Elise. Come, child, there's no need to hover at that distance."

Moving with a tentative step, Cara came to a neighboring table and sat down. The innkeeper, Elise, lifted her head and wiped her eyes. She stood quickly, mumbled something about work to be done, and scurried away. The clothman was an older fellow, well into his fifties, and had white hair that made his pale skin seem translucent. He sighed, running a hand through his thinning tonsure.

"My child, you look troubled," he said, his kind brown eyes meeting Cara's.

More than you could know, Cara thought. Aloud, she asked, "Why did they burn that woman?"

"Ah. How long have you been in town?"

"Just arrived this morning."

"That was Marta Jamison, Elise's sister. Marta...ah...had a son. And, well, he was bitten. We all thought it was the plague at first, but he turned prowler after he died. She didn't tell anyone when he passed, and she didn't have the heart to burn his body."

"How many others did he infect?"

The clothman shook his head. "There's no knowing. He wasn't the first prowler we've had, nor will he be the last. But the people wouldn't listen to reason; they've wanted someone to blame since the first person turned."

Cara shivered, her skin still damp under her clothes. If a village burned an innocent woman for her son turning prowler, what would they do to *her*?

"What do you know of the prowlers?" she asked.

"No more than most. I know that they were once men but turned into monsters. I know that their numbers are growing, and that people are afraid."

"Are they evil?" *Am I evil?*

"None of the gods' creatures are inherently evil or good," the clothman said. "But, the prowlers must be of Autorus, mustn't they? He is death, and his fingers corrupt the goodness of our world. The prowlers are unnatural. I would say that they are, indeed, evil."

Cara's throat tightened. "Can they be redeemed?"

"Can Autorus? But why do you ask, dear child?"

"Because it wasn't their choice. No one *wants* to become a prowler."

"Such is life and death. Is either just? Autorus corrupted their souls, and now they cannot see Lyael. And for one's family to succumb to it...it is a great tragedy."

Lyael, the domain of the gods, was the final death. All souls wished to go there, but Autorus trapped many in his afterlife, keeping them from the gods. He was the greatest evil of all.

"Surely there must be potential for good in them," Cara said.

"I wish it were so. But I fear that evil can only beget evil."

But how did evil come to dwell inside me? Cara thought. She wanted comfort, but this clothman only brought her confusion.

Am I, too, corrupted by Autorus? Am I barred from Lyael? But why? I did nothing to deserve this! More than ever, Cara wanted a cure, to be rid of her beast now that she knew what it was.

Cara rose suddenly. Merick would know. Even if he'd lied to her before, he *must* know something. The clothman bowed his head. "Shall I pray for you, child?"

"No." *He's a good man. He can't pray for evil, even unknowingly.*

The inn door slammed open. A rush of wind surged through the room, bringing with it the acrid smell of burnt flesh. Sandu stood in the open doorway, his eyes wide. He saw Cara and ran to her, grabbing at her arm.

"What's–" Cara started, but he spoke over her.

"It's Merick. We went to the healer while you rested, and–"

"What happened?" All anger at Merick drained from her, leaving only dread.

"He's vomiting this black...vile..." Sandu gestured helplessly, apparently unable to find the words.

Cara ran to the door.

CHAPTER FOUR

Cara

OUTSIDE THE INN, the air swirled with smoke. The taste of the burnt woman settled on Cara's tongue when she opened her mouth. She coughed, but ran after Sandu. They wove through the remnants of the crowd, ignoring shouts and jabs, until they reached the far side. There, Sandu led her to a white-washed building with an apothecary's symbol painted on the door.

The room inside was clean and tidy, and shelves on the walls groaned with hundreds of glass bottles and vials. A counter separated the back half of the room, with another door behind it. Beyond that door, Cara could see a short man hovering beside a low table.

A pungent smell assaulted her nostrils, stinking of decay and rotted fruit overlaid with a coppery sweetness. It was the same smell from that dreadful night, when the Hooded Man stood before the yawning purple void and black tentacles struck Merick while Renna vanished into the darkness.

At that smell, the beast wriggled in her belly. Cara didn't just build a wall around it: she constructed an entire castle, moat and all, to ward it away. She wouldn't let the beast overcome her now. Not when Merick needed her.

Cara took a deep breath to ready herself before stepping into the room. Merick lay on his side on the table, one arm held around his gut. On the floor beneath his head, a black puddle of oozing vomit sank into the sawdust, reeking of that awful smell. Merick groaned, then spewed forth yet more. Careful not to step in the muck, Cara sank onto the bed beside Merick. He spared her a grateful glance before burping up another chunk of the unnaturally thick, oily stuff.

"How long has he been like this?" Cara asked.

The short man said, "It started a little while ago. He came into the shop complaining of pain, said his wound was open and needed stitching. I had him sit on the table to examine him, and then..." He gestured helplessly at the quivering mercenary.

"Did you see his wound?"

"No."

Cara reached for Merick's shirt, but he grabbed her arm. He stared wildly at her, and rasped, "I 'eard a voice, Cari. Like Death 'imself. Said he were come'n to claim me."

"It was only a dream, Merick," Cara said, brushing a hand on his fevered cheek. "It can't hurt you."

"But it 'urts!" Merick babbled, eyes as wide as a child's. He grasped Cara's arm so tightly she thought he might rip it off. She gritted her teeth, blinked back tears from the pain, and put her other hand over his. There was fear in his look, fear such as she'd never seen in him before. Even after the prowlers, Merick had seemed calm and collected. But now, he looked like a scared old man who still wished his mother could hold him. *I have to be strong for him*, Cara thought. The idea terrified her. He was supposed to be *her* protector, to always know what to do and where to go.

What do I do? All three of the men looked to her.

Cara again extended her hand for Merick's shirt, and he let her. That concerned her just as much as the vomit. Pulling the cloth up, she had to quickly turn her head away before she lost her last meal.

The gash on Merick's stomach was inflamed, each inch swollen and bursting with pustules. The blackened edges had grown, darkening the skin for a finger's-width all around. A reddish-brown fluid seeped out, the source of the coppery smell. *Dark magic.* Just as Freebane had said. Would it infect Cara, too, if she touched it?

"Is it bad?" Merick asked, his sweat-drenched head leaning against the pillows.

"It doesn't look pretty." Cara turned to the others. "Healer, we need to wash this out. I–"

The healer shook his head, gazing at the wound. He made a sign over himself. "This is witchcraft."

"Veck it, man, he needs our help!" Cara said. She pushed to her feet and came nose-to-nose with the healer. "Unless you do something, he'll die."

"It's not right. First the prowlers, now this...it's a bad omen, he'll bring Autorus' wrath on us, I can't–"

Cara drew her sword. She didn't need the beast to urge her on. "Do what you can, or tell me where a man with a stronger stomach might be found."

The healer's eyes slid along the length of the blade. "There's nothing to be done."

"You haven't tried anything!"

"Not even Shepherd Jerloam in Copefield could heal a man at this stage," the healer stammered, backing away from her. Cara stepped toward him, but he turned and ran, pushing past Sandu to flee his own shop.

"Vecking hell!" Cara swore, slamming her sword back into its sheath. "Sandu, how far is Copefield?"

"Almost a full day's ride northwest, out of our way."

Cara paused, chewing her lip. If she didn't take Merick to Copefield, he'd die. But if she did, then they might lose valuable time in finding Renna.

One is here with me, and the other is not. Gods forgive me, but I have to save him while I can. More selfishly, Cara couldn't let him die without learning the truth – whatever he knew of it – about herself. "I'll be damned if I don't do something. Go get our packs and saddle the horses. Meet us outside." Sandu nodded, then ran out after the healer.

It would take a quarter of a candle at least before he met them. Cara searched the apothecary's shop, locating supplies for cleaning and stitching the wound. She tipped a water bladder into Merick's mouth before she set to work.

But Cara paused, watching the slow liquid. Would it infect her, too? Even if it might, what choice did she have? Still, perhaps if she kept it from touching her skin...Cara raced to the front door, where she found a thin pair of sheepskin gloves left behind by the healer. She pulled on the gloves and returned to Merick. The beast beat at the castle walls, but she reinforced them. There was no time for fits.

Swallowing her nausea, Cara wet a cloth and dabbed it along the wound. She cleaned the black edges before washing the gash itself. But as she wiped away the fluid, she saw that Merick's organs had gained an awful grey tint scored with black veins. More of the substance exuded from some unseen place, trickling up toward Cara's hands as she tried desperately to wipe it away.

"Merick..."

"It still 'urts," Merick mumbled, black vomit dribbling from his lips.

"I know, I know, I'm trying to help." But what use was it? She was no healer.

She had to try. Merick had done so much for her, she couldn't just let him die. Not yet, not when she still needed him.

Little Cari, only seven years old, fell and bruised her knee, tripping over her own feet, the wooden practice sword too heavy in her hands. She stifled her sobs, because Merick always said that a warrior didn't cry.

Despite her efforts, two fat tears rolled down her cheeks. Merick leaned down and cupped her chin. "Now, lass, it's only a bruise. C'mon, get up, show me what you're worth."

"But it hurts," Cara said.

"I know, lass. But there's naught to do for that. Push past the pain, there's a girl."

Cara shook herself. *Push past the pain.* She wove a line of catgut through Merick's flesh, stitching it together with trembling hands. Yet as she stitched, she saw the pus flow between the thread. The catgut melted away in front of her eyes.

What is this dark magic?

The quarter-candle must have passed by now. She was out of time, and nothing she did helped him. She tore a long strip from the bottom of her dress, wrapped it around Merick's torso, and secured it over the wound. It wouldn't last for long, but it was all she could do.

Merick moaned, only half-conscious, as Cara put one of his arms over her shoulder and helped him from the room. He mumbled and drooled black liquid all the while.

Outside the shop, a small group of about a dozen people had gathered, the healer among them. He pointed a finger at Cara, screeching something incomprehensible. Beyond the people, the pyre had burned lower, only fragments of the doomed woman remaining as she crumbled into ash.

The people murmured. One man, taller than the rest, had a scythe held ready in front of him.

"What are you doing here, outsider?" the man asked, leveling the scythe at Cara. "What witchcraft have you brought to us?"

"I'm trying to leave," Cara said. The beast stirred, and she gritted her teeth, holding it at bay. "Is traveling forbidden now?"

Some of the people shifted, looking at their leader, but he snorted. "And what caused that poor man's wound, eh? Your coven of hags?"

"If I did this to him, would I be trying to save him?"

"Could be you're saving him for worse, for a sacrifice to the dark ones."

Damn him, it won't matter what I say. Their blood is riled up. In the distance, Cara saw Sandu across the field with the horses. He hesitated, though, at the sight of the crowd. *Don't you abandon me, Sandu Crin, I swear by the gods—*

"Strange for a woman to carry a sword," the leader said. "It ain't right."

Cara scoffed. "And you expect your farm tool to be any good against it?"

"Are you threatening me?"

"I'm telling you that I'm leaving with my friend, and you're not going to stop me." Cara eased Merick to the ground, and he lay slumped, his breath shallow. The beast roared at the opportunity for action, and Cara subdued it with great effort. Her castle walls were weakening.

The villager raised his scythe, uttering a war-cry. With the ease of an experienced swordsman, Cara ducked under his too-high blade and rammed her pommel into his stomach. He wheezed, bending over. Sliding out from under him, Cara slammed her arms onto his back, driving him to the ground. He lay stunned in the dirt. The people around her gaped and backed away from her.

Cara rushed to Merick as Sandu ran to meet them. They heaved Merick into the saddle, and Cara vaulted behind him, shouting, "Take my horse's lead, Sandu."

The townsfolk gathered themselves and ran at them, yelling and brandishing their simple tools.

Cara spurred Merick's charger, her arms tight around her mentor. She prayed that he would stay upright as they raced from the town, the sun not even at its zenith.

The forest closed around them, muffling the thud of the horses' hooves and hiding the sky from sight. Cara put her heels to the animal's flank, urging it to go faster. *We can make it in less than a day, we have to make it.*

Merick's head rolled on his shoulders, his weight heavy on her. Her arms began to shake, but she pressed forward. Then Merick leaned far to the right, his mass buckling her arm. Cara tried to heave him upright, but he was too heavy. Her arm gave way, and he crashed to the ground.

Heart in her throat, beast in her lungs, Cara sprang to the ground and ran to Merick. He sprawled motionless in the dirt, staring up into the sky. His breath came ragged and harsh, and when he coughed, the black liquid flew from his tongue. The cloth Cara had wrapped around his wound was already falling apart, destroyed by whatever cruel magic ran havoc through his flesh.

"Merick!" Cara shouted, tapping his face. His eyes were glazed over, and he blinked slowly. "Merick! You're a fighter, don't you die on me now!" *Don't you die before you tell me what you know. Don't you die before we find Renna.* The beast flowed hotly into her limbs, and Cara thought savagely, *Don't you dare, you bastard.* She shoved it down into her feet and imagined it trapped in the castle, which itself was buried beneath a mountain with no tunnels out.

For a moment, Merick's gaze cleared, and he looked at Cara, mouthing her name though no sound came out. Sandu crouched beside Cara and said in a low voice, "The jirriloe."

Too much will kill, Freebane had said. The bottle was in Cara's hand before she realized what she was doing. She stared at it, the little vial of death.

"He's not going to make it to Copefield, Cara," Sandu said. "Give him a dignified death. He deserves that much."

"I can't kill him," Cara said, aghast. "He's like...he's...I just can't." Her mind turned in circles, the smell from Merick's vomit reminding her of that fateful night. "If I'd run forward, if I'd taken the blow or done something–"

"Then you'd be dying in the dirt, too." It was blunt, but spoken gently.

"No! There has to be another way, I'm not going to just let him–"

Merick took another strangled breath, coughed, and nearly choked on the vomit. His frightened eyes pleaded with her, but she shook her head. "I can't do it."

"Then let me," Sandu said, reaching for the jirriloe.

"Stop it!" Cara yelled at him, holding it out of reach. "You've no right, you can't just–"

"C-Cari..." Merick's voice was faint. "Please..."

Cara looked from Sandu to Merick, her chest tight, as if all the air in the world compacted inside her, squishing her very heart with its weight. It was lucky the beast had retreated, for if it tried to control her, she couldn't stop it.

But I have too many questions, and he has the answers, she wanted to say.

But I can't do this without him. He's the closest thing I have to a father.

If I can't save him, how can I hope to save Renna? Or myself?

Merick's eyes begged her. He had done so much for her, yet she couldn't bring herself to give him one selfish wish.

Tears pricked her eyes as Cara took hold of Merick's hand. In a low voice, too low for Sandu to hear, she said, "I wish I could have been better for you, Merick. You've given me everything, and I've been nothing but a brat. But I promise, I'm going to find Renna. I'm going to save her." *And then, I'm going to save myself.* "May you reach Lyael before Autorus takes you."

Tenderly, gently, Cara lifted Merick's head. She looked one last time into those care-worn, loving eyes. She tipped the vial into his mouth and let all the jirriloe cascade down his throat. Merick swallowed, then smiled. He tried to speak, but his words were too soft to hear. His stressed breathing came slower and slower, an eternity between each pause, until finally his lungs filled no more.

Cara sat beside her dead watchman, staring down at his pockmarked cheeks, the scars upon scars on his skin, his slack jaw. No breath filled his lungs to yell forms at her, no spark lit his eye. He should be moving, constantly moving as he used to. It reminded her of Ulton, once so full of life, now empty on the table in the great hall.

Grief filled her, too much, overflowing from her heart. The weight of it shook her. Memories flooded in, one after another, and she wept.

"C'mon, Cara!" Renna called. She ducked through the hedge bordering the manor lands, then poked her head back through. "We're going to miss the festival!"

Cara, only twelve at the time, hesitated. Renna reached out and tugged at her arm, but still she looked back to the manor. "Merick'll kill me."

"Not if he doesn't find out," Renna insisted. "We'll be back before he realizes it."

Cara smiled to herself. They hadn't made it back in time, and Merick had given her a good whooping for leaving the grounds without permission. But later that night, as she settled into bed, he had come to tuck her in.

"I'm disappointed in you, Cari," he said.

"I know," she whispered, ashamed. She wiped away stubborn tears, her bottom still sore from his punishment.

Merick sighed, and closed the window to keep out the chill night wind. "You're growin' up too fast. Soon I'll have to be scarin' boys off."

Cara giggled. "Only from Renna. They don't look at me."

"No?" He sat on the bed, his calloused hand stroking her hair. "They will, someday. But remember, if'n they break your heart, you can beat 'em in a fight."

Merick leaned down and kissed her forehead. It was a rare thing, him showing affection like that, and Cara savored it. She looked up at him with her innocent eyes.

"Merick?"

"Hm?"

"You'll never break my heart, right?"

He smiled down at her. "Never. An' I'll kill anyone who tries it."

Through a fresh haze of tears, Cara squeezed Merick's limp hand. She murmured, "You kept your promise." *Until today.*

In that moment, Cara wished for Renna's presence at her side. Her friend would know what to say better than Cara ever could. *I'm not fit to give a eulogy.* When Lady Nellestere died, Renna wrote a beautiful poem to be carved into the headstone. There wouldn't be such lovely words, nor a marker, for Merick. *I just hope I don't have to find words for Renna, too.*

Cara didn't know how much time had passed when Sandu said, "We'd better burn him, else the prowlers will come."

"They won't want him. No predator likes spoiled meat." *Gods, did I really just say that about Merick?* Cara slowly climbed to her feet, then put her hands under the old man's arms. When Sandu made to help her, she glared at him, and he stepped aside. With great heaves, Cara pulled Merick from the road and dragged him to a nearby tree whose roots were festooned with flowers. It seemed odd, laying the rough mercenary in a bower of beauty, but at the same time fitting. He'd never had time for loveliness in life, but perhaps he could enjoy them in death.

Red and black stained Merick's armor and skin. Cara poured water on him, cleaning him as best she could. After she arranged his arms over his chest, she slid his sword and sheath from his belt and wiped them on the grass. She would use them from now on, to remember him by. Then she went back to the horses, retrieved a blanket, and laid it over him. The whole time she worked, Sandu stood awkwardly to the side, sometimes opening his mouth to speak before shutting it again.

Once Merick was covered, Cara whispered a short prayer over him. Then, she stood and returned to the road.

"Let's go," she said.

"We can stay for awhile longer," Sandu said. "We can bury him if you want."

"He wouldn't want us to linger over him. And I never want to see this place again," Cara said, mounting Merick's black charger. She kicked the horse to a trot, wishing nothing more than to get away from that sorrowful place.

Goodbye, Merick.

Long after Cara and Sandu abandoned Merick's corpse, when the sun had fallen from the sky and nightcats prowled the woods, a purplish light filled the forest, shaking the trees and filling the air with the odor of decaying flesh. A void opened, blurring the lines between natural darkness and deep, deathly murkiness. Black tentacles curled forth and wrapped around the old mercenary's body.

CHAPTER FIVE
Jagger

VECK EVERYONE. Veck life. Veck it all. At least liquor provided some sort of solace, however short-lived.

"Another drink?" the fat barkeep asked. Tall and stout, he had these great muttonchops that really, truly should be shaved off. Maybe take the rest of the balding hair with it. Maybe his whole head. Could be a bit of fun.

Jagger nodded. He watched disinterestedly as the barkeep refilled his mug with a dark ale, then downed half of it once it was back in his hand. Raven had always chastised him for his drinking, telling him the solution never lay at the bottom of a glass. *Might as well try. Maybe I'll be the lucky bastard who finds it there.*

But he didn't find an answer at the bottom of the mug. Just dribbles of spit mixed with that little bit of drink that somehow always lingered. He wiped his mouth with the back of his filthy hand. Once, those hands were clean – or at least, cleaner – but that was before it all. Before the fire. Raven would make him wash his hands, clean the grime and blood from under his nails, rinse his greasy hair with cold water. Without her to care for him, Jagger didn't put any thought into his appearance or hygiene. He knew that he smelled like a dead dog left to rot in a muddy ditch.

Beneath his loose, simple rustic's garb, Jagger's body

reflected a hard life. Scars crisscrossed his back, white and ragged on his pink skin, signs of whippings from his youth. Thievery at the tender age of thirteen had given both his pinkies to the justiciar's knife.

Yet Jagger would have sacrificed the rest of his fingers to have Raven back.

At just past midday, he was the only one in the tavern. Taken to ale like it were his own brother, the barkeep had joked. Jagger only glowered at him from under the fringes of his lank blonde hair.

The door burst open, sending a gust of wind into the peaceful bar. Not quite autumn yet, but here in the high mountains the cold days were already taking over the hot ones. Jagger barely glanced at the group of soldiers that stumbled inside wrapped in heavy red cloaks. Dolts. Probably from the lowlands, didn't know how to handle a bit of cold.

If Jagger were younger, with stronger arms and that recklessness his middling years had robbed him of, he would fight them all then and there just for the fun of it. Only four: a tough fight but not an impossible one. Especially if they were drunk. They'd be cocky, thinking that their numbers and youth would help them against a nearing-forty man, but he was fast, and vicious. For good reason had he lived past all his enemies.

As they sat down, Jagger noticed the crest emblazoned on the soldiers' chests. His jaw tightened, hands clenching. These were Realm's Protectors.

Jagger turned his back to them. These likely weren't the ones from Daggenhelm, weren't the bastards who killed Jagger's wife and destroyed his livelihood. They were just uppity commoners thinking they'd gain fame and fortune by patrolling backwater shitholes like this, all fresh-faced oafs with no real fighting experience. *Not one o' them's seen a man bleed to death, his guts spilling out and the ground slippery with the stuff, much less been the ones to do it.* The four young soldiers couldn't be the ones from Daggenhelm. That was miles away, miles that Jagger had purposefully put between himself and the massacre – all the way through Havish Pass, then halfway around Red Peak for good measure.

Just let them be. No sense bringing attention to yourself. The four soldiers ordered a round, jabbering loudly at each other. Jagger tuned them out as best he could.

"...c'mon, Blike, tell us. What happened at the fortress? We're aching to know."

"Aw, it weren't no big hassle. And the commanders don't want us talking about Daggenhelm no-how."

Jagger spluttered into his ale. He coughed and glanced around to see if the soldiers had noticed. They hadn't. *Morons wouldn't notice a fly on their nose.* They were huddled together, three of them all leaning toward the fourth, the one they called Blike. Blike shook his head, but had that smile which said "Two more drinks and I'll spill any secrets I know, damn the consequences."

Patience, a word that had not come into his vocabulary until recently, made Jagger sit and wait. He agonized, wanting to hear what this freckled vecking soldier had to say. His instincts kicked in, past his drunken ideas of vengeance, and he ordered water while the group drank yet more liquor. He wanted a drink for courage, but some water would grant him sobriety along with a vecking headache.

Nothing could have been more difficult than that wait. Jagger wanted nothing more than to spring up, run at them, stab them in their vecking hearts until no blood was left to bleed.

Patience was a bitch.

Finally, over a candle later and three drinks in, the one called Blike set his mug down, wiped his chin, and said, "Alright, I'll tell you. Y'know we've been looking for Fauste's Shiv for damn near ten years. Slippery little shits, they were always one step ahead. Seemed to know when we'd strike, and moved before we could. All over the highlands, they'd gone.

"But we found 'em. One of their own sold 'em out, and we found 'em before they could run away. Over a hundred of us snuck up on 'em in the dead of night. We set fire to their keep and waited for 'em to be flushed out. It didn't take long. Those bastards tried to run, and we gutted every last one of 'em."

Not every last one, Jagger thought savagely. *You left one alive. Dug your own grave, really.*

The soldier took another drink. "Some of 'em jumped from the windows. Splat! They didn't stand a chance."

Jagger's fingers curled around his cup, his anger rising. But with the anger came fear, and a memory he had tried so desperately to forget...

...The bells clanged, crashed, and rang furiously. What the hell was going on? It was the middle of the night, what the veck was happening?

Shouts echoed up into Jagger's small room.

"Fire!"

"Fire in the keep!"

Jagger leapt from his bed, still dressed in his clothes from the night before. His head pounded, a soreness building behind his eyes. The effects of his drinking had caught up to him, but he couldn't think about that now. Gritting his teeth, he grabbed the washbasin, dumped it over his head, and gasped at the cold water.

Shouts were joined by screams of pain and confusion. "Enemies at the – arrrrrrrgh!"

Jagger took hold of his knife belt and strapped it across his chest. In a sudden wave of fear, he realized what was missing.

"Raven!" he shouted as he dashed out into the corridor. Where was she? She hadn't gone to bed with him, hadn't been there as he drunkenly kicked off his boots. "Raven!"

The tower. Hadn't she told him she would be helping the Archmaster tonight? A new collection of stolen scrolls had come in, the elders needed help sorting them, Raven had offered her services...

As he ran headlong down the corridor, Jagger thought only of saving her. Through open windows, he could see the tower rising above the rest of the keep, flames bursting from its shutters. His fellow Shivs scrambled past him, all desperate to escape. Smoke filled his lungs. He coughed, but kept running. Raven. My love, I'm coming.

Rubble blocked the fastest way to the tower. He'd have to go around. Throwing people aside, Jagger sprinted down the stone stairs, slipping once or twice, grabbing at the rails to keep himself from falling but never stopping his wild descent. In the courtyard, everything was wrong. Soldiers in armor ran through a blasted gate, their helmets hiding their faces. Their shining blades flashed as they rose and fell, hacking apart the frightened Shivs.

Jagger didn't pause, didn't hesitate to throw a knife at a Protector who ran at him, barely registered the man's bloodied neck and gurgling, dying breaths. Raven. He ran to the lower entrance to the tower, and found his path blocked by more rubble. "Shit!" He scrabbled at the stones, his hands coming away broken and bleeding. "Raven!" he screamed, staring up at the tower.

Glass rained down, and Jagger ducked back under a wooden overhang. Way up, he could see a silhouetted figure tossing objects down, books and scrolls that clattered to the ground. As he watched, a sudden boom *cracked the cobblestones below his feet. It sent the figure above flying out into space, its body falling at a feather's pace before it gained speed and rushed to its inexorable death. The body lay mere feet from Jagger, mangled and broken and burning, its blood soaking through the parchment beneath it.*

Jagger pulled the body toward him, turned it over, brushed aside its long dark hair. Its face was shattered, ruined, but its eyes stared emptily up at him. Raven's eyes. He choked as he cuddled her disfigured body, not caring that ash and blood rubbed off on his clothing. "Oh gods, Raven, oh gods, veck, Raven, wake up, please—"

Jagger's mourning was cut short by another explosion, this one sending chunks of stone and balls of flame at him. He lost consciousness then, and had woken with fresh burns that made him cry out in pain whenever he tried to move. The soldiers made their rounds, stabbing at anything that still moved. But Jagger crawled, slowly, and found a place to hide. There he had fallen asleep, and there he had come awake to a wild dog sniffing his leg and sunlight giving stark definition to the piles of dead bodies, the broken walls, the ash...

...The soldier finished his tale, taking a long drink as his friends gaped at him in admiration. They looked so smug, so pleased with themselves, though they weren't the ones who were there. Sins of the father, so it went. They'd all pay for it.

Jagger's knuckles were white around his mug. His other

hand, he realized, had been closed in a tight fist, and he slowly unfurled his fingers. Fingernail marks in little red crescents imprinted his skin.

The group sat, drank, told stories, laughed; one would occasionally stand up to go piss. Jagger stopped listening to them. What they said now didn't matter. He didn't look at them. Looking might make him second-guess himself. They were fresh-faced men after all, and no amount of training could prepare them for what he would do to them.

At last, one stood and pulled on his cloak. The others did the same, and all four of them stumbled drunkenly from the tavern, the wind whipping the door as soon as they opened it. They didn't bother to close it. *Self-righteous bastards.* Jagger tipped his head back to finish his mug of water. His head felt clear, if not perfectly painless. He wiggled his fingers and wondered why they didn't shake, then chuckled at himself. *Never been much for trembling when the quarry is near.*

Jagger paid then shuffled out, pulling hard on the door to shut it. *Courtesy goes a long way in these small towns.* Squinting against the wind, he saw the group of four heading down the road. They wove across the dirt and into each other. Jagger followed them, just close enough to keep them in sight.

Four against one. They'd think those great odds. *How wrong they are.*

He didn't own much, but Jagger had his knives. Strapped across his back, his chest, to his legs, tucked up his sleeves...more than twenty, at least, sharpened over months of misery where his only companion was the sound of steel scraping steel. Oh yes, very sharp. Excellent for this job.

But Jagger wanted the storyteller alive. *I need to know how they discovered the Shivs' location.* Which one was it? He couldn't quite tell with their backs to him. Some townsfolk braved the wind, hunched over on their way from shop to home. Still, too many witnesses.

Jagger whistled tunelessly. One of the soldiers glanced over his shoulder, grinning. Smiling back, Jagger gave him a little wave. Friendly, unassuming. He was just one of the rustics to them. But the soldier that looked back wasn't the one he wanted. He couldn't attack until he was sure.

"Oi!" Jagger shouted at them.

"What do you want, you Skallish bastard?" one of them yelled back. The others stopped and turned to watch. The storyteller, Blike, staggered backwards a little as he spun, putting his hand on the speaker's shoulder.

"I'm lookin' fer a friend," Jagger said, moving forward casually. "Big bloke, brown hair, face like a cabbage."

Another of them laughed. "As big as you? Haven't seen him, mate. Maybe you can help us?" His words were slurred, his eyes crossed.

Jagger forced his smile wider. "Aye, I kin do that."

"Any brothels around here? Kosca here has a craving." They all laughed at that. *Worst joke I've ever heard.*

Rubbing his chin, Jagger pretended to think. He didn't know of any, and didn't care to know. "Down that side road, around th' third corner. Red lantern."

Without any sign of gratitude, the party tripped over their own feet as they made their way. Jagger let them get ahead of him. No use in their suspecting him yet, not that they'd even notice. The further they got from the main path, the worse the road and fewer the bystanders. Perfect.

Three blocks down, the group went into an alleyway, no doubt expecting to see a shining red light. A wooden fence and piles of manure met them instead. *Bad for them, good for me.*

For a second they gaped, confused. Jagger reached into his belt, drawing out two small knives. With a practiced spin of his wrist, he sent one into the back of the soldier closest to him, the loudmouth. It sunk deep between the soldier's shoulder blades, the only sound his surprised exhalation. He pitched forward into the man in front of him, scrabbling at the other's jacket and dragging them both to the mud.

It took a second for the attack to register in their minds. *Typical.* But they were trained, after all, and they spun to face Jagger, drawing their weapons. One fell, a knife sticking from his throat. *Too slow, friend.* The remaining two raised their swords and advanced. Their boots squelched in the mud, their legs trembling as their eyes rose up Jagger's nearly seven-foot height to his hard blue eyes.

Two more knives came to Jagger's hands. He shifted his body, moving his weight to the balls of his feet. They had reach, but he was fast, and sober. Blike lunged at him, yelling a drunken war-cry. Jagger waited. He inverted his knife, handle ready to strike. At the last second, he dodged, cursing as his foot slipped. The soldier's blade caught his shirt and barely missed his side.

"Veck you!" Jagger shouted, throwing his left arm backwards, hilt out. His hand vibrated as he felt the pommel connect with Blike's back. He heard the man curse behind him, but didn't look. The other one, a spare, crept forward with sword held high.

With a flick of his hand, Jagger sent a knife at the soldier's neck. Steel rang as the soldier hit it away with his sword. Jagger threw himself forward, tackling him around the waist. They crashed into the wall, the man's head kicking forward. It hit the top of Jagger's scalp as stars sparked in his vision. With one hand, Jagger bashed at his enemy's head, nails scratching at his eye, muttering, "Vecking little shit." The other hand sought another knife and finally located a smooth handle. He drew it, snagging at the back of his breeches.

Holding down the soldier's head, Jagger raised the knife and plunged it, over and over, into any fleshy part he saw: neck chest, eye, it didn't matter to him. Blood squirted up at him. The man gurgled, blood foaming at the corners of his mouth.

"BASTARD!"

Jagger heard Blike's shout and quickly rolled away from the soldier's corpse. He narrowly avoided Blike's sword, which sank into the dead man's neck. Jagger tensed, braced for another blow. It didn't come. He scrambled to his feet. Blike tried to regain his footing, having slipped and reeled after pulling his sword from the corpse.

Drawing the long knife concealed in his boot, Jagger advanced, panting. His lank hair was dirty with mud and blood soaked into his clothing. His fingers felt stiff and cold, barely holding onto the knife's handle. Blike fared no better. The front of his fancy tabard was streaked with dirt, his handsome face grimed up. *Ha.*

A smile crept onto Jagger's gaunt cheeks. He may be tired, and sore as hell, but this soldier was young and stupid. Blike wouldn't try to charge again, he'd be cautious now, and that would kill him. Swords were no use in close quarters.

Darting forward, Jagger feinted to the left, then when the soldier swung at him, ducked right instead. His blade snicked out, catching the soldier's stomach. Not a deep cut, but the man still shrieked in pain. Using the mud, Jagger dropped down and spun, then thrust his knife in the back of Blike's knee. Blike screamed and fell. Jagger dragged him back by the hair, knife at his throat.

"Tell me what I want to know," he growled, "and I let you live."

"You'll be vecking executed, you bastard." *False bravado. Admirable, but stupid.*

"Apparently I've died already."

"I won't tell you anything," Blike spat. Jagger hauled him up a little, pulling at his scalp. He yelped.

"You were at Daggenhelm," Jagger said, his voice cracking a little. "Is that right?"

"What does it matter to you, Skal?"

Jagger pressed the knife lazily into his skin, a few errant bits of blood trickling down. In an easy manner, he said, "Ever heard of the Bloodied Giant? Eightfingers? The Heartless?"

"He's dead. We didn't let a single vecking Shiv past us."

"Ha. Really now? *Cause I'm the Bloodied Giant.*" Jagger felt the soldier's neck move as he swallowed nervously. "You thought you were so brave, didn't you? Murdered hundreds of people in the middle of the night, in their sleep? Very brave."

"You're Jagger Cross," Blike whispered, his eyes rolling up in a terrified attempt to glimpse his attacker. *Can't be having that.* Jagger pulled his hair erratically left to right, making him yelp again.

"The same. So you'll know exactly how merciful I am. You tell me what I want to know, and you'll go free. Might be lacking a finger or two, maybe an ear, but you'll live. If you keep your mouth shut in an effort at 'dignity' or 'honor,' I promise that you will die slowly, painfully, and lacking any honor. You'll scream like a little girl, you'll wet yourself, you'll beg me to stop and promise me that you'll suck my cock for a chance at life. You'd even let me sodomize you if it meant the pain could stop. But it won't, not until Autorus comes to drag you yelling and crying into the afterlife. Now, Blike – that is your name, isn't it? – you're goin'ta tell me how the Realm's Protectors found Daggenhelm. Who told you? Who did you pay to find it?"

"I don't know!" the soldier squealed.

"Not a good answer," Jagger said. He sliced his knife down the side of Blike's head. An ear bounced with bloody splatters to the ground. Blike howled in pain.

"Who told the Realm's Protectors about the Shivs' location?" Jagger asked, deceptively calm. Inside, he longed to gut this man now, drag his intestines into a drawing on the ground, but he needed information.

"Some peddler, a young man I think, I didn't see him clearly!" the soldier sobbed.

"Name!" Jagger hissed.

"Sandu Crin, I think. He worked there, he sold you to us for–"

The soldier's words were cut short as his blood sprayed down his body, a red cascade from the vicious slash across his throat. Jagger had nearly reached the man's spine. *Huh.*

Now he knew. Jagger shoved the man's body away from him and wobbled to his feet, thoughts spinning through his furious mind. *Sandu? No. No, it's a lie, Sandu would never...Sandu was my friend! Sandu died in the attack, he must have...*

Jagger remembered, though, that Sandu had left a mere deshe before the massacre, saying he'd be back once his business was completed. He had never returned.

That bastard. I'll make him eat his own guts.

Jagger's anger overpowered him. Grasping Blike's head, he

bashed it, again and again and again, against a pile of old bricks, smashing it, yelling incoherently, until his strength was spent, the battered face unrecognizable.

Jagger mumbled to himself, "I'll hunt Sandu down. I'll kill him, I'll break him, I'll destroy every bastard that ever looked favorably on him. I'll make him pay for it, Raven, I promise."

CHAPTER SIX

Gwen

HER MAROON-COLORED DRESS rustled softly against itself as Gwen folded it carefully. Such an ordinary action, yet her hands trembled. *This shouldn't be happening.* For a moment she paused, gathering herself. She had worn this dress at last autumn's Hymn Day festival, when the men started paying attention to her and her brother jokingly protected her from their guiles. Her brother Wullum had told her, "Little Gwen, stay a child one more year; adulthood comes far too quickly!" Gwen smiled at the memory and moved to place the dress in her traveling trunk. It was already crowded with more dresses, shifts, bodices, under-linens, and jewelry. She hesitated, holding the dress in one hand while sorting through the packed trunk with the other, before shaking out the red fabric and laying it back down on the bed. There wouldn't be much room for fancy clothes on the road.

The next half-candle Gwen spent laying out the remainder of her dresses, occasionally exchanging one from her wardrobe for one in the trunk. Only so much could fit, and she wouldn't be able to change her mind later. Not much time remained, but still she dawdled. *It's for my own good,* she reminded herself. *Wullum wouldn't have me leave unless need required it. I have to leave Lordstown, and never come back.*

Never was a very long time.

Wullum and his advisers told Gwen she would be safer in a foreign land, away from the Trials here in Demarren. But she didn't quite believe them: what could be safer than being with her brother, the Liegelord of the kingdom?

And if she left, she would be completely alone. Though she might feel lonely here sometimes, she knew the faces of her servants and the Demar courtiers. Everyone would be a stranger no matter where she went.

Before the servants came to take her trunk, Gwen called her favorite, most loyal attendant. "Rinar, you must do something for me. When I am gone, look underneath my bed. There's a loose slab of stone. I want you to take everything you find there and burn it. You must do this before the Inquisitors make it into the palace. Do this for me, and my brother may have a chance at life."

Rinar nodded. "It will be done, Your Highness."

"Thank you." Gwen watched the last of her luggage be taken out, then sat at her mirror, picked up a brush, and played with her dark hair. It calmed her, running her fingers through the silky strands and curling them around and around her thumb. Her mother had always said, "A woman's hair is her pride, my Gwen. When you are older, you will understand the way a man looks at you when your hair shows – just so – your heritage." And her mother, the gods bless her grave, had been a rare beauty.

"Gwen?" Wullum stood in the archway to her rooms. He was every bit a Liegelord, with golden rings on his fingers and tattoos on his dark, bald head. In the warm summer, he dressed only in a long, white, open-faced robe over loose breeches, his feet bare. "I've come to make my farewells."

Gwen nodded, the realization that this may be the last time she would ever see her brother settling on her, clouding her head like wine. When he held out his arms, she stepped into his familiar embrace. He smelled of chocolate and sweet fruit, his robe soft against her bare arms; the comfort she gained from holding him cracked by the fear of leaving, and anger that he was the one to make her go. Though she was seventeen and almost a woman grown, she felt like a child again, desperate not to let go of her older brother.

"No words, my bird?" he asked, his cheek buried in her braided hair. She shook her head against his chest. She didn't know what to say. Goodbye was too short, too empty, yet anything else seemed too long.

"Then I'll talk for both of us. Stay wary, even once you've left our shores. Spies and assassins are as fleas in this world, it seems. Never let a man take advantage of your innocence, and never let women prey upon your fears. It won't be a pleasant journey, I'm afraid. A merchant, Master Hamon, has a way out of the city for you; he'll take you to the port by land. The rivers are infested with Inquisitors checking every ship. Once at sea, the ship's captain has been given instructions to take you wherever you please."

"But why?" Gwen blurted out.

"The Inquisition will not take long to come into the palace, sweet bird. When word of your escape has traveled to the Skals, they'll use it as proof of our guilt."

"They won't get past the soldiers," Gwen said with a certainty she didn't feel. Her violet eyes darted to the window, as if she expected to see enemies creeping in at that very moment.

Wullum smiled sadly. "I'm afraid they will. There's too many of them, with too many fearful rustics on their side. Once they've come into the palace, they'll torture me to learn where you've gone. If I don't know the answer, then I can't betray you. Don't you see, Gwen? You'll be safe."

"Come with me," Gwen pleaded, clutching at his robes. "They can't torture you if you're with me! Don't let them do this."

"If there's a way to halt the Trials, then I'll find it here. What would the people say if their Liegelord fled the country on the hearsay of fear-mongers? I must stay, whether it be folly or courage. You are a princess of Demarren and will obey me, so I order you to find a new home and live happily. When the Inquisition's leaders have been executed for crimes against us, then you may return an innocent woman."

"As you command, my liege," Gwen said to her knees.

Her brother's strong arms tightened around her, then he left, almost running, as if he were trying to conceal a grief it would be unmanly to reveal. Gwen stood, an emptiness filling her, and watched him go. Soon after the last traces of his scent dissipated, she shook herself and went to change for the road. Instead of her usual silks and satins, she wore a simple linen dress, torn in places and stained with dried mud, and simple boots of rough leather. A cowl wrapped around her head and hid her dark brown face, replacing the opaque veil she normally pinned to her hair. She looked the same as any peasant.

Before her brother's trusted steward, Falil, bundled her away to an uncertain future, Gwen looked one last time at her rooms. Here she had played as a little girl with her dolls and her pets. Here she had bled for the first time and been comforted by her mother, who was delighted by Gwen becoming a woman. Here old Ebarren had found her soon after she chanted imaginary words and caused her doll to float untethered across the room.

Maybe I should confess, Gwen thought desperately as Falil tugged at her arm. *If I confess to having magic, perhaps the Trials will end and they will leave my brother alone.*

But even as she thought it, she knew that her confession would only hasten hers and Wullum's executions. Magic, no matter who practiced it, was forbidden in Demarren, and now an Inquisition had been built to root out the wizards and witches and bring them to justice. The accused were tortured until they confessed and then hanged publicly. Not even members of the royal court were immune: Udrina, Wullum's adviser, had been dragged from her home twelve days before.

Falil led Gwen through the servants' low, dark, twisting passages. They darted from hall to stair as if the very walls could betray them to the Inquisition. Putting a finger to his lips, Falil peered out from a concealed doorway. Then he took her hand and led her across an empty room and into another set of hidden warrens. More than one cobweb caught in Gwen's clothes.

"Have the lead Inquisitors been named?" Gwen asked. When the Inquisition began, accusations came from the mouths of children who claimed that magic had been used to hurt them. But as the Trials grew, Wullum confided in Gwen that there must be leaders behind it, urging the children to name those closest to the Liegelord.

"Your Highness, with all due respect, you shouldn't think of such things now. These matters are best left to–"

"I need to know whose names to give to the gods, as protection for Wullum," Gwen pleaded.

The steward glanced back at her and said, "It is as our liegelord suspected, Your Highness. Councillors Rolf Rahskken and Olfrick Kron have joined with the Faith to lead the Inquisitors. Both have been expelled from the high council."

Skallish traitors. Of course. Wullum had complained for years that the native Skals were continually resisting his rule: they claimed that he and his Demar kin had no place on their island. The great First Liegelord, Hasifer Zaman, had taken his beleaguered people from their native land and traveled north on the sea for months until they landed on this beautiful yet harsh island. Disparate Skallish tribes dwelled here, but they were too divided to withstand the invading force. Liegelord Hasifer established his people here, but now his hard work was threatened by Skallish traitors. Few of the accused were the pale-skinned Skals.

Her breath coming harder, Gwen didn't ask any more questions. She and Falil wound down through the palace until they reached a small courtyard where deliveries and supplies came in. Sooner than she would have liked, Gwen found herself lying among sacks of potatoes and beets in the back of a horse-drawn cart. She could see the sun setting beyond the wall until the merchant covered her and his cargo with a heavy cloth.

"Don't move, don't make a sound," the merchant said softly. "Hide under the sacks as best you can." He gave her a small smile, which she returned. He had a round, jolly face, and the light skin and hair of a Skal. *A better Skal than those traitors.*

Gwen did as he said and shifted the sacks until she had made a small nest, then drew a lighter sack over herself. Only a small sliver of light made it through the layers of rough cloth. She heard the merchant, Hamon, cluck to his horse, and the cart shifted beneath her. A few minutes later, the smooth stones of the courtyard turned to the rough cobbles of Long Way.

From her hiding place, Gwen could hear the cries of people in the street. "Hang the witches!" "Kill them!" The shouts faded as the cart traveled further from the palace toward the city's high halls. Gwen bumped and jostled with the produce, biting her cheek to keep from crying out. Her hands grew tight from clinging to the sacks, her back sore from crouching. The sliver of light faded, and Gwen closed her eyes. She couldn't see anything even if she tried.

The quarter-candle journey from the palace to the city wall stretched out interminably, though Gwen couldn't tell if Hamon drove the cart slowly or if she was imagining it. It felt an eternity since she had been swaddled among the vegetables.

Gwen wished Wullum were with her, or, even better, she could be home asleep with no Trials to worry her. If the Inquisition succeeded, and the Skals took her brother's throne, she would no longer be a princess – just a scared little girl.

At last, the cart stopped, and she heard a man's voice, "Just made it in time, Hamon. We were about to close the gates. Usual load, then?"

"Yea, just vegetables and wares. Not a good economy in the city, what with the Trials and all."

"Aye, it's a shame alright. Go on through."

Gwen let loose the breath she held as the cart jolted forward once more, the merchant whistling a jaunty tune as he goaded the horse to a canter. Some time later, he stopped and brought Gwen up to sit with him. He chatted away with an air of pretend nonchalance, but she didn't listen. Her eyes closed, she leaned against the backboard, homesick already. Strange, how she had never missed Lordstown on all her travels away from it, but now that she couldn't return...

Hamon hummed a merry tune and watched the road with a

steady eye, his hands sure on the reins. Gwen turned her face away from him, only sniffling a little as she began to cry. She felt a nudge on her arm as he held a handkerchief out to her.

"To dry your pretty eyes, Highness," Hamon said with a wink. "I'm sure you'll return before too long."

"Thank you," Gwen mumbled.

"Don't mention it. Settle in, then. It'll be a few days to the harbor."

A quinn later, Gwen stood, unsure, on the road next to a long dock. The harbor teemed with life: crewmen scurried about their ships, sods lay drunkenly amidst nets and crates, and ladies held their kerchiefs aloft to wave goodbye to their loves. Smoke and meat perfumed the air, with a touch of sweat and more than a hint of salt and fish, while the slip of waves lapping wood underlaid the heavy fall of men working their hammers. Gwen sweated under her linens. She hadn't bathed the entire journey, and must smell as poorly as everyone else here.

"Perhaps a letter has come for me, saying I can return?" Gwen asked Hamon hopefully.

"I think not, Your Highness," he said.

Taking her arm, Hamon led Gwen along the dock, past Skallish longships, Dedarian galleys, and Dotsch holks to an Empire-fashioned cog with a single tall mast. Gwen saw no other passengers.

A serious-looking Demar man stood bellowing orders on the dock, one hand on his hip and the other stroking his chin. In the middle of shouting to his crew, he glanced their way. "Put the trade goods below, Carsey, it should've been done candles ago! And secure the riggings, Blewsley. Lawson you better not be touchin' the sour afore we set off! First watch for you, lad!" Satisfied that the crew were behaving, he turned fully to Gwen and Hamon and made a sweeping bow. "Maid Zaman, a pleasure it is. I'm Gaulin, the first mate. Captain Longwood is inside; he's waiting for you. If you'll follow?"

Gwen hesitated, turning to Hamon. He gave a small shrug. "It's out of my hands at this point, Your Highness. These are good, honorable men. They'll keep you safe."

"Thank you, Master Hamon," Gwen said. "The gods bless you, for everything you've done."

"Gods' mercy on your journey," Hamon said before donning his hat and hurrying away. Gwen didn't blame him; he had a family to return to.

The captain greeted her in his sparsely decorated quarters. Sitting at his desk, his elbows on the maps in front of him, he said, "Our orders are to carry you wherever you please, Your Highness. Once there, we have letters of introduction for you. You'll be welcomed anywhere in D'Ehsen."

Welcome anywhere but home. Gwen almost turned around, thinking that an adviser would magically appear at her shoulder, but there was no one there but Gaulin. She didn't know much of the wider world except for stories of great cities and beautiful lands: Con Salur, the city of cliffs and seat of the benevolent king of Dotschar; the vast Empire, stretching from D'Ehsen across the water into the far west; Dedaria, Rengu Forest, Skålland...so many distant, foreign lands, each as intangible as the rest. Then Gwen remembered a tale her mother had told her of the most beautiful city of all: Riverfen, the city lit by hundreds of lanterns in fantastic shapes, glowing gems that lit even the poorest of streets and held magical fire that never went out; a city ruled by a renowned earl who seated even the lowest of beggars at his own table on feasting days.

Her guilty heart knew another reason why she wished to go to Dotschar: there, magic was allowed. Curates learned healing spells, and each court employed its own array of wizards and mages. Perhaps there she could find someone like her. With fear pumping her heart, and miraculously no stutter, Gwen said, "Take me to Riverfen."

CHAPTER SEVEN
Gwen

AFTER NEARLY a month at sea, thrown about by stubborn winds, every pore and scrap of cloth inundated with sea-salt, Gwen finally alighted in Riverfen. The terror of her escape had subsided, leaving only her fright for the future. The stewards of the Cascade Palace had welcomed her after reading Wullum's letters of introduction, but Earl Seastone had not yet returned from visiting his vassals. Nearly an entire deshe passed before the stewards brought word to her that the earl's arrival was imminent.

The day he returned, Gwen would learn her fate in Riverfen's court, if there was any destiny there at all. She meandered the palace as the moment drew closer, its beauty doing nothing to assuage her fears.

If anything, the stories told of this place did it an injustice. The Cascade Palace, built on a plateau in the middle of Riverfen's many waterways, was a dream come to life. Blue and green tiles underfoot depicted elegant patterns of flowers and ocean waves, so intricate that sometimes she felt as if she strolled through an elven story rather than a castle. A slight breeze drifted through the airy halls and delicate arches, carrying with it the smell of salt. Multiple wings were built out from a central hall, though the grounds and gardens behind the palace dwarfed it, spreading down from the top of the plateau in multiple wide rings.

From the palace front, circuitous streets zig-zagged down to the twisting canals and roads of the main city. Wealthier homes and businesses occupied the higher layers of the plateau, but as one went further down, the elevated, controlled waterways that flowed alongside the streets devolved into muddy mires as the paved cobblestones of the upper city gradually turned to dirt. From her room, Gwen could see the bay's waters twinkling over a mile distant.

But it was not the rivers, nor the grand palace that Gwen had wanted to see. What drew her to this beautiful city were the lanterns. Hundreds of them – no, thousands! – lit the city at night, crisscrossing over the streets and strung up on gables, blue and red and green and purple and every other color imaginable. In the merchant and plateau districts, teams of simple wizards cast magic to light them. In the slums and fishermen's wharves, where they used cheap paper instead of glass, paid men went to each one and lit it by hand. Every night, Riverfen turned into a festival of lights and colors, reflected by the stars above and the water below.

But in the palace, Gwen felt alone. Every nobleman she passed failed to meet her eye and every fine lady frowned at the floor. They dodged around her as if she were made of porcelain, or worse, some monstrous creature bent on their destruction. *Aren't I a princess? Then why...?*

In her heart, Gwen knew the answer. She was a young stranger with darker skin, an accusation thrust on her, and no man to protect her. If the earl failed to take her as a ward...Gwen didn't want to think what she would face if he turned her out.

The day came, warm and humid. Druam Strilu, Earl of Seastone and the River Valley, had sent word that Gwen should meet him that afternoon. Dressed in the confining finery of Riverfen fashion – a bodice that laced tightly across her chest, underskirts swirling about her ankles, and a weighty overdress with floor-length sleeves – Gwen waited. Though she could now forego the veil across the bottom of her face (one she had worn in public since the age of eleven), she missed the privacy it lent to her expressive lips. She had never learned to hide her smiles or frowns, for the opaque cloth had done that for her. Without it, she felt naked, even with heavy brocade covering her from the shoulders down.

Gwen waited for her summons with her hands pressed to a side table to prevent their trembling. How would she introduce herself? Might the steward, Eigbrett, be there to do it for her? Did she call him Earl Seastone, Lord Strilu, Sire Druam, or 'Your Distinction'? The etiquette here baffled her; what if she ruined her prospects by addressing him incorrectly? If only Wullum had come with her, he would speak and she could simply listen and smile behind her comforting veil.

At last Lord Eigbrett appeared at the door to her antechamber. He bowed and said, "His Distinction awaits you in the covered walk."

"Thank you." She followed the steward down from her rooms, through the long tiled halls with their open windows and sun-drenched tapestries, and into the sprawling gardens.

A wooden walkway circled the outer border of the gardens, marking the boundary between the nobles' space on the plateau's top and the public walking areas on the lower terraces. A vine-laden roof muffled the sunshine overhead and grass cushioned her feet. Benches dotted the walkway at frequent intervals.

Eigbrett pointed down the walk. "Your Highness," he said before bowing once more and leaving her. Gwen hesitated. How many turns of the path must she endure before seeing the earl? But he waited for her, and she mustn't linger long.

Lifting her skirts from the green-staining grass, Gwen began the infernal journey down the path, her feet keeping her in the sunshine and away from shadows. Her heart beat on her ribs and her lungs wanted to burst with air and her hands nearly dropped that weighty cloth, so sweaty were they. She had to scold herself for running, to slow down, breathe, go back to one step at a time. Her dark cheeks flushed with heat.

She had walked for nearly a quarter of a candle – she must be halfway around the gardens by now! – before she saw him.

Druam Strilu stood straight, hands clasped behind his back, his body facing her. He didn't move. As she drew closer, she saw his head turned to the side, his eyes on the city. He had a handsome profile, though his eyes were deep beneath his brow. Dark hair, slicked back with oil, gave him an air of youth, and his olive skin was unblemished.

When Gwen paused a few feet away, Strilu cocked his head to look at her. She sank immediately into a deep curtsey, the fingers of her right hand pressed against her collarbone in the Dotsch manner. She peeked up at him from under her lashes. His expression was unreadable.

Once she thought her curtsey long enough, Gwen rose and gave her hand, upon which the earl pressed a short kiss. The formalities concluded, he pivoted on one foot and offered his arm. "Walk with me."

As she took his arm, Gwen became horridly aware of the various emotions flitting across her mouth: a slight smile at the breeze, a frown at the silence, lips pressed together nervously. She did her best to control her rebellious face as they walked slowly together, her in the sunlight and him in the shadows.

Strilu spoke first, "I hope you have found your accommodations pleasing."

"Yes, Your Distinction, thank you. My rooms are lovelier than those in my brother's castle." Despite longing for home, Gwen truly meant it.

"Good. You are welcome to stay as long as you wish as my guest. I would send no one back to suffer the Trials."

"Your Distinction, I...I mean to say that...thank you. Your kindness is most appreciated."

He nodded, but said no more. Though Gwen's heart had lifted when he asked her to stay, it sank at his continued silence. She stumbled a little and grasped his hand. He helped her right herself, and when she looked into his eyes, she couldn't tell what emotions dwelled there. Apathy? Suspicion? Kindness? His face was as a statue's, blank and still.

But then, the hint of a smile graced the corner of his mouth, and for a brief moment, he placed his hand on hers. He removed it, his cool touch lingering on her skin, and said, "I would be honored if you might join me again tomorrow."

Every day for a quinn, in the hour following luncheon, Gwen promenaded with him. On one particularly sunny afternoon, the earl stopped as they strode through the menagerie, his eyes fixed on a small wildcat. His fingers were cold on hers.

"Sire Druam?" Gwen said, glancing up at him. She had long since been given leave to address him informally. "Is something the matter?"

He blinked, then smiled down at her. The more time Gwen spent with him, the more she had seen the subtleties of his expression. Rather than stained glass, its story accessible to anyone, his emotions were more like a manuscript, readable only to those with the knowledge and experience. After a moment's pause, he said, "Nothing. I was simply thinking about the brevity of our lives."

"And? Did you find it a comforting or a chilling thought?"

"Rather comforting. It forces us to move, to act, whereas if one had hundreds of years in front of them, they may linger too long in the past, thinking rightly that they have all the time to pursue their desires."

"I find it terrifying."

They sat together on a stone bench.

"My lord, if I may venture to ask: what is to become of me?" Gwen licked her lips, then continued, "The days here have been pleasurable, but I cannot aimlessly wander forever."

"I had thought much on this. You cannot return to Demarren, and...should you leave here, it would sadden me greatly."

"I didn't think myself to be such an excellent guest. I suppose I should find a husband, though I don't know your courtship rituals."

He smiled sadly. "I suppose you should."

Gwen glanced at him, misreading his questioning look. "How does one choose their partner? How do they know it to be a good match without their family to guide them? I suppose, when you married, it was not so difficult a decision."

"I'm not married," he said. "Though I ought to have long ago. My father died before he made a match, and I have felt no urge to pursue any of the ladies throwing themselves at me. Until now."

"Why now?" As Gwen said it, she noticed the intensity of his look, the weight of his hand on hers.

"Maid Zaman – may I call you Gwen? – Gwen, I am painfully aware that I'm twice your age and you likely desire a younger husband. But you are the Liegelord's sister, so bring with you the means to lasting alliances. There are few men in D'Ehsen, other than myself, deserving of such a political match. Therefore, I make an offer of marriage to you."

During his speech, Gwen sat still, ever so conscious of the flitting corners of her mouth. She let his hand remain on hers, but didn't squeeze it in return. Her mind ran circles as he spoke, dancing between delight and fear. Delight at the thought that an earl should wish for her hand, but fear, too, for she had no idea how to respond. He had status, wealth, good blood...though nearer forty than thirty, he retained a sense of the handsomeness he must have had in his youth. Above all, he was unfailingly kind to her.

Despite his fine qualities, Gwen hesitated. She, like many maids, longed for romance, for a handsome knight to throw down his sword and take her up instead. Though too old now to deny the existence of duty, she was still naïve enough to hope that she alone was unaffected by it.

I wish Wullum was here to make this decision for me. What if I send a letter...no, it would take too long, and by the time it returns to me the earl may have moved on. If I marry a man as powerful as he, I might yet find a place here and earn the trust of these Dotsch strangers.

"I can see you have no answer yet for me," Druam said. He kissed her hand, then pulled away. "Think on it for as long as you wish. I will await your answer when you are ready." With that, he strolled away, his hands held loosely behind his back. Gwen couldn't tell what emotions he had felt at her silence; his expression had slipped back into the blankness she didn't understand.

For a few moments, Gwen breathed deeply and contemplated the offer. She could not consult her brother, and had no friends here to ask for advice. The sunlight followed her as she walked to the only place she thought she could find help: the novum. Though the novum possessed statues and altars to the nine Dotsch gods, Gwen liked to think that the gods of her faith could still hear her there. If anyone in this foreign place could help her, it would be them.

When Gwen entered the palace, her skin prickled. She paused, glancing around, but saw nothing out of the ordinary. A cluster of nobles was gathered not far from her, but they only spared her a disinterested glance before returning to their conversation. She shook off her wariness and turned toward the novum.

"A word, if I may, Your Highness?" One of the nobles disengaged himself from the group and approached Gwen. He had blonde hair cut to his chin and dressed in a style Gwen recognized as Skallish. The scent of mint clung to him.

"I'm sorry, my lord, but I don't think we've been introduced," Gwen said. She held her hand back from his extended palm, and he withdrew, his warm expression turning colder.

"Then let me remedy the situation," the lord said. He offered his arm. Not wanting to offend him further, Gwen took it and let him lead her away from the others. He said as they walked, "I am Lord Einar Daghorn, the ambassador from King Arvid of Skålland. You need not introduce yourself; I know that you are Gwendolyn Zaman, the princess of Demarren. I had been hoping, ever since I heard of your arrival, to speak with you."

Even without his condescending tone, Gwen would have felt suspicious of this man. The Skallish people in Demarren still held close to their kin in Skålland.

Lord Daghorn held tightly to Gwen's arm, his smile frozen above his long mustache. She said politely, "I am sure I would have little conversation to interest you, my lord."

"Oh? Surely you must know why I would seek you out. You see, I am rather interested in the Trials. My kin have anxiously awaited news of the Inquisition's success in rooting out foul witches, and I wonder why, in such circumstances, Demarren's own princess would flee."

Gwen swallowed and looked straight ahead. "My brother wanted me to learn more of Dotsch culture in order for me to gain a marriage offer. He hopes to make a lasting alliance."

"Is that so? I only question, for I had heard rumors – nasty ones, not oft heard in polite society – that you had been charged for possessing magic. Of course, I would never believe such horrid accusations, but your presence here does force me to wonder if there may be some truth in them."

"Lord Daghorn, I–"

"Rest easy, child. There is nothing I can do to you...not at the present, anyway. But my kin in your country would be delighted to hear of your safe arrival in Riverfen." Daghorn withdrew his arm and made a sweeping bow, his eyes glittering. "I hope we may speak again, Your Highness. I am *fascinated* to hear more of your brother's plans for alliances." He swept away, the smell of mint lingering where he had stood. Gwen hugged herself. *The Inquisition knows where to find me now; what will they do to Wullum?* She didn't think that Daghorn knew the truth of her magic, as only Ebarren and Wullum had seen her use it, but even his suspicion could put her brother in danger.

Gwen tried to put her thoughts at ease, but they swirled in her head and made her stomach turn over. She smoothed her skirts, clammy hands comforted by its softness. Perhaps she could send a letter to her brother, warn him...but that might only make things worse. She could do nothing for Wullum now. She, at least, was safe under the earl's protection. But that idea, of course, reminded her of the proposal, and her guts only churned more.

Thankfully, no one else was in the novum, and Gwen shut the door behind her. She sank to her knees in the middle of the calming space and stared at the nine statues arranged around her, each lit by a multitude of long candles. Not having learned the names of these new gods yet, Gwen whispered her own familiar ones: "Ittar, father of all; Rebir, mother of Earda; Junan, brother-and-sister-in-one: I pray that you still hear me in this strange place. I'm sorry for not turning to you sooner, but I feared that my voice wouldn't carry to you. I seek repentance for my sins, and ask you to help me."

As she looked up at nine statues, Gwen imagined the three images she knew. Ittar, his beard long enough to wrap around his torso three times, sat in the middle. Rebir was always placed to his right, her body rounded, and Junan to the left, a figure both man and woman. Securing their visages firmly in her mind, Gwen prayed, "Keep Wullum safe. I will do everything I can to live well and happily, as he asked me to, if only you keep him safe. I don't know what to do with Earl Seastone. He is kind and handsome, but I don't know him." Gwen paused to think about Lord Daghorn. "Without Wullum to help me...I must turn to the earl, mustn't I?" The nine unfamiliar gods gazed down at her, their faces blank. However, one of them, a woman, had her hand held out in a friendly way, her smile apparent even in the semi-darkness. Gwen thought her to be the Dotsch version of Rebir: motherly and warm. The more Gwen looked, the more she thought the statue to be kindly rather than strange. "Earl Seastone is good to me. He wouldn't let me come to harm, and he would treat me well. Rebir had only known Ittar for three days before he impregnated her with Earda, and she has loved him ever since. I will take Druam Strilu as my husband, as Rebir took the highest father."

Gwen clasped her hands and finished her prayer. "Let my decision be the right one. Protect Wullum, and keep all creatures of Earda within your hearts. *A'alatar*."

Gwen gathered her skirts to stand, then stopped, for there was something else she must atone for. Bowing her head, she whispered, "The Inquisition has taken innocent people and hanged them. I am guilty of possessing and using magic, and yet I am free. I promise that I shall never again cast magic. I will be an obedient wife and a good mother, if I am blessed to be such, and I will not let my talents tarnish this new life you have granted to me. *A'alatar.*"

CHAPTER EIGHT
Seanna

THE QUEEN of Dotschar languished in silk sheets, delighting in the touch of her partner's skin, its dimples and moles, the bumps of bone along her spine. She traced her hand up the other's back, waiting for the undressing to be done. Already naked herself, Queen Seanna tried not to look down at her five-month pregnant belly: it was horrid and huge with blemished skin. Ugly.

The rest of her, though, was beautiful. Everyone thought so. With Eadron blood from her grandfather, Seanna had ochre skin with dark hair and darker eyes. Like her mother, she wore her hair in relaxed curls that made her round face seem thinner. She had a look, when peeking up from under her thick lashes, that made men's hearts tremble with lust.

"Why are you stopping?" Seanna asked when she noticed her lover, Larka, hesitate.

"Your Grace, I...I'm sorry. I can't."

"Why not?" Seanna demanded. "You've done it plenty of times before."

"Yes, but...but you weren't with child then. Carnal acts are dangerous for the baby, so says Shepherd William, and I can't be responsible for hurting it."

"Horseshit. There's ways to do this without upsetting the child. I could pleasure you, make you scream such things as would make the gods themselves blush. Come, my dear, my sweet, my own–"

"No, Your Grace. It's not just the child; it's the symptoms." Larka paused and gave a significant glare to Seanna's belly. "Could you love me if I were deformed like that?"

The queen's mellow mood darkened and twisted into a sour temper. Larka had been her lover for the past eight months, but the royal family had only just announced Seanna's new pregnancy now that she started to show. In that time, Seanna had showered Larka with gifts and jewels far above the girl's station. But if Larka could abandon her so easily, Seanna could do far worse. "Mind your words, Maid. I could have you executed."

"And I would bring you down with me," Larka snapped as she pulled her dress back over her shoulders. "A queen making love to her handmaid, who rejects her king's bed for that of another woman? I think your head would find the block far sooner than mine."

"No one would believe you." Seanna put on an air of nonchalance, though inside she seethed. The fiery words that first attracted her to Larka spun around onto Seanna, and she greatly disliked the feeling. She rolled to her back, her head on the pillow, and regarded her lover with a bored expression. "No one would care."

"Wouldn't they? The courtiers hate you, the king hates you...everyone knows that his bad humors worsened after he married you. They'd all cheer to see you dethroned."

"How dare you speak to me like that," Seanna said, and though her tone was sharp, she betrayed little of the fury lodged in her heart. *Damn this common whelp, she should be grateful to lick my boots, let alone be allowed in my confidence! She's a liar and a whore.* "I am the queen of Dotschar."

"The king's whore, they call you. The Empire's slut," Larka said fearlessly.

Seanna picked at her fingernails. She was too practiced at apathy to shiver. "And yet history will remember me as the mother of the finest king D'Ehsen has ever known. What shall you be remembered for? Nothing. When you die in filth, you'll wish you had not scorned me."

"With empty threats such as these, Your Grace, you cannot expect anyone to take you seriously." With a firm thud, Larka shut the servant's door behind her, the seam blending into the wall.

Seanna glared at the seam. *Vecking slut. Once I bear the king's heir, I shall have the power to do as I please, and Larka will find herself tied to a stone in the bottom of the channel.* If she kept up her anger, perhaps she wouldn't notice her heart's pain.

"You would never hurt me like that," she whispered to her belly. "I'll raise you to love your mother above all others."

The main door to her chambers slammed open, and she rolled her eyes. *Henrik.* Of course the king had come without announcement. Though her pride still prickled at Larka's scorn, Seanna was glad that they hadn't been caught together. Despite her confident words, she knew the king would be furious with her.

"My dear?" Henrik called from the antechamber. "Are you decent?" Both questions were said flatly and without tenderness. The pet name was a courtesy, etiquette at this point, for the people expected their king and queen to care for each other.

Seanna bothered only to put on a pair of slippers before shuffling from her bedroom to the antechamber. Her breasts, just recently heavier, sagged more than she liked, and she couldn't see her dainty feet past her protruding belly. From her large window, she saw the glimmering sea, blue with white flecks. She was to set sail that day for the Masque, and could have sworn departure was scheduled for the afternoon. *Though Henrik could have changed it just to spite me.*

King Henrik waited in the large entrance room. It had tall windows hidden by red curtains, multiple Eadron rugs, couches, chairs, and an empty fireplace that would be roaring come winter. A legged mirror stood to one side, reflecting the king's rear. Henrik's hands were clasped behind his back, and he stared at the floor, his brow wrinkled in thought. He was not the tallest man, but had a thickset way about him that made him seem larger. From a pure Dotsch bloodline, he had thick brown hair, grey eyes, and fair skin.

As Seanna entered, Henrik groaned at her nakedness and turned his back to her. "Must you?"

"Oh, my dear," Seanna said, coming to stand in front of the mirror to criticize her reflection. "You know I must."

"If only to frustrate me."

"Show what you've neglected, you mean."

"You neglect me as oft as I neglect you."

"Have you even thought of me since I became with child? Your child, I should say."

Henrik's shoulders hunched, then relaxed. He still didn't look at her. "Our child, Seanna. And it is unwise to threaten its health. I cannot bear another loss." He paused, then said, "I haven't come here to discuss our marriage. Too often lately have you spoken of things best left unsaid. I have heard complaints, too, that you stay silent at the woes of the minor nobles and rustics rather than offering solutions and sympathy. As my queen, and therefore my mouthpiece when I am absent, you must reflect my opinions and condolences at all times."

He blathered on as Seanna stopped listening. *I know this already. And what if I state my own thoughts? I am the queen.* And queen she had been for four years, though since her wedding she had, mostly out of spite, gone out of her way to be contrary to Henrik's wishes.

At first, of course, Seanna had been the image of the perfect queen. Her father, the Earl of Stillmeadow, spent months cajoling the king into marrying Seanna rather than another earl's daughter. Though her beauty brought many wealthy suitors to her door, her barbed words often frightened them away. Knowing her tenuous position in the court – and knowing how beloved Henrik's first queen had been before her untimely death – Seanna tried to hold her tongue and present herself as sweet and modest.

That lasted about as long as her first failed pregnancy.

Henrik paused, and Seanna realized he expected her to say something. She smiled blithely. "Of course, darling. Anything you say."

"Did you listen at all?"

"Here and there, though I must confess I have heard better sermons from drunk curates."

Henrik shook his head. "I've tried to help you better understand royal politics. I am finished. Make an embarrassment of yourself if you must." After he made a minuscule adjustment to his robe, he continued, "Get dressed and have your things sent to the docks. The ship launches at noon."

Seanna chose a loose, comfortable linen dress for the trip. Instead of her heavy crown with its egg-sized gems, she placed a beaded circlet on her brow. Before she left, she sent for a steward and ordered, "My handmaid, Larka Fellsworth, is no longer capable of acting in my service. Dismiss her at once and dock her pay for insubordination. A quinn in the stocks may also help her understand that rudeness to royalty will not be abided." The steward bowed stiffly, and, her commandment given, Seanna left her rooms satisfied.

The carriage she and Henrik took to the docks could easily carry ten passengers, but they were its only occupants. It carried them away from the Silver Keep and across the bridge into Midtown.

Con Salur, the capital of Dotschar, was a work of architectural art. It held four districts, each the size of a lesser city. King's Berth (lovingly called Midtown) sat on the shelf of a red-stone cliff and housed the city's nobles and wealthiest citizens. The second district, Seawind, rested atop the cliffs. It held the Grand Novum and most of the city's residents. All around, both sea- and land-side, a wall seventy feet high guarded Seawind from both enemies and elements. At the very base of the cliffs was Dockside, where the wharfs, warehouses, and homes for sailors and fishermen could be found. Sprawling docks berthed the king's navy, as well as various merchant ships and foreign envoys.

But the most amazing district, and the most mysterious, was Darkroad. It stretched from Seawind, to Midtown, and then down to Dockside, a series of underground switchbacks, alleyways, and buildings carved inside the cliffs. The main thoroughfares were wide enough to accommodate three wagons side-by-side, while the smallest alleys had barely enough room for a starving urchin. The only entrances to Darkroad were stone doors in the three other districts, and if those doors were to be shut, no one could go from one district to another.

When Seanna first came to Con Salur, she had been overwhelmed with its size and intrigued with the secrets built into its very heart. Now, she twitched the curtain shut as the carriage trundled into Darkroad and made its slow, laborious way down to Dockside.

Inside Darkroad, though, the wind died, and Seanna soon sweated through her linen. Despite the grandeur of the Silver Keep and the beauty of the ocean from the cliffs, to travel between districts was intolerable. It took too long with little entertainment on the way.

"Is Prince Udolf coming?" Seanna asked as the carriage jostled them for the hundredth time.

"No. I've left him as Steward of the Court, as practice." The king didn't say it, but Seanna knew the implication. *As practice in case I fail to bear a son.*

Henrik's sister, before her death, had borne a healthy son. Unless Seanna produced an heir, the kingdom would pass to the king's nephew, Udolf. Often, Seanna had nightmares of Udolf cutting the unborn child out of her or poisoning her so that she would lose the baby. He was an ambitious man, and she was a threat. She was glad that he would stay in the city for the months she and Henrik were gone.

The carriage rolled along beaten planks, making a rumbling sound that reverberated through Seanna's chest. She felt her heart lift instantly at the sound and sight of the sea: waves climbing hungrily up the beach, gulls croaking overhead, the occasional splash on the tumultuous surface as a fish rose to snatch its meal.

"How long will your trip take?" Seanna asked when the carriage came to a stop. Henrik was to travel overland to visit his estates and break bread with vassals; Seanna had happily chosen the faster route by water.

As he helped Seanna out of the carriage, Henrik gave her a smile that she disliked immensely. "Actually, I have decided to travel with you by sea. The vassals will have to wait until after the Masque."

Veck. Vecking hells...damn him!

Seanna stopped on the last step, her foot hovering over the ground. She saw the fancy holk sitting heavily in the water and sailors waiting for her to board. Members of the court stood to either side to wave farewell. They all watched her. *A whole deshe trapped in a vecking ship with my vecking husband.*

"Henrik, you–"

"Manners, my dear," Henrik said, grinning smugly as he waved. She glared at him with despise in every bone.

I had a lover in Brin you took me from, she thought savagely. *I've lost two children before birth because of the way you treat me. The curates told me that a man's cruel words will poison a pregnancy. They were right. And you'll poison this one, too.* Sudden inspiration struck her. *I'll see those vassals he's neglecting. They'll learn to love their queen and her son far more than they ever loved Henrik.*

"I'm taking the wagon house by land," Seanna hissed.

"You can't possibly mean–"

"Of course I mean it. Tell the men to unload my belongings and take them up to Seawind, where I expect the caravan to be prepared for me. I don't care how long it takes me to reach Riverfen; I refuse to spend any more time with you than I have to."

Her proclamation given, Seanna ripped her hand from Henrik's and climbed back into the carriage. From inside, she could see the disdainful looks people sent her way when Henrik made the announcement. He could have ordered her to go, but she expected he was just as tired of dealing with her as she was with him.

Seanna feigned apathy and tried to convince herself that she was in the right. She whispered to her child, "They are merely envious of me. I am the queen."

But down, down in the hidden places of her heart, she knew that they loathed her.

CHAPTER NINE
Seanna

THE BED Seanna had been given was carved from stone, hard and unforgiving. *How do they expect me to sleep on this thing?* The room itself held no appeal: clean and sparse, no unnecessary decorations nor rugs. The window had no shutters or glass, leaving her room open to the late summer air. In winter, great stone blocks would be used to seal the opening and keep in the warmth. Seanna couldn't imagine living in a completely enclosed space for months straight with no means to look outside or feel the sharp breeze.

All in all, it was a disappointing room. *They call this fit for a queen? Does absolutely everything have to be made of stone? The bed, the desk, the washstand, even the damned pisspot.* Seanna had always been fond of spindly chairs with cushioned seats, long fainting couches, or feather-soft four-poster beds. This was ugly at best, insulting at worst. Did even the High Earl himself sleep on a bed such as this in his own home? She put one arm on the windowsill and looked out over the city.

Mostly built from light grey rock streaked with blue or green or vivid red veins, D'Clet stretched out across the mountain valley, bordered on three sides by towering peaks. Roofs constructed from bronze tiles reflected the summer sun. Far in the distance, at the mouth of the valley, a great wall rose to protect the city.

Nothing broke the monotony of stone and metal, save a chasm that split the city in two. On one side lay the majority of the city. On the other, where Seanna now stood, were expensive homes, monasteries, and libraries, built up from the valley floor and into the mountainside. A road curved up above the vast complexes, leading to temples that soared over all.

The ravine disappeared from sight to the right and left, traversing miles of mountains. Here in D'Clet was the only bridge that spanned the dark depths, wide enough for two wagons side-by-side but still frighteningly narrow. A single spanning arch, forty feet in length, with no trestles nor bracing, and only chest-high rails to halt a plummet to the rocks far below, it crossed the divide at its narrowest point.

Seanna couldn't help but be slightly impressed.

Only slightly. After all, Con Salur had far greater feats of architecture and engineering; only D'Clet's bridge surpassed it in sheer technical construction. *And the beds here are still made of stone.*

"Your Grace?" Sir Eric stepped into the room, his blue cloak swirling about his ankles. A tall man with a grim face, he was precise in everything he did: from his polished mail to his clean boots, his shaven cheeks to his trimmed nails, he had not a buckle out-of-sorts or misplaced. His greying hair was shorn in the military style. He rarely spoke, and then only in the shortest sentences possible. Seanna couldn't recall if she had ever seen him smile.

"Is it time?" Seanna asked, still staring out the window. She heard Sir Eric shift slightly, the links in his mail making a tinkling sound.

"Yes. His Distinction requests you wear something warm, as the feast will be held on the terrace and may last into the night."

"Thank you, Sir Eric. You may attend me later," Seanna said. Sir Eric bowed and turned sharply on his heel to leave.

Seanna prepared herself for dinner with the High Earl. Egil Rask, whom she would address as Earl Hjalder, had a reputation as the shrewdest, least trustworthy lord in Dotschar. He controlled most of the mines in the southern Seldar Mountains, as well as all the passes from the lowlands to the River Valley; the only man wealthier than him was Earl Seastone. Most lords treaded lightly around him, for his allegiances had shifted back and forth over the years from the gods to the king to the earls and back again. Some even suspected him of questionable deeds in order to win and keep his power: he had outlived all of his younger brothers, two wives and multiple children, and four other High Earls before earning the title himself. Seanna had heard whispers that Rask had hired necromancers in an attempt to prolong his life.

At this point, Rask had no loyalties. He held disdain for Henrik and the other earls, and had recently withdrawn donations to the predicants in the Grand Novum. Though she knew she would not gain an alliance with him – for Henrik's first queen had been Rask's daughter, and Henrik had chosen Seanna instead of another of Rask's children for his second marriage – Seanna hoped to at least leave a good impression. She had even taken the long way to Riverfen to see him: a powerful man such as Rask could prove useful to her in the future.

Clothed warmly in red fox fur and grey wool, Seanna let Sir Eric escort her through wide stone halls lined with extravagantly carved pillars and hundred-foot rugs. They went up, up a huge curving staircase that led to a balcony of enormous proportions. It had two sides that, if one cared to peer over the graceful bannister, dropped straight down into the bottomless ravine. Not wanting to feel that head-spinning, stomach-unsettling sensation that such a sight would bring, Seanna glided straight to her seat. A round table, smooth on top but ragged rock underneath, held room for fifty chairs all similarly sculpted from mountain stone. Nobles milled around the balcony, sipping wine and laughing.

Two chairs painted with gold and silver faced the ravine. Seanna sat heavily in one. The baby shifted restlessly, as it had been all day. *I hope he settles soon.* Gods, she wanted nothing more than to take a nice long sojourn over the chamberpot, then go to sleep.

"His Distinction, Egil Rask, High Earl of Dotschar, Earl of D'Clet and Hjalder," a steward announced. "And his wife, Lady Hjalder." From the hall stepped an old man, nearing seventy, with long white hair streaked with grey and a groomed beard to match. He, like Henrik, was pure Dotsch, though his fair skin was blighted with age. Though his shoulders bent and his back curved, his eyes glared out with steely authority. Moving slowly but deliberately, he made his careful way to his seat, his eyes darting about the company as if trying to decide who he wanted to hang the most. Beside him, a young woman – she must have been younger even than Seanna, barely out of her teens – shuffled nervously. Her expression reminded Seanna of a deer's, startled at the attention and debating between fleeing or staying.

Those sitting at the table rose as the high earl and his wife made their tremulous way along the balcony. Only Seanna remained seated. When the old man finally reached her, she leaned forward and held out her hand. He took it with a surprisingly firm grip and planted a dry kiss. Seanna's skin crawled as his eyes met hers. *You're the queen, you have nothing to fear from this worm,* she reminded herself. But the man in front of her appeared an elderly wolf rather than a worm: hungry, feral, not caring who he should destroy in the search for his next meal.

"Your Distinction," Seanna said, a false smile stuck to her lips.

"Your Grace," Rask replied. He sat with a sigh of relief. "It has become quite a trial for these old bones to travel those long halls."

"I empathize," Seanna said, patting her belly. "Different causes, same results."

The earl now arrived, dinner began. Course after course of highland foods appeared over Seanna's shoulder: roasted ox legs, medleys of carrots and beets, freshly-caught salmon with scales that almost melted off, berries mixed with heavy creams and spread on sugary bread, cinnamon apples, balls of dough filled with savory lamb, chicken breasts dipped in white gravy...half of it made her want to send praises of delight to the kitchens, but the other half made her gag. *I used to love steak, now*

I can't even smell it without wanting to puke.

Full of food and lolling in their chairs, the nobles soon turned to swapping inane political speeches. *Their favorite pastime.*

"Lord Bladefell, what do you think of the recent corsair attacks?"

"A travesty, my friend! We should gather all our resources and hunt those wretches down. With my archers and your ships, we'd make the coastlines safe again."

Years of listening to such drivel, plus a full stomach and a kicking child, helped Seanna tune out the nobles' nonsense. She watched the gathering with little interest, judging the ladies' hairstyles or jewelry with a bored glance or trying to decide how easy it would be to hide an entire chicken in a lord's sleeve.

"–I do believe that Manderly has a chance at the position, if only he would spend more time in the Novum itself," the lord Osney Deering said with a shake of his head. Seanna sat up, a pulse of excitement flaring in her chest.

"Does my lord support Predicant Manderly?" she asked.

"Well," Lord Deering drawled, "he *does* have a certain...rustic appeal, if you will. The commoners seem to adore him. As for myself, I find the whole process to be utterly droll. Holding an election within the Grand Novum for the next Exalt...it hasn't been done in over a century! It's more fascinating to me how effectively the candidates have–"

"It seems to me," Seanna said over him, "that Manderly has the support of the majority of the kingdom, and without resorting to blackmail or bribes. Even as a curate, he walked the slums giving his sandals from his feet and his cloak from his back to those in need. A man such as Manderly would earn money for the Novum through nobles' desire to do good, while Ropaz might spend it all in order to keep his power. What think you, Earl Hjalder?" Seanna asked, turning toward Rask. A flush of pride crept onto her cheeks at what she thought to be a fine argument.

Before Rask could speak, another courtier said, "Ropaz is a good friend of mine! He would never–"

"But Manderly does have the support of the people..." someone else interjected.

They talked over themselves, only snippets of conversation audible over the din. *Damn, Rask's just going to let them jabber on.*

With utter casualness, Rask leaned forward, plucked a grape from his platter, and chewed it slowly, his eyes drifting over the guests. Seanna's sweaty palms gripped her armrests and the nobles quieted as they waited for him to speak.

"My, my. A broad collection of opinions here, and not all of them good," Rask said, his soft voice slithering across the table. "I am perhaps the only person alive here who remembers the last time an Exalt died; a truly tragic waste, but too much mead will do that to a man no matter how holy. He had chosen his replacement, which of course meant that the issue of succession was nonexistent. A historic moment, this, of the Novum predicants choosing one amongst their numbers to lift above all, the closest to the gods any of us could hope to be."

He paused, took a sip from his silver chalice, and smacked his lips. "A good vintage. Now, you ask my opinion, Your Grace, and you must not be angry with me for speaking it plainly. The truth of the matter is, you are as ignorant as a rustic child."

What? Seanna gaped dumbly at him before remembering her station and shutting her mouth.

Rask's bright eyes mocked her as he continued, "Manderly, though a kind man, has no knowledge of politics or the work that goes into running the entirety of our religion. You call him charitable, yet those paths are oft taken by men whose attempts in other areas have failed. Did you know that he once worked to divert donations for the poor back into his novum when his actions brought it to near ruin? It was years ago, of course, but I remember it quite well. Later, he blackmailed brothels into paying him a monthly stipend so he wouldn't send his righteous soldiers after them. That, too, proved unsuccessful. His 'charity' is a last resort, not a deed born from compassion.

"Besides, Ropaz has demonstrated himself to be far superior in negotiating with foreign ambassadors, and has a keen mind for money. The important thing to remember about rustics, Your

Grace, is that they only have to *think* they are being treated well. If they are given their holidays and the occasional tax break, they count themselves fortunate."

"But, Your Distinction–" Seanna interjected.

She only got that far before Rask said loudly, "Of course, how can any of us expect our queen to know the inner workings of religion? The function of layman politics escapes her. A queen, if she knows little of our world, should be seen and never heard. You may carry the king's child, but we all realize that is your only purpose in the court. At least my daughter, the gods bless her grave, knew what Henrik needed and wanted, and provided him with a queen worthy of the title," he sneered. Her eyes focusing on nothing, Seanna swallowed hard and pressed her nails into her palms. *The nerve.*

Nobles around her snorted, then giggled, then laughed, bursts of mirth echoing in the ravine. Seanna stewed in silence, the earl's words like a knife in her chest. No one, not even Henrik, had ever spoken to her like that before.

"That's better," Rask said with a condescending glare. "Red cheeks become you, as does silence. Your only redeeming quality is your beauty, and that shall fade with time. I wonder what will happen to you when even that has disappeared and your child has outgrown you? The gods be good, you'll meet the same fate as my daughter."

"How *dare* you!" Seanna gasped. "Only the gods and the king may judge me. I am still your queen!"

"Only they can judge, that is true, but the rest of us can appraise you as we would a fine jewel. Though, in your case, the rusted chain and broken pendant kept in the bottom of the drawer."

I won't hear him insult me any longer. Seanna pushed out her chair, standing as forcefully as she could. She earnestly hoped she seemed magnificent rather than petulant. "I thank you for the fine dinner, Your Distinction, though I found the conversation trite and offensive. Good night."

As Seanna swept away from the table, she heard the courtier's whispers and Earl Hjalder's barking laugh. Hot tears poured from her chin onto the floor, trod seconds later by her slippers. *I'll be the most beloved queen D'Ehsen has ever known,* she thought savagely, her hand closing in a fist over her belly. *Even more than Fleta vecking Rask. My son will rule a kingdom shadowed by his mother's legacy.*

CHAPTER TEN
Gwen

WILL HE be kind to me? Gwen thought as she sat at her wedding feast's groaning tables. *Mother told me that some good men become monsters when they are married. Please, Rebir, let him be good to me. Let him treat me well.*

The whirlwind of their ceremony had left her little time for thought: *The predicant gestured to Gwen. She stepped forward, as did Druam, until each stood beside a basin of water. With her hands in Druam's, she waited for the predicant to place a long ribbon over their heads. As he draped it over their shoulders, she took a deep breath.*

"Princess Gwendolyn," the predicant said," invoke the names of your maternal ancestors."

"Mother Sardra, Grandmother Gwendolyn, Great-Grandmother Hidara," Gwen said softly.

"Your Distinction, invoke the names of your paternal ancestors."

Druam intoned, "Father Ephraine, Grandfather Ansel, Great-Grandfather Beniarnyn." As he spoke, a drowsy feeling came over Gwen. She blinked, and it faded. The predicant used the blue ribbon draped around their necks to tie their hands together. Dipping his fingers in the basin, he sprinkled water over their joined hands and said, "By the blessing of Jarico and Milen, I tie the lives of these two people together, sanctifying their union with holy water. From now until their deaths, never to part, may they be of one soul and one heart." The nobles clapped politely for the new Lady Seastone.

The feast, though splendid, held little appeal for Gwen. She barely picked at the quail and quite ignored the mutton. Even the various kinds of loaves, made with all sorts of spices, failed to make her mouth water. Only a handful of fruits and pastries made it to her plate, and these she only nibbled at. Meagre mouthfuls of wine and cordial stuck in her throat. Gwen hoped Druam would be a kind lover, but all men changed once they saw a woman naked, or so her mother had told her years ago. *And will I conceive a child tonight that I can tell such things to?* She watched the surrounding lords with wary eyes, knowing that soon they would carry her to the bedchamber and rip off her clothes as they went. She wished she could have married at home in Demarren, where there was no such barbaric tradition.

During the dancing, Gwen partnered with a score of lords, all whispering in her ear. Some, a word of congratulations; others, a petulant warning. "You are quite lucky, my lady. He will bring you great happiness." "He cares only for the land and its people; even his brothers could attest to his lack of warmth." The lords became indistinguishable from one another until one, younger than all the rest, took Gwen's hand during the *galliar*. Long black hair hung around his high cheeks, green eyes met hers unabashedly. His ivory-white hands were soft. A gleaming amulet lay on his chest, a halo of clear gems around a white central stone.

"I'm Mavian Strilu," he said as he guided her around the circle of other dancers.

"My husband's brother?" Gwen asked. The earl had mentioned his younger brother in passing, but this man looked nothing like Druam.

"No," he said with a short laugh. "His cousin. I doubt Xandro would have pulled himself from his books for this affair, and of course Verdon is...well, I really shouldn't speak of it."

"Speak of what?" Gwen was intrigued. The man's name and description sparked a memory, but she couldn't recall it exactly.

"My lord's middle brother vanished years ago. Left, and never returned. But we shouldn't speak of such sad matters on this happy day. Though all the interesting gossip is macabre, isn't it? Some interesting rumors have begun circulating. People say that prowlers have come close to the city."

Gwen laughed. "That's preposterous! How would they hide?"

"Think what you will," Mavian said, a smirk edging into his cheek. "Druam tries to keep the peace, but we all know the prowlers are spreading faster than ever before. It's only a short time before they appear in the city. Besides, they're not as wild as some believe; I've seen them myself, coordinating with each other, plotting, using strategies to stalk and corner their prey. My castle borders on wild lands, and I've watched from the walls as their packs descend on farmers and travelers, always sending my soldiers out too late to help. Quick little bastards."

He's always studying those prowlers,' Lady Smithen said. 'Sending his men out to find the victims and capture the beasts. Tries to get them alive, so I've heard.' Gwen had overheard the conversation between nobles. *'Why Earl Seastone allows such behavior is beyond me,' Lord Smithen had replied. 'He's not right in the head.' 'Oh, too true, but the earl loves his cousin far too much. I think he dotes on him because of Verdon.'* Here and there, Gwen had heard talk about Mavian Strilu, none of it good. Everyone disliked and avoided him, yet he acted friendly to her.

Gwen hadn't much time to think about it. The dance ended abruptly, and bells, like silver chirruping birds, rang out around the gathering. Guests shook them with gusto, excitedly looking between Gwen and Druam. For the new couple, the public festivities had ended; the bedding had come.

A lord caught Gwen around the waist with the blue ribbon, pulling on the silk as if he pulled a horse by the reins. More lords clustered around Gwen and lifted her skirts just enough to grab her lace garter. The victorious noble held it aloft, spinning it around his finger and laughing uproariously. Fingers pulled at Gwen's dress, coming away with the carefully sewn embroidery.

Many hands lifted her aloft to carry her to the bridal chamber. She craned her neck to see the women pushing Druam along, their grasping talons ripping off his tunic. By the time they reached the chamber, Gwen had lost her shoes and stockings.

Finally, the invasive men put her down beside the bed, some jeering at her, others still laughing from the fun of it. *Beasts*, she thought sourly, reaching up to touch the jagged edges of what used to be her sleeves. *And they suffer their own daughters to undergo this humility?* Her gown had been ruined, its skirt filled with gaping holes. Druam stumbled into the chamber having fared a little better.

Then Gwen realized that the noblemen had not left. They and a few women filed into a small gallery which had been filled with seats, four rows that rose one above the other. Many more courtiers gathered outside the room, their painted cheeks pushing against each other to see. *Am I to be an animal on exhibit, rutting with my mate?*

Gwen turned her back to the crowd. *They can't see me cry.* She bit her lip to keep a wail from escaping. The bed was a large, four-poster thing with curtains all around. On both sides of it, wooden partitions hid the back of the room from view. A servant took her arm and guided her behind one of the partitions. Another took the bed's curtains, drawing them shut to the crowd.

Once hidden from the nobles' eyes, Gwen felt anticipation crawling up her spine and down her arms, a quiver that made goose pimples break out over her dark skin. Her mother had told her that consummation could be a pleasant experience, if the husband took his time and ensured her pleasure. *'But that is very unlikely, my dear. Pleasure is nearly impossible for a woman, so expect it to hurt at the worst and feel awkward at the best.'* Despite her mother's warning, Gwen felt a tingle of curiosity.

Her flesh prickled, naked and exposed to the overpowering heat in the room. A fire had been lit on top of all the bodies packed in. With a bow, the maid pulled aside one part of the curtains to hide Gwen's body as she climbed into the bed. Some light filtered into the small space, glowing through the fabric. She waited, shivering despite the heat, for her husband.

The curtains on the other side of the bed opened and Druam entered. His body, pale in the darkness, was long and lean. Dark hair traced down his chest, soft as the down between Gwen's legs.

"Are they still out there?" Gwen whispered, hugging her legs.

"Yes. They'll wait until they hear us finish." Druam's voice was gentle, though his eyes ran over her. His thumb brushed her cheek and caught one of her tears. He made no move to get on top of her.

"I'm sorry," she said, wiping away stray droplets. "I should be grateful, I should be pleasing you–"

He exhaled, a soft snort of amusement. "You're a virgin in her wedding bed. I'd be more surprised if you didn't cry. We have to do this, but I want you to promise me that you'll stop me if you ever feel mistreated."

Gwen nodded.

Tendrils of warmth followed his fingers across her body. Her stomach fluttered as he traced across it. His hand slid over her hip bones and thighs, reaching for the darkness between her legs. A sudden intrusion inside made her gasp, filling a space she hadn't known she possessed. Was this it? She didn't know it could feel so...so strange.

Gwen tensed, her whole body tightening, her arms rigid on the pillows, her legs crunching up against him. The full feeling went away, and she felt a warm wetness brush against her thigh. *Remember what Mother said: I have to please him. I have to do this.* "Keep going," she said through gritted teeth.

"Try to relax. Please, I know this frightens you, but it'll hurt less."

To do as Druam said seemed difficult, but as he caressed her and whispered sweet things, Gwen's body melted back into the bed. Not completely, but enough that he tried again, moving his fingers inside her. Sometimes, he would hit a place that made her shudder, a new feeling of delight welling up from a hidden spot.

Some minutes later, he levered himself on top of her. He hesitated, and she said, "I'm ready, I think. Do it."

The pain Gwen expected didn't come; instead, she felt an

odd pressure against her bladder and a stretching sensation where he entered her. She wondered if she would ever become used to the fullness, and how any woman could take delight in this event. She let him take her legs and wrap them around his hips. That tingling warmth again spread from inside her, causing her thighs to twitch against him, her heart to race. It felt nice. Not the divine ecstasy her mother had spoken of, but certainly a small, good feeling.

The bed frame creaked ever so slightly, the pillows and blankets soaked with Druam's sweat. Gwen didn't know for how long he moved inside her. From outside the curtains, she heard once more the nobles' polite clapping, and remembered that this had been a spectacle for them.

Druam's hand found itself on her leg, resting there in a private supplication, as the sound of many footsteps and low voices signaled the nobles' retreat. At last, the door closed, and Gwen was alone, truly alone, with her husband.

"Is this where I'll sleep now?" she asked in the burdening silence.

"No," he answered, his hand still on her thigh. "This chamber was readied specially for tonight. You will still have your chambers, which I'll visit regularly, or you may come to mine. This room, I expect, will be given to guests paying a high price to sleep where the earl's marriage was consummated."

Bitterness colored his tone in the last sentence, though at what she couldn't say. At the consummation itself? Or that their marriage bed would be tainted by money?

Curling up against him, she asked, "Will we take meals together now?"

"Yes, once the Masque is over and most of the court has returned home."

"What is the Masque?" Gwen said. Word of it had spread throughout the palace, but no one had taken the time to explain it to her. "I've never heard of such a thing."

"It's a new fad," Druam replied. "Started by King Henrik. Like a ball, but where each patron dresses in costumes and wears elaborate masks. No one should reveal their face throughout the entire thing. A night for anyone to speak without repercussion."

"Is each earl hosting one?"

"No, just myself, though the king's court will hold one at the beginning of spring. The Treaty of Riverfen, signed here a hundred years ago, marks the end of the last war Dotschar has been in. All of us hope that the peace may last another hundred years."

"I hope so, too," Gwen mumbled as she snuggled deeper into his arms. Eventually, she fell asleep, exhausted by the anxieties of the day.

Deep in the early hours of the morning, she woke, aware that a heavy blanket covered her now and that Druam was not beside her. Paltry light, the first hints of dawn, filtered into the room. She pulled on a robe and stepped barefoot to the floor to explore the room. As her eyes adjusted to the low light, she saw that Druam had left, though his wedding clothes were laid out. She wandered over to them, touching the cold fabric. A table had been set behind his partition, with an empty goblet and plate of food placed on it. She upturned the goblet, watching as red liquid dripped to the floor. Then she crawled back under the covers. Her nether region felt sore and stretched, and a musty smell made her wrinkle her nose.

Sitting up, the robe on her shoulders and the blankets on her legs, Gwen waited.

At last, she heard the creak of the door, light footsteps on the carpet, the rustle of fabric – no doubt Druam undressing – and the curtain pulled gently open. His head poked in, and he saw her awake. "I'm sorry to wake you, love. Pressing matters required my attention."

"I thought perhaps it was all a dream."

Druam chuckled and climbed into the blankets beside her. "I hope it was a decent dream for you. Sometimes I wonder if all my life is a dream, especially now. Are you hungry? Do you need anything?"

"I was just thinking about my brother," Gwen confessed. She hadn't spoken of him in days; who could she talk to? "I pray every night that the Trials have ended, that he's safe, but...how would I know? I'm afraid for him, and I don't know how I could ever hear any news." It all came out suddenly, those nights of silenced worries. "I'm afraid, too, that no one here can ever learn to like me."

"If they see what I see, they will," Druam said, pulling her into his arms. "I'll arrange for some gatherings for you. As for your brother...whatever I find out, I'll tell you, as soon as I know. I'll send one of my men there now as my eyes and ears for the Trials."

"Thank you."

"Anything for my wife," he murmured as Gwen cuddled against his chest. She finally felt like she had found a new home.

CHAPTER ELEVEN
Sandu

IT'S BETTER Merick's gone. Makes my job simpler. Sandu wanted to think such thoughts, but his weak heart instead urged him to comfort Cara. She had been nearly silent for two days, staring into the trees or at the road.

Sandu whistled a strain from "Dilara the Fair," a song his grandmother used to bellow next to the campfire on long winter nights. He had taken the spare horse's lead, as Cara seemed apathetic.

Sandu noted her morose expression, eyes unfocused, mouth slack. Her ruddy cheeks had turned redder, her nose pink. The green flecks in her eyes were brighter than usual. She looked the same as Sandu's father had after Mumma's death: vulnerable, lost, and not quite sure how to deal with her grief.

"How are you feeling?" he asked, immediately regretting it. *She's a product to be delivered. You're in this for the gold, don't forget that. Don't get attached.*

Cara raised her eyes, gave him a blank look, and said nothing. *For the better. She's nothing more than an assignment. Just get her to Riverfen and be done with it.* For once, the small voice in the back of Sandu's head stayed quiet. A relief, though a minor one.

Drizzle turned the clay-textured dirt into sticky mud as day wore into evening. Sandu's cloak soaked through, his clothes clinging to his wet skin. No matter how many times he had lived through such an experience, he shivered at the cold and cursed the heavens. *No one likes being rained on,* he mused. *Not even the farmers who need it to grow their crops.* Beside him, Cara had pulled her hood up, only the tip of her nose visible from its depths.

Galen struggled on. The rain sleeted down in cold sheets, masking the surrounding mountains in misty grey droplets. Water trickled down their horses' necks and tangled their manes into fierce messes. The morass underfoot sucked at Galen's hooves, making dreadful, squishy sounds. Sandu hated mud.

"What's that?" Cara asked, pointing in front of them. A path, barely visible through the rain, cut away from the road.

"I don't know. Maybe a trail to a farm or an outpost? Could be made by animals."

"Let's take a look." Cara climbed from her horse, dropping into the mud like a stone. Eyeing with distaste the brown slime that coated her boots, Sandu reluctantly followed suit. He led the way, wincing with every step. Gods, he hated mud.

Sentinel pines and granite boulders marked the way, nature's statues that had stood solemnly for centuries. After about fifteen minutes, during which Sandu had been tempted no fewer than eight times to just turn back, they emerged into an open space bordered by trees and a rocky slope. A ruined keep interrupted the greenery, its roof crumbled in and its stone walls scorched from some long-past fire. Filthy water filled the parts of its moat which weren't strewn with rubble, and three of the four towers had collapsed, covered now with nature's slow green hand.

"It must be ancient," Cara mused, one hand pulling her hood back slightly. "Abandoned years ago, to be this worn down. Is it safe, you think?"

"Safe enough, though I'm guessing we're not the first ones to have found it. Wait here; I'll take a look around inside, make sure no one's holed up in there. If I'm not back in half a candle, go back to the road and continue to the next town. Leave Galen, though."

"Be careful."

As he drew closer to the keep, Sandu listened for voices and watched for tell-tale smoke. He scurried to the walls, flinching as mud squelched under his boots. No hollers, no silhouettes at the broken windows; good signs, all told.

Double doors must once have guarded the entrance, but only fallen hinges and wood scraps remained now. Scavengers had picked the place apart, leaving only the most worthless or heaviest objects. Sandu passed as quickly as he dared through the haphazard maze of rooms, met only by bare walls and cold floors. Just as he thought about turning back to fetch Cara, he stumbled on an inner room which smelled of woodsmoke and onions. It had no windows and no other doors. A wool blanket had been spread against the far wall, and a fire pit made of old stones occupied the center, still full of ashes and barely burning embers. A pot lay to one side, scraped clean by whoever lived there. *Only one*, Sandu thought, frozen at the threshold. *A hermit, perhaps, or another traveler?* Still, the keep was large enough to fit all of them, and no one had to know the other passed through.

Retracing his steps, Sandu padded down a different main passage than before and found a decent-sized tower room on the far side of the keep. Just down some stairs from it, a small scullery door let out into the woodlands. It was a perfect place to rest and keep the horses.

After collecting Cara, Sandu led her and the three horses to the scullery door. When the horses were taken care of, he pilfered the saddlebags for food. For the last two nights, when they slept beneath wayfarer pines and couldn't risk a fire for fear of prowlers, they had eaten only meat, bread, and an apple split between them. Tonight though...tonight they could make a vegetable broth flavored with spice, with bread to dip. And an apple each. A veritable feast in Sandu's eyes.

Cara left to gather firewood as Sandu set up their sleeping place. He laid out their blankets, placed stones in a circle for the fire, and chopped an onion and potato. By the time he had finished, Cara returned with an armful of large and small sticks. Most were wet, so Sandu used some of his paper to get the flames going. In a few minutes, a happily spitting fire warmed the room, and the stew began to smell of home, flavored with Valadi herbs.

Sandu watched Cara. *Why does Laris Stanthorpe want her? What did she and Merick hide from me after the prowlers?* Having never been tactful, he asked, "Why do you want to find your mistress? Why not leave it to the soldiers?"

Cara shrugged. Almost as if the question had started a chain reaction in her, she buried her face in her arms, then looked up again, her eyes sparkling with tears. With an anger Sandu thought rather unjustified, she wiped them away, took a deep breath, and another, until she calmed. His palms tingled with the temptation to reach across and place a comforting hand on her shoulder. *I shouldn't have asked. I shouldn't have opened that door.*

Outside, the rain danced a *tarreta* on what remained of the roof. Scooting a bit closer to the fire, Sandu watched the hungry flames devouring the sticks and branches, feeling the heat on his cheeks.

"Merick practically raised me," Cara said softly. She stared at the shadows, the firelight reflected in her eyes. "I was five when I first met him. He terrified me, but he's not all bad. Wasn't all bad. He brought me to the Nellesteres, to Renna. They were my family more than anyone else. Renna and I grew up together. Mumma only came to visit once in a red moon. Sometimes just once a year. It's been two years since I've seen her."

"I'm sorry."

"I thought it was normal at first. Until Merick came, Mumma took me all over, though I don't remember much of it. I wanted Mumma to stay with me. Every time I saw her, I begged her." Cara hesitated, eyes flicking over to Sandu's.

"What did she say?" Part of him really didn't want to know more, the small part that cautioned him against this bounty in the first place and reminded him of what he did to Jagger.

"She hugged me and gave me toys, books, dresses. Never promised anything one way or the other; always ended up leaving." Cara laughed a little, a sad sound.

"Where is your mother now?"

"I don't know." Firelight softened Cara's cheeks, made her hair a myriad of reds and ambers against dark brown. Wisps from her loose braid drifted across her face. It made him think of a Lofalin doll he had seen once in Brin, made from thin clay and painted white, a fragile and lovely thing.

"Renna's all I have left," Cara said. "We played and shared stories. She thought it great fun that I could fight like a boy. She'd get me into trouble sometimes, daring me to beat one of the farmer's sons in a brawl or mud fight. As she grew older, she became beautiful. I knew some rich man would come take her from me one day. When I told her that I was afraid of it, she promised me that wherever she went, I'd go too." She gave a bitter laugh. "I guess neither of us expected her to go where I couldn't follow. But now I have to find her, to make sure she's safe. She'd do the same for me."

But Sandu thought he caught something left out of her explanation, some secret she didn't want to share with him.

"What about you?" Cara asked. "Do you have a family?"

"Once," Sandu said. From the past, his mother's laughter welled up in his ears, his father's grumbling praises, the smell of Nan's sweet apple crumble, the creaking of wagon wheels through the dry ruts from D'Clet to Riverfen, mist kissing his cheeks in the hour before dawn on the morning when the prowlers attacked, screams all over the caravan, blood pooling beneath his feet, Mumma's last painful sighs before she passed and Father grabbing him, running, running for hours until they no longer could. Then Tambrey's voice whispered in his memory, her soft arms holding him as the children played–

Sandu took a deep breath and pushed the memories back down.

"Once?" Cara said. "What sort of answer is that? Don't you have any family, or a lover?"

"I've sworn off romance. It doesn't work for me." Sandu didn't want to tell her about the Valadi caravan he grew up in and its end, or about Tambrey and all that happened what seemed like a lifetime ago. Not about Father, unjustly imprisoned, and his own cowardice.

Veck bringing that up again. What right had she to his hard-won life? What right had she to know anything about him? She was his target, his key to wealth and freeing his father, nothing more. Not to mention the secrets she kept from him, too. His fists clenched, heat rising into his chest.

Anger is worse than the memories. It'll lead you down a road you don't want to travel again. Stop it, Sandu told himself. In the span of seconds, he willed himself to calm down. *What harm can a memory do? Pick one of the easiest, and tell her that.*

"My father raised me," he said. The safest – the only – story he could tell now. "We lived in Dunfrey, in the Barrowfort lands. Father was a brewer, like his old man; wanted me to be one, too. But I made friends with the wrong lads and spent all my time gambling. Lost what little money I had, and then my father's. He never hated me for it, though. When the debt grew too much, and to the wrong people, men came to take me to debtors' prison. Father hid me and claimed the debt as his own. So I left; I've been working ever since to pay it off and free him."

It seemed so...so horrible, when Sandu said it like that. Blunt. Like he didn't care at all. For the first time in months, hatred for himself reemerged. What must she think of him now?

He realized that, after he had finished, he feared Cara's judgment.

Damn. Vecking damn.

And still Sandu waited for her to speak, hoping she would not hold his past against him.

"I'd say we're about equal in tragedy," Cara said. "But there's always tomorrow, isn't there? There's time to make things right again."

Damn, it's going to be Jagger all over again. And the small voice piped up, *Well, maybe not. She hasn't been delivered to Stanthorpe yet.*

CHAPTER TWELVE

Sandu

A CRICK in his neck finally caused Sandu to abandon all hope of sleeping more. With a loud groan, he kicked off the blankets. As he pulled on his boots, he looked over to where Cara had slept. She was not there.

"Aw, vecking hells," he muttered. Cara's blankets had been neatly rolled and tied to the bottom of her pack, which was propped against the far wall. With his old, damp-smelling blanket around his shoulders, Sandu wandered into the keep. Voice low, he said, "Cara? Where are you?"

Sandu had gone through what felt like half the keep before he spotted her. She sat on a window bench, arms wrapped around her legs and head resting against her knees as she gazed out at the forest below. At his approach, she turned to look at him.

"I've already readied the horses for us...I couldn't sleep," Cara said. The darkness beneath her eyes told the truth of that. "I was thinking about Merick."

"It's..." Sandu couldn't think of anything cheerful. "It's going to be a long time before the grief is gone. Even then, it'll pop up now and then, when you don't expect it to."

"I shouldn't have left. I should have stayed in Kell, or gone to Stonetree like Havershim said. I should have realized–"

"And what would have happened if you stayed? Even if

you had known that the wound would reopen, Merick would still have died. There's nothing to do against dark magic." Sandu sat across from her on the bench and looked down at the forest, grey and blue in the pre-dawn light. "You lost your friend. It'll hurt for a long time. But you have to move past it if you want to make something of yourself. Would Merick want you to give up what he died for?"

Cara gave a slight shake of her head. Gathering his thoughts, Sandu said, "I don't even know Renna that well, but I intend to help you see this through. We'll find her." The moment the words left his mouth, he regretted them. Gods, he had a job to do!

In the early morning, though, sitting across from Cara and seeing the expectations in her expression, Sandu weakened. Five marks, compared to a human life? Sickened by his own turmoil, he stood abruptly, unsure whether he'd actually deliver her to Laris.

"We should get going," he said brusquely.

"Sandu...thank you."

He didn't look back at her. "Come on, then."

Sandu remained silent as they trekked back through the keep. *Damn, damn, damn! Befriend your target and you'll end up with guilt as your bed partner. Sandu, you weak-hearted bastard. Don't trust her, don't give in. Gods give me the will to see this through and see my father out of prison. Five marks, and he'll be free.*

In the first days after giving his report on Daggenhelm to the Realm's Protectors, Sandu had drunk himself to sleep every night and woken only to drink again. Hadn't it been for the greater good? Jagger was no longer a threat to the people of Dotschar, no longer an assassin for hire by those with too much money and too little conscience. Fauste's Shiv deserved to be culled.

But this girl is innocent. She's no longer a child, but only barely; a child that seeks to rescue her lost friend. Isn't that a noble cause?

Through the keep came the snort of their horses and Galen's high, braying whinny. Sandu sprinted past Cara, dashed around corners and leapt crumbling stairs, desperate to reach the bottom. Behind him, he heard Cara yell, "Sandu?"

"Our horses!" he shouted back. "Someone's trying to steal them!"

His small dagger in hand, Sandu ran onto the grass outside the keep. Still picketed, the horses perked when they saw him and Cara. Sandu slipped on the grass as he came to a stop.

In front of Galen was a tall, tall man with blonde hair, his back to Sandu. He reached up, stroking Galen's nose, and she pushed back at his hand playfully.

No. Gods no. He shouldn't have survived. He couldn't have.

Galen whinnied over the man's shoulder, turning her large brown eye to Sandu. The man turned.

Oh, gods. Jagger. Scarred and thin, but alive. He smiled at Sandu, showing every last one of his yellow teeth. Jagger's eyes bored into him with a hard blue look. Like a dancer's, his hands crept out to his sides, fingers splayed. In anticipation? Sandu swallowed, hands shaking as he lowered his dagger. *Veck.* He tried a nervous smile, forcing his lips in what came out as more of a grimace.

"Jagger! What's happened to you, what happened at the keep? I returned on my route and found everyone dead!" Sliding his dagger back into its sheath – *I'm going to regret that.* – Sandu held open his arms, still smiling in what he hoped was an agreeable fashion.

"Don't lie to me, little bastard," Jagger growled. He rushed forward, pressed his hand to Sandu's chest, and pushed him hard enough to fall. The air flew from Sandu's throat as he crashed to the ground, and he shook his head, trying to regain it. He gripped the wet grass and stared up at his one-time friend.

Jagger pushed down on Sandu's chest with his foot. He towered over Sandu, his weight pressing the air from his lungs. A dagger, conjured seemingly from nowhere, twirled between his fingers. Trying not to piss himself, Sandu spread his hands in a peaceful gesture. *Lot of good it'll do. Mercy is not one of Jagger's virtues.*

"I hadn't expected to see you again," Jagger said, his tone even, almost placid. "A great gift, isn't it, two old friends *happening* to meet in the wilderness. When the walls crumbled around me, when my wife's body burnt in front of my eyes, I thought of you. Thought how lucky you were to have escaped the carnage. Counted myself fortunate for having known you."

"Jagger..." Sandu reached out a hand. Immediately, Jagger stiffened, his foot pressing into Sandu's chest hard enough to hurt his bones. From the corner of his eye, Sandu saw Cara frozen a few feet away. *Get out of here,* Sandu thought desperately. *Save yourself.*

"No!" Jagger yelled down. "Time for you to listen, Sandu! Time to realize all the damage you caused me! I may have become a beast made man, but I deserved a good death. I deserved that at least."

He rambled, cohesive words mangled by obsessive madness. *What has become of him?* Sandu marveled, unable to tear his eyes from the...the *thing* above him.

"I searched for candles and candles, hoping to find one other alive. My hands pulled the wreckage off their cursed corpses, and found only death. The blood of all their lives, soaked into my skin," Jagger muttered. "It wasn't supposed to end like that."

Jagger went suddenly quiet, staring into space at something only he could see. His dagger slowly, slowly, lowered to his side. Sandu licked his lips nervously, hands trembling at his sides. He had barely mouthed *Go!* to Cara before Jagger snapped back to attention and leaned down, his cruel blue eyes fixated on Sandu's, his blade inches away.

"It's your fault," he growled. Sandu could only look back into his unblinking glare. "You spied on us, you *used* us. For what? For money?" He spat, as if the word were poison. "We were friends! My closest friend in that hellhole, the only one I could count on. Why did you do it, Sandu?"

Sandu said nothing. What could he say? *'Yes, Jagger, I betrayed you for coin. I am everything you claim and more.'* He merely shook his head, holding Jagger's gaze, full of regret. Regret, sorrow, guilt, and fear. So, so much fear. He would die today, before the sun had even risen.

Cara inhaled sharply. She stiffened, and, as Sandu watched in confusion, the skin of her face bubbled and stretched. Ridges grew on her forehead, her eyes sunk, glimmering with a red light, and long, pointed fangs protruded from her lips. Sandu's mouth dropped open, his heart clenching. In the place of his companion, a prowler now stood, the feral features hers yet not hers.

Without a cry or any warning, she threw herself at Jagger, knocking him off of Sandu. Jagger's shocked expression turned to anger, then pain as Cara's sword tore through his shirt and ripped into his chest. Sandu scuttled to his feet, his lungs throbbing.

"Get the horses," Cara shouted in a coarse voice that sounded only faintly like her own. For a second, Sandu stood there, a deer caught between a wolf and a bear, his mind blank. A part of his brain screamed, *Run, you mad shit, run* and he dashed past Jagger's groaning form and leapt onto Galen's back. He pulled her reins hard, kicking her to a gallop.

Sandu heard the other horses behind him, but didn't look, didn't slow. Galen raced across the small meadow and onto the woodland path, hooves pounding detritus and dirt. Sandu's breath felt like it had overtaken his mouth, his ears dominated by the pounding of his heart. As the sun rose over the mountains, illuminating the world in sweet, sweet light, he tried to stop the mad crowding inside his brain. *How did Cara...Why? What happened? How far behind is Jagger? Will he ever stop? I'm a dead man. I'm so, so very dead.* But the rush of thoughts refused to calm, and the more he suppressed them, the greater the overflow when the dam breached.

Veck.

Eventually, Galen slowed, her coat lathered in foam, harsh breath pushing out her nostrils. Her legs shook as Sandu dismounted. He patted her side and rubbed her forelegs up and down, murmuring apologies. Cara, on an equally tired horse, rode up behind him, her face thankfully returned to normal. Still, Sandu walked around Galen, putting her mass between him and his companion.

"You want to explain what happened back there?" Cara demanded.

"I...I explain?" Sandu spluttered. "I'm not the one who turned into a vecking prowler! Explain THAT to me."

"I didn't think you'd need to know," she said, mouth turned in a hard line. "You wouldn't have believed me if I told you."

"I don't believe you now, despite the evidence of my eyes."

For a moment, neither said anything. Then, with a sigh, Cara said, "I don't know what I am. I think Merick knew. At least, he knew more than me. I've always had this...power, or curse. When I'm angry or frightened, I turn into it. Somewhere, I can feel myself at the back of my mind, but the rest of me turns into this...this...beast. It terrifies me."

"What are you going to do about it?" Sandu asked.

Cara shook her head. "Nothing, except maybe find a cure. I don't want this at all. But I have to find Renna first." She paused, then said, "Now your turn. What happened back there?"

For a second, Sandu hesitated, then decided to tell her the truth. Or, part of it, at least. "That man back there...his name is Jagger Cross. For a time, I worked as a peddler, and I sold to his people. Fauste's Shiv. Have you heard of them?"

Cara nodded, expression neutral. *Is that distrust behind her eyes? Or am I imagining it?* Sandu continued, "I was one of the few who knew where they were located. They often spent a lot of money – more than most minor lords – so I kept my mouth shut. I traded goods, I brought them strange items that I couldn't fathom had any purpose, I did what I had to. For people like me, who can't see past the next day and spend whatever comes into hand...it was a great route. I spent a day or two whenever my route brought me to them, and I befriended Jagger. I knew his wife, even. A sweet woman, she was. I always felt at home with them.

"A couple of months ago, I had a special order that took me farther off my route than usual. In years past, I might only go a quinn or two between visits. This time, it was over a month. I went up to the Shivs' hiding place and found it burnt to the ground. Not a soul left alive. At least, so I thought. Jagger, that son of a bitch, survived somehow. I don't know who attacked, but I guess he blames me. Maybe because I had been missing for so long. Maybe because the grief drove him mad. I don't think he's meant to live without his wife."

He didn't tell her that he had taken the Shivs' location to the Realm's Protectors. He didn't tell her that he had been tasked to kill Jagger himself, and couldn't face it, so he put it on the *honorable* knights of the realm. He didn't tell her how many sleepless nights he had passed because of his betrayal.

He didn't tell her that she was his next good to sell.

Cara saved him from his guilt. "Then we need to put as many leagues between him and us as we can. I don't fancy another scene like that; he's clearly a lunatic."

"Agreed."

"I'm glad he didn't kill you."

"I'm glad you didn't turn me into a prowler." Sandu grinned. "Can you even do that? Turn people into prowlers?"

"I hope not. I've not exactly tried it." Cara smiled. "How does a man like that find a wife? A sweet wife, at that?"

Laughing, Sandu mounted Galen. "I've no vecking clue. For a hardened killer, Jagger does have beautiful eyes. Maybe Raven liked that about him? Or maybe he stole her, like Autorus stole Hebta to live with him in the underworld."

"No, no, you've got the story all wrong," Cara said. "Hebta wasn't taken, she went willingly. She didn't love Autorus, you know; she loved his second-in-command, Donte."

"That's not how Nan used to tell it." They bickered that day about old tales. When evening came, they settled beneath a wayfarer pine. Cara soon fell asleep, but shivered in the cold. Looking through Merick's saddlebags, Sandu found a wool blanket and draped it over her before he climbed beneath his own thin cover.

Sandu did not sleep that night. Jagger's gaunt, maddened face lurked beneath his eyelids, though he did his best to ignore it. *Take this burden from me*, he prayed to the gods whom he too often turned from. *And help me to make the right decision this time.*

CHAPTER THIRTEEN
Cara

"WHERE TO next?" Sandu asked. They stood at the top of a switchback overlooking a valley.

Cara patted her horse's neck, thinking. In the days since Merick's death and Jagger's attack, she hadn't thought beyond the next day. She knew that they had to reach Riverfen before the Masque, else risk losing any opportunity the festival granted them. She said, "We should head to Riverfen as quickly as possible."

"And then?"

"We find Renna and kill the Hooded Man."

"That's all well and good," Sandu said, "but you don't know how to kill him. His magic took down Merick without much effort."

Cara toyed with her braid and considered this. *Perhaps I can kill him before the magic gets to me...* Even with the beast's power, she doubted she could outrun those dark tentacles.

"We had spoken about going to Mott." Sandu pointed below them where the road split into two, one branch going south and the other continuing west. "There's the crossroads for it."

"That'll just waste time," said Cara. "Time that Renna may not have."

"It only adds a few days to our journey, and the scholars there could have answers for us. If there's anywhere in Dotschar that holds arcane knowledge, it's Mott." Sandu mounted his horse and gazed off into the valley. "If the Hooded Man wanted Renna dead, she'd already be buried back in Kell. Wherever she is, I bet she's alive."

Cara climbed onto her horse and nudged it to walk. "I hope you're right."

They passed from the ridge down into the valley, reaching the crossroads just as the sun touched its zenith. Sandu pulled his horse to a stop and looked to Cara. "Which way?"

Riverfen for Renna, or Mott for me. I could tell myself that we go to Mott to find more about the magic the Hooded Man used, but that would be a lie. I want the beast gone forever, and the scholars there might be able to help me.

Cara knew she was stalling, but she asked, "Have you ever been there?"

"I've passed through Mott before. It's...can you imagine a city where silence is the dominant sound? It's meant to be a haven for scholars, but I found it eerie. And they have a library filled with too many scrolls and books to count. All the secrets of our world, they say, lie within those walls."

Cara tried to imagine it and couldn't. The concept eluded her. And excited her. All the secrets of the world?

Would Renna last long enough for them to scour all those scrolls?

And if we don't go, will I be able to suppress the beast forever? The thought of the beast overtaking her body, her own mind trapped forever in itself, persuaded her. Cara turned her horse south to Mott. *Renna's still alive, and we'll reach her. Just not yet.*

Sandu followed with a knowing look.

The weather took a shift from the breezy, calm days of summer to end-season squalls, with great winds blowing Cara and Sandu's horses into each other. The air chilled their hands as rain hassled them. Between these sudden storm bursts, the sun beat down, giving them harsh red marks that stung at the touch. Unlike the plains, where the beginning of autumn often marked a serene change of pace, the high mountains only brought worse and worse storms that gradually turned from rain to sleet to snow. In another two months, the snow would grow so high that many of the roads from the plains into the River Valley became impassable.

On the third day since leaving the crossroads, a large snow-covered mountain loomed in front of them. It dominated the sky all that day and the next as they descended into a large vale. A river emptied into a clear blue mountain lake at the foot of the behemoth. Nestled between the lake and mountains was a small town.

"There it is," Sandu said. He pointed at a large building in the middle of the town, which boasted a bell tower and multiple spires. "That's the university compound. All the classes and the library are there, as well as the novum. Don't be deceived, it's much larger than it looks from up here."

Cara gaped at the town. She had never seen a building so tall. The town around it held hundreds of homes and businesses, more than she'd ever seen before.

"Come on, country girl," Sandu said with a smile. "I want a hot dinner and a bath."

The oranges and pinks of sunset had just started to color the sky when they rode into the town. Despite Sandu's earlier words, Cara had expected such a large town to be bustling with noise and people. The quietness unsettled her, though she saw townsfolk passing and speaking softly.

Keeping her own voice low, Cara asked, "How do they convince everyone to be so quiet?"

Sandu shrugged. "It's been this way for years. I expect the rustic folk simply grow up knowing how to act in this town. It's louder in the outskirts, where people are farthest from the university."

The sun touched the mountains, and bells rang out over the town. After the quiet of nature and the strange stillness of the town, Cara jumped at the noise. The bells sang out a beautiful melody, not a single note discordant or jarring. They sounded for a quarter candle before the air grew silent once more.

"Why are there eyes everywhere?" Cara asked, pointing to symbols of an eye surrounded by leaves. It seemed every building had at least one painted or carved on it.

"The all-seeing, all-knowing eye. It's the university's symbol," Sandu replied.

Cara and Sandu arrived at the town green, three sides of which were surrounded by university buildings. Each one was built of the same ivory limestone that had grown grey over time. The bell tower rose from the center of the middle building, brass bells shining in the last of the sunlight.

At the far side of the green, multiple wagons lined the cobblestone street. Men in orange robes and tonsures scurried about carrying boxes and scrolls.

"What's happening over there?" Cara asked.

Sandu peered at the activity and said, "I'm not sure. Perhaps the university received some books from a lord?"

Cara watched a moment longer, then shook her head. "They're loading the wagons. See? All the boxes are being put in, not taken out. Do the scholars here ever take their scrolls elsewhere?"

"Not that I've heard of. Let's go closer, see if someone will tell us."

They dismounted, tied their horses to a hitching rail, and walked over the green. After so many days on the road, Cara enjoyed the springy grass below her feet. She wouldn't feel that simple pleasure again for months after the snows came.

"Excuse me," Sandu said, pulling at a monk's robes. "What's going on here?"

The monk shrugged him off and bustled away. Just as Sandu reached for another, a tall man strode over to them. He wore a fine tunic stitched with an eye, but his dirty blonde hair wasn't shaved in a tonsure. He wore a cape draped over one shoulder, and Cara saw by the cleanliness of his boots that this man was not a rustic. The man stepped in front of Sandu with a suspicious glare. "Who are you? Who gave you permission to be here?"

"No one," Sandu said, "but seeing as how we're all outdoors right now, I didn't realize we needed permission to enjoy the fine evening."

"This is university property," the man said. His eyes swept over Sandu and Cara's travel-stained clothes. "And university business."

"We were only curious," Cara said before Sandu could insult the man again. She shot a warning glance at her friend. "We didn't mean any harm."

"Then satisfy your curiosity elsewhere." The man turned away, but Cara quickly grabbed at his cloak.

"Before you go, sir, perhaps you could help us?"

"The closest inn is down the road," the man said. "I–"

"We need to speak to a scholar," Cara said, determined. "One who knows about dark magic or prowlers."

That made the man pause. He turned back, his pale green eyes assessing her once more. "And why would a rustic need to know such things?"

"Because both have accosted us in the last month, and I fear we will meet one or both again before the year turns." Cara bit back the words, *and because I think I'm related to them.*

"You don't speak like a rustic." He crossed his arms, his gaze turning to Sandu. "Are these the ravings of a madwoman?"

"I dearly hope not, otherwise I'd have pledged myself to lunacy." Sandu winked at Cara.

The man's brows drew together. "A woman leading a man? Are you of noble birth?"

"My mistress is," Cara said, snatching onto his words. "Her name is Lady Renna Nellestere of Kell. She was kidnapped through dark magic. We're trying to find her."

For a moment, it seemed as if the scholar would turn them away again. His expression darkened, but then he nodded. "Follow me."

The man swept away, and Cara glanced briefly at Sandu before following. He led them into the main building, up a grand staircase, and into a wide, airy corridor. Near the end of the hall, he opened a large wooden door and ushered them into a spacious study. Each wall was lined with bookshelves, and though there was a desk in the room's center, most of the books and paperwork were spread out over a smaller table by a stained glass window. The man sat behind the desk and gestured at the chairs opposite.

Cara gingerly took her seat, too aware of the fine cushion beneath her muddied dress.

"Tell me everything," the man said.

Sandu looked to Cara, and she hesitated a moment before she began to speak. She told of Renna's disappearance, the Hooded Man's magic, and the prowler attack before Merick's death. Though time had lost many of the details, she remembered the feeling of the magic and the sight of her mentor's horrible wound.

Cara said nothing of her beast.

When she finished, the man rubbed his chin. He said, "An interesting tale, if true. Why would a woman pursue this 'Hooded Man'? Why not send for the Realm's Protectors?"

"I've been trained since childhood to protect her," Cara said. "I have to see her brought home safely."

If I can succeed in that, maybe it'll mean I'm not like the prowlers.

The man looked between them, though his eyes lingered on Cara. "I'm afraid this university has little resources on dark magic since the last king forbade its study. We cannot help you there."

Cara's hopes fell a little. She looked to Sandu with her wordless question: *can we trust him?*

Sandu spoke up, "We've also encountered a creature similar to the prowlers, but not...well...as animalistic. Something that can control itself and appear human. Have you heard of those?"

Thank you, Sandu, Cara thought with a sigh of relief.

The scholar leaned back in his chair and crossed his fingers. Beneath his carefully composed features, Cara thought she detected a hint of delight.

"You mean the *fampir*?" he asked.

"The what?" Cara said. She exchanged a confused look with Sandu.

For a moment, the scholar's composure broke, and excitement shone out in his bright eyes and white smile. "Few have heard of them. Have you really seen one? When? Where?"

"Perhaps," Cara said carefully. "What exactly are they?"

"I've studied prowlers a long time – the university's foremost scholar, you might say – and I've found that they aren't the only undead." He stood up, nearly bouncing on his heels. "In my research, I came across tales of the *fampir*. They're common in all the Valadi tales, and legends of them go back to the Dead's War. They are the ancient ones, older than prowlers and far more dangerous. Most people have stopped telling their stories, but the Valadi still do."

"I remember those tales," Sandu interjected. "Nan used to tell me by the fire on long winter nights. She said they'd come for me at night if I didn't eat all my supper. I'd forgotten about it."

The scholar cocked his head. "What tribe are you?"

"Sarga," Sandu replied. "Are you Valadi?"

"I am of the Dalscra lineage in old Belleslye, though I wasn't raised in a caravan. I sought out my tribe some time ago and spoke to our elders. Everything I learned, I wrote down. I must be the first in centuries to have done so."

Before the two men could devolve into talk of their tribes, Cara asked, "So, these *fampir*...are they like prowlers?"

"In many ways, yes. They spread their affliction through their bite, as the prowlers do, and need living blood as sustenance. But prowlers are feral creatures; *fampir* can masquerade among the living, keeping up their deceptions for years. I've heard of some that are centuries old."

Not like me, then. Cara looked at her hands. *Fampir* living for lifetimes...it all sounded so strange, like a fairytale. All her life, she'd known of prowlers in the same way she knew of bears or nightcats: creatures of the dark to be feared and avoided. But *fampir*?

Sandu reached out and took her hand, giving it a reassuring squeeze. She met his eye and nodded. *Thank the gods I have him beside me.* Cara took a deep breath and said, "What you're describing...that's not what we saw."

"Oh?" The scholar deflated and returned to his seat. He

flipped through his books, visibly disappointed. "I'm not aware of any..."

He paused, his eyes flicking over a notebook. Cara held her breath, hoping that he knew something more.

"What did you say your name was, again?" asked the scholar.

"I didn't. I only mentioned my lady, Renna Nellestere of–"

"Of Kell. Right. What's *your* name?"

Sandu gripped her hand again, though she didn't know if it was a warning or another reassurance. "My name's Sandu Crin."

The scholar didn't even look at Sandu. His eyes burned into Cara. She swallowed past a suddenly dry throat and said, "Cara Gellder. And yours?" She hoped he would look away soon.

"Alex. Maid Gellder, can you read?" She nodded, and he handed the book over to her. She looked down at it, noting the scrawling handwriting and sketches in the margins. Scanning the page, she didn't understand why his demeanor had changed. She opened her mouth to ask what was going on when she saw it:

Sura Gellder.

The last time Cara had heard that name, it was whispered between Merick and Madame Freebane. They thought she went in for supper, but when she returned to grab her practice sword, she overheard them speaking about her mother. Mostly how long Sura had been gone, and whether she would ever return. Merick had said that the money for Cara's upkeep still came every year, but Sura herself...no one could know.

Cara had been eighteen at the time, and her mother hadn't visited again. This clean, tidy study, with its smooth wood shelves and comfortable rugs, was the last place she would ever expect to see Sura's name. Hundreds of questions sprang to her mind, the foremost being, *Why would she come here?*

"Do you know her?" Alex asked. Cara could only nod. He waited another moment for her to speak, then said, "She visited me a few years ago, and asked many of the same questions you have."

"She's my mother," Cara said softly. The word felt odd in

her mouth, an acknowledgment of a lost relationship. In all her conversations with Sandu, she had been able to hide her feelings from herself and pretend that she didn't mind Sura's absences. Now, with answers within reach, with the slap of the name appearing in this place, she didn't know how to feel. Curiosity, resentment, and anger all fought within her. The beast stirred, awakened by her turmoil.

The scholar nodded. "She told me she had a daughter in Kell. At first she didn't say why she wanted my knowledge on *fampir*. But after some time, she told me the truth."

Cara's head shot up, her fingers tightening on the little notebook with her mother's name written inside. "What truth?"

Alex's eyes flicked to Sandu. "Are we in trusted company?"

"Yes, of course. *What truth?*"

Cara's breath caught in her mouth, her eyes fixed on Alex. Whatever he said next could change everything she knew about herself. She wanted desperately to know, and at the same time to be back in Kell not a whit wiser.

"Your mother asked many questions, mostly about the *fampir*. What would happen if an undead and a mortal woman were to mate. Eventually, she admitted to me that she had successfully conceived a child with a *fampir* man, and borne a daughter." Alex's eyes rested on Cara's, but she stared past him. "By all logics, such a thing should be impossible: life and death mixed in one person. Honestly, I didn't believe her when she said it."

"What changed your mind?" Sandu asked. Cara didn't return his hand squeeze. Her mind whirled with questions and fears. If prowlers were evil – as the clothman said – and *fampir* were worse than prowlers, then the beast inside truly was sinister.

Cara vaguely listened to Alex.

"I wrote to a contact in Kell, Madame Freebane, and asked her about Cara. She told me about fits and strange conniptions. That spurred me to further research. Deep in the archives, written in dead languages, I finally found some evidence of a half-mortal, half-*fampir* woman, called a *sulpari* by the old texts.

The creation ritual matched what Sura told me."

"So I'm a *sulpari*?" Cara asked. *Surely Mother would have mentioned an undead father at least once.* Now that she thought of it, though, she remembered Sura's disturbed expression and blunt rejections at any questions of Cara's father. *Did she realize the wickedness that she brought forth?*

"Describe your fits to me." Alex picked up a quill, ready to take notes. The beast moved uncomfortably inside Cara's belly, its heat rising up her throat. *Why not just show him?*

The hot hatred poured into her limbs. It consumed her, washing over her features until little of Cara remained. Her teeth elongated, sharpening into razors over her lips, and the smoothness of her brow rippled into rough, hardened ridges as her cheeks sunk into the bones of her face. She knew her eyes had taken a red glint, her pupils turned catlike and narrow.

Sandu exclaimed and sprang out of his seat, and Alex cringed back in his chair, one hand raised as if to ward her off.

"Is this proof enough?" Cara growled. The beast colored her voice, making it harsher. Its anger and hunger flooded through her. Her gaze fixed on a vein in Alex's neck which pulsed sweetly with blood. She wanted to draw that blood, spill so much that she could bathe in it. Some tiny part of her resisted, knowing the error of her thoughts.

To her surprise, Alex regained himself quickly. He stood up, his hands held up in a placating manner. "Easy, there. We won't hurt you."

His words pierced the feral portion of her head, coaxingly soft. Cara's claws twitched, the beast questioning this stranger. Her eyes fixed again on Alex's pulse.

"Easy now. Aren't you just a wonderful thing?"

The beast stilled at his serene voice.

"There. That's it. Won't it be nice to just rest? Rest, and let Cara back in."

Her heartbeat slowed, the blood behind her eyes receding, her skin smoothing back over her features. She took a deep breath. Then another, and another, until she no longer felt the beast's consuming rage.

Cara sank into her chair, shaken by what she'd just done. Never before had she just...allowed the beast in. It both thrilled and terrified her. All that raw power, but all the hunger, too. Had Alex not spoken, she was sure she would have leapt for his throat.

"You're sure I'm not *fampir*?" Cara asked once she felt calm enough to speak.

"Do you require blood to live? Were you once mortal, but underwent a painful transformation into undead?"

Cara shook her head. "I've always just been me."

"Then you were born with that tainted blood, not given it at a later time. I can't imagine the magic required to create you, but you are mortal. Same as Sandu and me."

But you don't have evil living inside you. Cara took a deep breath and asked, "Can it be cured?"

"Cured? But–"

"I don't want this. I never asked for it. I just want to find my lady and go home." Cara stood abruptly and walked to the stained glass window. She stared out into the darkness. "In all your research, did you ever find a cure?"

"I...No. No, I've never found such a thing." Alex joined her. With his closeness, she could smell pine and fresh soap. "But if it exists, I can help you find it."

"I can't stay here," Cara said. "I have to go to Riverfen and find Renna."

"As it so happens, the earl has called for myself and my scholars to bring our research to Riverfen. He fears the prowler threat, and wishes us to work with his wizard to find a solution. Our caravan leaves in the morning. You could join us." He gave her a sidelong look. "And, when my work is done, I can help you find your cure."

Cara caught his green eyes and quickly looked away. A flush crept up her skin, and she turned to the window. *Just the effects of letting the beast in.* "I'd like that. I think Sandu and myself have been traveling alone for too long." She met Sandu's eyes. "If that's alright with you, of course."

A strange, pained look crossed Sandu's face before he

smiled. "Of course. The more the merrier."

"Excellent." Alex put his hand to the small of Cara's back. "I have to finish preparations, but the scholars will find a room for you. Nothing elaborate, but the beds are comfortable enough."

His hand lingered just a moment before he ushered them out the door. Another scholar led them to a small, whitewashed room with two beds and a washstand.

As soon as they were alone, Sandu said, "I don't trust him."

"He's the only one who knows what I am," Cara said. "We don't have much of a choice."

"The way he looked at you..."

"I didn't notice anything." She had, but she wasn't about to tell Sandu that. *Plenty of men have looked at Renna like that. Why not me this time?*

"It was a longing look."

Is Sandu interested in me? No, he's never done anything to suggest that. He's a concerned friend, is all. "I am a pretty girl, despite my rough edges."

"If he ever asks for your hand, I expect him to ask me first, as the closest thing to a father you have." Sandu caught himself and corrected, "Well...without Merick here, I mean."

Surprisingly, Cara found that she could hear the name without a rod of melancholy ramming through her. It stung, but like a bee's nip instead of a bear's sharp teeth. She smiled and laughed. "Merick would quite enjoy my predicament. A rustic or a lord's son...do I marry for love or riches?"

"Riches, every time. Never consider someone like me for a husband; we're shit at it."

As they readied for bed, Cara watched her friend. Nothing in his joke had a sense of denial, nothing suggesting that he did, in fact, love her romantically. For that, Cara felt immensely grateful.

And then there was the beast. Sandu had seen it, and didn't care. Even Alex, though he'd only known her a few candles, had embraced it with excitement instead of fear or rejection. Would Renna do the same?

Of course she will, Cara tried to tell herself, but she knew it to be a lie. Perhaps, after all this was over, she would ensure Renna's safe return home and then leave Kell. That simple, quiet fief was no place for a monster like her. *Even if I save Renna, I'll always have this beast inside. She doesn't deserve the pain of dealing with it.*

The thought of leaving Renna, once incomprehensible, didn't hurt as much now. Cara reflected somberly on the revelation, but didn't try to quash it. Perhaps it would be best to leave her childhood behind her. *Renna and I have simply grown too different.*

Chapter Fourteen
Sandu

SANDU CURSED softly, then held his thumb up and sucked the droplet of blood. The needle had slipped in his fingers yet again. Cara stirred a bowl over their fire, pausing now and then to taste it. She grimaced at the latest spoonful.

"I can't believe the scholars eat this every day," she said. Though she and Sandu preferred to make their own fire, the scholars had been kind enough to provide them with rations each day. Nearby, the other men talked quietly around their larger fire.

"Here, let me help," Sandu said. He put down his mending and reached for his pack. As he searched for his sack of spices, his finger brushed the bounty list. He paused, then grabbed the sack. Even with the slow-moving caravan, they drew closer to Riverfen each day. Closer to the man who would pay good money for Sandu to deliver his only remaining friend.

Cara watched him, and Sandu gave her a quick smile. "Valadi herbs and spices," he said, holding up his sack. "I never leave home without them."

With careful fingers, Sandu added a pinch here and a handful there, mixing his favorite blend of home into the watery soup. The simple movements soothed him, as did the scents drifting up from the bowl. *Like Nan used to make*, Sandu thought. He tasted it, nodded, and held the spoon out to Cara. She sipped at it and smiled.

"It's good," she said.

"Old family recipe," Sandu replied with a wink. He divvied the soup up into two smaller bowls just as Alex stepped into their little camp. The scholar carried a loaf of bread and a wine bladder.

"May I join you?" Alex asked. Sandu gestured at the fire, then pulled out another bowl. Over the last few days of travel, he'd watched the scholar carefully. He noticed that Alex usually ate with his men, but also assisted with the cooking and cleaning. *Unusual for a lord.* When the scholars made watches, Alex insisted on taking one every night. He helped repair a wagon wheel, and knelt into the mud to work without complaint. For the most part, Cara and Sandu held back from the others, feeling out of place among all the monks. Yet Sandu's suspicions of Alex had slowly dwindled. *Most lords wouldn't stoop like he does. Maybe he is as genuine as he appears.*

Alex seated himself and broke apart the bread, giving the larger portions to Sandu and Cara. Sandu dipped his bread eagerly and dove into his supper without hesitation. As he did, though, he noticed the glance the other two exchanged. A quick, flirting look that reminded him too painfully of his courtship with Tambrey.

Don't think about her. Or the children. Just enjoy that Cara's happy. Focus on that. Sandu banished the thoughts of his family, knowing that even memories could send him into a long-lasting melancholy. He had grown efficient at hiding those thoughts over years of practice.

"Tell us more about the *fampir*," Cara said. She accepted the passed wineskin and took a deep drink.

Alex blew on a spoonful of soup. He swallowed the broth and nodded at Sandu. "Tastes like what my mother used to make. I haven't had good Valadi soup in years." Then he turned to Cara. "What do you want to know?"

"Where'd they come from? How do they become undead? What does that even mean?" Cara held tightly to the wineskin, her eagerness clear. Sandu smiled into his bowl; he hadn't seen her this carefree since Merick's death. *But happy for the knowledge, or that Alex is the one giving it?* He decided it didn't matter. She was happy, and that was enough.

Alex put down his supper and clasped his hands over his knees. "Most accounts trace the *fampir* back to the Dead's War. The records of how, exactly, they were made is long lost, but we know that powerful magic created them out of elven slaves. Each side of the war forged their own version of the undead, and many believed that all the undead slaughtered each other by the end. But we know that a few *fampir* survived to pass on their curse. Whatever that magic was, it connected them to Autorus and the underworld. Any who turn into *fampir* or prowler die first, then are resurrected into undead. Blood is the tie there: blood makes them into beasts, and then drives them forever. We're not sure exactly, but we believe *fampir* retain part of their soul even into undeath. The prowlers, though, appear soulless. No one knows what created them, only that they pass their curse along same as the *fampir*."

Sandu ate his supper quietly as he listened. Cara watched Alex with rapt attention.

"You said that the undead slaughtered each other," Sandu said between mouthfuls. "So they can be killed?"

"Yes, but it's not as easy as it would appear. Some have been hanged or decapitated, yet came back – though I believe losing a head will kill a prowler. Fire destroys their bodies, making it the surest way. I've read, too, that a stab in the heart is as final as fire."

"What about novums and herbs? All the stories say that prowlers hate them," Sandu said.

Alex shook his head. "It's not the 'godly presence' that drives the undead from the novums. It's the incense; they're quite sensitive to smells. And garlic sears them, though why I don't know."

Sandu's spoon scraped the empty bowl, and he put it down. He reached for the wineskin and drank. It tasted fruity, with soft undertones that he couldn't quite place; certainly the finest wine he had ever had. Feeling almost guilty for drinking it, he handed it back to Alex. The scholar leaned in closer to Cara, explaining more about the *fampir*. Sandu looked away from them, reminded again of those first days with Tambrey.

He stood abruptly and gathered their bowls and utensils, muttering about cleaning them. The other two barely glanced at him. As he walked toward a small stream, Sandu peeked over his shoulder at them. Envy burned in his stomach, for he had once had such attraction, and then lost it. *My own damn fault.* Sandu again pushed the memories deeper. *She's gone. You can't go back to her.*

Sandu scrubbed at the bowls, his thoughts growing dark. *If you turn Cara in, you'll be ruining what they have. Just like you did with Tambrey. Just like Jagger.* He scowled, and mumbled to himself, "There's gotta be an easier way to get five marks than to betray everyone you know." Maybe he could grab Galen and leave in the middle of the night. Cara would be hurt, but no worse than if she learned the truth. The thought made his head hurt. He couldn't just leave her.

I'm going to give up the job, Sandu decided. *I can't have this guilt shadowing me my whole life.* He returned to camp and settled into his blankets. Eventually, he heard Alex say his goodnights and walk away, and then Cara settling down to sleep. When he heard her breath turn slow and steady, he reached for his pack.

By the light of the fading fire, Sandu looked over the bounty list. Names had been added and crossed out, and other hunters had marked their intention to locate Cara. He tasted stale regret, staring at her name. *Five marks. She's worth more than that.* Sandu pricked the back of his hand with his quill and crossed out his name. *I'm done.*

For a moment, the blood shone bright on the parchment. Then something happened that had never happened before: his line sank into the paper, leaving no trace he had ever made it. Sandu gaped, his thoughts running wild. He tried again, and again the mark vanished. *What's happening?* Almost frantic now, Sandu wildly crossed out his name, his quill biting into the parchment with his ferocity.

The lines all disappeared.

Sandu thrust the list into his pack, his breath catching in his throat. *Why won't it work?* The headache from earlier returned, more painfully this time. Sandu threw off his blankets and stumbled to the stream. He tossed water over his face, the chill refreshing on his flushed skin.

The pain grew and grew, building in his temples and behind his ears. His eyes watered with it. He shut them, but it didn't help. It felt like his whole head would burst.

He opened his eyes, then quickly shut them, sure he had gone mad. He waited a breath, then tried again. This time, the vision came more clearly. An old man had appeared in front of Sandu. He wore a tunic with long, wide sleeves under a heavy robe. His outline, though, was blurry, almost wavering, as if he wasn't quite there. Every time Sandu's eyes focused on a new spot, the man shifted there.

"What in the—"

"Shut up and listen," the man said, glaring. "This is a tricky spell and one I hate to use for long. Gives me a damned earache."

"Are you a wizard?" Sandu asked, feeling dumb.

"No," the old man replied irritably. "Stop asking questions, it only makes you sound like an idiot. I'm Laris Stanthorpe, the master of your guild. Stop your tongue, boy. I know you've found the girl, I wouldn't be here otherwise. No, I don't care to tell you how I know. What's important is that you bring her to me, as quickly as you can."

"What do you want—"

"I said shut it." Stanthorpe waved a hand and muttered something, and Sandu's tongue lodged itself firmly behind his teeth. No matter how he tried, he couldn't budge it. Stanthorpe continued, "Now then. I noticed you trying to back out of the job. It's unacceptable. You belong to me, remember. I made you what you are. If you won't bring her willingly, I'll find other ways. Unpleasant ways." Laris stepped forward, his blurred shape growing large. He grabbed Sandu's chin, staring into his eyes as he whispered in a strange language. Sandu felt a cold sensation creeping through his skin. His tongue didn't respond, though he wanted to demand what was happening.

"There," Laris said, releasing Sandu. "I'll be able to find you wherever you go. You can't escape from me. Bring the girl to Riverfen. Once you're there, write me a letter and say these words: *Exus marinel causin.* It'll find me, don't worry about that. If you don't, if you let her go her own path...let's just say that Autorus will meet you far sooner than you'd like."

Sandu's vision blurred as the old man shimmered and disappeared. His tongue slid itself free, and he mumbled, "Vecking bastard."

He thought of his father, rotting in a cell and waiting desperately for each penny Sandu sent. Five marks would erase the debt Papa had taken for him with plenty to spare. *But Cara needs me, too. Even with Alex here now...who knows if Renna is still alive? And after all this, I doubt Cara can return to Kell as if nothing's changed.* Deep in his gut, Sandu knew that he wanted to stay with her. How long had it been since he had a true friend?

Not since Jagger, and Sandu had picked money over him. *See how that turned out?*

Then before Jagger...there was Tambrey. He lost her because of money. Every time he tried to do something right, it had hurt others.

Sandu remained by the stream for a long time, his thoughts dancing around in his aching head. He couldn't sell Cara, but if he stayed Laris would find her anyway. *I don't trust him, and I don't think he'll do right by her.*

The only right thing is to leave and hope that no one else finds her. Alex is with her now; he'll keep her safe.

Sandu walked back to the camp on numb feet. Without thinking, he rolled up his blankets and tied them to Galen. His horse blinked at him, but didn't make a sound. "Good girl," Sandu murmured. He heaved his pack onto his shoulders and led Galen away.

Cara turned over in her sleep, making a small sound. Sandu looked back at her. "I'm sorry, but this is the only way."

He left her sleeping. Maybe he should have written a note, but he didn't know what he could say. Besides, if he lingered too long, he'd lose his courage.

Sandu led Galen away from the caravan, despondent yet sure that he was doing the right thing. He'd ride as far as he could get that night, then start early in the morning. The "where" and "what he'd do now" he had no idea, but he knew that anything was better than endangering his friend. *I could be a farmhand, or a scribe for a minor lord. Become a peddler again, though how I'd buy the wares I don't know...*

A shadow disconnected itself from a tree in front of him. Sandu jumped, his hand flying to his dagger, before he realized who it was.

"Alex, what are you doing out here?" Sandu asked. In the scarce moonlight, he couldn't see the scholar clearly.

"It's my shift," Alex said simply. He wiped at his hands with a kerchief. "And I had to relieve myself."

Sandu held onto Galen's reins, painfully aware of how he must appear. He said, "Well, then. I'm no threat, so I'll just–"

"Where are you going?" Alex's tone was friendly, though Sandu thought he heard some suspicion in it.

"Away," Sandu answered truthfully.

"Does Cara know?" When Sandu didn't reply, Alex sighed. "Sneaking away in the middle of the night often speaks of nefarious deeds."

"It's none of your concern," Sandu snapped. "It's for her own good."

"You're her friend, aren't you? Tell me how abandoning her does her any good."

"You wouldn't understand."

"Not if you don't tell me."

Sandu gritted his teeth. He had hoped to slip away with no one the wiser, but now that Alex had caught him, he felt caught between his conscience and his desires. He said, "It's a long story."

Alex moved closer to him, his face hidden by shadows. "We have all night. There's a log over there; sit with me."

With his courage ebbing fast, Sandu felt compelled to obey. He dropped Galen's reins and joined Alex on the mossy log. He stared at his hands, not meeting the other man's eye.

"Are you afraid of what Cara is?" Alex asked bluntly.

Sandu shook his head. "No. She wouldn't hurt me. But if I stay, I'll hurt her."

"How?"

"I've made a lot of mistakes in the past," Sandu said. *Maybe I can skirt around it.* "I've lost people because of them. I'm afraid I'll make another mistake."

"You seem a loyal man. I don't believe you'd leave just for fear of a mistake yet to be made." Alex's voice was soothing and warm, and Sandu relaxed slightly. *I can trust him*, he thought. *He's harbored many secrets at that university.*

"I'm a bounty hunter," Sandu said. He spoke quickly, trying to just get it all out. "I'm supposed to bring Cara to my guildmaster; she's worth five marks to him. But my last bounty...I ruined his life. His wife's dead because of me. But I need the money for Papa. I need it badly. Yet I can't betray Cara. Not after all we've been through together."

"Then don't betray her. Don't bring her to the guildmaster."

It sounded so simple when Alex said it, but Sandu knew it to be a false hope. "He spelled me. Says he can find me wherever I go, and that if Cara's with me, he'll get her. So you see? I have to leave for her own good."

Alex shifted beside him. Sandu wished he could bury his head in the mulch and be left alone. But the scholar stayed, and after a moment said, "You're not alone anymore. I have contacts in Riverfen. We can protect her."

"But his magic–"

"He's not the only wizard in the world." Alex stood up, brushing off his breeches. "You're her friend; she needs you. Come back to camp with me."

Sandu wavered, hoping that Alex spoke true. *If he's right, then I can stay with her and Laris won't come between us.* He took Alex's proffered hand and stood. "You won't tell her all this?"

"It's not my truth to tell."

After a moment's hesitation, Sandu nodded. "Alright. Let's go back to the camp."

His heart was lighter now, for he wanted to be with his friend, but he couldn't help but second-guess his decision. Then Alex fell into step beside him, and Sandu felt more confident. *Together we can help her.*

CHAPTER FIFTEEN
Jagger

JAGGER'S CHEST throbbed, the cut in it congealing too slowly. He made his way to his packs, found the hooked needle and catgut, and collapsed to the ground. No water to clean it. Not that it mattered. A cut this shallow wouldn't do much harm, not to him. He'd been cut far worse in his time. His fingers shook as he threaded the needle. Harder than it looked, this. Astounding how women did it without any trouble. He laughed at that, then coughed, a coppery taste filling his mouth. He spat. *Vecking bitch.*

He stuck a piece of wood in his mouth, bit down, *hard*, then stabbed the needle into his flesh. Sharp thrills of pain shot from the new, tiny wound. Jagger grunted. A tailor working in living fabric, he closed the cut with rudimentary stitches. Every once in a while, he had to pause, to wait for the agony to subside, but he never waited long to start again. Might get too scared that way and not finish the job. When all was said and done, fourteen jagged black stitches held the oozing wound shut. He tied off the gut and used a small knife to cut it. The threat having passed, he looked around him, regaining his bearings. Sandu and his monster friend had fled back to the main road, no doubt. Which way from there? Down into the valley, probably. Coming from the mountains, going to the rivers and streams. He should've killed Sandu when he'd had the chance, but he couldn't resist the urge to tell Sandu that he knew, to see the fear of certain death in the bastard's eyes.

Another head-on attack would not end well, that much was certain. The prickling cut he had just closed was proof of that. The girl – whoever she was – was strong. Strong and dangerous. Where had Sandu found her? Was she a lover? Perhaps he could get to her, use her against Sandu. But if she meant nothing to him...no, there had to be something else. *Sandu has to suffer before he dies. What does he love? Himself, that damn horse. Me and Raven, once upon a time. Clearly not anymore...*

...The young man stood dripping in the rain, his dark hair plastered against his wet forehead. His soft brown eyes looked up cheerfully at Jagger.

"Who the veck are you?" Jagger asked, peering from the cracked doorway. "What do you want?"

Shrugging, the man said, "Food and a bed for the night, and a place to keep my horse. I have goods to barter, too."

"Peddler?"

He nodded.

"What happened to Dirrard?"

"Broke his leg under a fallen cart, poor fellow. Asked me to take his route up here, at least for the time being. Oh, here, I have a letter from the Guild that allows me to trade in this region. What can I call you, good sir?"

Jagger held the letter inside to peruse it. Seemed genuine enough. Handing it back, he said, "I'm neither good nor a 'sir.' Jagger works for me. I'm goin'ta have to take you up to the Archmaster afore you can trade or sleep."

"Thank you, Master Jagger. My name's Sandu Crin."

"Didn't say I cared." At last opening the door, Jagger stood aside to let the man pass. Crin smelled of horse and dripped all over the Lofalin rugs that had been imported just last month. If Jagger had a mind for expensive things, he would have rebuked him. Instead, he wordlessly walked up through the keep, already regretting taking Hepel's door shift for the night.

He wished Crin would have been quiet, too.

"I haven't been through Daggenhelm before. Never heard of this keep, neither. What sort of business would you run all the way in the middle of the mountains, a hundred miles from nowhere? Had to ask all throughout Havish Pass for directions, I did. Most people didn't seem to want to say anything. Say, Jagger, that's an unusual name, I've only heard of one...man..."

The man stopped in his tracks. When Jagger glanced back, he was met with a horrified expression. Crin stammered, "You're...no. You can't be...but..." His eyes darted down to Jagger's fingers. Jagger, a glint of humor in his eye, held up his hands, missing pinkies and all.

"You're Jagger Cross, the Heartless. Eightfingers. The Bl-"

"Bloodied Giant, yeh, yeh. We've all heard the stories. Veck, I've lived them. Welcome to Daggenhelm, Master Crin. Home of Fauste's Shiv. Dirrard traded with us, made good coin, and kept his mouth shut. Now you can either follow me and swear an oath of silence to the Archmaster, then barter and partake of our hospitality as you wish. Or, Master Crin, I can drag you outside like a dog and rip your lungs out. Your choice."

"I'll speak with the Archmaster, please."

Once the peddler had been properly threatened and his compliance assured by the Archmaster, Jagger led him down to the dining hall and gave him a bowl of soup and some mead. At this hour, just after the seventh bell, guards, laborers, and Shivs all sat shoulder to shoulder drinking and laughing. Jagger always liked it at this time of day. Most of the others didn't speak much to him, but he liked to sit and watch them. Pretend he was normal, at a tavern or the like, just a normal man.

"How'd you lose your pinkies?" Sandu asked, blowing on his soup to cool it.

Jagger didn't look at him. "None of your damn business."

"Fair. They're old scars, though. Probably sometime in your youth, I'm guessing. Vandalism? Or thievery? I've seen the like many times before. I wandered the streets for a time, too. Me and the whole gang, we thought we owned Dunfrey." He laughed a little. "Can't say how many fingers ought to have been cut off me, if the law was as good as people like to think it is."

Despite his usual aversion to people, this lad didn't irk Jagger *overly much. Jagger looked curiously at him. Apparently taking that as a sign, Crin continued, "I never in my life thought I'd meet you. Mumma used to tell me stories of the Heartless. I remember us sitting around the fire, wagons at our backs, and she'd always warn us that if we didn't behave on the road tomorrow she'd call for Jagger Cross to come get us."*

"I never kidnapped anyone," Jagger said. Well, maybe he had, but only as part of a larger job. Murder, extortion, and torture were his oats and honey.

"No? Honestly, that surprises me. Well, in any case, it scared the shit right out of us. And now here I am, sharing a meal with the storied monster of my childhood."...

...Jagger made his slow way through the trees and onto the road. A few rain clouds had gathered on the horizon as sheets of grey poured down on unseen regions, a gust of wind bringing the tantalizingly sweet smell to his grateful nostrils. After he resettled his pack on his shoulders to ease the pain in his chest, Jagger walked stiffly down the road, his mind spinning around a thousand thoughts of revenge. Sandu had once told him that he came from a Valadi family. Those Gallic bastards were close, weren't they? The Sarga tribe, that was it. Striking at them would hurt Sandu to his very core.

With each slow, measured step, rage built itself from his feet to his crown, stacking in jagged layer upon layer. His thighs warmed as the heat of it traveled up, his chest wound throbbing in dull harmony, his fingers twitching with the thought of Sandu's life choked out between them. With each step, the anger threatened to boil over, to force him to stab a passing farmer or throw knives at the bright trees. But he resisted. He had to save it, hold it inside until his job was done.

By the end of the day, the anger subsided – leaving his limbs cold and shaky – and settled in his belly in flame-hot slumber. Jagger remembered the way Raven would hold him at night, when his temper nearly exploded from him, and calm him. In her arms he had felt the rage bubble away into nothingness, but without her cool hands pressing against his sweaty skin, it merely waited for its chance to spring up once more.

Raven would not like this. She would want him to find a new life, to escape the death and destruction, tend a farm or start a business, something reputable that would bring honor and peace to her dead name.

No, Jagger thought fiercely. *You'd never be at rest. This is the only way, my love.* Let his own soul be damned; he'd kill a thousand children so she could be truly at peace...

..."How long will you be gone?" Raven asked. The three of them — she, Sandu, and Jagger — sat in a quiet corner of the dining hall, drinking ale and listening to one of the lads play a mandolin with a broken string. It was a night of celebration for the Shivs: two members had returned, bringing money and reputation to the company.

Sandu shrugged. "A quinn, perhaps a deshe if the weather is unkind. There's a mining camp up on Mount Kriener that's in need of supplies and offering my guild a pretty penny for some decent ones. Since I'm the closest peddler...they didn't exactly give me a choice in the matter."

Raven tipped her head back to finish her drink. After wiping her mouth, she said, "Taavi thinks there's a blizzard coming. What if you get stranded up there?"

"I'll be fine. I have more than enough in my packs to rig myself a nice little shelter."

"That I don't doubt. But have you ever built a lean-to, or made a fire with wet wood?"

"It can't be that hard."

Raven turned to Jagger and said seriously, "He's going to die." She looked back at Sandu. "At least bed poor Gilly before you go. The girl's been eyeing you since the day you came sodden to our doorstep."

"Wha-?" Sandu spluttered into his mug. Laughing, Jagger shook his head at his wife. "He's not only an idiot, he's an idiot who can't see when a lass wants to fuck him dizzy."

"Now wait just a minute," Sandu started.

"I'll let you handle this one," Jagger said. He grabbed Raven's and his empty mugs and lurched from the table, his head slightly fuzzy

from the strong drink. Behind him, he could hear Raven's giggling and Sandu's indignant exclamations. Smiling to himself, he weaved his way to the barrels on the far side of the room and filled their mugs to the brim with Marwin's latest batch of barleybrew. It was a strong, deep amber ale with light froth and a hint of apple to it. Lately, it was all Jagger wanted to drink.

As he returned to the table, he noticed Raven and Sandu speaking more seriously to each other, both leaning forward with the slight intensity only seen when two people are so focused on their conversation that nothing could intrude upon it. Jagger decided not to disturb them, and perched on a stool some twenty feet away, nearer the lad with the warbling voice.

Jagger watched Raven as she spoke, noting the graceful lines of her neck, the wide gestures her hands made, the brightness of her eyes. She's still the most beautiful thing I've ever seen. *It constantly bemused him that a creature such as her, something so perfect she could have been of the fae realm, could have fallen in love with a monster like him.*

One of her hands rested on the table, her fingertips touching Sandu's wrist. She smiled sadly, and Jagger could only guess what the two had shared.

Ever since Sandu had started making regular visits to the keep, Jagger and Raven had laughed more. Having a friend – not a fellow murderer, but a normal man – had been a balm for them. I should get him something nice, *Jagger mused.* Maybe a small barrel of berrymead, or a new cloak. That one's nearly ratted to nothing...

...Jagger's dreams had lately been full of memories. Each morning he woke with a sour taste in his mouth, as if the sweetness of such things had turned rotten in the remembering. Had Sandu been wearing the cloak Jagger had bought for him? Jagger spat. Some thanks Sandu had shown.

You've done worse for the Shiv, a small part of him said. Betrayed and cajoled and murdered and tortured and manipulated. How is what Sandu did any worse?

"Because he was my friend," Jagger muttered out loud. He picked up a stick, then snapped it in two and threw away the broken halves. "I trusted him. Raven trusted him. He drank with us and swapped stories by the fire. There's sacred things you just don't break. He did."

Would you do the same thing to him if it meant saving Raven?

"You bloody well know I would. That's not the issue here. Sandu didn't have anything but us. And he betrayed us. Traitorous Valadi bastard."

How do you know that he didn't go back to his family? Maybe he finally reunited with them...

"Shut up!" Jagger yelled, his voice echoing around the empty woods. "Veck Sandu! Shit on him and his whole Gallic bloodline!" His throat felt raw, but rather than stopping, he laughed; a loud, long sound, more like that of a strangled cat than a man. "I'll kill you Crin! You're a dead man walking!"

No reply came from the woods.

For days Jagger marched, his sore feet driven by purpose. Find the Valadi. Find the Sarga. Make Sandu regret ever coming to Daggenhelm. He didn't know where it came from, but he had always had a knack for finding whoever he was looking for. Some of the Shivs called him a bloodhound, for once he put his mind to it, he always found his target. *Maybe there's some magic in me*, Jagger had once thought. Now, though, he didn't question his abilities. He only hunted.

At each village he passed, he asked about the wandering caravans. Most stewards kept logs of the Valadi, to track their comings and goings, to see if any thievery or murder discovered in the night could be attributed to the bastards. When they asked his purpose, Jagger told them, "My daughter ran off with a troupe. I want to find her and bring her home."

Most times it worked. Sometimes, though, the steward would glance down and see the missing pinkies. His eyes would widen, his mouth gaping open as words tried and failed to come out. Jagger was used to the way people would sidestep from him in the streets or fearfully duck into their homes as whispers of rumors swept through the town ahead of him. It used to bother him, and many long nights in Raven's arms comforted him that *someone* in the world was unafraid of the Heartless. In her arms he became simply Jagger, a man as any other.

Now he wore the fear like armor, using it to twist his smile into something a knight would quail at.

At last he came upon the Valadi. Evening had just coated the sky in dark blue tones, a cool breeze sweeping across the hills with the coming of night. Down in a dale, Jagger could see their fires as well as three large wagons and a fourth smaller one circling the outer edge of the camp. Music drifted on the wind, its melody composed of laughter and stories.

On the hill above, Jagger found a smooth stone, still warm from the sun, and perched on it. His eyes were not as good as they once were, but he could count the silhouettes around the fires. Maybe fifteen in all, maybe two more or less. Three of the shadows made regular circuits of the camp, the watchmen for the night. Some of the shapes were much smaller, children no doubt sitting and listening wide-eyed to tales told by their elders.

All in all, an easy mark.

Jagger raised a hand to wipe his brow, then realized it was shaking. How long since he had last eaten? A day, perhaps two? His dogged determination had carried him farther than mere food ever could, but hunger tremors could ruin the entire plan. Besides, these caravanners would likely take candles to fall asleep. He could wait. In his pack he found some old jerky and fruit. The fruit was moldy, but he didn't care. He had eaten worse before in the high mountains of the north when the winds had been too strong for any fire to burn and raw goat was all he had. He spat out the first mouthful, then forced himself to down the rest. His stomach churned threateningly, so he quaffed his water, then sat still as a stone, waiting for the queasiness to pass.

Dammit, he couldn't let himself starve before finding Sandu again. He'd have to be more careful about eating. *Don't forget. That's the key: don't vecking forget to eat.*

The campfires below were damped down as the Valadi went to bed. Those three silhouettes still prowled the perimeters, one of them stopping every quarter candle or so to stoke the remaining fire into a semblance of life. Jagger waited until midnight had passed and clouds drifted across the face of the moon to darken his path.

He slipped from the rock, checked his pack to make sure nothing in it would make any sudden noises, then threw it over his shoulders. With deliberate steps, he descended the hill and strode into the forest. Autumn had already breathed into the trees, crunchy leaves fallen everywhere on the forest's muted carpet. He put each foot down with careful grace, testing the ground before allowing his full weight to bear down on a dead leaf or stick. What would normally have been a ten minute walk turned into half a candle of crouching and near-crawling. His thighs burned from the stance, his eyes straining through the dark trunks to see the camp and its guards.

At last he heard the murmur of voices:

"...damn cold out here. Can't we go south this winter?"

"With the feast coming up? We'd be fools not to try and convince the earl to let us perform for his guests."

"Damn feast."

Their soft conversation faded as they walked away. Jagger crept to the edge of the clearing and looked more closely at the camp. The smallest wagon stood twenty feet away, but too close to the fires. If he kept to the trees, he could get within ten feet of one of the large wagons.

Melting back into the forest, Jagger made a circuit of the clearing until his target stood between him and the fires. He could see two of the watchmen standing across the camp to his left and staring into the trees away from him. The third, though...

If he waited too long, he'd lose this opportunity. Darting from the cover of the trees, Jagger scurried to a rear wagon wheel, his heart thumping in his chest. His mouth had gone dry. He licked his chapped lips and swallowed nervously. Even after all these years, the thrill of the job still made him anxious.

Which was probably why he had managed to live so long.

No outcry rose up, no cold, hard steel bit into his flesh. He let out the breath he had been holding, then secured his pack more tightly against himself and fingered one of his small knives. In the dark, in unknown territory...he could maybe take down one of the guards, two if he were lucky, before the rest of the Valadi woke and drove him away or killed him.

He paused, realizing his stomach hadn't dropped at the thought of death. *That* was unusual. Maybe, after all this business with Sandu was through, he would be ready to die.

Jagger placed one foot on the wheel's spoke and pushed himself up until he could grab the edge of the wagon frame. His limbs shook with the effort of keeping his body pressed as close to the wood as possible. One hand on the frame and one foot still on the spoke, he swung his other leg up until it found purchase on the back of the wagon. With his free hand for balance, he placed all his weight on one leg as the other lifted from the spoke and rested atop the wheel well. He stopped to regain his breath. His legs threatened to collapse from beneath him. The scars stretching across his back ached, the wound on his chest feeling as if it would burst.

Perched precariously on the back of the wagon, Jagger could see more of the camp as well as the third guard. The man squatted near the fire, back to it. If he so much as turned his head to one side, he'd see Jagger. That'd be the end of it.

But the man didn't turn, and Jagger quietly opened the door to the wagon and slipped inside.

Four shapes lay against the walls in tiny bunks, two on each side. A knife appeared in Jagger's hand. He found the first sleeping form, its back to him. He peered over until he could see its face: a lad, perhaps sixteen or seventeen years old. Olive skin and sandy hair, like Sandu's. His mouth had dropped open in his sleep.

In the span of a second, Jagger gripped and held shut the boy's mouth and slit his throat. He died without a sound. Jagger crept to the next form. An older woman, perhaps nearly as old as Jagger himself. The mother, no doubt. With the same cold efficiency, Jagger killed her. Then the father, whose soft snores had filled the wagon.

Jagger turned to the final form. This one, smaller than the rest, had a blanket pulled up over its head. Gently folding the blanket down, Jagger held the knife ready.

His breath caught in his throat as he stared at the sleeping girl. A child, really, thirteen at the oldest. Her cheeks were still round and flushed with the rosiness of youth; her dark eyebrows were held ever so slightly together, making a wrinkle in her forehead; her pink lips were parted just enough to breathe. She reminded him of Raven when he had first met her a lifetime ago.

The knife trembled in his hand. The girl made a muffled sound, her fingers drawing up to partially cover her face. Despite himself, Jagger could not pull away, could not bring himself to ruin the peacefulness of her dreams. *Dammit, she's nothing to you. A Valadi brat. Kill her and be done with it.* Yet still he lingered, hardly daring to draw breath.

"How far is Riverfen?" The quiet voice outside broke the moment. Jagger shook himself, raising the knife.

Then he lowered it and ducked out of the wagon. He readied three throwing knives, then stood tall. Two guards faced away from him, backs to the fire. The third stood at the edge of the camp, his trousers loose around his hips, his head tipped back in satisfaction.

"...but if the roads get any worse–" The speaker's words were cut short, a knife sticking from his neck. His partner gaped, eyes widening. Before he could sound the alarm, Jagger's knife buried itself between his shoulder blades.

"Mar–" The third had turned, his member hanging out, a spot of flesh in the darkness. Red dripped down the man's chest, and he stared in amazement at the steel stabbed into him. He looked up just in time for Jagger's second knife to fly into his eye.

Jagger drew a deep breath. His turbulent mind settled itself from hurricane to calm skies. Methodically, like a butcher preparing his meats, he went into each wagon and quickly dispatched the sleeping Valadi, his hands stained black in the darkness.

After pilfering each wagon for supplies, Jagger returned to the first wagon that held the only other living person in the camp. Jagger harnessed and saddled two of the horses using equipment he found. Then, he crawled back into the wagon and gagged the girl. Her eyes flew open, she struggled and tried to scream against the rag stuffed in her mouth. His implacable hands held her firm, dragging her from the wagon and hoisting her into the saddle. One of her feet kicked out, hitting his face.

Jagger felt the bruise welling up. His first urge was to slap her. His second, to draw a knife and cut the tendon behind her knee. He stopped just before his blade touched her flesh, and glared up at her. "Kick me again, and you'll never use this leg again. Understood?"

She nodded, terrified.

"Good." Idly, Jagger wondered what he'd do with her. A problem for the morning. He mounted the second horse, took the lead for hers, and rode away from the camp, as far as he could get before dawn.

Chapter Sixteen
Seanna

RIVERFEN AT LAST. The famed city of lanterns, with its perfect white marble palace and thousands of canals and streams, its resplendence the inspiration for poets and ballads for hundreds of years.

And yet, Seanna found no joy in gazing at the multitude of colored lights reflected in the waterways, the smell of salt permeating her chambers in such a way that her childhood memories floated up constantly to remind her of happier times. In the interminable days since her disastrous dinner with Rask, she could think of nothing else. Any other expecting mother would, at this time, seek bright swaddling clothes or wooden toys. Prepare the baby's room. Find a nursemaid. Begin to withdraw from polite society in order to embroider pillowcases or practice lullabies.

Seanna was determined not to do such things until she must. She would have years to love and raise her babe into a far better king than Henrik, but only months before propriety forced her into reclusion until after the child's first birthday. In those months, she would build a societal empire for herself.

At least her king husband often dined with his own cohorts, leaving her to herself. She had arranged to dine with River Valley nobility, few whom she knew well. A field of persons ripe for harvesting. Her words, she hoped, would be her scythe, drawing them to her.

To her disappointment, Earl Seastone and his new wife had given their apologies and failed to attend the dinner. Seanna didn't let the feeling linger long; instead, she listened to the verbal spars between her guests.

"Ah, my Lady Greenswell...still trying to find a new tailor?" a lord said, leaning over to look at the noblewoman's ill-fitting garb.

"It must be difficult to smell with that monstrosity atop your lip," Lady Greenswell retorted. "Surely you must release your barber? At least," she said with a glance toward Seanna, "I don't pretend to be smaller than I am."

There was a round of polite laughter. Seanna blushed, smiled, and took a sip of wine. *May the sharpest tongue win.*

Seanna said, "Well, perhaps I can speak to the tailor you had when you were pregnant." The lady colored, flashing an angry look. It was a low jab, Seanna knew – the lady had miscarried three times and borne no children – but others laughed with her.

When dinner was done, more snide remarks having been spat than food swallowed, Seanna excused herself, her appetite for spite satiated. She stepped into the hall, soon joined by Sir Eric and the silent handmaids that followed her everywhere. Her mind caught up in the whirl of gossip, she ignored the beautiful tile mosaics underfoot. Rumors she had heard months ago flitted in and out of memory, each one crueler than the last. She hadn't given thought to voicing them then...but now perhaps–

"Pardon me."

A lady, only a year or two younger than Seanna, dipped low, moving out of the queen's way. Her chin, however, remained lifted, a smirk resting in an infuriating way on her red lips. Even curtseying, she was taller than Seanna, her fashionable snood doing nothing to lessen the discrepancy. Golden curls flowed from beneath the pearls and velvet. Pink cheeks blushed in a fair face. Pale blue eyes, cool and derisive, peeked from beneath dark lashes.

Seanna stopped, staring this stranger up and down. She

was a beauty, to be sure, but a beauty with little respect.

"The proper address for the queen is 'Your Grace,'" Seanna said.

The young lady sneered. "Of course, Your Grace. I had forgotten." Never before had Seanna heard so much condescension dripping in the title. A quiet arrogance pervaded this woman's entire demeanor, from the words she spoke to the way she held her arms at her sides.

"What is your peerage?" Seanna asked.

"My father is Lord Ecurio Westerburg of Resta, my brother the champion knight of the Holly Tournament. Our lands are renowned for grapes and wine."

"I have never found western wine to be particularly pleasant. Far too dry, like the people who produce it. Your name?"

The woman's face grew red, though she hid whatever shame she felt behind a lovely smile. "Maeria Westerburg, Your Grace." She curtseyed again and made as if to leave. Seanna put out a hand.

"Maeria. A pretty name." She remembered a comment one of the courtiers had made earlier that night: *'The Westerburgs are lucky not to have lost their flower in that fire. Tactless, I've always believed it, to send a daughter away to a convent until she comes of age.'*

Seanna's smile held no warmth. "You are fortunate not to have been burnt in the fire, else your best quality would have been ruined."

"Not nearly as thoroughly as yours, Your Grace. I hear a woman's body is never the same after pregnancy."

"You have a quick tongue, Maid Westerburg. If only vineyards afforded dowries that tempted lords into marrying a shrew."

"I should think the miles and miles of bountiful farmland surrounding the orchards to be tempting enough. I have been in society all of a month, yet already received four offers of marriage, as our line is untainted by foreign blood."

How dare she! Seanna forced a smile. Her maternal

grandfather, an Eadron ambassador, had married into Dotsch society, and she, like her mother, had inherited his dusky color.

Maeria, taking advantage of Seanna's silence, dipped then glided away, her skirts whispering against the mosaics. Seanna stilled the faint tremors of her angry heart with a deep breath and carried on down the corridor, her encounter with the maiden sliding into the back of her mind. *She is nothing to me.*

A striking portrait caught Seanna's attention, its subject a beautiful woman with cascading chestnut hair and a radiant diadem atop her curls. She regarded the painting a moment, drinking in the woman's knowing smile, her jeweled dress, the sheer confidence of her posture. *I will be like her,* Seanna decided. *Beautiful, yet in control of all around me. I daresay no one sneered at her. She may have even kept her husband under her thumb.* Seanna couldn't envision a greater aspiration than that. *And she could have any lovers she desired, and none could argue against her. Beyond that, any children she had she loved deeply, and raised into noble, good rulers.* She moved on, picturing herself with such a wondrous life. The baby shifted, and she cooed softly to it.

As the sky outside the palace darkened, Seanna's mood improved. She imagined the warm, scented bath waiting for her in her rooms and the soft sheets on a bed far too large for her, beckoning her to sleep.

But the moment she entered her chambers, peace crashed down into broiling hatred. Henrik glared at her with those scornful grey eyes, the room filled with his kingly presence.

"Henrik." Seanna waved a hand at her maids. "He won't be staying long. Prepare my bath and bed."

The handmaids rushed through the room, grateful to escape the crackling tension between the king and queen. Never taking his eyes from her, Henrik sat, his robes arranged perfectly on the seat. Seanna sat more slowly, feeling ungainly in front of him. Neither spoke.

"You made a fool of yourself in D'Clet," Henrik said at last, his lips tightened in a straight line, his mouth barely opening. "You made a fool of *me.* They think me a weak king who can't control his own wife. Can you even comprehend how dangerous you are to my very rule?"

"Then perhaps you should respect me more. After all, I–"

"Speak when asked to," he said in his deep rumble, the threat of a distant roar in his tone. "I stand behind Predicant Ropaz, and if you had known your place, you would have agreed when asked by my vassals. Your temper got the better of you, and rumors already circulate about your storming out like a petulant child. I offended him when I decided to marry you, and I had hoped, after your outburst on the docks and your insistence on traveling overland, that you might at least prove yourself to him as a queen worthy of the station. I was a fool. Rask is the most powerful man in this kingdom, no matter the praises sung of me in the streets. He is dangerous, and should he so choose, could secede and take most of the earls with him. I have kept his alliance on a thin thread, and here you come along to ruin everything I have worked for! You stupid, ignorant woman!" Henrik shouted, looming over Seanna, casting a shadow across her stony expression. Seanna refused to show him the fear that had sprung into her throat, gagging her. He paced now, still shouting at her.

"What have I done to deserve a disobedient wife such as you? Have I angered the gods in some way? Vecking hells, Seanna, I tried! I did everything correctly, and yet you still failed when it counted, miserable bitch that you are!"

"At least I don't snivel and grovel to Rask," Seanna blazed back at him.

"You're pathetic and weak-minded. You'll find yourself losing the few allies you have been lucky enough to gain. You've already lost the love of your husband."

"As if to suggest I *ever* had your love!" she sneered. "I did my best to please you, yet you treat me like the dogs in the kennel. Of course I turned from you; you had turned from me before our wedding day."

"You...the impertinence! The absolute – the nerve that you should speak to me with such a tongue." Henrik lifted his arm, the back of his hand large against the shadow of his face. Seanna did not flinch. Slowly, his expression growing darker, he lowered it, clenching his hand into a fist at his side. "Only for the sake of our child do I resist."

"As if you would dare even were I not pregnant."

"You would be unfit to be seen in polite company for weeks if I did what I wished to now." Henrik stalked from her chambers, slamming the door behind him hard enough to shake the portraits on the walls.

Falling back into the divan's cushions, Seanna pressed cool fingers to her hot cheeks. The baby kicked, and she placed a hand protectively over him. "I'm sorry, little one. I didn't mean to scare you. Mumma will always love you, even if your father doesn't love me." The child calmed, and she rubbed her belly, thinking again of the portrait she had seen in the hall. *I will prove Henrik wrong. I'll be a better queen and mother than he believes I am, and show the world how pitiful he is beside me.*

CHAPTER SEVENTEEN
Gwen

BESIDE HER, Druam smiled and waved, his bronze circlet glittering on his proud brow. He looked younger, as if marriage had wholly rejuvenated him. Gwen felt it, too: with him beside her, fears of Daghorn or the nobles' rejections had nearly dissipated. Though she had often turned to her magic to comfort her in Demarren, here she felt secure in being simply Gwen.

Her cheeks sore from beaming, she turned her attention to the crowd. Hundreds of people, mostly nobles or wealthy merchants in a sea of shining jewels and shimmering velvet, screamed and shouted as they pushed against the rails separating them from the arena.

The last tourney of the year, in all its violent glory, commenced as soon as King Henrik and Queen Seanna took their seats. Under the beating sun, Gwen sweated in her silks and fanned herself for some small relief. Before the tournament even began, a hedge knight passed out in his armor and had to be extracted from the heavy chainmail. Other knights ordered their pages to pour water down the backs of their necks as they waited to ride. The smell of body odor and blood combined in a sickening way, and, were it not for Druam's excitement, Gwen would have retreated to the cool rooms of the palace. She wished that he had let them sit under the awning, where the shade provided some reprive. But Druam had decided that if his fighters were to be subjected to the heat, so would he.

All day, knights came and went, bowing to the royals and then riding around and around each other, dueling with sword, spear, mace, or axe, hitting and unseating their foe or completely missing and falling onto the ground themselves with sickening crunches, only to rise slowly a minute later with blood flowing down their necks and crusting into their mail. In the third duel, one man's sword clanged into his opponent's helmet, then slid into his neck. As the knight tore his sword away, the other collapsed from his blood-coated horse, falling thickly into the dirt, unmoving.

As the sun rose to its zenith, so too did the sweltering heat grow and fester in the humidity. Glancing at her husband, Gwen saw his manic smile, his skin pale and clammy to her light touch though not a drop of sweat beaded his hair. "You should spend some time in the shade," she murmured, grasping his cold hand in both of hers. "You look ill, my love."

"If the knights can stand it, then so can I," he replied hoarsely. His hand grew warmer and warmer until it felt like fire between her fingers.

"Please, Druam..."

The hard grip of his hand slackened, his eyes rolling back in his head as he stiffened and fell from his seat on the hard wooden stand. Gwen tried to catch him, to ease his fall, but too slowly, her mind dim from the sunlight beating on her black hair. There were shouts behind her and the box shook beneath them as lords dashed to their side. On the field, swords collided in a harsh knell.

Gwen didn't know what to do. Eigbrett knelt at Druam's side, feeling his forehead and trying futilely to cover him from the sun's harsh glare. Druam's eyelids fluttered, his mouth moving with no sound. His breath came in short, rapid bursts, as a man running or making love. Others crowded around them and pushed Gwen away. She scrabbled at them, desperate to return to her husband's side.

"Don't move him! It might disrupt his humors," Queen Seanna shouted.

"Call for a curate and bring him into the shade," King Henrik commanded.

Just help him! Gwen wanted to scream, but her mouth wouldn't work. Her hands felt heavy, her vision too bright. She almost felt like she would faint, too. She stood still, dazed and terrified, until some voice within her told her to do something. Druam needed her; she couldn't give into fear now.

Four sturdy servants grabbed Druam's arms and legs and lifted him into the shade. Across the arena, the crowd surged and screamed, unaware of their earl's condition. The knights still rode around and between each other, their weapons clanging over the din of fans and hawkers.

Her hands clutched anxiously, and Gwen finally pushed back to Druam's side. Shepherd Marin scurried over in his curate's heavy robes. He dipped rags in a bucket and wrung them over Druam's head. Suddenly, Gwen didn't want to merely watch as he treated her ill husband; she wanted to do something, anything, to make Druam better.

"Let me help," Gwen said.

"Take the rag and hold it to his forehead," Shepherd Marin ordered, handing the warm, moist cloth to Gwen. She obeyed as he held two fingers to Druam's neck. Then he ran his hands up and down the earl's body. "His heart is weakened. Bring a carriage with a roof; we'll take him to the palace."

"When will he wake?" Gwen asked as she mopped Druam's brow. His eyelids barely moved, and she could feel the heat radiating from his body. She hadn't known anyone could be so ill so quickly; it frightened her, seeing the confident earl in such a state. *What if he doesn't wake?* A tear fell from her cheek onto his nose.

Marin leaned back on his heels. "It should be any minute now. It's not good if it takes much longer."

"Is there anything else you can do?"

"Not until he wakes. Then, we'll give him water and fruit. But he needs to return to the palace as soon as possible."

"I'll take him." She silently dared someone to contradict her, but no one did. Then she remembered that she was now the

Lady of Seastone, and must play hostess. Gwen looked to the king and queen, who had not moved from their thrones. "Your Graces, please do not worry for him. I'm sure he would want you to stay and run the tourney in his stead."

"Of course," the king said. "Give him our blessings when he wakes."

Druam did not stir the entire journey through the city back to the palace. Gwen sat with him in the carriage, stroking his head and humming a Demar lullaby. Not once did she look out to see the city pass by. Druam filled all her sight, and she prayed over him, lips moving silently as she begged the gods to be merciful. Even after he had been carried through his suites and placed in his down feather bed, Druam did not wake. His skin, grossly pale, still felt hot to her touch.

Marin checked him over. "He has a fever. We must bathe him with cool water. Help if you wish it, my lady." He beckoned a servant and whispered a few quick words in her ear. She hurried out of the room as he mopped his brow. "Once she returns, I must leave and prepare the earl's draught. It helps him when he is most ill."

"You've seen this before?" Gwen asked.

The curate nodded. "Ill humors in his family line cause it. But this may be the worst I've seen him. For other ailments, magic might be used, but not for this. The draughts, I've found, are more effective than anything else."

"Then we must pray that it works," Gwen said, her throat tight. "Can the court wizard help?"

"Avallune? He's not a healer. If I went to him, he'd only suggest turning the earl's skin to stone to prevent it from happening again."

Gwen almost laughed, but Marin's expression was serious. *If I told the curate of my own magic, perhaps I could help him.* Yet when she tried to speak, she found the words didn't come. So she turned back to her husband to hide her shame.

Blood had drained from Druam's lips and cheeks, though his forehead burned when she placed the back of her hand to it. The servant girl returned bearing a basin of water and a stack of linens. With the curate's help, Gwen undressed Druam and lay him atop the sheets, then placed water-soaked cloth all over him. Marin left then, promising to return as soon as the draught was ready.

"Leave us," Gwen said to the servant. She and Druam were alone now in his vast bedchamber. With his hand clasped in one of hers, she stroked his cheek. Fear struck her, fear that he may never wake. What would become of her? She had yet to bear him an heir...

In the silent, mournful air of the room, Gwen's worries began to take hold, and she paced about to ease her mind. The sun caressed her cheeks when she peeked out onto the balcony. She paused for a moment, then opened the paned door and stepped out into the light. *Only for a few moments.*

Taking a deep, wonderful, humid breath, Gwen shut her eyes. Her lids glowed, giving half-sight to an otherwise strange inner world. Wullum would often spend the hot afternoons with her playing card games. She pictured him next to her, their dark skin absorbing the sunlight, sitting together as they so often did.

"I'm surprised to see you abandon Druam's side." A familiar voice startled her. Gwen whirled to face the one who intruded on her fantasies. Mavian Strilu stood against the doorframe, a tiny frown making a crescent of his thin lips. "Given up hope?"

"I merely wanted some fresh air. He will wake soon," Gwen replied, hoping it was true. Beyond Mavian, she could see the darkened room and Druam's still form. "Who let you in? The servants didn't announce you."

Mavian shrugged. "I know my way around, and my cousin doesn't expect such courtesies from me. I came to see if he had woken."

"Not yet, I fear. If that's all...?"

"It is." Mavian's black hair, pulled back into a long braid, swung over his shoulder as he came to lean against the balcony next to her. "I always come to see him when he's suffering bad humors such as these."

"How often do you visit the palace, Lord...er...." Gwen realized she had no idea which fief he ruled.

"Far-eyes," he prompted. "And I stay most months of the year. I was brought here as my cousin's ward when my father died."

"I am sorry to hear of your father. My parents went to Autorus some time ago, too."

"There wasn't much we could do for him. The prowlers attacked during an evening hunt."

Gwen waited politely for him to continue. He merely looked out over the city, seemingly content in their silence. As the quiet grew too awkward for her, she asked, "Have you ever captured a prowler?"

"Oh yes," Mavian said. "Though it died not much later. Hard to care for, those beasts. But I learned much in the brief days it lived. They can talk, but only in strange, gibberish tongue. They see, and they learn; it killed one of my guards during its feeding after it had observed the routine. But, most importantly I should think, it has no soul."

"No soul?" Gwen could not think of a more horrid fate. "But what happens to the souls of those that become prowlers? How can they find peace in the afterlife?"

"They don't. I believe they must wander purgatory until their bodies find rest."

"But it's not their fault! No man would turn prowler of his own will."

"True. But, life has never been fair, has it? Why should death be any different?" he said. Gwen pondered before realizing the truth of Mavian's words. Autorus was the most powerful – and the most hated – of the Cythra: elusive, semi-godlike beings. It was because of Autorus that so many feared death, for they must pass through his domain before joining with the gods.

With a sigh, Mavian pushed back from the bannister and glanced inside at Druam. "He still hasn't woken."

"Do you know of anything that can be done for him? Other than the curate's draught?" Gwen stepped gently back to Druam's side as Mavian followed. "I feel so terribly useless."

"Shepherd Marin knows the best remedies, and so we must

wait for him. If I knew of any healing magic, I would cast a working that might ease the sunfever, but...well...some that are interested in magic are not so fortunate as to be blessed with it."

Gwen looked guiltily away from him. *Does he know?* But Mavian's expression held no suspicion, only concern. She said, "I don't know how long Marin will take. I can send for you once Druam is awake."

"I would greatly appreciate that. In the meantime, I will see what duties I can take from him while he recovers." Mavian gave her a slight bow, then disappeared behind a servant's door. When she was sure he was gone, Gwen laid one hand on Druam's forehead and the other on his bare breast. She had promised the gods she wouldn't use magic again, but surely they would understand Druam's need.

Before Wullum had discovered them and put a stop to it, Ebarren had taught Gwen a spell of health and longevity. He had recited it in a crisp, dry voice, but Gwen found she cast the working better when she sang it. As the words tripped over her tongue, she felt a tendril of sparks forming at her breast. Magic fluttered beneath her skin, dancing down her arm until it reached her fingers. There, it shuddered and cavorted. "*Lilintim, orohro, lilintim, edralen,*" Gwen sang, pouring all her heart into the magic. It pushed out from her fingertips, a collection of blue energy that hesitated, then sprang into Druam's cheek. His skin glowed faintly, then gradually returned to normal. His breath slowed, became measured and easy, as his hand cooled in hers.

"I'm sorry," Gwen murmured to the gods. "I promised not to use my magic, but I couldn't let Druam suffer. I swear, on all things above and below Earda, that this will be my last working."

Tired and sticky from the heat, Gwen climbed onto the bed beside Druam, careful that the only part of her that touched him were her fingers. *I wonder where the curate is,* she thought drowsily before dozing.

A soft knock came at the door, and Shepherd Marin poked his head in. "My apologies, my lady. I have finished the draught."

"How long has it been?" Gwen asked. She sat up in the sheets and rearranged the damp cloth on Druam's body.

"Barely a candle, my lady. Has he stirred at all?"

"No."

"Well. Perhaps this will aid his recovery. I'm going to bring him forward; fix the pillows behind him so we may give the draught with no fear of choking."

Gwen stacked the multitudes of pillows against the headboard. The curate eased Druam onto them and propped him in a sitting position. Druam's head lolled, his mouth dropping open.

Marin said, "I'm going to hold his head back. Pour the draught straight down his throat until I tell you to stop." The curate took Druam's chin and pushed down on his forehead to tip his head back. He nodded to Gwen. She took the goblet and tipped it, allowing the sweet-smelling liquid to flow slowly into Druam's mouth. The concoction looked like mud and smelled of copper and herbs. When the cup emptied nearly all the way, the curate said, "That's enough for now. Let him rest, though stay if it pleases you. I've prepared extra measures of the draught if he sends for me."

"What do I do if he doesn't wake?"

"Wait a candle. If he still gives no response, call me at once. Though by that time, I'm afraid the gods will have taken him into their hands. Pray, my lady. I will pray too."

Too awake now to sleep, Gwen did pray. She asked forgiveness once more for her use of magic – how many innocent lives had the Trials now taken? – and begged for Druam's health. She would never touch her magic again, if only she could be a courtly wife to her healthy husband. *I will work to gain favor with the people here, and I will forget all Ebarren has taught me. Just bring Druam back to me.*

"Gwen?"

The sheets caught around Gwen's legs. She cracked her eyes open and looked around blearily, caught in the half-state between sleep and wakefulness. Outside, night had coated the land in its cool blue tones, and the lanterns twinkled in their thousands. For a moment, Gwen forgot why she had slept in her husband's chambers. Then she started and turned over, hands seeking him in the darkness.

"Gwen?" Druam asked again, voice raspy. Gwen sought his blue eyes and held his face between her palms, thanking all the gods. She didn't dare speak for fear her words would be overcome with sobs.

"You're here," Druam said. She only nodded, holding him like he might vanish if she let go. His weak hand cupped hers. "I'm so thirsty, Gwen."

Gwen slowly let go of his face, though she kept hold of his hand, as she reached for a cup on the side table. She held it to his lips and helped him drink. After he had his fill, he asked, "I suppose I missed the archery contest?"

Gwen laughed, tired and magic-worn and so, so relieved. She buried her cheek in his shoulder, weeping and laughing in turn as he held her.

CHAPTER EIGHTEEN
Seanna

THE RIVER VALLEY council met in an immense circular chamber called Lord's Hall. Pillars lined the outer edge, tall as trees and carved with patterns of seaweed and ocean creatures, and painted in blues, greens, purples, and deep reds, making the watery scenes come to life. On warm days, the wooden walls between the pillars came down and opened the room to the elements around it. A smooth, long stairway ascended from the palace into Lord's Hall, spewing forth in the center of the majestic room. As Seanna climbed upward, she stared at the ceiling: a series of arches curved in and around each other, tiled with mermaids and sea dragons cavorting about magnificent underwater cities.

Finally tearing her eyes away, she looked around the wide hall, feeling the breeze on her cheeks. Directly in front of her was a gigantic table carved from a single block of red-veined marble. Henrik, already seated there, stood and offered his hand to help her take her chair beside him. Voices murmured, rising and falling in the natural way of conversation. The smell of salt and rain filled her nostrils, a reminder of that morning's light showers.

"Ostentatious," Seanna muttered, watching a crowd of rustics gawk.

Seated along the high table with her and Henrik were

various other lords, their entourages standing discreetly nearby. She recognized the Earl Stonetree – Edsel Hawk – as well as the Skallish ambassador, Lord Daghorn. The largest chair, Earl Seastone's place, remained empty.

"Has the earl recovered?" Seanna asked Henrik.

"He is in better health and high humors, according to his steward. Here he comes now."

All gathered stood, except Seanna and Henrik, as Earl Seastone made his slow way up the stairs with Lady Seastone on his arm. Though still pale, some color had returned to his cheeks. Remarkable recovery, for having collapsed just a few days before.

Once he reached the marble table, Seanna stood and kissed his cheek. "I'm glad to see your humors have returned to balance."

"Thank you," he said. "Without my dear wife, I rather think I would have taken longer to regain health." He continued to his place, then turned to address his subjects. "Dear people of Riverfen and the River Valley, let it be assured that I am fully mended and shall once again walk the streets to see and hear you."

The nobles clapped softly while the rustics gave a resounding cheer.

"We are honored to have our esteemed king and queen join us for open council. Please, bring forth your grievances as you would if I were sole arbiter of this court. We beseech the gods to look down on this meeting with favorable minds."

From there, the council continued as it does everywhere: first the greater nobles, then the lesser, then finally the rustics stepped forward to ask for money, or resolution to a conflict, or for permission to execute a wrongdoer, on and on and on and on like that for over a candle. Druam did his best to move along the procedures, but occasionally one of the appealers would blather on regardless of the queen's obvious boredom.

At one point, Henrik argued with Druam, the two men nearly shouting at each other. Seanna rolled her eyes. She thought savagely as she stroked her belly, *I'd rather you die than turn into a pig like your father.* A moment passed, and she realized the threat she had made against the only child she had carried this far. *I'm sorry, my love. No matter what, I shall never leave you.*

Finally, no more petitioners came and the council disbanded. Those at the high table left first, the king and Druam leading with Seanna and Gwen trailing after them. Once the airy hall had been left behind, the king nodded curtly to Druam and stalked away, his shoulders tight and jaw set. Druam, too, took his leave.

"Shall we walk together?" Seanna suggested, taking Gwen's arm.

"If it pleases you," Gwen answered, smiling up at her. Seanna, though not a tall woman by any means, still stood a half-head taller than the girl. Their handmaids and Sir Eric followed a respectable distance behind them as they strolled amiably to the gardens.

"How fares your husband? We have all been praying for his quick recovery." Seanna noted the girl's nervous lick of her lips, and wondered at it.

"His recovery has been fast, thank the gods. I try not to leave his side; when we are alone, he allows his fatigue to show."

"Men must be ever strong, mustn't they? Especially in front of their wives. I believe Henrik's heart is wood rather than meat. He has no sensitivity."

"Your Grace!" Gwen exclaimed. "To talk of the king in such a—"

Seanna laughed over her, patting her hand. "Trust me, Lady Seastone, no one cares what I say of the king." Gwen's arm was warm in hers. Though young, and certainly naïve, she had a sort of...charm about her that attracted Seanna. *I've never slept with a Demar. Though she seems content with her husband, the latent desire might be there.*

"You wear Dotsch fashions well," Seanna said, rubbing the cloth between two fingers. "Have your people any interest in it?"

"Not much, no. If anything, the Skals and their customs influence our own. I thank you for the compliment, Your Grace."

"Please, my dear girl, to you I am Seanna. And to me, you

are Gwen. Friends cannot have such formalities, can they?"

"Thank you, Y– Seanna. May I ask, what does it feel like when you're with child?"

Seanna thought for a moment. "Like your stomach is tightening, and everything else is tightening, while the child itself grows and grows. I'm nearly always hungry, and far more irritable than I ever was before. Why? Do you think you might be...?"

"No!" Gwen's eyes widened. They were a dark shade of purple, and so very pretty. "I don't think...it takes months, doesn't it?"

"My dear," Seanna laughed. "You can fall pregnant your first time with a man! As long as his seed ends up inside you...he has done that, hasn't he?"

"I...I don't think this a proper topic for conversation."

"My dear, if your cheeks could blush, they would be crimson. In Demarren, is it custom for a lady of breeding to preserve herself before marriage?"

"Yes. Although we are allowed many suitors afterwards."

"Really? That I do find surprising. Is married life as wonderful as you thought it would be?"

Gwen was quiet for a second, then said, "Not as wonderful, perhaps, but certainly not terrible. It is as I should have expected: sometimes I am happy, yet sometimes I feel terribly alone. Do not mistake me, though, Seanna. Druam is very kind to me, and I am fortunate."

"Fortunate indeed."

"But, I suppose..." Gwen trailed off.

Seanna asked, "Suppose what, sweetling?"

"That I wish I had known more about men before marriage. Been in childish love, perhaps shared a kiss, but just..."

"More."

"Exactly."

"Well, my dear," Seanna said as they turned to walk in the gardens, "who's to say that you can't do the same now? You are married, not imprisoned. It may not be looked upon as common here, but plenty of young women have affairs. Not just with handsome lords, either." She glanced at Gwen's lovely face. The girl looked aghast.

"Even if we lived in Demarren, I simply cannot imagine betraying–"

"Betraying? Oh no, not as dire as that. Straying, perhaps, but it's never a betrayal. Especially not when your husband is usually shaft deep in some maid or other while you stroll the gardens with your ladies."

"Druam would never–"

"All men do, my dear. But we women stick together; 'tis natural, Gwen." With one finger, Seanna stroked the girl's cheek, delighting in its softness. But Gwen drew away, ever so slightly. Hoping that the girl was simply naïve, Seanna said, "Seek pleasure where it is offered. Don't deceive yourself; Druam is a man, just as any other man, and his needs couldn't be filled by one woman alone."

For a moment, the girl was silent, and Seanna nearly reached a hand to touch her waist, tempted to trace along that finely-shaped back. Her fingers just brushed the cloth when Gwen said, "I do sincerely believe that Druam has not strayed from me, and I would honor him by doing the same." She smiled with innocent lips.

"Then I wish all the happiness for you both," Seanna replied sweetly. Inwardly she seethed. Ever since Larka had left her, Seanna had felt the loneliness of a cold bed. *Why don't noblewomen ever see how much better a lady is as a companion?*

"Thank you, Seanna. You are a finer friend than ever I could have hoped for." Gwen's tone was annoyingly sincere. "Ah, Eigbrett is waiting. If you will excuse me?"

Gwen tripped away to take the steward's arm. Both turned, bowed, and left, Gwen's maids rushing to follow. With a flick of her hand, Seanna dismissed her handmaids and gestured for Sir Eric to step forward. He took his place beside her as she strode sedately from the gardens back into the palace. Her nethers were warm and tingling, but Gwen had scorned her. Seanna longed to find someone – *anyone* – to pleasure her. Part of her even wished she had brought Larka along. *Though Larka wants nothing to do with me now.* A thought intruded, and at first she rejected it. But as she walked, and the desire for intimacy grew, she gave into it. *If I can't find a lover, perhaps my husband will do.*

"Where are Henrik's chambers?" Seanna asked Sir Eric.

Minutes later, she knocked at the doors to her husband's suite. A silent guard stood to either side. A second passed. *Oh well, he must be away. It was futile, a stupid idea.* But one of the doors cracked open and the steward's tousled head appeared.

"Ye-oh, Your Grace. Shall I call your ladies for you?"

"No, Jacobi. I need to speak with my husband. Alone, if you please."

"Of course. I shall announce your presence; if you would step into the drawing room?"

Leaving Sir Eric outside, Seanna followed the steward into a sumptuous chamber, then seated herself on a couch as the little man disappeared behind a paneled door. Though she had at least five or six rooms in her suite, the king had been given what amounted to a small manor: a drawing room, bedroom, dressing chamber, washroom, study, library, antechamber, meeting chamber, and so on. Half the rooms would likely remain unused, but were there should the king require them.

Eventually, Henrik appeared, a robe wrapped around his burly frame. His bare feet shuffled across the thick carpet, and the imprint of his crown was shown in his hair. He poured a cup of wine, then leaned back and ran his fingers through his hair. He surveyed her for a moment.

"What do you want?" he asked. "Are you displeased with your rooms?"

"I want to start again," Seanna said. "I carry your child, and I realize now that my lack of obedience will poison him in my womb."

"Liar." *He always could tell. Damn him.*

"Fine. I want someone inside me, and I thought to seek my *husband* before another man." *Or woman. I would have preferred Gwen's sweet little malkin, but...I suppose one must make do.* "Or would you prefer your queen to bed some servant or a petty lord?"

"Hm." He said idly, "That would be treason, you know."

Which is why you'll never find out. Seanna continued, "Henrik, don't you hate what we've become? The silences, the arguments, the pettiness? I once loved you as any vassal loves their king, and I thought I would love you as a woman loves a man. Does all the blame lay with me? Please, Henrik. Can we at least be civil toward each other?"

Her tone, Seanna thought, had the perfect mixture of pleading, wistfulness, and tenderness. A good show all around. She waited while Henrik swirled his cup. After a few seconds, he said, "I find myself needlessly angered whenever I see you. I had hoped, when we first married, that you would be more like Fleta. Demure, soft-spoken."

Vecking Fleta. Must he always compare me to her?

He said, "That was unfair of me, and I treated you poorly because of it. For that I am sorry."

That truly surprised her. *An apology, from Henrik?*

He continued, "Perhaps I have been too harsh on you. I cannot say that I love you as I did Fleta, and I am certain the feeling is mutual. But we are tied together, for better or worse, for the rest of our lives. I want to raise my son without the shadow of his parents' animosity darkening his brow."

"That's...thank you."

Silence deepened between them, though not nearly as uncomfortable as the silences of the past. Henrik tipped his cup back and drank deeply, his apple bobbing on his throat. Seanna bit her lip and stared at nothing, rubbing her belly. The gesture had become a sort of comfort for her, one she had often sneered at before.

"Come to bed," Henrik said. A command, albeit a soft one.

They disrobed separately, each carefully folding their garments. Seanna purposefully kept her gaze to his face and arms. The quilt was warm beneath her, and she tried her best to smile up at him. He gave her a tight-lipped grimace in return. They both hesitated, then he reached down to cup her cheek and give her a dry kiss. She returned it dispassionately. The parts of her which had so quickly excited at the thought of touching

Gwen now remained dry. Henrik, too, was lackluster. His fingers found her cunny, but no wetness, and he sighed. Still, he pushed his finger inside her, trailed kisses down her neck and along her collarbone, and she nibbled at his ear in a faint attempt at reciprocation. Minutes dragged on before he pulled back and looked at his woefully limp john. With a frown, he tugged at it, and rhythmically stroked his fingers inside her. *If I wasn't so apathetic to him, this might feel good. Gods, if only this could be anyone else...I'd take the steward over him. Something new, at the least. I wonder if it's this difficult for other women? Damn Gwen, if she hadn't been so painfully naïve, I might be showing her the wonders of her own body, I could kiss her where Druam has never kissed her, I could–*

"Finally, you're getting somewhere," Henrik grunted, pulling her from her daydream.

"You're not."

"You were thinking of something else."

"I must confess I was."

"We can't even do this right."

Seanna shrugged. "Maybe the gods never meant for us to join."

He finally took his fingers out and wiped them on the quilt. Climbing out of the bed, he draped his robe back over his shoulders and cinched it. "I'll be in my study. I trust you can find your way out?"

Seanna left more miserable than before. *At least I tried.* She knew that their beds would forever remain separate save for the times they must come together to make more heirs. To her surprise, a hint of sadness crept into her heart at the thought. *Perhaps there's something wrong with me. Every other lady would kill to be the king's wife.* Yet she knew, too, that another woman's bed would never be safe.

Seanna walked up and down the long corridors, her mood as sour as their lovemaking had been. She nearly ran into an old curate, who bowed and smiled. "My child, you seem distressed. Is anything pressing your mind and heart?"

Nothing but rejection. Gwen's parting smile, Henrik's

resigned shake of his head, the ghostly sound of nobles' laughter...None of this was Seanna's fault. She didn't deserve to be brushed aside and cast down by those miles beneath her. Gwen's ringing laughter, at first joyful, grew into frantic howling derision. *The foreign girl. An easy target; not yet assured of her place in this world, in my world. When they see what I do to her, no one will dare go against me.*

The idea grew, and she smiled. Seanna said, "All is well."

CHAPTER NINETEEN
Gwen

THE QUIET murmur of hushed voices and soft singing filled the room. Ladies in their silk dresses and fine jewels, their hair braided in such complicated twists and turns the eye could barely follow them, sat in clumps of three or four with embroidery or instruments in their laps. A harpist played in the corner, crooning an old hymn to attentive spinsters who nodded appreciatively and sang along in quavering voices. Thirty or so women of status had gathered to spend the afternoon together. Handmaids lined the walls, standing on their toes, ready for their lady's call. Servants circled with platters of wine, fruit, chocolate, or pastries, somehow never getting in the way.

Gwen sat with three other young women and chatted idly about autumn events. Her embroidery, one she had been working on all that quinn, was simple yet elegant. It depicted the Strilu crest, a blood-red wyvern circling on a field of dark grey. She had sewn jewels as its eyes and scales, and held it to the light to marvel at the play of reflected colors. If she were lucky, the crest would adorn her baby's shawl. *Now that Druam is well again, I can forget my powers. I will be the perfect earl's wife, and soon we'll be blessed with a child.*

After they bored of idle chatter of the upcoming masque, the ladies passed rumors back and forth. Gwen listened but didn't comment. Back in Demarren gossip had rarely traveled to her ears; who would bring it? Ebarren had no interest in it, especially not when teaching her to cast workings.

No. That's a part of me I must forget. What would Druam think?

Gwen wondered if the Trials were still ongoing. Had Wullum discovered where she had gone? Had Lord Daghorn sent word to the Inquisition's leaders about her? But surely the long tentacles of the Trials could not reach this far, could not touch the earl's wife in the great marble palace above the sea.

"Lady Seastone," hissed the maid next to her, suddenly coming to her feet. Startled, Gwen looked up to see Queen Seanna glide into the room, a grand diadem resting on her brow. All the women curtseyed; Gwen peeked from under her lashes at the beautiful queen. Despite her pregnancy, Seanna moved with grace and poise, one hand resting on her belly with the other held out to accept kisses.

"Lady Seastone," the queen said, her hand extended to Gwen.

"Your Grace," Gwen replied, kissing the proffered palm. "An honor to see you." Gwen smiled at the queen, hoping that she may be invited for another private conversation. *Druam would be proud of me for befriending her.* For a moment, Seanna's smile wavered, but then it returned kinder than before. *I must have imagined it*, Gwen thought, lowering her eyes in what she hoped was a demure expression.

"My dear lady, would you care to show me the library? I've heard it's quite lovely." Seanna held out her arm. Gwen took it, keenly aware of the jealous eyes of the other ladies. The library in these chambers wasn't quite a library at all, more a small collection of books and statues. Still, the queen had asked to see it, and Gwen would oblige.

The two women went through a side door into a wood-paneled room, their footsteps muffled by a thick red and gold rug. Sunlight warmed dust motes through gaps in the heavy curtains, and marble statues on plinths or shelves stared unseeing at the intruders. The heat was stifling for that time of year, and Gwen felt sweat dripping down her arms.

"The statues were commissioned by my lord husband's

father. One to represent each season. I think the sculptor did quite a marvelous job, don't you?" Gwen said. Seanna had stayed by the door, and now pushed it almost closed. She went to a side table which held a jar of wine and silver goblets. After pouring one for each of them, she at last met Gwen's eyes with a hard look.

"Seanna?" Gwen asked as she took a goblet.

"You seek my favor, do you not?" the queen asked softly.

The heat was overwhelming. Gwen longed to sit in one of the many cushioned chairs pushed against the walls, but could not while the queen still stood. "I seek your friendship, Seanna. I – I hope I have received it."

"You are to address me formally," Seanna snapped. "You have earned, and will receive, nothing but my disdain. For such a pretty flower, with so much potential...'tis a shame, really. I had hoped better for you."

"I don't understand, how have I–"

"Do not presume to speak."

Gwen's mouth snapped shut, her eyes widening in confusion. The queen shook her head, speaking loud enough for the ladies outside to hear.

"The queen of Dotschar stands before you, you foreign, ignorant wretch. You were granted a high privilege in marrying one of our respected, beloved earls, and you marred his name! You...you disloyal child, you traitor to the sanctimony of marriage. If I took you for a woman, I would petition for your banishment from court."

Her own anger rose, and Gwen spat, "Did you not counsel me yourself that I should stray from my husband, that I–"

Seanna grabbed her wrist, wrenching it painfully. Gasping, Gwen blinked through sudden tears as the other woman nearly shouted, "You twist my words and dare to blame me for your own foul deeds. We are good Dotsch women, loyal to our husbands and our king! Do you seek to destroy the earl's name, little snake? Make him seem weak, unable to control his whore of a wife? We will not fall for your foreign tricks, Demar slut. We know that Seastone is a far better man than you deserve."

Gwen tried to blink back tears. She couldn't. They dripped onto her dress, staining the silk. Her thoughts emptying through her eyes, she shook her head and mumbled, "Please, Your Grace, let me go. Please, I want to leave."

"You shall stay until I am done with you!" Seanna shook Gwen's arm, her fingers white. But she released her. Gwen drew back, holding her hand to her chest, still shaking her head, thinking, *What have I done? Why does she hate me? I never betrayed Druam!*

Seanna blocked the door. Gwen could do nothing but stand there, shoulders drawn in, throat shutting as she tried not to make a sound. She stopped listening to the queen's words. They didn't matter. She stared at the wall and shut her eyes. *Just let it be over soon,* Gwen prayed. She didn't know what she'd done wrong, and part of her wanted to plead with the queen for mercy.

A hard grip forced her eyes open again. Seanna glared at her, her nails clasping Gwen's chin. Lowering her voice for the first time, so only Gwen could hear her, she leaned close, those flint eyes locking onto Gwen's. "You are nothing but a pawn of your birth. I offered you agency, freedom in your limited life, and you rejected me."

The details of their conversation played out in Gwen's mind. Had...had the queen been flirting with her? Gwen stammered, "I...I didn't mean...I didn't know–"

"Listen to me, little bitch. You have a pretty face, a fresh malkin, a malleable disposition – but you are nothing great, you will never be anything great, and you will die in the shadows. I hope your husband annuls your marriage before he is brought to dust because of you."

The queen's hard eyes pierced Gwen's fragile confidence. Deep inside Gwen's chest, she felt her magic pulsing, an ever-present comfort. *I should never have come,* Gwen thought. Tears renewed and coursed down her cheeks, and she knew that she couldn't bear the idea of never knowing Druam. *But how can I be his dutiful wife if everyone thinks I've betrayed him?*

At last, the queen freed Gwen. A mask of sincerity and

sweetness settled on her treacherous face, and she smiled bitterly, then turned on her heel to float to the door.

Gwen said softly, "You're wrong about me." *I have to believe that.*

"Am I?" Seanna replied without stopping. "Wait and see."

"You're wrong," Gwen said again with no one but the statues to hear her. For a minute, she could not move. Her mind had gone blank, all she had thought she knew washed away by the harsh flood of words. The heat of the room gave her a headache. Realizing she still held the goblet of wine, she sucked it down. That, at least, gave her some feeling. A dizzy, half-nauseous feeling, but enough to bring her back to her senses.

With great effort, Gwen straightened her shoulders, then found a dusty mirror to examine herself. At least she hadn't worn much paint today, for only her red-rimmed eyes displayed her grief. With a quick, habitual action, she wet two fingers in her mouth and wiped her eyes. She tried smiling at her reflection.

The queen had left the door open. At the threshold, Gwen could sense the gazes of the other ladies. When she glanced to meet them, their eyes darted away. *I survived the Trials of Demarren, and I will survive this, too.* Gwen took a deep breath and lifted her chin. Taking her long skirts in her hands, she made her way around chairs and food-laden tables to her friends.

Abruptly, the other ladies stood, abandoning their embroidery as they turned their backs on her. Left alone, Gwen bit her lip to try and remain calm. She motioned to one of her attendants and handed off the piece she had been working on earlier. "Take this to my rooms. I wish to walk the palace."

The quiet room remained tense as Gwen stood and walked to the door. She almost looked back, almost shouted, "It's not true," but she knew that the ladies would never believe a foreigner over their queen. Her dreams of being the grand Lady Seastone, loved by the court, had shattered.

Gwen shook, her whole body nearly convulsing with shame. *You are nothing great, you will never be anything great, and you will die in shadows.* The queen's sneering face loomed up, and Gwen nearly choked on the sobs that rose from her chest into her throat only to escape her mouth in hot, sour gargles.

A hollowness settled on her heart. Her throat closed; she swallowed with difficulty. She remembered the tourney, only a quinn ago, when she had stayed by Druam until he woke. She remembered Mavian Strilu's mention of magic.

You are nothing great, you will never be anything great, and you will die in shadows. Gwen had scorned her magic and promised the gods she would not use it. But perhaps, if she learned how to wield it, she might prove her worthiness to the court. First she must hammer her resolve, turn it from ore to iron, fold it over and over as a blacksmith his steel until it became strong enough to protect her when she went to Mavian. Though the rest of the court rejected him, he had been kind to Gwen. *And I've been rejected as harshly as he.*

CHAPTER TWENTY
Jagger

THE GIRL stared up at Jagger, her face scratched and bruised. She had fought him when he pulled her from her saddle, and he threw her onto the forest floor. Jagger left her to fumble to her feet, tied up the horses, then removed their saddles and rubbed them down. All the while, he watched her from the corner of his eye. She didn't try to run. Smart, or simply too scared to do anything? She stood perfectly still, her bound hands held in front of her. After a moment, Jagger realized she was trying to protect her nethers.

"I'm not goin'ta rape you," he muttered. The girl didn't say anything. *Probably cause of the rag in her mouth.* Jagger said, "If I kill you, it'll be clean. No pain, nothing. I'm not in the torturing business. Not anymore, at least. Don't imagine you've ever heard of me? Naw, why would you? I was in my heyday when Sandu was still a pup, but not for a long time now. Parents don't need to warn children about the Heartless anymore."

During his rambling, Jagger puttered about their makeshift campsite, setting up a bed for himself, making a fire pit, and tying the girl's rope to one of his knives before driving it into the yielding dirt. It'd be pretty easy for her to escape that, if she had the nerve to.

At last, he took out her gag and threw it away in disgust. Thing was wet. Smelled rotten.

Jagger crouched in front of the girl. She didn't meet his eyes, and did her very best to look anywhere but at him. Her lower lip trembled, and a few wayward tears dripped down her cheeks. In a quavering voice, still with the high pitches of girlhood, she said, "You killed Ma and Pa and Dustin."

"Yes," Jagger replied matter-of-factly. "Everyone in that caravan's dead now. Everyone except for you. We'll see how long that lasts."

He didn't mean it as a threat; he honestly had no idea what he'd do with her. Taking her and letting her live were impulses he didn't know himself to be capable of. But damn her, she had soft, brown eyes like Raven's, full of that *something* he never saw in his own. Compassion, probably. Basic human decency.

The girl burst into full sobs. Her ugly grunts echoed in the treetops, but Jagger quickly clamped a hand over her mouth. He ignored the moisture on her lips and cheeks. "Stop that. I've found us a good hiding place, somewhere they'd have to look pretty hard to find. But your blubbering would make it easier, and then I'd have to kill you. I don't have a mind to meet the noose. The gods gave me another chance at life, and dammit I'm goin'ta use it to kill Sandu before I get knocked off. I'm not goin'ta kill you. But I'll gag you forever, or cut your tendons, or cut off your fingers. Make you like me, missing your pinkies. If you don't want that, you'll shut up."

The girl's eyes blinked above his dirty hand. Jagger could hear her gulp, then she nodded slowly, and he took away his hand. He rocked back on his heels, contemplating her. She swallowed again, but did not cry out. Jagger cocked his head to one side. *Why did I bring you with me? Veck me, but you look like Raven. Could pass as her little sister.*

The girl opened her mouth, then closed it. She licked her lips, then finally gained the courage to speak. "Why are you doing this?"

Jagger shrugged.

"Are you really the Heartless?"

He held up his hands and showed her the stumps where his pinkies used to be.

That made her pause. After a minute, she said, "I don't have gold, or anything like that. I'm a virgin, but–"

"I said I'm not goin'ta rape you. It'd be disrespectful to Raven."

"...oh." At last she looked to the ground and stopped asking inane questions. Satisfied that that was the end of it, Jagger went to his newly-supplied pack and pulled out food and a bottle of mead. He ate his fill, took a swig of the honeyed drink, then offered the girl the remainder. She took the food and ate greedily. He held out the bottle.

"Ma doesn't like me drinking."

"She ain't here now. Drink. It'll put some color in your cheeks." The girl hesitated, took a sip, then pulled a disgusted face and handed it back. Jagger smiled, downing the rest of the bottle's contents. "Good stuff, this. Your tribe had fine taste."

She teared up, but did not sob. *Smart lass.* Jagger stood up and stretched, then laid down across from her. The sun climbed higher and higher in the sky, but he didn't feel the need to sleep. Instead, he watched her.

After she had her quiet cry, the girl stretched out her arms and legs as best she could. *Raven used to stretch like that. This girl could be our daughter, if we'd ever had one.* The girl rolled her head around on a long, tan neck. But she didn't try to escape.

She's just another job. Treat her like you'd treat your other targets...But I had Raven back then. She'd always be at the gate when I came home from a job, and hold me when I couldn't bear it anymore. I hated the Shivs. I was damned good at killing, and I hated it. The girl sat, buried her head in her arms and cried. *Just like Ryton's boy during the Ivering job. I didn't tell Raven that I had to kill the boy, too. She'd love me less for it.* Jagger tried to think of this girl in the same way as the boy. *Just part of the job. She'd slow me down, eat my rations, drink my water. People'd learn about the caravan. They'd question me. It's the best option, really.* Gods knew he'd gone back on his word more times than not. And the girl wouldn't care once she was dead. *Just another job. But I'd only done them to feed myself and Raven, to keep us going when we hadn't a thing left but each other. I won't get paid for leaving this girl's corpse in the woods.*

"Can I have some water, please?" The girl's lips were chapped, and she sweated through her clothes even though they were in a shady, secluded spot. Jagger gave her a full water bladder and watched her gulp it down. He wondered if she was related to Sandu. A cousin, perhaps, or a niece. Would Sandu be sad to learn of her death? Would it hurt him? *Killing her would be awful easy if I pretend she's Sandu, just for as long as the deed takes. Picture his lying eyes instead of hers.*

He fingered one of the many knives tucked in his shirt and thought about it some more. *How silly. The Bloodied Giant, scared to kill a child? Gods know how many tiny graves have been dug 'cause of me. What a silly, foolish thing to be caught up in.*

The girl met his eyes.

And Jagger remembered that night, Raven's dead brown eyes staring up into his, her forehead smeared with blood and dirt, fire scorching his skin as he dropped her and crawled into the ash and debris, leaving his wife's corpse to rot with the crows.

"Veck," he muttered when he realized he'd drawn the knife and dug its point into his palm. He tossed it into the dense trees. *Never goin'ta find that one again.*

Glaring at the girl, Jagger drew another knife. Her eyes flicked from his to the blade and back. He began to rise, and she said quickly, "Who's Raven? You keep muttering her name."

"Dead." Despite himself, Jagger slid back down onto the blanket and sat cross-legged, the knife held loosely on his knee.

"I'm sorry to hear that. It's because of her, isn't it? What you're doing to me."

He didn't answer. *Smarter than she looks.*

"Are you going to turn me into a monster like you?"

The question surprised him. It made sense, though, in a twisted way. *My wife taken from me, so I take someone else's family, and so on and so forth.*

"Hadn't considered that," Jagger said truthfully.

"You murdered everyone I know," the girl said, and he heard it: the fury in every word she spoke. "If you let me live, I'll kill you. I'll learn how. I'll track you down and make you pay for what you've done."

"I'll already be dead. I've one mission, lass, and that's my own revenge. Mourn your family." Why was he saying such things? Jagger had never been one to comfort others, but he found himself still talking. "I don't intend to live much longer after I've made my peace. Piss on my grave if you must. I won't care. Your family's dead, and no one but Autorus can bring them back. And I don't expect he'd do anything of the sort."

"Then kill me and be done with it."

Not a bad option. And yet Jagger stayed his hand. Had he grown soft? The girl stuck her chin out, but her eyes betrayed her. *She don't want to die yet.*

"What's your name?" Jagger asked. The girl only glared.

One of the horses pawed at the ground and huffed quietly. Jagger listened to the sounds of the forest around them: crickets chirping under a bush, squirrels chattering in the trees. He even thought he heard the tell-tale cry of a lantern faerie. *Good luck when the sun shines, bad fortune after it sets.* Never one for enjoying nature's myriad noises, he said conversationally, "I was goin'ta be out of it soon. The Shivs. Nearly earned my freedom. Two or three more good jobs, I reckon, and Raven and I could've bought ourselves a little homestead in the mountains somewhere, maybe in Skålland, maybe Dotschar. She'd have liked a little herb garden, some wildflowers in a shelf under the window, some goats and pigs. Don't know how well I'd do settling down, but I'd try it for her. Maybe have a young one. A daughter that looks just like her mother. Someone gentle. Not like me. Bring a little good to the world, you see? Just once in my life."

He stopped talking suddenly. Even when he and Sandu drank together, he never strung more than ten words together. *Raven talked enough for the both of us.*

"I'm glad you'll never have that," the girl spat.

Jagger nodded absentmindedly. That's what he wanted for Sandu, after all. *Might not even kill him, if I can take everything from him first. Though killin' him would be easiest. Like killin' her would be the easiest thing to do. Damn, if Raven had a daughter, she'd look just like this girl.*

"If I had had a daughter, I'd name her Dilara," Jagger said. "After the old song. Always liked the name. I think I'll call you that."

"Bastard."

"Mind your tongue. I can go cut a switch and be back in a quarter candle to whip you."

"I'm not your vecking daughter."

"You're not anyone's daughter anymore. An orphan, like I was at your age. You're what, twelve? Thirteen? I'd already lost my pinkies by thirteen."

The girl spat at him. He wiped it off; he'd been spit on too many times for it to bother him anymore. "If you're trying to get me to kill you, you'll have to try harder. Insult my mother, or something like that."

Dilara shut up. She sulked, the rope going taut as she pulled as far from him as she could get. Her dark eyes never left his. *If looks could kill...*

"You're bleeding," Dilara said suddenly. Jagger looked down at himself, and saw that some blood had seeped through his shirt. He cursed and pulled it off. *Damn.* Some of his crude stitches had pulled loose, probably from all the dragging and lifting he'd done to kidnap the girl.

Rifling through his pack – muttering curses as he did – Jagger found the old catgut and needle he'd used the first time. The string had started to fray all along its length. "Veck," he said, though not terribly concerned. He'd healed from much worse than this.

"It's going to fester," Dilara said with a hint of delight. "I hope I get to see you die."

"And then what'll you do, Dilara? Find some farmer's boy to marry so you don't die alone? Join the Rangers to feel like you've accomplished something in your life? Hope to gods you don't get raped and left for dead by some scoundrel or other? Watching me die won't help your problems, lass. And you've got plenty of 'em now widout a family to help you."

"But that's not my fault!" Dilara sobbed. "*You* killed them, *you* dragged me away, *you* ruined everything!"

"Aye. And I'm not in the business of repairing what's been done by my hand. I'd have joined the clergy if'n I wanted a life of mending others' problems. I don't feel guilt for what I've done; never have, never will." Well, maybe sometimes, late at night...but she didn't need to know that.

Jagger didn't have the heart to do the proper thing and kill her. A strange feeling, that.

Dilara cried into her knees. Jagger pulled a bottle from his pack, his decision made. It took him a minute to find the other thing he was looking for: a small vial, unlabeled and corked tight. He popped out the stopper, then poured the concoction into the bottle, swishing it around a little. *Lucky I kept this.*

"Here," he said. "Drink this."

She sniffled, "What is it?"

"Mead."

"I don't want it."

"Either drink it willingly or I'll force it down your throat."

Dilara took the proffered bottle and sipped it. He shouted, "Down it, girl!" and she quaffed the rest, her throat moving up and down as she swallowed. When she finished, she threw the bottle back at him, resentment festering in her eyes.

"Good lass." Now Jagger just had to wait for the concoction to work itself into her system. Dilara didn't speak or look at him, instead preoccupying herself with cleaning under her fingernails. Jagger found a short stick and whittled it. He hummed a tune Raven used to sing as she went about her chores. He had never been much of a craftsman; the carving was supposed to be of the girl, but instead looked like a rotten turnip. Eventually he gave up and tossed the failed carving into the trees.

The girl's eyelids drooped, her chin dropping to her chest. She tried valiantly to shake it off, but Mother's Kiss was a potent thing. A few minutes later, Dilara lay sleeping on the dried pine needles.

Jagger threw a stone at her to make sure she wouldn't wake. Not even a muscle twitched.

The sun began its descent, and Jagger packed up the camp as quickly as he'd made it. He loaded one of the horses with everything he needed, then laid out an old blanket and placed some food, a bladder of water, and the coins he could spare in its center. After wrapping it and placing it by the girl's head, he untied the rope binding her and retrieved the knife he'd used as an improvised stake. He left one horse for her.

Jagger looked down at her. "I'm sorry for not offing you when I did the rest. Would've made my life easier, for damn sure. I'm as sorry as I can be for dragging you into my mess. Make something of yourself. Piss on my grave, if you can find it. If there's even one made for me."

As evening's shadows lengthened into night, Jagger rode away. With each mile put between himself and Dilara, renewed anger built up within him. *This is all Sandu's fault. If he hadn't betrayed me, then I wouldn't have killed the girl's family.*

Some small part of him finally understood the old saying, *An eye for an eye makes the whole world blind.* But Jagger had one more eye to put out, and he intended to do it properly this time. No talking, no allowing for escapes. Sandu was as good as dead now that the Heartless was well and truly after him.

CHAPTER TWENTY-ONE
Sandu

AT LAST the caravan reached Redgull Pass. All paused at the height of the road to look out over the River Valley. Verdant greens and blues painted the rolling hills, forests, and farms. In the distance, Sandu imagined he could see the glistening sea, though he knew it was still too far away.

Home. He breathed in deeply, the scent of pine soon to give way to fresh-tilled earth.

"It's beautiful," Cara said, her wide eyes lingering over the sight.

Alex grinned. "We're almost there."

"There's still the swamp to get through," Sandu said. At the bottom of the pass, a large expanse of deep green and brown separated the mountains from the plains, stretching for leagues beyond the foothills. Sandu shuddered looking at it. He loathed swamps. All mud and mist-folk, and little sunshine.

"How long will that take?" Cara asked.

"Two days if we move quickly," said Alex. "More if the wheels get stuck or the mist-folk spook the oxen."

"Mist-folk?" She looked between them.

"You haven't heard of them?" Sandu asked, incredulous. His whole life he'd been told stories of the swamp's denizens. He even knew of an uncle who had been lost to the creatures. When she still looked confused, he said, "They lure people off their path. Then they drown their victims and eat their corpses."

"Sometimes they appear as specters of people you know," Alex said. "Their imitations can draw you off the road. It's not a pleasant way to go."

Cara stared out over the swamp below. "Is there any way around it?"

Alex shrugged. "Yes, but it would take days."

"We may not have that time." She chewed her lip, then nodded, as if she'd made up her mind. "It's a risk we'll have to take."

The scholars whipped their oxen into movement, and the caravan lurched down the mountainside. Alex, Cara, and Sandu rode at the rear.

In the days since their conversation, Sandu had gained a new respect for Alex. The scholar ate most meals with them now while Sandu regaled them with stories of his childhood with the Valadi. They passed around wine or mead as Alex spoke about the university and his various studies, and Cara sometimes joined in with what she had been taught. They felt like a comfortable band, a trio against the world's woes.

When the fire went out, though, and the rest of the camp slept, Sandu often stayed awake. He thought of Jagger, wondering how he'd survived and whether it was right to end Fauste's Shiv. Then there was his father, locked in a cell for a crime he didn't commit, growing old without watching his grandchildren blossom. And Tambrey...tears pricked Sandu's eyes most nights, leaving moist spots on his blankets.

If he heard Alex up and about, he would join the scholar. Together, they would sit and watch the stars pass by overhead.

As they descended into the swamp, Sandu let his mind wander. He worried about Laris, for he'd never seen such magical prowess before. He trusted Alex, but doubt niggled in his mind. Could the scholar actually do anything against a wizard?

The caravan reached the foothills, and from there followed the road into the swamp. It began to rain, large drops carrying yellow leaves to the mud. The world hushed, listening to the rainfall. The trees changed, aspen and spruce replaced by twisted willow and oak. Wagons lurched and horses slowed with the soggy ground.

Deeper into the swamp, daylight grew scarce. Thin yellow shafts only occasionally pierced the trees, too wan to properly light the way. A dense fog shifted over the road, coating Sandu's lashes and brushing against his hands on the reins.

Lost in his thoughts, Sandu didn't notice the wagons grow more distant, nor Alex and Cara gradually moving farther ahead. He stared morosely into the fog and fancied that he could see his loved ones in those curtains of mist.

A bird's cry distracted him. Sandu glanced up to find the animal, but the fog was too thick. When he returned his gaze to the road, he realized that the caravan had vanished. He shivered, drawing his cloak around him as he kicked Galen to a faster pace. The mud sucked at her hooves as she trotted forward.

The road twisted and turned, offshoots going haphazardly into the swamp. Sandu kept to what he hoped was the main road, but he couldn't tell in the gloom. The longer he was alone, the more he began to worry. He pulled Galen to a halt and listened.

He didn't hear the creaking of wheels or the scholars' hushed conversations. He couldn't see Alex and Cara's horses.

Sandu's mouth went dry, his hands clammy with fear and fog. He urged Galen slowly forward, every nerve strained for some sign of the caravan.

"Sandu!" A distant call came from the swamp, barely audible.

"I'm here!" Sandu shouted back. He stood in his stirrups, staring desperately into the fog. "Cara!"

"Sandu!" The voice came from his right. He turned to see a wavering figure through the mist. A woman, with long yellow hair.

"Tambrey?" Sandu turned toward the woman, pulling at Galen's reins though she resisted. He shouted, "Tambrey?"

"I've lost you!" Tambrey's voice, sweet as he remembered it, echoed in the fog. "Sandu, where are you?"

Sandu kicked Galen, and she plunged through shrubs and over sodden logs, her nose pointed toward the hazy figure. A tree branch whipped in front of Sandu's face. He ducked as water sprang onto his neck. When he blinked away the moisture, Tambrey had disappeared.

"Tambrey!" Sandu shouted again, looking frantically in every direction. Deep in his bones, he felt a thrill of fear, as if his body told him not to go after her, that it was a trap, that she didn't know he'd changed his name...But she was so close for the first time in years. He had seen her, he had to go before he lost her again.

There! He saw Tambrey, and with her two small figures. The sight of them pierced his heart; how the children had grown! He spurred Galen forward. The figures drifted further away, and Sandu couldn't understand why they'd be running–

Squelch! Galen's chest plowed into black mud. Trailing branches snagged at Sandu's legs, reaching for him. Ooze sucked at Galen, drawing her further into the bog. Sandu struggled out of the saddle, grabbed his pack, then clutched at a branch overhead. It bowed with his weight, dunking him into the mire, but he clung on. He pulled hand over hand until his feet touched dry land.

He grasped at a vine to throw over Galen's head and pull her out. He had to get her back. She was his oldest companion – strange as that was – and each desperate kick pulled her further into the mire. He knotted the vine, his fingers slipping against the fibers, as Galen's eyes rolled. He flung it out over her, but missed.

"You'll be fine," Sandu said, mostly to himself. Galen's legs made a sucking sound as she tried to pull free. Sandu stared at her. If he went after her, he might never come out again.

But Galen trusted him. Her big brown eyes looked at him as all faithful animals do, with a certainty that he wouldn't leave her. Sandu gritted his teeth and knotted the vine around his waist, then tramped into the mud. It clung to his boots and breeches, his feet sticking with every step.

Sandu latched onto Galen's reins, his hands fumbling with the muddy leather. Vague shapes rose up around them with strange transparent arms that dragged them further into the mire. His vine grew taut, straining against the mist-folk that held him.

If I don't let go, I'll be dead too, Sandu thought. Would it be so bad a thing, to slip easily into death now? Laris would never find Cara then. The mist-folk murmured around him, coaxing him.

Sandu stared at Galen, only her long neck and head exposed now. He let go of the reins.

"I'm sorry," he whispered as Galen's head drifted under, a smooth patch of algae and weeds sliding in to cover where she'd vanished. Sandu dragged himself back out of the bog, hand over grueling hand. The mist-folk challenged each step, imploring him to stay. They spoke with different voices: Tambrey and Eaton and Elvy and Papa. Sandu cried, but didn't listen to them.

When he reached solid earth, he collapsed into the dirt. Relief, terror, and mourning filled him. He had escaped, but his loyal friend hadn't.

Soft laughter emanated from the mist, sounding of wind and chill nights. Goosepimples broke out on Sandu's arms and neck. He drew his legs up, burying his face in his arms as that horrid laughter grew and grew until it felt like it would overcome him. The mist-folk had lured him off the road. He'd lost Galen, and didn't know how to find his way through the fog.

The mud dried on his clothes, sticking to him with freezing tenacity. He shivered, his teeth chattering. His numb hands searched in his pack for his flint and steel, but the branches he gathered were too wet to light. The gloom grew deeper, and though the fog lifted, no sunlight filtered through the trees.

Sandu wrapped a blanket around his shoulders. *So this is how I die,* he thought. *Not the worst way to go.*

At least he would rejoin Mumma and Nan at their campfire in the afterlife. He pictured them with their colorful Valadi skirts spread around them, their faces shining in the firelight. "I'm sorry, Mumma," Sandu mumbled. "I didn't have the strength to free Papa." He laughed bitterly, for he knew he could never enter Lyael. His soul was simply too corrupted.

"I wish I could have seen the children again," Sandu said to himself. "I wonder if they're still as blonde as their mother." Tears pricked his eyes at the memory of Eaton and Elvy holding hands as they ran through a field of flowers, their shrieks of joy the sweetest sound he'd ever heard. *They were so little when I left,* he thought. *I wonder if they'd even remember me.*

Somewhere in the distance, golden lights floated through the trees.

"Not going to fool me this time," Sandu said. "Vecking mist-folk."

The lights moved slowly as voices carried to him. They called his name, but he ignored them. He wouldn't be tricked again.

After a few minutes, the lights halted, and then began to recede. He watched them go with dull eyes. Just as they drew too dim to see, Sandu had a sudden thought. *The mist-folk didn't run until I chased them. And they didn't have lights.*

He tried to stand, but fell back on sore legs. He caught his breath, pulled his blanket tight, and ran as fast as his aching feet could carry him.

"Wait!" Sandu shouted. His voice was too hoarse to penetrate the swamp. "Please!"

He stumbled and fell, his hands going into a puddle. His fingers splayed in the mud, and he stared at them. Pale hands in the dark earth. He smiled, his fatigued mind enjoying the simple contrast. He began to laugh, first a chuckle, then a giggle, then a screeching guffaw. It hurt his ribs and chest, but he couldn't stop himself.

His vision wavered, and he coughed in between bouts of laughter. *I'm going as mad as Jagger,* he thought. From the corner of his eye, he saw the bobbing lights growing brighter and closer. *Just end it. Pull me under and be done with it.*

The lights drew near. "Sandu! Is that you?"

The mud made a squishing sound as Sandu withdrew his

hands. He sat back on his haunches, the laughter finally dying down. *It was too good to be true. The mist-folk have only invented a new game to draw me in.*

"I'm ready," he whispered. In a shout he said, "Come get me, then!"

"Sandu!" Cara's face materialized in the gloom, illuminated by a glowing lantern. She smiled in relief. "You're alive."

"Just kill me," Sandu said, unconvinced that this wasn't another trick by the mist-folk. "Don't make it last."

Alex rode up beside Cara, holding a lantern at the end of a stick. "Why would we kill you?"

"You drowned Galen, just drown me, too."

"Sandu, it's us," Cara said as she slid off her horse. She knelt in front of him, worry clouding her relief. "We're real."

"No you're not," he said. *Neither were Tambrey and the children. They led me astray.*

She looked up at Alex. "What do we do?"

Alex dismounted and joined them. He tentatively reached out a hand and touched Sandu's face. Sandu flinched back, but the scholar's touch was merely cold, not the chill life-ending fingers of the mist-folk. Alex said slowly, "We're real. We're here. The mist-folk are gone for now."

Something about the scholar's peaceful voice penetrated Sandu's fear.

Sandu grasped at Alex's hand, then reached out to grab Cara's. He held them for a moment, savoring their tangibility. *I'm safe*, he thought. Tears came to his eyes, and he flung himself into Cara's arms.

"Gods, I thought I would die," he said. "Galen's dead. They took her."

"Shh, Sandu. We're here." Cara held him close. "You'll survive another day."

All the grief and terror built up inside him leaked to his cheeks. He clung to her, as he hadn't held anyone since he was a child. Somewhere, he thought he heard the mist-folk call in his family's voices. He shuddered and held her tighter until the voices died away.

They'll always haunt me, he thought. *And Cara will, too, when she learns the truth.*

Suddenly, he no longer felt safe in her arms. Would her beast come out if she knew? Would she force him away, as Tambrey had? Sandu met Alex's eyes, and prayed that the scholar kept his promise.

CHAPTER TWENTY-TWO
Gwen

"HOW LONG will you be staying in Riverfen?" Gwen asked. Her hands shook as she poured the wine for Mavian. *Just ask him,* she thought. *He'll accept.* Still, she stalled the conversation, keeping it as light and trite as she could until she regained her courage. Her eyes flicked occasionally toward the silent maids standing against the wall. She would rather they not know of her magic, but she couldn't be alone with Mavian. Not after the queen's accusations. Even this was a risk, but she didn't know who else to turn to.

Mavian took the goblet and said, "I shall be heading back to Far-eyes shortly after the Masque. I generally winter there and spend the rest of the year here. You'll find, I think, that many courtiers prefer doing the same; they can't abide missing any tournaments or festivals."

"How do they tend to their vassals' needs if they're hardly ever home?"

"They let the stewards handle all that. Our duty as nobles is to secure our place in our hierarchy, make alliances, and deter our enemies from doing the same. Isn't that why you sought me out? You found yourself placed on a low, low rung, and need an ally."

"I need a *friend.* Don't any of you ever spend time with each other because you actually enjoy it? And in my country, a noble's duty is to protect and serve his vassals. My brother only ever brings ten or fifteen nobles and their families to court at a time, and only allows them to stay for two months. He expects them to care for and listen to the rustics they have been trusted to protect."

"Your customs are different from ours," Mavian pointed out.

"And therefore worse," Gwen said. "If ever I discuss Demarren's way of life or traditions, those are seen as somehow inferior or barbaric. Yet I'm expected to adapt to Dotsch politics with ease."

"I didn't intend–"

"You may not have intended to cause offense, but you still dismissed my heritage as easily as the rest. Sometimes I feel that even Druam simply humors me whenever I discuss my homeland." Gwen's cheeks flushed, and she chided herself for her rash anger. *Remember, you're trying to befriend him.*

"Well...never mind."

"No, please go on."

Mavian hesitated, then said, "Demarren is enduring the Trials right now. Dotschar hasn't experienced any sort of internal power struggle or war for a century. Of course courtiers here aren't going to trust what you say. You're a refugee, a former *princess*, and therefore a reminder that bad things happen even to those with status. They convince themselves that the Trials are only happening there because it's a barbaric place with barbaric customs. You're an *other*, and if you stay like that, you can't threaten their way of life."

"That's ridiculous. Why would I want to bring the Trials here?"

"That's not what I said. It won't be the Trials, exactly, but something similar to upset the status quo, perhaps put some of them out of power. Despite your youth, you could put new ideas into Druam's head that – in their eyes – would bring about chaos. The queen only voiced what others feared. And, you're quite lucky that Druam never pays heed to rumors. He hasn't asked you about any affairs, has he?"

"No." Gwen had feared it after her public humiliation. She

had thought that Druam would be enraged, but he wasn't. He had only come to bed and complained about the king's stubbornness. "I don't know if he would believe them, either."

"Good. But be wary of the queen; she still has his ear."

"You don't think she'd tell him anything, do you? She's already made the entire court hate me; isn't that enough revenge for her?"

"Revenge for what?"

"Nothing." Gwen's cheeks burned.

Mavian raised his eyebrows, but didn't question her. "Even so: as long as you stay out of her path, I'm sure she won't come between you and your husband." He gave her a curious look as he sipped from his goblet. "Finding a friend isn't the only reason you've come to me, is it? There's something on your mind...speak it."

Gwen licked her suddenly dry lips., "You know of magic, do you not?"

"I do."

"I...well, I...it's a shameful thing, and I am not proud of its consequences in Demarren, but...you see, I..." Gwen stammered, still unable to get the words out. Mavian inched toward her with evident excitement.

"Do you possess such gifts?" he asked. When she nodded, he let out his breath, then stood, shaking out his hands. "I knew it! I suspected it when I first saw you – I read once that violet eyes were one marker of power. This is absolutely incredible, Gwen. Have you any experience casting spells? Any training?"

"Some," she said. "My brother's councilor told me what he knew before Wullum caught us. But you mustn't tell anyone, Mavian. What would they think of me?"

"They would think you a great coward, and guilty of all charges the Inquisition brought against you," Mavian said, sinking back onto the couch. "I will keep your secret. But why come to me instead of Avallune or Shepherd Marin?"

"As I said, I want a friend, not just a teacher. Show me what you know, and maybe we can practice together. You said you have some magic."

"Not truly, or in the way of most wizards. I stashed some old spell books and workings in my rooms. Wait here." He stood, gave her a quick bow, then dashed away. While he was gone, Gwen swore her maids to silence. After that, she had only to wait a half candle before he returned, arms laden with dusty tomes.

"Before we begin, you must understand how magic and Gaiar work," Mavian explained, pulling out one of the tomes. Gwen peered at the words, but none of them made sense to her. She could barely read Demar, let alone the Dotsch tongue. Mavian continued, "Most scholars believe magic to be the source of life here on Earda, although its presence has dwindled over the vast millennia. While we are still studying its uses, source, and limits, there are some things that are commonly accepted as the truth."

Gwen nodded, remembering bits and pieces of what Ebarren had told her. It was so long ago, though, that she sat and listened without interruption as Mavian spoke.

"Gaiar is a person's inner magic. Some possess great amounts, while others possess very little. I am one of the second, as are many that have magic. Cantrips – or workings of a simple nature – need only Gaiar to cast, while more complex workings require materials, precise wording, and so on."

"What happens if you can't cast a more complex working?"

"Every spell takes energy. Materials are sources of energy, so are animals or plants, and pieces of metal imbued with Gaiar. Moving elements such as fire and running water can be used, though only by the most talented wizards. A working that requires substantial energy can drain the caster if he's not careful, making him fatigued, giving him chills or a fever, or killing him. Many inexperienced casters have died from trying a spell that takes too much energy and Gaiar."

Gwen sat back, shivering. "How do you know if it's too much?"

"You'll feel it, or so I'm told. I've never attempted anything beyond a cantrip...my Gaiar is simply too weak." Pointing out a line on the page, he said, "These are the Principles of Magic.

Every Gifted should know them before they cast even the simplest working. Read them."

"I can't," Gwen said stupidly. "I can't read."

Mavian frowned. "I had hoped Demarren would educate its ladies better than Dotschar does. Still, there may be something here that can help you." He flipped through a different book, then exclaimed, "Aha! I knew I'd seen this cantrip before. It's a spell for reading other languages; one of the most useful I've ever seen. I cast it myself to read a book written in High Rengu. While looking at the words on the page, whisper under your breath the words *Fumult eri klimen eri polom*, and repeat them as you go. It'll give you a headache, but it's well worth it."

Nervously taking the tome he handed her, Gwen concentrated on the line at the top of the page. In a hushed voice, she repeated the words he'd said. Her temples pounded, and she felt the pool of magic in her chest flickering with warmth. Nothing happened. She shook her head and tried again, still whispering. Though she could feel the words tugging at her Gaiar, her magic didn't respond the way she thought it should.

Gwen set the book down, then held up a hand as Mavian opened his mouth. Tasting the spell's words on her tongue, Gwen experimented with their rhythm and sound. She repeated them, over and over, until she settled on an old Demar melody that elongated the words' vowels, making them somewhat slurred. Leaning back over the tome, Gwen sang rather than chanted the spell. This time, she felt the working draw up her Gaiar. The back of her eyes tingled, and she realized that she was reading the words on the page.

Humming the working, soreness gathering at her temples, Gwen kept reading, every word easier than the last. With every sentence, the pressure built behind her eyes until they felt as if they would burst.

Somewhat reluctantly, Gwen ended her working by humming the final note and releasing her flow of Gaiar. She sank into the cushions behind her, her heart racing. She took deep breaths, waiting for the pain to stop and her Gaiar to settle.

Mavian hovered nearby, his hands twitching.

"Look at the page again," he said.

To Gwen's astonishment, she found that, even without the cantrip, she still understood the words written upon the page. She looked up at Mavian, her eyes shining. "I can read it!"

He laughed, lines wrinkling his smooth face. Taking her hand, he said, "You've much potential in your Gaiar, I know you do. How do you feel?"

"Tired," she said, "but I could do more."

"I'm sure you could. You should rest for today, though."

Though some small part of her reminded Gwen that her gift was the cause of strife in Demarren, she ignored it and gave in to the joy that shot through her. After so many years of guilt, after so long of denying herself, she at last had access to not only the secrets of her magic, but to reading. Who knew what else she could do with time and practice? Her mind spun with possibilities.

Still, a small fear tickled the back of her mind. She turned to Mavian and asked, "Are you sure this is alright? That I won't be in trouble?"

"Of course you won't," he said. "Your magic isn't wicked here. It's a shame you had to hide it for so long."

"Should I tell Druam?" Gwen asked. She didn't want to keep it hidden from her husband, but would his opinion of her change? He knew the circumstances of her exile...how harshly would he judge her choice now?

Mavian sighed and looked away from her. "I don't think you should. Not yet, at any rate. For all his fine qualities, Druam can be rather old-fashioned. I don't know what he'd make of his wife practicing magic, much less the wife of an earl." He hesitated, shuffling his feet, and said, "And...I suppose there's the matter of the Skallish ambassador. The more people that know this secret, the more you'll be a target."

Gwen nodded and gave Mavian a quick hug goodbye. After he left, she wandered her room, feeling both high-spirited and afraid. She had never directly lied to Druam before, but Mavian was right. It would be far better to wait, and show him all she could do, than to ask his permission to pursue magic. *But I must always make sure to keep at least one maid in the room with us to prove that I'm not straying from him.*

Though Mavian had told her to rest, Gwen felt too excited to sit back and embroider. Using the reading cantrip, she sang her way through an entire chapter in the tome, though it took much of the evening and she had to rest frequently. By the time supper came, though, her Gaiar felt stronger and more capable, and her headache lessened until she barely noticed it.

I'll learn the most beautiful spells, she thought giddily, *and Druam will be proud of me. I may not be the social wife he wanted, but I will be useful to him as a talented mage.*

Despite her rediscovered joy in her magic, Gwen's contentment did not last. She woke in the early hour of dawn to an empty bed. Druam had disappeared sometime in the night, again. Shivering in the cold, she wondered if Seanna was right after all: perhaps her husband preferred to sleep with another woman. Perhaps she was not enough for him, no matter her talents or her potential.

Curled against the pillow, Gwen tried not to think of it and instead forced herself to dwell on recalling all her happiest memories: boating on a lake with Wullum, her father's voice as he read to her, her wedding day...eventually, she fell back into slumber, and when morning's warmth woke her, her youthful mind thought only of the spells in her chamber that waited to be cast. Druam had returned, and snored softly beside her. As she cuddled up to him, she hoped that his absence had been but a bad dream.

CHAPTER TWENTY-THREE
Gwen

"HAVE YOU tried any of the cantrips?" Mavian asked as he strode into the sitting room.

Gwen replied, "I've read the book you left me and tried out a few of the workings. Some of them were easy, but others took a couple of tries to get them to do what I wanted. I had always been under the impression that magic required only the right words, but they were more complicated than that."

"If they weren't, anyone could cast any simple workings."

"I wanted to try something from *Dunalan's Compendium*, but it all seemed a bit much. I felt my head swimming just reading the first working."

"That one should be put away for now; you're months, if not *years* from casting any workings from it. Not to mention some of the more dangerous spells – and even curses – it contains." In a brighter tone, he asked, "How is Druam?"

"His councils have been worsening his humors. Sometimes when he talks to me, it's as if he were seeing something far off. And then he'll resume the conversation as if nothing had occurred." Before taking a sip of her wine, Gwen uttered a cantrip that cooled the liquid in her chalice.

"My cousin, I admit, is an altogether unique man. You would not be the first I have heard belabor the point." Mavian frowned into his cup. "Even though I've known him my whole life, there are still so many secrets he holds close."

"Sometimes," Gwen said, speaking slowly, "in the dead of night, I wake in our bed and find him missing. He always returns before dawn, and there are nights on which I am positive he never leaves, but..."

"Druam would not stray from you," Mavian said, "but these disappearances are concerning. I have never heard of him hosting late-night councils, though perhaps he's more secretive than I thought. Have you ever tried following him?"

"Of course not!"

"Perhaps you should. Discover for yourself what he has failed to tell you."

"What if I'm caught?" *Would Druam send me back to the Trials if I displease him?*

"He may become angry with you, but he is a fair man. Short of treason, there are no laws allowing divorce between two nobles. At the most he may restrict your movement and your socializations, but that's already been done to you by the queen. You can only gain from this endeavor." Mavian's green eyes lit as he spoke. For a moment, Gwen wondered if he had any other motives to encourage her in this. *No,* she decided, *he is a concerned friend, that's all.*

"I'm too easily recognizable," Gwen said.

"Use your magic. There are a thousand ways to remain concealed without resorting to base sneaking."

She hesitated, and Mavian pressed, "Druam is an honorable man in public, but even he may conceal some dark secret. If you do not take this risk, you will forever live as his gullible wife who blindly accepts his deception."

For a long moment, Gwen sat and pondered. She didn't know if she could tolerate spending her life in ignorance of Druam's secrets, but if those same secrets would tear open her heart...why not remain unaware? Perhaps in time she would fall pregnant, and then her days would be occupied with caring for a child rather than obsessing over Druam's every action. *And wondering if any other woman carried his seed to fruition.* Her throat closed at the thought of Druam atop another woman in the darkness before dawn.

Mavian took Gwen's hands. "Don't lose your courage now, Gwen. Too many ladies bury themselves in accomplishments and wine to escape their husbands. I would lose all faith and love for you were you to do the same."

His green eyes looked so sincere, and Gwen felt her own curiosity pulling at her. *I would rather know than not*, she decided.

"Very well," Gwen said. "But if he discovers me, I'm telling him it was your idea."

"Excellent. Now, let's see if we can find anything that would help you." Mavian pulled one of the spell books into his lap, then scanned through its thick pages until at last he said, "Here! A working to be unseen. It says to chant the words '*metti non, urri urri non, ilrenn non*' and project a thought of yourself as beneath notice. Try it."

Gwen stood and moved a few paces away, then pictured herself as a scurrying mouse. In a singsong, hushed voice, she chanted the words, moving in a circle around the room. As she chanted, she felt her magic bubbling out onto her skin, coating her in a sheen of energy.

"Go out into the other room, then come back in. I'll close my eyes," Mavian said. Gwen followed his instructions, still holding the working as she chanted. The longer she went, the more she let the words slur together, creating a little song of her own. She walked back into the sitting room, and Mavian sat in a chair facing her. However, as she moved closer, his eyes drifted over her, unseeing. He craned his head, looking all around. Sometimes, his eyes focused on her for a brief second before they went blank and glanced elsewhere. Moving behind him, Gwen let the working fade, then tapped his shoulder. He jumped, then turned around, grinning.

"Very well done!" Mavian said, standing and sweeping her off her feet. "Once in a while I detected a shimmer in the air, but otherwise, I didn't really notice you. And I *knew* you were there. How did it feel?"

"It took concentration, but became easier the longer I held it. I wasn't even properly saying the words by the end." Gwen stepped away from him, suddenly aware of his closeness. If Druam had heard the accusations, this would only be evidence against her.

"Fascinating. Most wizards must be absolutely precise in their workings else they lose the entire spell." Mavian looked like a child with a new toy. "I have to research this more, to see if there are spells that work better for less rigid casters. Do you feel able to follow Druam now?"

Gwen nodded, but felt herself quite terrified at the prospect. Whenever she'd used magic before, it had been to practice or when no one could see. Would she be able to keep the spell while walking the palace corridors?

Gwen barely slept that night. A sudden emptiness beside her followed by the creaking of the bed told her that Druam had risen. Straining her ears in the darkness, she heard the rustle of clothing as he dressed and the sound of well-oiled hinges on the door not long after. For a moment, Gwen thought to follow him, but her courage failed her. Nausea roiled in her stomach, the back of her mouth tasting sour. She waited instead, her nerves too frazzled to return to sleep.

When the curtains glowed softly with the sun's rising, the door finally opened. Druam slipped inside and carefully shut it behind him, then started to undress before he noticed Gwen.

He went back to unlacing his breeches. "Did I wake you?"

"No," Gwen lied. "I had a nightmare, and couldn't sleep after. Then I wondered why you had left our bed."

"Urgent matters in the council. I am sorry to have been gone when you needed my comfort."

Gwen searched his eyes and thought she saw a glimmer of falseness. His tone had been light, but still she doubted him. *I must follow him*, she thought. But she smiled and rolled into his embrace, the picture of the perfect wife.

Gwen shifted in the muck, trying not to think what caused the stench beneath her feet. Her boots were soaked from all the puddles she'd walked across, and though she had wrapped her hands in her cloak, they were chilled through. Paper lanterns of all colors crisscrossed the street in front of her, their light doing nothing to brighten the alley next to the tavern where she waited. The whitewashed buildings around her were brown with filth.

At the sound of boots on cobbles, Gwen forgot the numbness in her hands. She crept forward, whispering her spell, and saw that Druam had come. He walked slowly, though not ambling, down the street, his eyes uplifted to the lanterns. Blues and reds flitted over his skin as he strode closer, illuminating his peaceful expression. Gwen's stomach churned, but he didn't notice her hidden in the shadows. She heard the tavern's door open, then briefly shouts and drunken songs from those inside before it shut.

For the last two nights, Gwen had followed Druam. The first night, she had reached the bottom of the plateau before losing him. On the second, she dogged him all the way to Fester's Wharves by the sea and saw him go into a tavern called Bertha's Bosun. Fear – for the crowded tavern would no doubt cause her to lose her spell and be seen – had caused her to retreat back to the safety of the palace.

But this third night, Gwen was determined to enter the tavern and discover Druam's secret. Was he gambling? Whoring? Taking poppin powders?

Gwen could barely see beyond the window's steamed glass. Along with a deep breath, she imagined Wullum at her back, encouraging her. Then she opened the door and released her spell.

First she noticed the noise, almost deafening, men laughing and yelling and the sound of flesh hitting against flesh followed by the roar of the crowd.

Then came the stench, sweat and beer, vomit and blood, body odors from scores of unwashed men. Gwen resisted the overwhelming temptation to cover her nose with a lavender-scented handkerchief.

Finally, the people. Sailors, farmers, merchants, and bums pushed against each other, shoulder to shoulder, all of them toting mugs of cheap dockside ale. A harried bar-wench hurried around the room, grabbing four empty mugs at a time and filling them as quickly as she could.

"Two copper pennings." A gruff voice, its owner a gruffer man, accosted Gwen not a second after she shut the door. He cornered her, his hand held out.

"Sorry?" Gwen's mouth had gone dry. The man could throw her out with one hand if he wanted to: he towered over her by nearly two feet, his biceps as large as her waist.

"Two copper pennings entrance fee," he said, sounding exasperated. "To watch the fights."

"Oh, of course," Gwen stammered. Thank the gods she had brought a small purse. She dug out a bronze penning, the smallest coin she had. "Here. Keep the rest."

"Two mugs of ale for ya, then." The man melted into the crowd. Gwen didn't know how he managed it. She pushed, pulled, and finally broke through to find a spot to stand near the fireplace. An empty stool sat next to the wall, so she climbed it for a better look around.

Tobacco smoke curled up to the ceiling. Tables were pushed against the walls, occupied by card players and some few brave men just trying to get a quick meal. An open space in the middle of the tavern held two shirtless men, their bloodied fists raised. The crowd around them erupted as one delivered a blow to the other's cheek, sending him crashing into the wall of bodies. He was pushed back to his opponent, who grabbed his head and thrust it down to collide with his knee. The man reeled. His opponent landed hit after hit, until finally the loser collapsed in a heap. The tavern's walls shuddered with noise as the spectators stomped and cheered the victor. A pair of bar hands stepped in to pull away the defeated man. The victor left to the bar, no doubt for a hearty drink.

Two more men, clean and unscathed, entered the now hushed circle. The one facing Gwen had tattoos crawling up his bare chest and scars roping across his muscled arms. He towered over the other man, who had lean muscles in his back and slick dark hair. A knot twisted in Gwen's gut.

She gasped when Druam turned to the audience. He basked in their cheers, his arms raised. The larger man cracked his neck. Druam turned his attention back to the ring when a third man stepped between the combatants. This man, slight and wiry but with an air of authority, spoke to the two fighters. His words failed to reach Gwen's ears, but when the fighters assumed position, she guessed that this man was a referee of sorts.

Then the brawl began.

The huge man moved gracefully on his toes, a bear circling his prey. Druam mirrored his movements with catlike fluidity. Even from across the tavern, Gwen could see the determination in his wide blue eyes.

Snarling, the large man pounced. His right arm hooked toward Druam's head. Druam ducked back and away, his left hand delivering a quick punch to the other's gut. The huge man barely grunted. He swung again, this time his blow connecting with Druam's chin. A spurt of blood fell on the closest onlookers. The crowd's thunderous roar shook the floor.

Druam smiled a feral smile. Red dripped down his chin onto the floor. His tongue darted out, smearing the blood across his thin lips.

Something stirred in Gwen, something far and below, a tingling excitement spreading from her nethers to make all her limbs tremble.

"Get 'im, Fris!" someone called out. The large man threw his head back in a primeval scream. But when his chin snapped back down, his eyes had a cold gleam to them. In the span of a second, he tucked his shoulder down and rammed it into Druam's stomach, his arms coming around to grasp Druam.

Druam vaulted over his back. Fris crashed into the crowd, carried by his momentum. He turned around dazedly. Druam did not wait for him to recover. He pressed forward, his left fist catching Fris's jaw. The large man teetered, but did not fall. Druam's right fist hit his shoulder. His left struck again at Fris's chin.

But Fris was ready. His face had turned from shocked to beet-red angry. He caught Druam's fist in his own, his hand nearly enveloping Druam's. Druam grunted. Fris grinned, and swung his free hand at Druam. The first hit connected, snapping Druam's head back. Druam caught the second, his smaller hand gripping Fris's wrist, knuckles white with the effort. They struggled, locked, turning in a slow circle. Fris pulled his head back, preparing to knock into Druam's crown.

Druam's forehead bucked up, striking Fris squarely on the underside of his jaw. Fris reeled, releasing his grip on Druam's hand. But Druam did not release him. He clung on, twisting Fris's arm around behind his back. The crowd cheered. With his free arm, Druam pulled the man's head back and locked it with his elbow.

Both panted. Sweat steamed from their bare chests. Fris yelped as Druam wrenched his arm back. Druam shouted, "Yield!"

Fris didn't answer. His meaty hand scrabbled at Druam's arm, but Druam did not release him. Fris's face slowly turned blue and he gasped for air. His eyes rolled back in his head. Druam let his unconscious body drop to the floor.

For a moment, the crowd was quiet. Then Druam raised his arms, victorious, and the tavern swelled once more, the rafters shaking.

Gwen's heart beat hard against her ribs, her mouth dry.

She had never wanted her husband so much before that moment.

It was incomprehensible, the rush of blood to her face, the dragonflies in her stomach churning and churning, the only thought in her head the *wanting* of him, no, the *needing* of him, inside her, right then, still bloodied and halfway broken.

The gruff man from the door materialized in front of her, two mugs of ale in his hands. "For the generous maid."

Gwen tore her gaze from Druam, at first not understanding the man's words. He stared at her and she gawped back before remembering. She held out a silver talent. "I want a room for the night, please. And I want that man who just won the fight to join me. Take him one of the mugs as my favor."

To his credit, the man barely flinched. He exchanged one of the mugs for the coin, then called over a maid before vanishing back into the crowd. The maid took Gwen's hand, led her through the mass of raucous men, and then upstairs. Beneath their feet, the floor shook with mens' shouts as another fight started. Gwen followed the girl down a dimly lit passageway to a grubby door which the maid unlocked and opened.

The room held a grimy bed, a small table, a washbasin, and nothing else. Still clutching her mug of ale, Gwen sank onto the bed while the maid said, "Your man may have gone to the back rooms, miss. Master Barles will get him up 'ere as soon as he can, never you worry."

"Thank you." Before the maid could escape, Gwen asked, "What's in the back rooms?"

"Just the private rooms, miss, for the better folk and the winners. Usually there's a girl or two, but most of the men just want the poppin."

"Oh." A picture sprang up in Gwen's mind of Druam sitting on a lounge sofa, a beautiful foreign girl dancing for him and sharing poppin.

The maid left and Gwen quaffed her ale. It had a horrible bitter flavor, but she needed it now. Her mind wandered back to the fight, to the feelings she had experienced watching Druam choke the other man into a faint. When she reached a curious hand between her legs, she found herself nearly dripping.

At that moment, a knock came at the door, and Druam opened it with a bewildered expression. He saw her and quickly came inside, shutting the door behind him.

"Gwen...? What are you...? How did you...?"

Gwen rushed to him, knocking the empty mug to the floor. She pulled his face down to meet hers and kissed him sloppily. He pushed her gently away.

"You're not bleeding anymore," she blurted.

"No," he said. "What are you doing here?"

"I had to know where you went," Gwen said. "I needed to know if there was another woman."

"No, no, my love, of course not." Druam's nose crinkled. "How much have you had to drink?"

"Only a mug, though I drank it quickly."

"We should return to the palace. I can't...you can't be seen here." Druam made to move, but Gwen stood firm, her hand gripping his tightly.

"I want to stay, if just for a candle or two. I saw you fighting, Druam. I saw you defeat a man in combat."

"You shouldn't have watched; you shouldn't have–"

Before Druam could protest more, Gwen blocked his lips with a kiss, tasted the copper still lingering there, and relished it. She pressed a finger to a bruise on his arm, and took pleasure from the groan in the back of his throat. Taking his hands, she pulled him to the bed. He seemed too shocked to stop her. Her kisses turned into bites. She ordered him to make love to her.

She had never before known such ecstasy.

Lying in the bed afterwards, their limbs entangled, dark against pale. Gwen's head snuggled in the crook of Druam's shoulder, and she asked, "Why do you fight?"

Druam's arms encircled her, squeezing her. "Because it makes me feel alive."

"You don't feel that way with me?" Gwen's half-drunk mind supplied the insecure words.

"Of course I do, love, but...brawling provides an entirely different thing. When I'm with you, and we're alone in the dark and the quiet, I feel safe, happy, secure. Being with you is a pleasure I had thought myself incapable of feeling again. But the fighting...you are a gentle girl, you couldn't understand the feeling as my own fists connect with another man's flesh. Of driving him to submission."

"You could do the same in the tourneys," Gwen pointed out.

Beside her, she felt rather than saw Druam smile. "Perhaps once, in my youth, I longed for the glory of the tourneys. But you saw how I fare in the sun, and being in mail on the field would far worsen that. No, I prefer the intimacy and anonymity of these brawls. No one here scrapes to me, nor do they care about my peerage. If I win, I am celebrated. If I lose, then I must earn my way back to victory.

"But you mustn't come back here, Gwen. There are too many dangers lurking on the streets at night. I promise you, I do not partake of poppin or the women; I only come for the fights."

Too sleepy and full of delight to argue, Gwen simply nodded against his chest.

CHAPTER TWENTY-FOUR
Cara

SANDU STILL shivered and mumbled, his hands tight around his blanket. Cara glanced back at him often, worried that he might run off again. But Alex held her friend tightly as they rode slowly through the swamp, their lanterns dim against the gloom. It hadn't taken long to notice Sandu's disappearance, but the fog had prevented searching for him. When it lifted at last, Cara had nearly run straight into the swamp. *Thank the gods Alex was with me,* she thought. He had the foresight to light their lanterns before sunset, and to mark their trail with dagger cuts on the trees as they followed Sandu's unpredictable path. Without him, she knew that Sandu would have died in the swamp.

Darkness had fully descended by the time they made it back to the main road. Alex dismounted, then carefully helped Sandu down from the saddle. Cara held Sandu and tried to warm him as Alex made camp. Their fire seemed pitifully small compared to the night's chill. Once Alex had it as large as it would burn, Cara settled Sandu close to it and wrapped another blanket around his shoulders. The three huddled together as they shared small bites of supper. Cara let her fingers linger on Alex's hand as they passed the wineskin. She gave him a furtive smile, her heart leaping when he returned it. For now, they would care for Sandu, but perhaps if they had some moments along the road...

"Where's the caravan?" Sandu asked between clacking teeth. Cara drew back from Alex and rubbed Sandu's shoulders. She hoped he would warm by the morning.

"It'll wait in the next town for us," Alex assured them. "If we don't appear in two days, then they'll move forward without us."

They finished their jerky and bread, and though Cara rifled through her pack, she couldn't find any more. "We're out of food unless one of you packed something."

The men shook their heads, Sandu seeming to hold back tears. "All my spare food was in Galen's packs." Cara took hold of his hand and held it tightly. *We've each lost someone on this journey,* she thought.

"And I didn't think we'd become so easily separated," Alex said. "We three fools indeed."

Loathe as she was to leave the fire, Cara said, "I should set a snare tonight; maybe we'll catch something for tomorrow."

"I'll stay here with him," Alex said. Cara nodded.

She had almost convinced herself to leave the fire's warmth when a cry rose from the swamp. She stilled, the hairs on her arms tingling. Sandu slapped his hands over his ears, and she heard the word "mist-folk" from his white lips.

"Not the mist-folk," she said, removing Sandu's hands and holding them. "Prowlers."

Alex straightened, listening intently. Another cry sounded, farther off, then silence. Cara reached for her sword, the familiar hilt comforting in her hand. "Do you have a weapon?" she asked as her eyes roved the darkness.

"Only a long dagger," Alex replied. "But I know how to use it."

"Good," Cara said. She squeezed Sandu's hand, then extricated herself from between the men. "You two stay here."

"Where are you going?" Alex asked the same moment Sandu exclaimed, "Don't leave me!"

Cara stooped to place a hand on Sandu's back. "It's alright. I won't be far, I just want to check around the camp. I'll keep the fire in sight."

"Be careful," Alex said. An intense light shone in his eyes, but Cara didn't think too much about it. They were all tired and emotional from the day's events.

With a lantern in one hand, Cara circled out from their camp, keeping the fire to her left, her ears pricked for any more cries. Another one sounded, but in the far distance. Cara peered into the trees, sure that she'd see red eyes, but none appeared. Still, she didn't want to take any chances. She doubted a dark flight through the swamp would end well, especially with Sandu in his current condition. With the dwindling firelight ever in her sight, she kept circling. At last, just as she could barely see the glow through the trees, she sighed in relief.

No prowlers nearby, she thought. *And no calls for a while now.* She desperately hoped that the monsters roamed far away from them.

Halfway back to the camp, Cara decided that her trip away from the fire shouldn't be wasted. She set a quick snare, paying little heed to the finesse of her handiwork. *It doesn't have to be pretty to catch a rabbit.*

As she approached the camp, Cara raised her lantern high and swung it a few times so that Alex didn't try to stab her. She rejoined her friends by the fire and blew out her small light. "Nothing out there."

"You rest for now," Alex said. "I'll watch until I need to sleep."

Cara nodded. She and Sandu curled up against each other as Alex stood up and stretched. Though Sandu soon drifted into sleep, Cara stayed up a little longer, her half-closed eyes watching the scholar. She liked the way he moved, the gentleness of his hands and the sharpness of his green eyes. She especially liked how he looked at her. *Sandu joked about Alex and I, but he was right. There's something here, and I want to find out where it goes.*

Eventually, her eyes drifted closed.

Though candles had passed, Cara woke after what felt like moments. Her sleep had been dreamless, and she gazed groggily into the still-dark swamp. Alex bent over her, his hand on her shoulder. "There's still a few more candles 'til dawn. Think you can take over for me?"

Cara nodded and gently pushed Sandu's head from her lap. He grumbled, but didn't wake. She stretched and yawned, sore and cold from the hard ground. As Alex settled down beside Sandu, Cara fed the fire. She asked, "Any more calls?"

"No. It's been quiet."

Cara opened her mouth, then shut it. Her mouth had suddenly gone dry, and she knew she should let him sleep, but...

"It always takes me awhile to drift off," Alex said as if reading her mind. "We can talk for a bit, if you'd like."

Cara smiled at him. In the firelight, his strong features smoothed into an almost boy-like quality. She asked, "Are scholars allowed to have wives?"

His knowing look made her feel foolish. "We are. Most of us aren't monks, you know."

"Oh." She was glad the darkness hid her blush.

"Of course, many noble sons get married off eventually. I'm one of the lucky ones whose family doesn't care about me passing on our blood. That honor is only required of my brother."

"Are your lands expansive?" Cara asked teasingly.

"Mine? Oh no. Mine are quite small. My brother's, though, will make quite the dowry for a lucky bride." He pulled his coat closer around him and asked, "What about your lady? Had her father arranged a marriage for her yet?"

Cara nodded. "The papers were signed just before he died. Renna didn't like the man, though. She asked for a full year's mourning to delay the wedding."

"A wise decision. If you rescue her, she could petition Earl Stonetree to nullify the contract."

"I suppose." Cara started to move away, but Alex caught her hand. As he pulled her close, her heart stuttered in her chest. Her skin tingled under his touch, and her breath hitched in her throat. He drew her in until their knees were touching, their faces inches apart.

"Why do you want to know about scholars and wives?" he murmured. His breath was hot on her cheek.

"Just...curious," Cara managed, too enamored by his lips to think any further. One of his hands entwined in her braid, and he leaned in. She had been kissed before, but never had she felt such a swell of desire inside her. She closed her eyes, ready, but the kiss never came.

Alex froze. Cara tried not to feel disappointed – after all, she was only a country girl, and he was a noble – but then he put a finger to her mouth.

"Listen," he said.

Cara pulled away, frowning. At first, she heard nothing. "Wh–"

Then she detected it. An absence of sound, like the swamp was holding its breath. In the silence, she heard the faintest hiss of breath between pointed teeth. It came from where she'd set the snare.

Cara drew her sword and indicated Alex to stay. He opened his mouth to protest, but she shook her head. She stole through the trees on quiet feet, eyes straining in the darkness. The beast uncurled from its slumber, begging to be released. Even as she pushed it down, Cara wondered if she'd need it for this fight.

Something moved in the gloom, and a high-pitched cry shot through the air. Cara paused, watching as the prowler's dark shape pounced on a rabbit caught in the snare. She raised her sword, ready to strike.

Light flared behind her. Cara whirled to see Alex with a raised lantern. But he didn't look confused or frightened; his expression was determined.

In the sudden light, the prowler hissed and crouched low. Cara turned back to face it, and went rigid.

The prowler was a child, its eyes rimmed red, forehead marred with bone-like ridges, fangs jutting out from its diminutive lips. Its talons dripped with the rabbit's blood. It had once been a boy, no older than eleven or twelve.

Cara drew back in horror. The prowler had only hunger in its eyes.

It lunged at her, low and fast. Cara pointed the sword at it, scraping its chest. It hissed. The primal part of her won out, and Cara let the beast rise to meet its kin. The hands clutching her sword rippled as her nails grew into claws. She pushed back at the creature with greater strength. It startled at her transformation, its red eyes widening, a keening cry escaping from its lips.

The beast's fury overrode Cara's terror. The prowler growled and swatted at her, but her reach was longer. It tried to leap again, and with deadly aim, she struck its head from its shoulders. The small body fell as its head landed inches from her foot.

Cara screamed, for she saw not the prowler's face, but Merick's, slack-jawed and empty. She shut her eyes tightly, but when she opened them, Renna glared back from bloodied blue eyes, tongue lolling out. Cara turned away and found herself in Alex's arms. He cradled her against his shoulder as she shuddered.

"It's alright," he said soothingly. "It's over. You did what had to be done."

Cara dared another peek at the head. The dead prowler stared up at the trees, its child's face innocent, not like a monster's at all. It once had a father and mother, maybe sisters and brothers that it played with in the sun.

She had killed a child.

No, Cara shook herself. *It was a prowler. Any trace of that child is gone.*

Yet when she looked again, she saw a boy's dim pupils, not the creature's hazy red ones. Blood gushed out of its hacked neck, both enticing and repulsive. For a moment, the beast sniffed, urging her to taste it, just a little drop on her tongue, nothing more–

Cara forced the beast back down. It surrendered, if unhappily, as her features and hands returned to normal. She clung to Alex, unashamed of the tears that stained his fine tunic.

"Shh," he said. "We're safe now."

He doesn't understand. I killed a child.

Alex led her back to camp, and though she protested, he insisted she sleep through the night. He held her head in his lap, stroking her hair, until she fell asleep.

But her dreams were plagued by the prowler child. It walked toward her, its head under its arm. *You did this to me,* whispered its pale lips. *You're no better than a monster.*

"Shut up," Cara said. "You're dead."

I know. But how did I die? Was I really a prowler, or just a lost child driven mad with hunger? A lost child that you murdered. Struck my head right off, you did. Well done. Don't all noble warriors start by killing children?

"You're not real!" Cara shouted at the shambling corpse. Worms crawled over its red-stained skin, brown flecks against stark white.

I'm as real as you. Gently must you treat the little children. Gently strike them through their little hearts. Little heart you could hold in your palm. Little heart you stopped from beating.

"Stop it! Stop it, you're dead," Cara sobbed, but she couldn't tear herself from the sight of a worm burrowing into the boy's staring eye. "I'm sorry, I didn't mean it, I didn't want to."

But you did. You wanted my blood, so tender and sweet. So good for one like us.

Cara recoiled. She shook her head even though she knew that the creature was right. It had felt good to deliver the killing blow. She *did* crave its blood.

Before the creature could say more, Cara sat up, suddenly awake as only one can wake from a nightmare. The swamp had lightened somewhat with the early sun. She rubbed her arms as she looked around for Alex and Sandu. Both were up and preparing the horses. They spoke in hushed tones.

"Is she hurt?" Sandu asked.

Alex replied softly, "No. But she's affected by it."

"I see." Sandu glanced at her and, seeing her awake, came over. He knelt beside her, his fingers playing with the edge of his blanket. "How are you feeling?"

Cara didn't know how to answer. She felt confused: pleased with killing the prowler, appalled at herself for doing it, disgusted with the beast's hunger for blood. Unconsciously, she watched the vein pulse in Sandu's neck. When she realized it, she tore her eyes away and said, "The child was in my dreams."

"It wasn't a child," Alex said. "I even looked this morning, just to appease you. It was a prowler."

"But it was only a child! It once had parents and playmates, and...and...and I killed it. And I saw horrible things, Merick and Renna dead in the creature's place, judging me. What would Merick think of me? What if Renna finds out? To know that I killed..."

"They would understand," Sandu said gently. "You did it to defend us."

"Prowlers aren't the humans they once were," Alex said. "The child whose body it stole was long dead already. You did what you had to."

That doesn't make it right. Cara took a deep breath and tried to listen to her friends' reasoning. *They're right, it was a prowler, not a child. But...how many more children out there have lost their lives to these beasts?* Another horrible thought struck her. *Are there* fampir *children doomed to immortality?*

"Can children become *fampir* too?" she asked, dreading the answer. Sandu's face blanched. When she looked to Alex, his expression had darkened.

"There shouldn't be," he said. "But it's possible. All the accounts I've read have forbidden their creation. It is the only law among *fampir*, though who knows if they all follow it."

Cara shuddered, and decided that the only recourse was to destroy any *fampir* and prowlers she found. *If they're dead, they can't pass on their curse.* With Alex's help, she climbed to her feet. He mounted the horse behind her, his arms wrapped securely around her waist. Sandu looked uncomfortable on an unfamiliar horse, but he tapped his heels to follow them.

"Your beast helped you against the prowler," Alex said softly as they rode into the swamp, morning light barely piercing the intertwining treetops. "Maybe it's not as bad as you think."

"I was faster, and stronger. But the beast made me feel

this...unnatural thirst. I don't want to become a monster that drinks blood."

"Once we reach Riverfen and unload the scrolls, I'll see what more they say of the *sulpari*. I might consult Lord Mavian Strilu as well, since he's conducted his own research into the prowlers. He could help us."

Cara leaned her head against his chest, enjoying the comforting feeling. She said, "If I try to drink anyone's blood, you'll stop me?"

"Yes."

That one word was all she needed. She relaxed at last, letting herself melt into the saddle and the circling touch of his arms. Every one in awhile, she looked back to Sandu, making sure he was still there. She smiled at him, and promised herself she would tell him that night how much she worried for him after he disappeared. *I want you with me, too*, she would say. *You and Alex are the only true friends I've ever had*. It pained her that she could no longer count Renna among her friends. *We've grown apart, and I don't think she'll want someone like me in her employ*. An ache for the past filled Cara's chest. She would find Renna and soak in all she could of her lady, basking in the memories they had shared together. Then, she would have to let her go. Picturing it was both relieving and terrifying: for the longest time, Renna and Cara had been inseparable. With each passing day, Cara found that she missed her less.

"Alex," Cara murmured, "when you went to Mott, did you leave behind people you loved?"

She twisted up to look at him. His jaw clenched, and he nodded. "But it was the right choice. My brother and I have very different ways of looking at the world, and it was best I leave him for a time. We still write, and occasionally visit, but it's best this way. We find we can love each other much better from a distance."

Cara pondered this as they rode. She said, "I hope Renna hasn't changed as much as I have, or we won't recognize each other."

He laughed. "You'll each be proud of the other. Change

sparks new life. It would be a dreary existence if one couldn't grow into one's old age."

Sandu came up beside them. "If Papa saw me now, I think he'd still want to take a switch to me. He'd call me an idiot for being taken in by the mist-folk."

Cara giggled. "Before or after he hugged you for facing down prowlers?"

"That would be just another switch for making clod-headed decisions."

Alex said, "You barbaric rustics. Nobles don't beat their children; they simply make them write lines for a day."

"I don't know which of those is worse," Cara said, "but I could tell you some of the punishments Merick came up with. He had quite the imagination."

Though their stomachs grumbled and the sunshine still struggled to reach the ground, they laughed and talked, the horrors of the day before slowly fading away. Yet when Cara glanced into the woods, sometimes she thought she saw a glint of small red eyes, and she couldn't quite shake the memory of the prowler child.

CHAPTER TWENTY-FIVE
Seanna

"WILL IT BE a boy?" asked Lady Marcha, her hands running over Seanna's small belly. Finally past the three-month mark, Seanna felt confident in announcing her first pregnancy to the court. Ladies cooed over her while gentlemen shook Henrik's hand in congratulations.

Seanna smiled. "I do believe so. My mother bore a son her first time, and her mother before her. 'Tis a likely thing!"

"Oh, that is marvelous."

The lady drifted away, and for the first time that evening, Seanna found herself alone in the giant banquet hall. Nobles gathered in small groups, the murmur of their individual voices indistinct in the overall babble. Seanna meandered to the nearest group of people she recognized. She stood at the edge of their circle, smiling and nodding along with their conversation.

Not one addressed her.

Seanna took a sip of her wine and tried not to feel disappointed. She had only come to Con Salur six months ago, after all, and recently married the king. Before that, her father had often refused to take her or her sister with him to engagements such as these. It was no surprise that few nobles knew her well enough to invite her into their circles.

Still, Seanna tried. After the failed event, she went to Henrik to ask his advice, but he merely laughed at her.

"Speak up for yourself, woman! Or don't say anything at all. Silence is preferred for a lady."

Later that quinn, Seanna tried to ingratiate herself with some of the courtiers from the area with a story of her voyage from Brin to Con Salur. They looked at her with disdain, then returned to their gossip.

Gossip, she found to her horror, that turned on her after her miscarriage a month later, and that only grew worse after the loss of her second pregnancy as well.

In the quiet dining room, her third pregnancy making her feet swell and giving her a headache, Seanna pondered the mistakes she had made a few years before. *Too kind, too sweet, too honest. The rustics love a queen like that; courtiers despise her.*

Earl Seastone entered the room and inclined his head. "Forgive me for my lateness." He bent and took her hand, brushing it with a light kiss.

"Come, sit down, let us eat and talk. The world moves fast enough without us lingering over my knuckles." Seanna gestured to the meal laid out on the dark-stained table. "Your chefs have prepared us a specialty from my grandfather's homeland. And done a marvelous job of it, if the smell is anything to go by. My mouth has been watering ever since I sat down."

"Then I am doubly sorry for keeping you waiting, Your Grace," the earl said.

"When we are in casual company, you may address me simply as Seanna. And you shall be Druam. None of this 'Your Grace' or 'my lord' nonsense. It wastes time."

"As you wish it." Druam said no more, and Seanna took that as a good sign. She waited for her plate to be filled with hot, spiced pork and boiled grains. Deciding that pregnancy was an excuse to ignore civilities, she tore into the meat with unladylike savagery. The juices dribbled onto her chin, and she wiped them off with the napkin in her lap.

Druam laughed. "I have never seen a noble woman treat her food as a man does. Gwen picks at hers with the utmost finesse;

sometimes I wonder if she eats enough to satisfy her humors."

"When she, too, carries a child, then she'll eat as I do."

A pair of servants pulled open the curtains to a large bay window, giving them a view of the city below and harbor beyond. Lanterns were lit in blues and greens, reds and yellows, purples and oranges, all flowing together in shining rivers of color. Druam carefully placed his pristine silverware onto the clean white tablecloth, then shifted to stare out at the city. Seanna could see the lanterns reflected in his eyes.

"Every year I commission a lantern from one of the glassmakers here," Druam said softly, almost to himself. "Shaped into dragons and wolves, kings and flowers, anything the craftsmen can dream of. Once they've finished it, I hang it in the slums of Fester's Wharves or Drycobble. You wouldn't believe what those glassmakers can do...and with only their hands and lips and the hot stirring sand. 'Tis the most wondrous thing to see."

"Do you often watch them?"

"Oh yes. As often as I can. And then I look at my own hands and the sand in the gardens, and I feel ashamed, for I could never in a hundred years make a beautiful thing from those few resources. Yet they can."

Seanna observed him carefully: the way his eyes shifted over a scene which only he could see, how his mouth curled up in one corner as he spoke. For such a reserved man, when Druam talked of the lanterns, there was a strange passion in his voice, as if all his emotions were contained in that one thought. She sipped at her mulled wine, waiting for him to continue. When he said nothing – merely stared past the window with a glazed expression – she asked, "Has Gwen watched the lantern-making?"

Druam looked back to her as if he hadn't just been lost in his own mind. "Not yet. I have made arrangements to take her after the Masque. She's often told me that the lanterns were what made her decide to come here after her escape. One could say I only met her *because* of the lanterns."

"You don't attribute your meeting to the will of the gods?"

"I doubt they would meddle in such small affairs. We live in a large world, Seanna; the gods don't have time to plan out the lives of each ant."

"My husband would have you whipped for blasphemy, you know," Seanna said teasingly. "He is a traditionalist in the faith. I suppose you don't favor Predicant Ropaz, since he wants to drive religion toward keeping the old ways?"

"I care not for religious affairs. Exalts come and go, and rarely affect the lives of those outside the monasteries and novums. Neither Predicant Ropaz nor Predicant Manderly would change my life in any real way; the rest of the nobles only care so that they may line the pockets of the curates and predicants to give sermons about the benefits of taxes." Now Druam's expression had shifted to boredom and irritation. Subtly, though. Only by closely watching the tics in his mouth and eyes could Seanna see the change. *No wonder others think him to be a cold man. Compared to his exuberant wife, he hardly shows any emotion at all.* The thought of Gwen soured Seanna's mood.

"How is your little wife?" Seanna asked, hoping for news that the twit had fallen off a high roof.

Immediately, the corners of Druam's mouth twitched up – barely noticeable – and his eyes brightened. "Every day, when I am tired and have bad humors, she brings me such simple joy. She is the most loving, sweet wife in the courts – with the exception of yourself. Though...she has complained that many of the courtiers have ignored or shunned her, including you. Is this true?"

Ha, Seanna thought. Seanna hadn't been a loving, sweet wife since her wedding night. Though she smiled at Druam, her stomach roiled with envy. *Damn that girl and her happy marriage. It's time to bring him into the ruse.*

Seanna's smile turned into a sympathetic frown. "She is a good manipulator. I cannot believe no one has had the nerve to tell you: Gwen is having an affair. Everyone knows, and we all shun her for the shame she has brought to you."

Druam sat stunned. His smooth hair rumpled as he ran his fingers through it, strands falling onto his forehead and into his eyes; he didn't brush them away. "With whom?" he asked.

"I...I don't believe it my place to say..."

"With whom?" Druam asked again, his expression darkening. When he met Seanna's eyes, she nearly quailed.

Seanna took a sharp breath. She hadn't thought quite that far, and said the first name that came to her head, "Your cousin, Mavian Strilu."

"It can't be...No. Why would Gwen betray me?"

Seanna pressed, "She told me herself that noblewomen in Demarren carry on multiple extramarital affairs and are *lauded* for it."

"This can't be true," Druam muttered, still running his hands through his hair. "What evidence have you?"

"Her maids have seen her, Druam. They've heard the cries of love-making while you are away, and helped Mavian leave her rooms by the servant's passages. Her girls love her too much to report on her, but still they gossip when they think no one to be listening. I am so sorry, Druam."

The earl's carefully constructed façade crumbled at last and he buried his head in his hands. With her own expression pristinely sorrowful, Seanna's heart sang triumphantly. No need to worry about the other nobles or maids betraying her story: a well-oiled palm would bribe the mouth to produce the necessary lies.

After extricating herself and her full belly from her seat, Seanna went to Druam's side. She knelt next to him, the picture of a serene, beautiful queen. Taking both his hands in hers, she ran her fingers over the soft calluses on his large palm, unconsciously feeling out the lines upon lines that spoke of a life she barely knew. His hands were cold, though not frozen, and when she rubbed them they grew warm. Side by side, she realized how very pale his skin was. *There must be Skal blood in him*, she thought idly, *or he is still ill from the tourney*.

"Use this to your advantage," Seanna said once the silence had grown too thick. She still massaged his hands. "Show the court that you will not stand for such things. Send her away and remarry, if you must, but prove that you are not weak. Who knows what poison Mavian breathes into her ear? Perhaps he shall convince her to get rid of you and take power for himself."

"Xandro would come," Druam said, though he spoke so softly she barely heard him. He stared listlessly at his half-eaten plate.

"Your brother is a scholar, not a warrior nor a leader. Mavian could do much damage before Xandro arrives. I know little of Mavian, but the snippets I have heard paint an ugly picture. He has already cuckolded you; would you allow him to take your lands, too?"

"You give him too much blame." Druam met her gaze. His eyes pierced her straight through: they were deep blue, as blue as the waters in the bay, and so very *old*. As if he had lived a hundred lifetimes, and had known every sorrow a man could ever suffer. He said, "Mavian is hungry for knowledge, not power. He yearns to discover the secrets of the prowlers. For his strangeness and lack of social etiquette, he has been unjustly labeled a coward and a schemer. In all the years I have spent with him – *raised* him – I have seen no evidence to support such claims. If he and Gwen have found each other, it has been as outcasts from the cruel world of politics. Mavian loves and respects me too much to dare touch her. I will investigate these claims and evidences to see if they are true." Seanna jolted as Druam gripped her arm, his penetrating eyes never leaving hers. "I have never loved a liar or hypocrite. Perhaps those beneath you have been mistaken in their reports; we are human, after all."

Releasing her, Druam stood, then offered a hand to aid her up. Disturbed by his last statement, Seanna took his arm and climbed to her feet. She swept from the room, pretending it had been her desire to leave, and not his clear threat, that drove her heels out the door.

Though Seanna tried to sweep away the memory of his eyes – so clear and so startling – they haunted her that night. She could not sleep for the thought of Druam standing over her, those blue eyes glowing in the dark, a knife in his hand. "You have lied to me and betrayed me, Seanna. You have broken my faith in my faithful wife, and for that you must pay." His knife plunged down, again and again and again, into her stomach, killing the unborn life inside her.

Seanna sat up, realizing she must have fallen asleep and had a nightmare. She shook the dream from her mind. *Druam is a calm, reasonable man. If he realizes the lie, I can claim that I only passed on what my spies told me. They were the ones with an agenda and false information. Not me.* Her alibi secured, she slept peacefully.

The next day, Seanna strode down the blue-veined marble corridor. Her footfalls were padded by an immense, deep rug while mermaids swam the murals overhead. Still half-enchanted by the beauty of the Cascade Palace, Seanna failed to notice Maeria Westerburg's approach.

"Your Grace," the gold-haired girl sneered, curtseying low enough to be deemed sufficient, but no lower. Though caught by surprise, Seanna didn't let it show. She smiled broadly.

"Ah, Maid Westerburg. I feel as if it has been a century since our last meeting." *And still not long enough.* Clad in a silvery blue dress with a matching snood, Maeria looked every inch the perfect noble lady. Running her eyes down the length of her dress, Seanna noted the slight curves at her breasts and hips.

Still an entitled bitch, Seanna thought bitterly, unconsciously rubbing her own round, stretched belly.

"A century would be *ages* too long," Maeria said with dripping sarcasm. "How ever would I survive without seeing you?"

"I suspect by showing off that fine silk of yours to every passing man, be he steward or prince."

"'Tis fine silk indeed, Your Grace. I noticed you looking; did you care to feel it?"

A slight blush rose in Seanna's cheeks, and she glanced away before she could stop herself. *Damn.* Despite the girl's uncouth mouth and horrid attitude, she was *extremely* attractive. Seanna said abruptly, "Not today, I fear. Good morrow," and rushed off, thinking only of Maeria's smooth skin, her perfect red lips, the soft down between her legs and her squeals of delight as–

Seanna shook herself and tried to ignore the fluttering in her chest. At afternoon tea, she spread the news of Gwen's supposed affair. All around her, courtiers gasped and whispered into their hands, fascinated by every word that fell from between her teeth.

"Your Grace, may I speak to you?" A tall lord caught Seanna's arm as she prepared to leave. He had blonde hair and a long, immaculately trimmed mustache. Seanna recognized him as the Skallish ambassador, Lord Daghorn.

"My lord ambassador, I always have time for our friends from the north," Seanna replied, taking his proffered arm. He led her to a secluded alcove.

"I have heard you speak of Earl Seastone's new wife," Daghorn said, his eyes glittering. "You see, my kin in Demarren have expressed interest in her, as her name had been listed among the traitors currently wanted by the Inquisition."

Seanna quirked a brow; she had already heard this information. "And? The girl clearly has no inclinations toward magic, else she would have shown it by now."

"That is where I believe the story to be incorrect. Give me time, Your Grace, and I may find conclusions regarding Lady Seastone's motives for leaving her country. It would be another arrow against her. And, should you yourself discover anything else, I am sure the Inquisitors would be delighted to hear of it." The ambassador planted a kiss to Seanna's palm. "I want only for us to be allies in this matter. There are many connections and favors I could provide, should you help me."

"I would be delighted," Seanna said. "Please, come to me once you have found out the truth."

The ambassador swept away, a cloud of mint swirling in his wake. Seanna felt a touch of pride. Already, powerful men sought her for the information she could give them.

When she returned to her chambers that night, Seanna found a small, velvet bag left on the table beside her bed. She opened it, her fingers slipping on the soft strings.

Inside, she found a lovely silver brooch inlaid with

emeralds and a note, which her steward read to her:

My dear queen, I hope you can forgive my rudeness. I have dreamt of meeting you for such a long time, and find myself too tongue-tied to be kind. Harsh words are my defense against affection. I do wish us to grow closer and become greater friends. — Maeria

Her heart beating as rapidly as a bird's wings, Seanna dictated a similar note, then folded it and placed it in the bag along with a ruby necklace. Once all was done, she sent the bag back to Maeria in the hands of the trusted steward.

In her bed, Seanna imagined Maeria's warmth against her own. She remembered the thrill of chasing Larka, and the sweet release after days of hurried discussions and quick touches. She relished the fantasy, hoping desperately that it may come true. With Gwen deposed, and Maeria, a well-liked lady, as her ally, Seanna knew she would soon rise above Henrik and even Rask. Her body spasmed at the image of Rask torn down and defeated, his power all but gone.

CHAPTER TWENTY-SIX
Gwen

DESPITE LOSING the friendship of most nobles in the palace, Gwen was happy. Her marriage had grown more intimate after that strange, yet incredible night with Druam in the tavern. They made love with an intensity she had never known possible, and now, when she looked at him asleep in the bed beside her or passionately arguing with the king during councils, she felt a warmth deep inside. If she could describe that warmth, she would say it felt like mulled wine nestling in her stomach, comforting and dizzying all at once. When the spell workings of the day drained her, she need only enclose herself in Druam's arms during the safety of night to feel buoyant again.

Yet she still kept her magic secret from him. She didn't quite know why she hadn't the courage to tell him, so she held onto it, promising herself each day that she would tell him on the next.

At Mavian's suggestion, they decided to move their spell practice from Gwen's rooms to the old, abandoned north wing of the palace, meeting there the first time that afternoon. When she walked into that silent place, Gwen's skin prickled at the sight of the long, dusty hall stretching out in front of her, its windows covered in dark curtains. Armed with a spell of light, she stepped into the dust-ridden, silent space, her maids hovering behind her. She saw no sign yet of Mavian, so opened the door on the right. Past it was a sort of dining room. A long table stretched from the disused fireplace to a pair of double doors on her left, all other furniture obscured by dusty sheets. Three large, covered windows dominated the wall opposite her.

A glint above the fireplace caught Gwen's eye. She stepped daintily toward the huge mantle, the fireplace almost taller than her. Over the mantle was a cloth-covered painting, though a gilded frame poked out and reflected the light. Reaching up as far as she could, her heels rising so she balanced on the balls of her feet, Gwen took the cloth and pulled it away.

The portrait was old, its bright colors faded and paint cracked in places. A beautiful woman, in the prime of her life, gazed out with a complacent smile. She was seated in a golden chair and wore a dusky orange dress of an ancient style, a blue sash tied around her waist. Her long, dark hair cascaded around her with thousands of star-like white jewels pinned to it. One hand extended out as if beckoning Gwen to join her tranquility. Behind her, the painter had shown a beautiful countryside with mountains in the distance and a single white tower flying a blue banner.

Something about the painting felt warm, comforting, and familiar, as if the woman it contained had a life's worth of care to give and a hundred lullabies to sing. Her smile was both haunting and enchanting. Perched on the edge of the table, Gwen stared at her.

"It is beautiful, isn't it?"

Gwen jumped at the sound of Mavian's voice and whirled off the table to face him. He smiled and entered the room, his arms laden with books. "I used to explore this old wing as a boy and make up stories for every portrait I found here. That one I called the Lady of the Plains, and I pretended she was trapped in a tower by an evil wizard."

Gwen peered at the tomes Mavian laid on the table.

"Did you follow Druam?" Mavian asked.

"Yes," Gwen admitted. "But it wasn't what I thought...he never betrayed me."

"Where did he go?"

Gwen hesitated, then said, "It's not my story to tell."

"I worried about you." Mavian paused, then asked, "Were you discovered?"

"Yes." Gwen saw no need to lie about that. "Why were you worried?"

For once, Mavian's cheery disposition faltered. "Druam can have a temper. You haven't known him as long as I have; he's as hard-headed as they come. I fear his reaction should he discover your magic. The more you use it, the more your Gaiar builds up inside you, like water behind a dam. Sometimes, that dam bursts through heightened emotions, a flux of your humors; anything could happen."

"And you think he'd cause that dam to burst?" Gwen was incredulous. She couldn't imagine Druam doing such a thing.

Mavian nodded slowly. "He could rail at you, stop you from practicing, and it would burst."

Never had she seen him so serious. Gwen shook her head, unsure how much she should believe. He could just be jealous of Druam, she thought. Maybe he doesn't want to lose his time with me. She said, "I don't want to hear any more."

"But–"

"Stop it, Mavian. Just...tell me about the spells you wanted to practice today."

Mavian frowned, but then leafed through one of the tomes. "I was thinking you could try illusion charms today. Some of them can imitate memories or create false images. Here's one: illutre vel imatre, chanted as the caster holds an image in their mind's eye."

"Illutre vel imatre," Gwen repeated. She held her hands on the table, picturing a bird laying on her palms. Before she could start the spell, though, one of her handmaids hissed, "My lady, the earl is here."

Mavian quickly closed the book as Gwen turned around. Druam stood on the threshold, his face marred in shadows. He stepped into the room, giving a poisonous look to Mavian.

"Get out," Druam said, his voice soft. "The maids too. I need to speak with Gwen. Alone."

Giving a worried look to Gwen, Mavian gathered his books

and scurried from the room. Druam stared at the ground and waited for the maids to close the door. "Sit down." As Gwen sat, he paced. "I couldn't believe it, but my own eyes didn't lie to me."

"What? I don't understand."

"I know of your affair," he said bluntly. The words punctured Gwen's lungs, and she gaped at him, speechless. Before she could say a word, he sighed as if trying to contain his emotions. "I know your Demar kin see such things as common, but I had hoped you wouldn't give in to your temptations. I know you thought I betrayed you first with my late-night excursions. But you saw the truth of what I do, yet still I find you here with Mavian."

"It's not true!" Gwen protested. "I wasn't...there is nothing of that sort between Mavian and I!" Yet she remembered the queen's threats, the ladies' scorn; too late, she realized her mistake. In her desperation for friendship, she had ignored the possibility of rumors. Her mouth had gone dry, her stomach twisting. Could Druam really think so poorly of her? She wanted to run into his arms and sob, but the pain in his expression prevented her. What could she say to ease his mind?

Druam said, "The whole court knows and looks upon me as a fool. I engaged lords and ladies on your behalf, yet none but the queen had the gall to tell me."

"She lied! I promise, Druam, on the graves of my parents, that I have never strayed from you. The queen turned all the ladies against me, and now she seeks to separate us, too." She prayed that the truth rang in every word. Tentatively, Gwen took Druam's hand, then wiped away a tear before it could fall to his skin.

Druam searched Gwen's eyes, his expression inscrutable. Running his fingers through his hair, he asked, "Then what are you doing with Mavian? Why are you meeting him in this secluded place?"

Gwen stared at him, afraid. She'd wanted to tell him for so long, but she didn't know how he'd respond. If she lied now, she would lose all his trust. If she told the truth...what would he think of her? Would he feel disgust at her cowardice in fleeing Demarren while innocent people died for witchcraft? Yet she saw no other way forward. It was time.

Gwen's throat closed, and she swallowed with difficulty. "He was teaching me."

"Teaching you what? I could have hired curates to work with you on all sorts of things: reading, writing, history, arithmetic, geography, even one of the sciences."

"It wasn't any of those things. He is teaching me to use my magic." Once the words had left Gwen's tongue, she couldn't retrieve them. She took a quick breath, as if the admittance had taken the same toll as a sprint.

Silence consumed the air around them. At last, Druam said, "The accusations made toward you in Demarren...they were not unfounded, were they?"

"No one knew but Wullum and one councilor."

"Tell me. I would have no secrets between us."

The emotion behind his eyes was unreadable. Gwen swallowed her fear and spoke.

"When I was a child, Ebarren – the councilor – noticed that I had potential for magic. He had traveled much in his youth, and learned secrets forbidden in Demarren. He taught me some, but Wullum discovered us practicing. His rage was awful, but he was also scared for me, worried that someone would find out and he would have to execute me. He made me promise never to do it again.

"So I hid all the spellbooks and materials under a flagstone in my room and kept to my promise. When the Inquisition came, they targeted me to get to Wullum. I doubt they know the truth." All the secrets Gwen had kept from him tumbled from her lips: using magic to heal him, her days of newfound joy in practicing her talents with Mavian, the spell to follow Druam to the tavern. When she had finished, Druam stayed quiet a moment, thinking.

"I am profoundly glad that you haven't strayed," Druam said. "But I am also unsure of your use of magic. Show me what you've learned so far."

A hundred cantrips and workings flowed through her mind, but none seemed right. Then Gwen looked at the portrait over the mantle, still beckoning to her. She took Druam's hand, led him over to it, and asked who the woman was.

"Her name was Imira Strilu, the matriarch of my family line," Druam said softly, a strange wistfulness in his tone. He reached up to touch the frame. "For years her smile graced the dinners of my forefathers, until newer and larger halls were built and she was forgotten. She brought the Strilu family out of Belleslye and to the River Valley after the Eadrons stole our country from us. Songs used to be sung of her beauty and compassion, her ferocity and quick wit."

"Do you know any of the songs?"

Druam shook his head. "There are Valadi storytellers who do, but I cannot remember them now. I know a song of Belleslye, but it is a song of longing and loss."

"Sing it for me."

Though he gave her a bemused look, Druam complied.

"My child, my child, come back home to me,
Tarry not in the woods where the wild beasts be.
Their swords and their knives know not the cries
Of my child who was lost in Belleslye."

The melody tugged at Gwen's magic, and she fed into it, harmonizing the words of the illusion working – illutre vel imatre – with the song. Picturing the woman's smile, imagining her warmth as she moved, Gwen chanted to Druam's singing.

"Dear child, dear child, oh where have you gone?
Hear the drums and the notes of the dark man's song.
Run faster than wind, so you'll never die
In the woods around dear old Belleslye."

Their voices filled the ancient air around them and the song grew stronger. Her hand held up, Gwen took the words of her working and imagined entwining them with the paint, infusing the portrait with the song's power.

"Twas there in my home 'neath the old oaken's gaze,
Where my child was lost,
Lost to me in the wintry caves."

The dust motes between Gwen's fingers and the painting glowed blue and green, shining like the sun hitting a fast-flowing brook. The glow sunk into the portrait, brightening its tarnished frame.

"My love, my love, sing once more for him,
Buried there in the dirt 'neath the tall oak limbs."

The ghostly form of the painted woman emerged from the portrait, her skin shining, her hair sparkling with jewels. She floated in the air before them, an angel brought to life by Gwen's illusion. Druam's voice faltered, but he faintly sang:

"Sing, else the wood will hear, and you too shall die
Never to again see sweet Belleslye."

For a moment, the air hung still, and though Gwen kept humming her magic, she did not need to say the words for the working to continue. The ethereal form of Imira Strilu bent down to Druam, her fingers caressing his cheek. Gwen tore her eyes from the illusion and saw that Druam's lip trembled as he stared into the matriarch's beautiful face. Gwen let the working fade, the illusion dissipating. Imira remained in her frame, her hand once more reaching out from inside the painting. Druam stepped forward, wordlessly reaching up to where the illusion had been only seconds before. Though the magic had gone, Gwen thought she smelled the scent of the plains after a thunderstorm.

Druam turned to face Gwen. "What did you do?"

"I brought an illusion of her." Without her Gaiar buoying her humors, Gwen's fingers shook with an effort she hadn't realized she'd exerted, her limbs cold. "I used your song as a guide."

"I see." Druam looked back to the portrait.

"I had never tried that spell before. It was more difficult than many others I've cast." Tentatively taking his hand, Gwen said, "Please don't forbid me from using my powers. It is one of the greatest joys in my life now. Without the threat of execution over my head, I no longer feel afraid of my own Gaiar. Please, Druam. Please. The queen has taken away all my friends in the court, and besides you, Mavian is the only one who speaks to me beyond mere courtesy. Please."

Druam hesitated, and there was a foreboding in his eyes that Gwen didn't understand. However, he tilted her chin to give her a quick kiss. "You must keep it secret. Lord Daghorn is seeking proof against you, and the king...may be displeased. I will put guards at the entrance to this wing so that you and Mavian may practice in peace.

"But," he continued, "You are still my wife, and I do expect you to fulfill your duties as the Lady Seastone. You have my blessing, provided you do all that your obligations ask of you."

Throwing her arms around him, Gwen hugged him close. "I promise I shall be as good a wife as you have ever wanted. Thank you, Druam."

CHAPTER TWENTY-SEVEN
Cara

DEEP IN the heart of the swamp lay a town that made most of its money from travelers seeking a safe place to rest away from mist-folk and prowlers. A few rice farms had taken over the marshes, but most of the townsfolk made their business through trade. Cara exclaimed in delight as the oppressive marsh gave way to large rice paddies and lovely wooden homes made from sturdy oak. She had never thought to be so happy to see the sun.

"This is Banyi," Alex said. "Home to the best artisans in the valley."

"And home to warm pies and pork," Sandu said, looking longingly at a bakery's display.

The town had been built on a series of raised wooden platforms connected by bridges. A wooden barrier with stakes circled the village, no doubt a small defense against prowlers. A wide stone bridge with a long, low ramp led from one side of town to the other, packed with wagons, carts, and livestock. Alex waved at their caravan and kicked his horse to a trot.

"Ho, Ronan," Alex called to one of the scholars. "Did you all enjoy your break?"

The scholars gathered around their horses, holding out bread and salted meat. Cara took her portion gratefully and ate while Alex explained what had happened. Sandu stared ashamed at the ground, but the monks only clapped his back and praised the gods that he'd been safely found.

Cara hugged Sandu after the press of people had diminished. "They won't judge you, you know. They're just glad we're all safe."

"I know," Sandu said. "But it's my fault any of us were in danger in the first place."

"You say that like danger doesn't follow us regardless."

"I suppose," he said, but he had a guilty look in his eyes that Cara didn't understand. She was about to ask him about it when Alex bounded up.

"Not much time to lose," he said. "We'll rest for a candle, then press on. I know a spot to make camp tonight."

"We're not staying here?" Cara asked, her heart sinking. She had been looking forward to a nice bath and a real bed.

Alex said, "We've already lost half a day's travel, and the earl is expecting us well before the Masque. But tomorrow night we've arranged to stay at the inn in Redbank."

One more night won't hurt, Cara thought with a sigh.

The candle's break seemed all too short, and before she knew it they were back on the road. This time, Alex rode his horse alone while Cara and Sandu shared. He liked to move back and forth between the wagons, talking with his scholars and making sure that everything went smoothly.

Sandu squirmed uncomfortably on the horse every few minutes until Cara asked, "You can walk, you know. I'm sure not every horse will ride as well as Galen for you."

"I'll be fine," he said. Then he sighed, "I miss her. You know, when she was first given to me she was a miserable nag of a creature. But she took a liking to me, and though she wasn't anything like a highbred horse, she always made sure I had an easy ride."

"I'm sorry."

"It's my own fault. And she was just a horse, not a man like Merick. I shouldn't be the one grieving when you're still mourning for him."

Cara had certainly thought that, but she didn't want to say it aloud. She hesitated, then said, "It's still a loss. It hurts. But we have each other and Alex now, and things will get better. I promise."

"Thanks."

Though she didn't know if she could really keep her promise, Cara wished she could. She rubbed Sandu's hands, then turned her attention to the swamp. Once again, trees blocked the sparse sunlight, and puddles and muddy spots gathered haphazardly over the road. In the distance, she thought she heard something calling her name. She shook off the thought, and stared resolutely at the wagons in front of them.

After a time, she asked, "What did the mist-folk lure you with?"

Sandu's arms tightened around her. "Someone from my past."

Cara started to demand a clearer answer when the forest shook. The horse stumbled underneath them, the wagons trembled on their wheels. Leaves fell from the trees into splashing marshes. A faint, familiar scent of mustiness and bad eggs assaulted her nose.

The quake ended quickly, and the scholars shouted down their line to make sure everyone was safe. Cara answered for herself and Sandu. As she spoke, her palms tingled. *This feels familiar*, she thought. She kicked their horse's flank and rode up to Alex as he helped get the wagons moving again.

"Strange," Alex commented when he saw her. "Never thought the swamps would get a quake like that."

"It's the Hooded Man," Cara said. "He's here."

"I didn't see a purple light," Alex said. "That's what you described, isn't it?"

"Yes," she said, "but–"

"We have to press forward. If this enemy is out there, we'll be ready for him." Alex called to the scholars, and the wagons rumbled forward once more. Cara held their horse back, waiting for the last wagon to pass before she kicked it to move. She knew what she had felt, but Alex was right. If the Hooded Man had appeared, he must be far away.

Candles passed, the swamp growing steadily darker around them. Bird calls and animal noises faded away until silence dominated the forest. Cara's hand strayed again and again to her sword as her gaze darted from tree to tree, sure that at any moment a hooded figure would appear.

The oxen pulling the wagons snorted and shuffled. Their nervousness affected the horses, which danced across the road and rolled their eyes. Alex rode back to Cara and Sandu, standing in the saddle as he surveyed the swamp.

"We're close to the campsite," he said. "Once there, we can set up a defensive perimeter."

"The mist-folk aren't calling," Sandu said. "I could hear them all day, but they stopped a little bit ago."

Alex chewed his lip, considering. "We should press forward."

"My lord," a scholar called from the front of the caravan, "there's a log in the road."

"It's a trap," Cara said, reaching out to grab Alex's sleeve. "We should turn back, now."

The words barely escaped her lips before a cascade of arrows fell from the sky. Some struck the ground, but more hit the wagons and scholars. Men screamed in the gathering dusk. Alex shouted, "Defend the wagons!"

Soldiers in black armor, their faces hidden with cloth, erupted from the swamp. They fell on the caravan as scholars rushed to defend themselves. Cara sat still a moment, shocked at how quickly it had all happened. Then she drew her sword and dismounted.

"Get away," she said to Sandu. "You and Alex need to run. *Now*."

Sandu stared at her wide-eyed. She didn't wait to watch him obey her. The beast rose up, and she accepted it. All around her, monks and scholars scrambled to fight with staves and daggers, but they were no match for the soldiers wielding spears and swords.

Cara danced between the combatants, her body liquid, her swings water that sliced through the soldiers. Their armor deflected her blade, but it was enough to distract them from the scholars.

The beast purred in her head, its hot presence guiding her. As she moved, time seemed to slow around her. The soldiers' arms swung with the speed of molasses, though their eyes were determined above their masks. Cara waited for the right moment; she had all the time she needed. She smoothly side-stepped one, her sword slicing into the weak spot behind his knee. He cried out as he fell. Another one ran at her, but his steps were too slow. She gracefully slid her blade into his neck, an arc of blood flowing out. Its coppery scent fell tantalizingly through the air, and she paused, distracted for a moment.

But the beast knew that the battle was not over. Though it, too, hungered for that sweet taste, it spurred her on. Cara lost track of the men who flowed around her, each slow as melting wax. Yet to them, she was a blur, a deadly creature that moved with inhuman speed.

Cara grinned, relishing the fight. Somewhere deep inside her, she knew that these were men with wives and children, that they were not the undead prowlers she had killed before. The beast didn't care, and in that moment, neither did she. They had come for her friends, and she would show no mercy.

From the corner of her eye, Cara saw the soldiers moving back. *Ha.* Alex, she saw, stood with his scholars by one of the wagons. She turned to him, ready to shout their victory–

The ground trembled, greater now than earlier in the day. Trees groaned at their roots, the wagons nearly falling to their sides. Men shouted in alarm, and Cara stilled, her speed crashing back to normal. She stumbled in the growing quake.

The stench made her gag, her late lunch churning in her stomach. Her ears rang, a high-pitched whine that drowned out all other sounds. She covered her ears, but it didn't stop. A purplish hue spread out from the center of the caravan, reaching not with the gentle changing of light, but with an aura of destruction and death. Black veins branched away into vine-like shadows that threatened to choke out trees and plants. The oxen pulled at their yokes, desperate to escape, as horses bucked and tried to run. Cara trembled with the memory of the first time she'd seen this dreadful void, of the too-slow run to save Renna, Ulton's death, the black tentacles flinging Merick off his feet...and the Hooded Man beckoning from the dark void.

The Hooded Man appeared now. Black tentacles surged around him, but they didn't attack. They dove into the wagons, drawing out boxes of scrolls. Alex shouted, and the scholars moved to stop the tentacles. The monstrous things threw them off easily, even as the soldiers renewed their attack.

Cara didn't care about the scrolls. She only had eyes for the Hooded Man. Though her nose still protested and her ears buzzed, she used the beast. It lent speed to her feet, counteracting the slowness of the void. Cara snarled as she ran past monks and tentacles and soldiers, her sword begging for the Hooded Man's blood.

He turned to her, and beckoned. Cara rushed to close the gap.

Something else stepped from the void. It was the size of a large man, and humanoid in shape. It, too, wore a dark cloak that swathed its face, and it bore a black greatsword in its grey-veined, blue-tinged hands.

Cara stopped to assess this new threat. Something about it seemed familiar, but she couldn't remember, her thoughts too muddled with the beast's instincts. Still, it stood between her and the Hooded Man, and she would defeat it to get to him.

The Hooded Man turned away as the new monster advanced on Cara. She backed away, giving only enough ground to move in. It swung its giant sword with ease, keeping her at a distance.

Cara ducked under the sword and slashed the creature's chest. It didn't grunt or move. It flung its arm out, catching her as she tried to dodge away. She crashed into a wagon, her head ringing. The beast pumped through her veins, and she staggered back up with a growl.

The creature was ready for her. Even with the beast's strength, she couldn't move quickly so close to the void. She ran at the creature, her blade cutting into one of its arms. Its sword swept at her, and she barely pulled herself under it. She backed away again, breathing hard. What was this thing?

The Hooded Man called out, and his soldiers raced back to the void and disappeared. All around her, Cara saw fallen scholars and soldiers, and empty wagons. She couldn't see Alex or Sandu.

Rage filled her. She wouldn't let the Hooded Man escape again. This time, she ignored the monster and raced straight for the cloaked figure. He turned to her, his hand flicking dismissively. She braced herself for a tentacle, but they were all gone.

The creature crashed into her, sending her sprawling. She panted on the ground as it loomed over her. Its foot stepped on her leg. Cara gasped and squirmed. Her sword hand struggled in the mud, but she brought her blade up and cut into the monster's flesh. It pressed her leg harder into the ground.

"Enough!" The Hooded Man's shout was cold and harsh. "We have what we came for."

The monster hesitated, then it turned its sword around. Cara screamed as the creature drove the blunt pommel into her leg, cracking it with brute force. She lay in agony as the creature walked back to the void. Tears flowed down her cheeks as the Hooded Man and his monster vanished.

The void closed with a pop, leaving spots in her vision. She still tasted the stench on her tongue. Her ears cracked with the lack of noise.

Gone. Cara slumped back on the ground as the beast retreated back inside her. *He's gone again.* She gasped in pain as her leg twitched, her calf bloodied and fractured.

"Cara!" Alex's white face swam up out of the darkness. His skin was smudged with grime. He knelt beside her. "Are you hurt?"

Cara could only nod, the pain too much for words. She grasped his hand, holding it tightly. Sandu pushed through the surviving scholars.

"He escaped," Cara gritted out. "He escaped."

"You did what you could," Alex said before turning to the

scholars. "See what's left. Make a litter for her, and try to calm the oxen."

He turned back to Cara, stroking her face as Sandu knelt to her other side. Alex said, "Be still now. We'll take care of it all."

Cara let out a sob, and then the pain grew too great for her. She fainted, the world growing black.

The prowler child's face lunged at Cara, its laughing fangs tearing into her skin. Its poison shuddered through her veins, turning her blood black. Her desperate heart pumped harder, unknowingly spreading the infection faster and faster. The rushing blood boiled in her ears. Red tinged the rings of her pupils, darkening her vision. Inside her, the beast celebrated. It rose up into her mouth, delighting in the lust that danced savagely in her chest.

Cara spun around. Behind her, Alex and Sandu lay face-up on the floor. She advanced on them. Each claw on her hands twitched, and her tongue ran over her ready fangs.

Sandu opened his eyes as Cara loomed over him. He struggled back, his hands scraping against the floor. He pleaded with her, but she paid him no heed. The skin of his throat was soft as she tore into it with a single claw. Staring at her bloodied finger in interest, she listened to him gurgling in his own blood.

Then, slowly, gently, like a girl bending over her sleeping lover, Cara put her lips to his throat. She drank deeply, the sweet, coppery taste sliding over her tongue. Sandu's moans of pain grew quieter as his life essence slipped away.

Cara was not satisfied. Blood coating her chin, she stood, letting Sandu's lifeless body drop to the ground. She turned to Alex, who lay peacefully asleep. With panther-like grace, Cara crept forward on all fours.

Alex did not have time to wake. He sluggishly flailed as Cara's claws slashed his chest and stomach open, his entrails painting the ground in red and pink hues. This time, she didn't drink. She watched, fascinated, as Alex tried to pull himself away, dragging his splattered insides through the dirt. When Cara had had enough, she grabbed his leg, ignoring his pleas and cries of pain. Without thinking, she plunged her claws into his flesh and tore out his heart. It pumped for a moment longer in her hand, a dark spot of red beauty.

"Cara..."

Cara whipped around. Renna stood behind her in a gleaming white dress, her long blonde hair floating around her head. Cara hissed and dropped Alex's heart.

"What have you become, Cara?" Renna asked. Cara scooted back, baring her teeth. Renna shook her head sadly, then turned away. Cara growled low in her throat, then sprang at her.

A black tentacle wrapped around Cara, halting her. She growled and turned to see the Hooded Man. His eyes blazed beneath his cloak.

"You think you can ever match my power?" he whispered in that cold voice. "You have no idea what you're facing."

Cara twisted and squirmed, her claws swiping at him. He only laughed. The laughter grew and grew, heightening in a feverish pitch, until she shut her eyes and plugged her ears, wishing it would stop.

Cara woke suddenly, her limbs glued by sweat to the litter. She shook her head to dislodge the dream. It drifted away, back to the realm of her unconsciousness. Her calf burned, though not as horribly as before, and though she wanted nothing more than to sleep, she found she couldn't ignore her heart's racing. She sat up as best she could and looked around.

A few scholars huddled by a fire, and Alex and Sandu sat nearby. Cara made a noise, and her friends turned to her.

"You're awake," Sandu said. He held out a skin of water.

"We set your leg as best we could; you were in and out. I'm afraid our only potion to ease your pain is quite unpleasant,"

Alex said. "But I'm glad to see you awake."

"What happened?" Cara croaked, her throat still parched even after the refreshing water.

"He stole everything," Alex said, his face crestfallen. "All our scrolls, our books. Most of the horses ran off or were killed...and many good men died. "

Cara swallowed past a sudden rage, and pushed down the beast. "What do we do now?"

"My men will return to Mott to recuperate and research. We three push on for Riverfen and tell the earl."

"And then we kill the Hooded Man," Cara said, half to herself. She ignored her friend's worried looks. *I'm going to rip him limb from limb, and then I'm going to throw him to the prowlers.* The beast assented, and for once Cara didn't feel repulsed. She remembered her own brutality in the battle, but didn't regret it. After all, Merick had trained her well, preparing her to kill or be killed. *And the beast slowed time.* She wondered at that, and resolved to ask Alex in the morning.

CHAPTER TWENTY-EIGHT
Jagger

JAGGER KILLED for the first time at thirteen years old. The owner of two new stumps where his pinkies had once been – stumps that still bled and caused him to cry out in the night – he had come across a beggar wrapped in blankets clutching an entire loaf of fresh bread. Jagger's stomach hurt, for he hadn't eaten in days, and his limbs shivered from the cold. He had asked the old man to share, but the man refused. Jagger's hands moved as if of their own accord, and he watched in fascination as his fingers closed around the man's throat and choked him until his lips turned blue and his eyes rolled back into his head.

Jagger took the blankets and the man's ratted coat, feasting that night on good bread.

He had always been good at killing. Liked it sometimes, too, when the Shivs turned to him because he was the only man good enough to track and hit the mark. At least he'd been paid for it then.

Now, Jagger was more bloodhound than human. The beauties of the autumn world meant nothing to him. He trailed his prey with supernatural intensity, his inner compass an inerrant guide. It was for good reason that he had gained a reputation as inescapable back in his prime. His knives remained satiated, for he killed nearly every Realm's Protector he came across; a swift slash of the throat or a blade in the back did the job quickly and quietly. Thoughts like *How many widows have I created?* or *Perhaps that man had nothing to do with the Daggenhelm massacre* flitted only briefly through his mind, but he paid them no heed. He'd made widows before. Like a dog, he didn't consider the consequences of his actions. His task became mindless, something he did only to further his goal: ride, kill, seek, kill, drink, ride.

He tore through the mountains and valleys, through Mott, and to the hill overlooking the swamp. His quarry was near, and Jagger felt his fingers tingle with the promise of blood. He spurred his horse down the mountain, uncaring of its sweat and lather.

The horse died from under him in the swamp, and he went forward on foot, ignoring the aches in his legs and pain in his chest.

Darkness had fully descended when he arrived in the town at the middle of the swamp. His sore feet carried him into the bunkhouse. As soon as he had a beer in hand, he asked about Sandu

The owner scratched his chin doubtfully. "Lots of folk passing through. Plenty of young men in the Mott caravan." He turned to a few scholars huddling together. "Some came back, said there was some sort of attack."

Jagger scanned the scholars, but Sandu wasn't among them. He paid for his drink and settled back to watch the bedraggled group. They spoke nervously to each other, jumping at every little sound. When one of them stood and went upstairs, Jagger followed. He saw a door close, and before it could be locked, he shoved it open.

The scholar went sprawling. Jagger shut the door behind him and drew a knife.

"Who are you?" the scholar asked fearfully. "I don't have any money–"

"Not here for money," Jagger said. He knelt over the man, letting his knife trail along the man's leg. "I want information."

The scholar spluttered, and Jagger laid a hand to the man's shoulder. "I hear you've been traveling with a man named

Sandu Crin."

Jagger pressed the knife harder against the man's breeches, letting them rip just a little. The scholar yelped. Jagger waited. After a moment, the man stammered, "He...he was with us. A guest of our lord's."

"Where is he now?"

"They made camp in the swamp," the scholar said. "After the attack, the woman was injured. They're staying there until she's fit to travel."

"How many are with them?"

"Just my lord. He sent the rest of us back."

Jagger contemplated the man's words. Fear could make a man babble, but this scholar seemed to be telling the truth. After a little more thought, Jagger nodded and stood. "Better clean yourself. Your friends will notice your wet breeches."

With that, Jagger turned and left the blubbering scholar.

His hands sweated, and he felt the familiar burning ache in his stomach that marked whenever his prey was at hand. He would not rest tonight, not until Sandu's neck was between his fingers. For a second, the Valadi girl's accusing eyes tangled themselves in his mind, but he shoved them aside brusquely. No need to think about her now.

Even as night closed about him, Jagger hunted. He walked along the damp path, straining through the darkness for signs of life. His stumps tingled. A nauseous lump rose in his throat, threatening to choke him. Strange. He'd never felt sick about killing before.

Voices called to him from the misty swamp. He knew the tales; hell, he'd sent some to the mist-folk himself. Jagger shook off their cries and kept going.

Then he saw Raven. She stood, ethereal and perfect, on the road before him, her dark hair floating in the breeze. Jagger stopped still, drinking in the sight of her.

"You'll not drive me off the road," he said at last when the mist-folk didn't speak. *Don't mean I can't enjoy seeing her again.*

"Killing him won't bring me back," said mist-Raven.

"It'll make me feel a fair sight better," Jagger grunted. He cringed back as the mist-folk stepped forward. She laid a hand to his coat, and he started. Mist-folk touches were chill as death, but her hand felt warm.

She cupped his face, and Jagger stared at her. "Is it...is it really you?"

"Remember when you first met Sandu?" asked Raven. Jagger nodded...

...Jagger watched the new peddler curiously, his fingers twirling a knife under the table. It was a habit he'd picked up a while ago, a sort of physical distraction while he thought. The peddler always had a smile on his fresh cheeks, but there was something deeper to him: in the way he held his cards – close to his chest, his fingers gripping them tightly – and the way he quaffed his drink as only a man running from his sorrows can. Yes, there was something more to him than merely a carefree demeanor.

"Mind if I join?" Jagger asked, pulling a chair to the table occupied by the new peddler and three others. All but the peddler were hardened Shiv men: Ipter was a burglar, Yennef a forger, and Orien a cold-hearted mercenary. The peddler seemed a hen in a fox's lair.

Orien dealt a new hand. "We're playing Yennef's version: princess takes high card, and soldier yields to merchant. How much you in for?"

"A round of drinks to start," Jagger said. He gave a tight-lipped smile; he and Orien had notoriously failed to maintain civility for years.

"Pity your woman won't let you gamble more," Orien snickered.

It was bait, and Jagger knew it. But he didn't quite like the mercenary taking jabs at Raven. His smile widened a touch. "Pity you won't be able to pay your whores after you lose."

Orien's expression darkened. "Tread carefully, Cross. The walkways are slippery after the rain. It'd be a shame if you were to slip, but you're a known drunkard. No one would be surprised. And who'd be there to comfort your poor, grieving widow?"

Jagger snorted. "As if to suggest any woman would sleep with you without coin."

"And after she's had a giant, she wouldn't want a man lacking

endowment." This – to Jagger's surprise – from the peddler. All the men stared at him, Orien too shocked to make threats. The peddler shrugged. "That is, of course, if what they say of tall men is true."

A moment of silence, then Jagger laughed, long and loud. Yennef chuckled with him, while Ipter only gave a weak grin. Orien stood abruptly, mumbling something about grabbing more beer.

"What was your name again?" Jagger asked at last after his laughter subsided.

"Sandu Crin," the peddler said.

Jagger took Sandu's outstretched hand, and felt as if he might actually have a friend in that godforsaken hellhole.

Some quinns later, Sandu clunked his plate down next to Jagger's. Without so much as a "hello," he dove into the meat and potatoes as if he hadn't eaten in a month.

"Slow down there, Sandu," Raven said, laughing. Jagger's shoulders loosened ever so slightly at the beautiful sound. She continued, "Are you getting ready for winter or something?"

Sandu shook his head, his cheeks ballooned out like a chipmunk's. Jagger laughed. Now he was thinking up similes...whatever next?

Jagger shoved a full cup at Sandu. "Saved some of the good stuff for you."

Sandu took it and quaffed a large mouthful. Music drifted over the full dining hall, and Jagger relaxed. Something about the lad made him feel untroubled. It could be Sandu's easy smile, or how Jagger felt at ease with him. He found himself telling more jokes, being less cross with the other Shivs, and looking forward more and more to Sandu's visits.

In bed that night, Raven's head cupped against his shoulder, Jagger sighed deeply. Not the sort of sigh one has when one feels weary or overcome by some inner tragic thought, but the sigh of contentment. Raven noticed – as she always did – and asked, "Are you bothered by something?"

"No. I'm happy for once, if you can believe it."

Raven's piercing eyes met his in the darkness. "No one else here would, but I do. You've livened up quite a bit since Sandu came along. He's good for you. Better than I am." This was said without bitterness. Jagger would have cut a man for claiming his wife had a bitter bone in her.

"You're pretty damn good. Should I marry him instead?"

"Maybe it'd help you not be such a grouch all the time. He brings out that side of you that you've only been like with me. If I didn't know you better, I'd say you love him."

Jagger frowned a little. Love? Until he met Raven, he never knew what the word meant. No parents had been there to love him, no kindly curates shared the love of the gods with him. Love was Raven's arms, her smile, her laughter, the scent of her neck as he kissed her, the way she stroked his hair when he couldn't control the hurt and rage anymore...

"I don't think so," Jagger said slowly, really mulling over her words. "Love is you. It can't be anything else."

"You can love more than one person, you know."

"Can I?" he said, bringing her down to kiss him. She tasted of skin and warmth, her long hair falling onto his cheeks, and for a moment, like so many moments with her, he could pretend he wasn't the Heartless.

But the next evening, sitting alone with Sandu in a corner of the mess hall and drinking, Jagger felt himself relax. His hands weren't balled into fists, the ache that lived in his temple had left for a time, and he kept laughing. Days were once when he'd laugh less than once a month, and now he was doing it multiple times in one evening.

As the night drew longer and darker, and the hall's occupants ebbed and flowed in their comings and goings, Jagger felt his head light with drink. Usually, when he'd had as many ales as he had, he would descend into cycles of anger, guilt, and doubt. Even Raven couldn't help him then. But the lightness this time came with a whirring dizziness that made him feel buoyant and happy, and a recollection of the good times he'd lived through, few though they were.

"How'd you come here?" Jagger asked Sandu, his head leaning close.

"I was hired as a peddler."

"But how'd you come to be a peddler? It's a lonely life on the road, going where people don't want to go in winter. Why'd you do it?"

There was something distant in Sandu's eyes. His words slurred,

"I...I need the coin. For my father. And for Tambrey. For the twins. If I can pay off my father's debt — my debt, really — then maybe I can go home."

"Tambrey? The twins?"

"My wife and children," Sandu smiled sadly. "Eaton and Elvy, a twin boy and girl. They're six this year. And Tambrey, the girl from the harvest who fell in love with me. I couldn't believe she wanted to marry me. And then she gave me children, both blonde like their mother."

Jagger couldn't picture Sandu with a wife and children, living in a little house with chickens in the yard. Normally, he wouldn't give a rat's ass about anyone else's miserable life. But this was Sandu. He asked, "What happened? Why'd you leave them?"

"She made me. The bairns were only about two when she threw me from the house. She said a blacksmith offered her a bigger house and more land to tend, promised he wouldn't gamble away everything he made, that he'd adopt the children as his own if I disappeared. Then the debt collectors came and Tambrey was done with me. She told the children and everyone else that I was dead." Sandu's head sunk to his chest, his eyes watering with memories. "I haven't seen them since. I was destitute, I'd lost everything I'd worked for, I hadn't a penny for myself much less for them. It had been so perfect. But I ruined it."

Jagger nodded. Without Raven, he'd have killed himself a long time ago. Or killed everyone else in the place. He couldn't imagine her forcing him to abandon their family, to claim him as dead to their children. The thought choked any words from his throat.

Sandu was still talking — rambling, more like — his words coming faster and more desperate. "I keep thinking, if I just make enough money, if I just prove myself, I can get them back. I'd ride in on Galen, with a new saddle and a nice wool shirt, a bag of gold at my hip. I'd free my father, and he'd come with me to that bastard's house, and I'd sweep Tambrey from her chair and lift her up. She'd smile and laugh and tell me how much she'd missed me, how the children begged for me each night, how the man she married was horrible to her and that she'd do anything to have me back. Sometimes I even think about changing my route to pass through Dunfrey so I can get a glimpse of them."

"Life can't ever go back," Jagger said, feeling more sage than he *was. "You can't forget her giving you the boot, and she can't forget what you did to deserve it."*

"I know. But maybe she can forgive. I already forgave her, a hundred times over. I've forgiven her for every cross word she spoke to me."

"But you've not forgiven yourself."

"No," Sandu said. "I don't think I ever can."...

...Jagger remembered that conversation from so long ago. That night, he'd gone up to his room and kissed Raven so deeply, she couldn't help but know how much he loved and appreciated her. He promised himself he'd drink less, for her sake. But then the fire came.

"Sandu took you from me," Jagger said to Raven's ghostly form. "He cried on my shoulder for losing his family – his own fault, too – and then took you from me. He don't deserve forgiveness, from me or anyone else."

Raven only looked sadly at him, then the mist swirled around her and she vanished. Jagger let out his breath, his hands shaking. *I am going mad*, he thought. *And they say the only cure for madness is murder.*

At last he spied a small camp just off the side of the road, its fire dying to embers and its three occupants stirring restlessly in their blankets. Their horse lifted its head but didn't make a sound. Jagger crept forward, the soggy grass underfoot dampening the sound of his footfalls, a knife already glinting in his hand.

Sandu moaned softly in his sleep, then turned away from Jagger, his hands unconsciously pulling his blanket tighter. The knife poised above the sleeping man didn't move, and Jagger hesitated. Sandu had done everything he had for the love of his family. Wouldn't Jagger have done the same and more to get Raven back? Hadn't Jagger already done worse in the name of revenge?

He looked up to see Raven watching him from the woods.

Slowly, very slowly, Jagger lowered the knife and stepped back. He went instead to the sleeping woman – *bitch sliced me open* – and grabbed her from her blankets. Her eyes flew open, and she struggled. Her splinted leg caught in the blanket. Jagger put his knife against her neck.

The other men startled at the noise and yelled, but they froze when they saw Jagger holding Cara. Sandu held up his hands.

"Jagger, please," Sandu said. "Don't hurt her."

With one hand holding the knife and the other squeezing Cara's hands behind her back, Jagger looked from Sandu to the stranger. "I won't. But I need somethin' from you."

"Kill me, but leave her alone."

"Oh no, I'm not goin'ta kill you yet," Jagger said, grinning. He adjusted his grip on the squirming Cara. "First you tell me what happened in Daggenhelm. Hm? Tell your little friends what happened there."

"He already told me!" Cara spat. "I know you blame him–"

"He lies," Jagger hissed in her ear. He looked to Sandu, and moved his knife so that the blade flashed in the firelight. "Tell her."

Sandu looked to his other friend, then faced Jagger and Cara. He ran his hands through his hair, and said, "I betrayed him, Cara."

Jagger's hands twitched. It felt so good to finally hear the truth from the traitor's lips. "Tell her more."

"He and his wife were my friends, but I was paid to find Jagger and kill him. I couldn't bring myself to do it, so I sold them out to the Protectors. It's my fault they're all dead."

Cara stiffened in Jagger's hands.

"That can't be true," she whispered.

"And why are you with her?" Jagger asked. "Surely you're not the type to go adventuring for the joy of it."

Sandu's face fell, and guilt washed over him. It took everything in Jagger not to hoot in delight. Sandu said, "You're my next bounty. But I tried to give up the job. I didn't want to betray you, too."

"Betrayed his father, his wife and children, me and Raven, and now you, too," Jagger said in Cara's ear. "And now he's going to pay the price for it."

Jagger shoved Cara at the other man, and they crashed to the ground together. Cara let out a yelp of pain. Before Sandu could react, Jagger grabbed him. He held his knife to the traitor's neck and turned to the other two.

"I'm taking him with me," Jagger said. "If you try to follow, I'll kill him and then you, too. If you leave us, I'll let you live."

With Sandu at knifepoint, Jagger left the campsite and delved further into the woods with his prey. Once he found a hidden spot, he tied Sandu to a tree, then took out a knife and began to sharpen it. Raven's ghostly face stared sadly at him, but he only smiled at it. Justice would be his. All would soon be right in the world.

CHAPTER TWENTY-NINE
Sandu

THE RAG IN Sandu's mouth tasted of sweat, dirt, and blood. His limbs cramped, held in place by rough rope. Sandu struggled a little, but knew it was fruitless.

Jagger knew how to keep his prey bound and ready for slaughter.

The sinister sound of knife scraping whetstone disturbed the otherwise peaceful night. Jagger sat nearby, intent on his work, his lank blonde hair hiding his face. The swamp around them was dark as a void, their small fire's glow only barely touching the tree trunks.

This is the night I die, Sandu realized. He slumped onto the ground, allowing himself to picture Tambrey and the twins, to remember their warmth and giggles and cozy home on the outskirts of Dunfrey. He cried as quietly as he could, grieving that Eaton and Elvy would never see him again, never know how much their father loved them. He thought of his father, stuck in the dungeons until the end of his days, unable to pay off his son's debt and live once more as a free man. The gag stifled the gasps that Sandu wanted to let out.

But he made enough noise for Jagger's head to snap up, his fierce blue eyes focusing on Sandu. Jagger stood, twirling the knife in his hand, and came around the fire. Sandu braced himself, ready for the cold steel. *Do it quickly, please. Surely we respect each other enough to give me a quick death?* Sandu shut his eyes.

"Look at me." Jagger knelt in front of Sandu, his face dark with the fire behind him.

Sandu peered up at his old friend, his throat closing up with fear. There was madness in Jagger's eyes.

Jagger stuck his knife in the dirt and removed the gag from Sandu's mouth before rocking back on his heels. Sandu licked his dry lips and spat out the rag's flavor. He dared not speak.

"I've had a lot of time to think about you," Jagger said in a strangely friendly tone, "during the deshes while I've hunted you. Imagined killing you. Lots of memories, too. We had a good time in Daggenhelm, didn't we? But now you're with new friends to betray for coin." Jagger stared into the woods. "I killed a whole Valadi tribe in my hunt for you. All of them Gallish bastards, no better than worms."

Jagger paused, then asked, "Why'd you do it?"

Sandu swallowed hard before he answered, "I needed the money for my father. But I've felt awful ever since, like I've betrayed my own family."

"Hm. Strange, that. I never felt remorse myself, though I am sorry for bringing Dilara into this." Jagger waved his hand distractedly. *Jagger never apologizes for anything,* Sandu thought. The tall man looked out into the swamp, but Sandu couldn't see anything. After a moment, Jagger said to the trees, "I'm doing what has to be done."

"What?"

"Hm?" Jagger plucked the knife from the ground and twirled it around. Sandu cringed away, his eyes following the moving blade. Jagger spoke as if he hadn't noticed Sandu's discomfort. "Raven liked you. She said once that I loved you, that you made me happy when even she couldn't. I didn't believe her."

Sandu tensed, sure that the blow would come any moment.

"I've had time to think about her, though, and you," Jagger continued. "I put the burden of my happiness on her, and she must have been so chuffed that you took some of it. You made me laugh for candles on end, and that's not something anyone else can claim. Not even her."

The knife spun and whirled through Jagger's fingers, but there was no anger, no hatred, in Jagger's voice. Madness lurked in his eyes, but it was of grief and resignation, the sort of madness only seen in those men who have found nothing in the world to live for.

Why did he go to these lengths to find and capture me if he doesn't mean to kill me?

"I've killed so many people," Jagger muttered. "Old, young, married, widowed, didn't matter to me. I was damn good at it, and it kept me and Raven fed and sheltered. I had my chance to kill you, and I didn't take it." His stricken eyes were haunting. "Why didn't I just kill you and be done with it, Sandu? Hm? Yours was just another throat to slit, something I've done more times than I've sung a song, and I couldn't do it. Listen to me, babbling on, when I haven't spoken this much since I was a kid. It's the end of my life, Sandu, and I think I've got some things to say before I go."

The fire flickered as a branch snapped in it. Sandu's heartbeat had slowed as Jagger spoke, and he licked his lips again.

"Do you believe that all the bad things in your life catch up to you eventually?" Jagger asked. "I didn't think the gods cared all that much for us down below; after all, I murdered my way through more years than some people get to live for. But maybe they were just waiting, biding their time for me to get my due punishment. They waited until Raven and I were near ready to leave the Shiv, to start our own lives away from all of that, and then they took her. You were just their tool. Well, I've learned my lesson. I'm done with it all."

Jagger leaned forward, his knife poised. Sandu gasped and tried to scoot back, but Jagger grasped him firmly on the back of the neck. Yet the cold slice into flesh never came. Jagger's blade swept through the rope, and Sandu was suddenly free.

Rubbing his arms and legs, Sandu inched away from Jagger. He froze as Jagger leveled the knife at his neck.

"There's one more thing you can do for me," Jagger growled. "I'm not goin'ta kill you, see? The gods took Raven from me, but they used you to do it. Wouldn't it be fitting for you to finish the job? Take husband and wife to Autorus." Jagger once again stared off into the trees. "Not much longer, love, and I'll be with you."

Sandu's mouth dropped open. *He's really gone mad.* He swallowed heavily, his normal witty replies dried up. What could he say? *Sure, old friend, I'd love to off you!* And what if he refused? Would Jagger kill him then?

Desperate to avoid any more guilt on his conscience, Sandu said, "Death isn't a way out anymore, Jagger. Look at the prowlers. Autorus isn't kind anymore to those wanting to pass through his gates. You could be stuck in an even worse limbo, far away from Raven's spirit. It's not the right way."

But Jagger ignored his pleas. Thrusting the knife handle into Sandu's unwilling hands, Jagger stood, his arms wide. "Strike quickly and be done with it. Let me die."

Sandu had no intent to kill him. With a quick movement he tossed the knife into the woods, then scrambled to his feet and said, "You need help, Jagger. You need a curate or a healer. I'm not going to kill you."

"Even now, you torture me further!" Jagger yelled back, dropping his arms. "There's nothing here for me without her. Can't you see that? There's n–"

Jagger stilled, his head swiveling, eyes widening. He took a step away from the fire and Sandu, his hands raised in a supplicatory way. He nodded, and said, "You're right. It'll be easier this way."

"Jagger..." Sandu moved closer to his old friend.

"Shh. Do you hear her? She's calling for me." Jagger's eyes glazed over, his whole body relaxing.

"There's nothing out–" Sandu started, but then he saw the ghostly form in the dark woods. The mist-folk. Rushing forward, Sandu grabbed at Jagger's arm. "It's the mist-folk, not her!"

Jagger threw him off as easily as a bear would a rabbit.

"She's out there. She's beckoning to me." Turning to Sandu, he smiled gently. The expression was unsettling on his scarred, pockmarked face. "I'm ready to go to her."

Sandu protested and tried to stop him, but Jagger merely swatted him away like a fly before running into the dark forest. Sandu heard the crunch of fallen leaves and the squelch of mud as Jagger disappeared from sight. For a moment, Sandu stood still, warring with himself.

"Veck," he muttered before he dove into the forest after Jagger.

The large man didn't bother to be quiet as he plunged into the marsh. Sandu caught up with him quickly and shouted, "Jagger! Come back! Please. You don't have to do this."

Jagger turned, still with that strange, soft smile. Behind him, grasping hands emerged from the water, reaching for his old friend.

"Come on!" Sandu called. He clutched a branch and held out his other hand. "Take my hand!" It felt all too familiar to losing Galen. Sandu blinked back tears and reached as far as he could go.

In the ghostly light of the mist-folk, Jagger almost looked radiant. He looked to Sandu, his blonde hair glowing, his blue-gold eyes holding no scorn or wrath. It looked like years had melted from him.

"Take my hand," Sandu urged again. "Please."

A warm hand rested on Sandu's arm. He twisted to see Raven, pale and lovely, her form ethereal. But she didn't look like the mist-folk; something was different about her. Sandu gaped, sure that he, too, had gone mad.

"Let him go," Raven said. "He must do this to find me again."

"But...you're dead," Sandu said. She nodded gravely and looked to Jagger. Sandu stared between them, feeling the warmth of affection that passed from living to dead. Raven walked to Jagger and rested a hand on his cheek.

"I'll see you soon," Jagger said.

She gently kissed him. "I wish it were so. When the blind

man comes, say yes."

Sandu could only watch as Jagger closed his eyes and fell backwards into the swamp, the mist-folk pulling him under. He stared at the empty water, his grief catching in his throat. When Raven turned back to him, he asked, "Why did you let him die?"

"It was necessary. And for what it's worth, Sandu...I forgive you." Raven smiled at him, then vanished into the mist.

For a long time, Sandu waited by the edge of the marsh, sure that his friend would reemerge. But when no signs of life came, he trudged back to where Jagger had first brought him.

Silence filled the night save for the crackling of the lonely fire. Sandu slumped on the edge of the firelight, his throat tightening with a hundred emotions. Relief, anger, confusion, shock, grief; all warred inside his breast, each anxious to make itself known. He didn't know how Raven had come, or why she'd let Jagger die.

Sandu sat awake the rest of the night, feeding the fire and remembering all those he had lost. First his wife and bairns, then his father, now Jagger. And Cara knew the truth of his bounty, too. Even if he found her and Alex again, would she take him back? Or would she send him away as Tambrey had?

The mist-folk started their cries again. Pushing his back against the wide tree trunk, Sandu plugged his ears and ignored them. They took Galen and Jagger, but they wouldn't take him. He sent up a silent prayer, to Autorus or the gods or whoever actually listened: *Take care of Jagger for me. Help me get out of these forsaken woods.*

PART TWO

CHAPTER THIRTY
Seanna

"DO TRY and remain civil, Seanna," Henrik said. He waited impatiently at the doorway with an extended arm while Seanna slowly adjusted her crown in the mirror and admired her reflection. She didn't look at him.

"Please, just try to be an obedient queen. I want no discussion of the Exalt, the trade disputes with Dedaria, or anything at all controversial. Speak politely of the weather, the upcoming Masque, parties you've attended, anything that can't be used against you. Rask is watching the both of us, and you cannot be the weakest leg of the throne." Henrik sounded tired, as if the woes of the kingdom followed him no matter where he traveled. Seanna spared him a glance, pursed her lips, then placed a hand in the crook of his arm and fixed a smile on her cheeks.

Henrik didn't move. "Seanna," he said in a warning tone. "Tell me that you will say nothing foolish tonight."

"I promise to say nothing to embarrass myself," Seanna said. "For once, we agree. Rask is no man to be trifled with." Inwardly, she promised to ruin the old earl. First, though, she must learn his weaknesses; then, she could exploit him.

Egil Rask had finally arrived in Riverfen for the Masque. He was the last of the earls to grace the Strilu doorstep, and so Druam had arranged a feast to officially welcome all the highest lords in the land. Not one had declined his invitation.

The king and queen were the last to arrive in the feast hall, appearing the joyous couple that many still believed them to be. They smiled and waved at the courtiers before proceeding to the crowded high table to join the earls and their wives. Egil Rask had been given the seat of honor to Henrik's right, with his wife beside him; next to Lady Hjalder were Druam and Gwen. Earl and Lady Stonetree were seated to Seanna's left, and Seanna's father, Ulmer Aylmer, the Earl of Stillmeadow, sat at the end of the table.

Seanna paused at her father's seat to give him a swift kiss on the cheek; it had been a long time since she had seen him. Nearing sixty, he was still a stout man, though his hair and beard had turned grey.

"Is Mother still ill?" Seanna asked, lingering behind him. Her mother had not come to Riverfen, electing instead to stay in their home city of Brin.

Her father patted her hand. "That's the claim she made. Your mother is the healthiest woman I've ever met, and gods only know why she mysteriously turns ill whenever an occasion comes up that she has no interest in attending." He winked at her, and Seanna returned it before following Henrik to her seat.

Egil Rask nodded to Seanna, then proceeded to ignore both her and Henrik. Henrik frowned, but then plastered on a wide smile and stood to address the crowd. They quieted as he raised his hands.

"Our friends, lords, countrymen! We have gathered from all over Dotschar to celebrate a hundred years of peace in our kingdom." A round of applause followed this. Nobles clapped each other's backs and raised their cups. *As if they're the ones who did anything to keep the peace these hundred years. The only one with any sort of claim to long term plans is Rask,* Seanna thought derisively. Henrik continued, "Many thanks to our generous host, Earl Seastone, and a congratulations on his new marriage; may she bear you many sons." There were some murmurs amidst the polite clapping. In a somber tone, Henrik said, "But there is growing strife in our kingdom. We have noticed the deaths from plague and the fear surrounding the rising threat of the prowlers. We have heard the cries of our people and seen the graves filling our cemeteries. In this historic moment, we will do all we can to speak with your people, to meet with lords great and small, and to work to create another hundred years of peace!"

It was a good speech, Seanna granted him that. She smiled serenely, as a good queen should, while the nobles downed their wine and mead. Henrik sat back down with a hint of smugness, then dove into his food. Picking at her own plate, Seanna let herself daydream about Maeria. She could see the blonde woman in the crowd, laughing and joking with those around her. It delighted Seanna to have such a beautiful young lady in her circle, and to have the ears of Maeria's friends in court. During the days while the men sat in council, the number of ladies gathering at Seanna's side grew and grew. Seanna eyed Rask's diminutive wife. *Gain her trust, and I'll have an ally close to my enemy.*

Seanna was pulled from her thoughts when she heard her name.

"–Queen Seanna is certainly a beauty, though I think that will fade as soon as the baby comes," Rask said, loudly enough for the whole high table to hear. "Not one of my wives retained their looks after childbirth, but at least they had wit to comfort me on cold nights!" He gave a barking laugh.

Seanna smiled as blithely as she could, though inside she fumed. Henrik didn't look at her, but he also didn't laugh nervously with some of the other lords. Instead, Henrik said to Rask, "Your daughter was both a lasting beauty and possessed a becoming wit, Earl Hjalder. I wish she had borne me sons to carry on our combined bloodlines."

"Yes. A pity." Rask's frown turned sour. "Though, given her past difficulties, I would not be so sure of your current queen's ability to produce any heir, much less a son. How many miscarriages has it been now? Three? Four?"

"Two," Seanna muttered, rubbing her stomach protectively. *Damn him, why won't Henrik stand up to this foul man?*

But Henrik merely sipped his wine. "The gods have their plans, Egil. I gratefully accept what is given to me, and pray that it is to the benefit of my kingdom."

"Bullshit," Seanna's father sputtered, dribbling mead into his beard. "Have a spine, man! My daughter the queen is no worse than yours, Rask, and you damn well know it. Insulting her to her face as if she's supposed to lay down and take it? Fleta was a dreadful flirt, and quite rude to those she deemed beneath her. Much like her troll of a father."

"You're drunk," Seanna hissed at her father. To the table at large, she said, "This is a day of celebration and joy! Why quibble over the past when we can look to the future?"

"What future? The one your Eadron spawn will drag us into?" Rask tore into a chunk of meat, his expression clearly showing that he wished to similarly tear into Seanna's flesh. "I'll be damned before I have one of those brown bastards as my king."

"You'll be dead before then," Seanna spat at him.

"I've outlived every wife, and I'll outlive you, too. Many women die in childbirth. And then who shall our king marry? Some guttersnipe with a pretty face and wealthy father?"

"Enough," Henrik said. "You reach too far, Rask. Let bygones be bygones, and enjoy the meal Druam has so kindly paid for."

Druam, who so far had remained quiet, acknowledged the king's words with a small toast. He looked worn through, like clothing that had been laid in the sun every day for a decade. Seanna had not spoken to him since she had lied about Gwen's affair; had he had a falling out with his wife? But Gwen smiled and laughed next to him; so why did he look so troubled?

The high table returned to idle banter. Seanna half-listened to the conversations. Earl Stonetree stood to make his rounds among the lords, and Ulmer soon took his seat. His nose had turned red, his cheeks rosy above his bushy beard. His breath smelled of mead.

"I'm sorry that that man treats you so badly," Ulmer said softly; Seanna strained to hear him over the crowd.

"Rask? He is a worm, nothing more."

"No, not him, my dear. The king. We shouldn't have married you off to him so young, and him still mourning poor Fleta. He's never healed from her death, and he's a bad husband now because of it."

"Hush, Father," Seanna warned, glancing at Henrik. Fortunately, he paid them no heed. "I am finely treated."

"You're miserable. I've only seen you smile once tonight. A real smile, I mean. I worry for you, Seanna. I thought your sister had the worst marriage to that dreadful Vladimir fellow, but they suit each other. You and Henrik are too similar, I think. Stubborn to a fault." He paused. "Lesser men than the king have beaten their wives to death."

"He's not going to beat me to death."

"No? Have a history book read to you, then. King Iverran executed three wives over the years. Do you think any court in this land would touch the king if the same happened to you? Hm? No, they would simply force him to pray for forgiveness, then give him a new wife to spit out his heirs."

Seanna glanced away from her father's concerned look. Henrik wouldn't have the nerve to kill her, even in his rage. Taking Ulmer's hand, Seanna said, "Trust me, Father. I won't die by such a common thing. I carry the king's son, and when I have given him an heir, I will be untouchable. Though sometimes I wish I could have had as happy a marriage as you and Mother, this is the lot the gods have given me. Sometimes we must sacrifice happiness for power. I fully intend to use my role to widen our family's reach."

"I have failed as a father," Ulmer said, "if that is what you believe this life to be about." He tottered drunkenly away, and Seanna wondered if she had seen a tear in his eye.

Later that night, alone in her bedchamber, Seanna thought about Rask. She had tried to win him to her side, but he scorned her and insulted her. Well, if that was how it was to be, she would play his little game. She called her most trusted servant and said, "I need you to do something for me, Ralston. Find out all you can about Egil Rask: his family, his connections, his opinions on matters great and small...everything you overhear, bring it to me. There will be extra gold tallied to your payment each deshe if you do this correctly."

The servant nodded, bowed, and darted away. He was a man in his middling age, good at his job and perfectly unnoticeable. No one would think twice if they saw him scurrying about.

Though midnight quickly approached, Seanna wasn't tired. She brought a steward to her drawing room, and there ordered him to write dozens of invitations, letters of welcome, congratulations, and regards. These she marked with her signet and sent off. When she finally went to bed, Seanna imagined Rask and Henrik kissing her feet as she drifted to sleep.

The next morning as Seanna ate, her reliable Ralston gave his first report. "My eyes and ears are still looking into Earl Hjalder, but I have heard dissenters speaking against you in the corridors, Your Grace. Lord Kellag of Haversdeep and Lady Fawin of Olwer both claimed you to be weak-willed and pathetic for supporting Predicant Manderly. I have since learned that Lord Kellag is a known gambler and lost half his estate to a merchant; no one knows except his servants. Lady Fawin is pregnant, but her aging lord husband is not the father; rumors say that she slept with the steward on multiple occasions."

"Excellent." Seanna sipped at her wine. "Anyone else?"

Ralston smiled. "How much time do you have, Your Grace?" He spent the next half a candle detailing the affairs, failures, and secrets of a dozen nobles, all of whom had spoken out against Seanna in some form or another. Seanna memorized every one.

"Where did you get this information?" she asked after he had finished.

"Servants, kitchen girls, guards...I have spent my working life hearing these rumors, and I remembered them all. For people such as Earl Hjalder, I will have to take more time and finesse to eke out the scandals, but rest assured, it will be done."

"Good. Find out all you can about Rask. Report to me each morning."

"It will be done, Your Grace."

CHAPTER THIRTY-ONE
Gwen

EACH MORNING Gwen woke feeling a vigor she had never known before. It had been over a quinn since she showed Druam her magic, and she practiced every day. As she cast more workings, her Gaiar grew from an ember in her belly to a near-constant fire that she felt every waking moment. Pulling from it now was much easier, and she had quickly progressed to some higher workings. She had grown beyond Mavian's own skill, so he merely studied her: her technique, her chants, her slurred words – everything she did, he made note of.

After kissing Druam, who still lay sleepily on the bed, Gwen dressed in a simple gown and hurried to the old wing. She found Mavian already there poring over a new tome. He looked up when she entered. "Look here – I've found a book in this wing. It mostly has cantrips, but there are a couple of higher workings that you could try. One of them is fascinating: it allows you to open a 'door,' so to speak, and step from one place to another. You could travel from here to your rooms in the span of a second."

As she read over the working, Gwen noticed the many lines of chanting as well as the materials required. "This is more advanced than anything I've done before. Look how meticulous it is: each material is used during a specific place in the working, and there are two pages of chanting. I don't know if I'm ready for it."

"But you don't always use the materials required," Mavian said.

"How do you mean? I thought I always cast my workings as near to written as could be."

"Well...not precisely. There are some I gave to you that I rewrote *without* including the materials. You still successfully cast those." Perusing his notes, Mavian pointed at a page. "See here? I noticed that you managed the cleaning charm without using the feathers that were called for. And here, I presented the 'passing unseen' working to you without telling you that it needed a live ant to be carried by the caster."

"Wouldn't that simply suggest that the workings were written incorrectly? That anyone with magic could cast them as I did?"

"Not necessarily. I've been reading more and more, and I don't think that you're a mage."

Gwen snorted. "Then what, pray tell, am I?"

"A sorceress." Mavian's eyes lit. "Look, I copied a passage here from *Ultar's Methods of Gaiar.* He said that mages and wizards, of any Gaiar, must precisely follow the instructions of a working in order for it to succeed. However, he noted that the sorcerers he'd studied could redo the working in their own style, allowing their more innate powers to guide the spell. It's how new spells are discovered or created: not by wizards, but sorcerers. They can manipulate their Gaiar to a greater extent, accessing Earda's magic in a unique way."

Gwen skimmed his cramped handwriting. "So...because I can cast the workings in a different way, that means I'm a sorceress? You said I could use magic in a unique way...how so?"

"I don't know. There have been very few sorcerers in our time, and the ones from the past like Dabolen Far-Seeing or Titania the Great were quite protective of their secrets. No one has found any of their writings. I met the king's sorceress, Milena Haubin, before she died a few years ago, but she refused to tell me anything more than what I've learned here. I don't know of any other sorcerers in Dotschar."

"Hm. What use is this knowledge if we can't use it? We might as well continue as we were and hope that we find someone who can teach me more."

"Indeed. Do you want to try this working?" Mavian said, referring to the door spell. Gwen set the book in her lap. She whispered through the words, not letting her Gaiar loose just yet. When she felt confident she was pronouncing it correctly, she stood and walked a few paces from the table. With the book in one arm, Gwen lifted her hand and pointed it at a spot in the air. She started the spell, letting the cadence of the words dictate the notes she sang as she went.

The first page went smoothly, her Gaiar easily flowing from her as a rend in the air grew wider and wider. It led into blackness, its edges cracked with flashes of light. As she deepened the working, the spell's words tugged at Gwen's Gaiar, pulling it from her faster than she could stop it. She grew breathless, the words coming now in a faster and faster rush. Her wide eyes sought Mavian and she shook her head. *I can't finish this spell,* she thought in a panic, her Gaiar burning as it left her body.

Mavian stepped quickly to her side and said, "Repeat that last phrase. Hold your Gaiar – don't let the spell take it from you."

Too scared to disobey, Gwen said over and over, "*Yraftei honild ir por, yraftei honild ir por, yrafteir honild ir por.*" Her Gaiar paused, rustling beneath her skin. The working hung in the air, crackling and popping, and she could feel that her magic yearned to go to it. She kept repeating as Mavian put a hand to her arm and chanted a working of his own.

As Mavian spoke, Gwen's Gaiar churned within her, the spell faltering ever so slightly. He fed his scant magic into her. Gwen took it and thought only of severing her tie to the failed working. Mavian's magic traveled down her arm, gathering at her hand. Gwen felt her connection to her Gaiar strengthening. She pulled her magic back into herself, using his working as a conduit. As she did, the portal collapsed in on itself, leaving a pocket of silence. Gwen fell to her hands and knee, gasping.

Mavian removed his working – she felt his magic recede, leaving an intangible hole in her – and sat down beside her.

For a moment, neither said anything. Once she had regained herself, Gwen rocked back onto her bottom. She asked, "What working did you use?"

"A spell of ending. It's meant to help end failed workings before they consume the caster," Mavian said, his voice raw. "Most casters won't attempt anything too difficult without a fellow mage there to help if it goes too far. Every curate and predicant I know has learned it by heart."

"Thank you," Gwen said. "I felt my Gaiar being taken from me, but I couldn't stop it."

"No one caster can stop their own Gaiar once it escapes them. You were lucky; there are others who have died losing their magic."

Movement at the door caught Gwen's attention, and she looked up to see Druam in one of his finer tunics. He quickly took in both Gwen and Mavian's exhaustion, then bent to look closely at Gwen. "You've over-exerted yourself," he said.

"Yes," Mavian answered for her. "I doubt we'll try that one again for awhile."

"Have you forgotten the date, Gwen?" Druam asked, helping her to her feet. "We are to attend Lady Stonetree's birthday festivities."

"I thought that was tomorrow!" Gwen said, mortified. She said to Mavian, "We'll have to practice more at a later time."

"Tomorrow, then," Mavian started, but Druam said over him, "We have yet more engagements for the next quinn, my love. You must postpone your practices for a few days."

"No!" Mavian exclaimed. Gwen and Druam paused, confused. His fingers clenching at his sides, Mavian said, "A quinn will turn into a deshe, and then a month. Who knows what could happen in that time? We need to stay focused."

"Just a few days," Gwen said, though she felt sorry for the stricken look on his face. "Then I'll be back, and we can continue as we were."

"Remember what I said?" Mavian's frustration bled into his

words. "About the dam that will burst?"

"Trust me," Gwen implored. "Nothing will go wrong."

Before Mavian could protest more, Druam took Gwen's hand and led her away. She glanced back at her friend, alarmed. *He's concerned for me, is all*, she thought. His earlier doubt of Druam crept into her head, but she pushed it aside. *I know Mavian lacks for company as much as I do, but I promised Druam I would attend to my duties.*

"What did he mean by 'the dam that will burst'?" Druam asked as Gwen dressed for the party.

"Nothing," Gwen said too quickly. She felt Druam's questioning eyes on her back, but she didn't want to cause strife between them. The small lie weighed on her, but she turned and smiled. "Mavian worries too much sometimes."

Lady Stonetree's party passed quickly. Still fairly shy – and still garnering glares from the other ladies – Gwen stayed with Druam. People crowded around them to listen to Druam's stories, and Gwen reveled in her husband's talent for engaging them.

When they returned to her rooms, they found a bottle of wine with an apology note from Mavian. Gwen and Druam cheered to reconciliation. The sweet liquor washed down any guilt Gwen had felt for his anger, and she resolved to write to him the next day.

In the morning her head felt fuzzy from the evening's festivities, and Gwen completely forgot to write. She spent the entire day in a whirlwind activity: first breakfast with the earls, followed by games in the gardens, then tea, and finally an evening dance that left her thoroughly tired of seeing people.

Though she wanted nothing more than to return to quiet rooms to practice magic, Gwen attended parties at Druam's side and on her own. Her days became a never-ending cycle of eating, dressing, attempting conversation, and drinking. The evenings often went on until past midnight, and she returned to her bed almost too tired to remove her gown and jewels. As the days went on, her appetite waned. She picked at her food, feeling queasy every time she looked at something too rich. *Too many grand feasts*, she thought. *And too much wine.*

On the fifth day, Earl Stillmeadow – the queen's father – invited them to a grand supper. Her face painted with gold, her legs swathed in finest silk and her arms bedecked with jewelry, Gwen should have felt finer than all other women. Yet, as she walked the mosaic corridors, she felt nothing but the churning of her stomach. An ache had developed in her temples, which grew to an incessant beating by evening.

The earl's feast was held in a small banquet hall. Druam found Gwen as soon as she arrived and walked her to their table. Queen Seanna was there, too, resplendent in blue silks and proudly bearing her growing pregnancy. The queen spared only a paltry glance for Gwen before returning her attention to the nobles crowded around her. Each of their faces lifted up to her beaming beauty. She said something, and all laughed at whatever joke she told. Then, Seanna leaned in conspiratorially, glanced pointedly at Gwen, and tittered. The rest whispered to each other, their jewelry flashing as they, too, peeked at Gwen. Her cheeks burning – *I did nothing wrong*, she reminded herself – Gwen stared away from them. The colors and movement in front of her blurred as she retreated into herself.

She found no solace, though, in her internal world. A roiling burst of Gaiar spasmed through her, and she tasted something foul in her mouth. The tempo in her skull heightened, pounding and pounding against every part of her head. Her cheeks flushed, her fingers trembling, Gwen grabbed at the table to stop herself from falling out of her seat. Each limb shook.

"I need to go," Gwen gritted, barely loud enough for Druam to hear.

"Are you well? Gwen?"

She only shook her head, her teeth clenched as she fought to keep down the paltry pieces of food she'd eaten that day. Clutching at Druam's arm, Gwen used him to stand, then leaned against him as they made their way around the sides of the room to the door.

But they didn't quite make it before Gwen shuddered, her throat tight. Her Gaiar pushed against the walls of her body, and she leaned forward. Vomit spewed from her mouth – she could hold back either it or her Gaiar – and coated the sleeve of a nearby nobleman. He shouted in disgust, stepping back as Gwen's stomach emptied itself onto the floor. Desperately, Gwen held back the tides of Gaiar that wanted to burst from her. Her head felt as if it would split in two.

She fell into Druam as his arms encircled her. Her skin was hot and flushed, veins of Gaiar running alongside her blood. Druam carried her from the crowd, the nobles' muffled laughter fading behind them. Soon all Gwen heard were Druam's boots on the floor and the beating of her own heart. She still felt sick, and it was all she could do to not let her magic consume her.

Mavian was right, she thought. *Damn him, he was right.* She would have to apologize to him at some point. Now, though, she must focus on retaining herself, on not letting the tides within overpower her.

The journey to her rooms was horribly long, but at last Druam deposited her on her bed. He dampened a washcloth and pressed it to her forehead, murmuring calming words. Soon after, a curate hurried into the room. He felt Gwen's pulse, pressed cool hands along her arms and neck, and looked in her throat while Druam explained what had happened.

"I don't know what to do for her," Shepherd Marin whispered. "It's not something I've seen before."

"Then don't blather about like an idiot," Druam snapped. "Fetch Avallune. I don't care what he's doing, just bring him at once."

Marin nodded and disappeared. Gwen groaned and tried not to cough. Avallune Martill was a wizard and talented alchemist, though not much of a healer. What Druam thought he could do...Gwen tried not to think about it.

She attempted a smile, but it came out as a grimace instead. When she tried to speak, Druam pressed a finger to her lips and shook his head. "Just rest, my love. Avallune would not dare refuse my summons."

A half-candle passed before Avallune came to Gwen's side. He was a tall man, with a groomed mustache and beard and long hair tied neatly back. His fingertips were warm where he touched Gwen's wrist. Though his lips barely moved, she felt a rush of magic drift through her. Her Gaiar calmed a moment, then pushed at her skin with greater vigor.

"You didn't tell me your wife had magic," Avallune muttered.

"We couldn't risk the knowledge spreading," Druam said.

"Fool," said Avallune. "Something has distressed her Gaiar. How long has it been since she cast a working?"

Druam squeezed Gwen's hand. "A few days, as far as I know."

"Her last spell?"

Gwen tried to respond, but her Gaiar surged again. It took everything inside her not to let it explode from her body.

The wizard moved his fingers up and down Gwen's body. Everywhere his firm hands touched, magic spread out into her skin with a bubbling sensation. Gwen's Gaiar recoiled from the magic, but didn't stop its assault on her. *Make it stop*, she wanted to say. *Please, I just want it to end.* Magic popped under her skin as white blisters spread up her arms and neck.

"Aha!" Avallune exclaimed. He had stopped above Gwen's right side. "Your liver. Whatever it is, it's in there."

"Can you get it out?" Druam's composed expression slipped, showing a fear Gwen had never seen in him before. Her heart hammered, her tongue feeling large in her mouth. *Tell me it will be alright. Tell me it will be over soon.*

"Hold her steady," the wizard said. His sharp eyes met Gwen's. "I'm afraid this will hurt, my lady." Magic crackled at his fingertips as he bent over her once more, his shoulders hunched in concentration.

Avallune's magic seared into Gwen's body. Her back arched, nails digging into the sheets. A cry escaped her lips, and with it a stream of Gaiar. Her magic spun around the room, drawing all the candlelight to it. The room grew dark as the ball of light shot out the balcony doors.

"Hold her mouth shut!" Avallune grunted. With a regretful look, Druam clamped a hand over Gwen's lips.

A battle of magic raged inside Gwen. Her own traitorous Gaiar fought against the wizard's magic even as it was pushed further and further inside her. First her skin burned from the inside, then her veins. Each organ made its own sensation of pain as Gaiar scorched its way past, Avallune's chasing hers to the liver. Gwen convulsed, her eyes fixed on Druam, her only solace in the agony.

Gwen wanted to scream. Her cheeks glistened with tears. Each passing moment brought such new torture that she wished to die and have it over with. All cohesive thought vanished. She twisted and groaned like an animal, desperate to escape.

"Hold on," Druam whispered as Avallune pressed down on her abdomen.

All Gwen's Gaiar condensed in her liver, churning like a hive of wasps that stung her insides. She shivered, her body wracked with torment. Avallune took a deep breath, then curled his fingers against her skin. He spoke quickly, his breath harsh.

The wasps slowed and slowed until they were still. For a brief, wondrous moment, the pain lapsed, and Gwen sobbed in relief. Then Avallune's nails bit into her, and another wave of magic blew through her, far hotter than the one before. Her skin glowed red with the heat. The Gaiar tried to flee, but was trapped within her. Gwen screamed against Druam's hand, and she saw true panic growing in his eyes.

Avallune's chanting grew louder until it was feverish in pitch. His forehead dripped with sweat. Gwen's organs scalded, as if magma was burning through her Gaiar. A dazzlingly bright tear slid down her cheek, then another, as if infused with a star's brilliance.

"Avallune..." Druam said, his skin sparking as her tears touched it.

The wizard didn't respond. He loomed over Gwen, his voice hoarse as he continued his chant. More starlight leaked from her eyes, at first so intense that they lit the room. After a minute, the shining lights diminished, until only Gwen cried with ordinary moisture.

Avallune swallowed hard, his eyes darting to Gwen with an

apologetic look. His voice nearly broke as he started a new spell. Cooling magic ran through Gwen's veins, a balm to the blisters inside and out. In moments, she felt wonderfully numb. Druam gently removed his hand from her mouth and stroked her cheek.

Gwen sobbed with relief. Her Gaiar flowed back to its resting place, calm and serene once more. She grabbed at Druam's hand, though she didn't trust herself to speak yet. The wizard rocked back on his heels and wiped his forehead. His hands shook.

Without the candlelight, the room had grown very dark. Druam stood and began lighting candles. Soft flames soon chased away the shadows. Though each part of her ached, Gwen slowly sat up. The sheets beneath her had been soaked with sweat.

"What...what did you do?" Gwen asked. It came out in a rasp.

Avallune examined his pale hands, as if surprised to have exerted such an effort. "I burned out the impurity."

"Impurity?" Druam returned to the bed and hovered protectively over Gwen.

"A...a poison of some sort which latched onto her magic. I've never seen anything like it before." Avallune settled heavily in a chair. "That's not something I can say every day."

"How did it happen?" Druam demanded. Gwen shivered again, though this time at the thought of a magical poison. Did someone give it to her deliberately?

Avallune shrugged. "It could have been passed through magic or ingested. Maybe put on her clothing and absorbed into her skin. Without seeing the initial contaminant, there's no way to know for certain."

"Surely others would show symptoms, then?"

The wizard shook his head. "Only those with Gaiar would be affected. Even then, I wonder if she's been exposed to it for longer than we know. For safety, all her wardrobe should be purified, her food and drink tested, and her jewels cleaned, but only by curates."

As Druam nodded, Gwen felt her sense of safety

diminishing. She had thought nothing could touch her in the Cascade Palace.

Avallune continued, "She must have rest for a deshe, at the least. I will bring a potion to keep her Gaiar subdued until she feels ready to cast again." He stood on trembling legs. "And...I must rest. I'm afraid that spell has drained me."

Druam dismissed him, and the wizard gave a shaky bow before leaving. When they were alone, Druam asked, "How are you feeling?"

Gwen didn't know how to answer that. She felt sore, hot, and cold, all at once. Fear had clouded her secure confidence, and her own Gaiar had nearly destroyed her. The dampness on the sheets made her shudder, and she wanted nothing more than to sleep and never wake up again.

But she didn't know how to say all that, so Gwen said, "I'm very tired."

"I'm here." Druam kissed her hand. "I'm so sorry, Gwen. Nothing has scared me more than seeing you like this."

But I needed you to be strong for me.

"Thank you," Gwen murmured as she gave in to her fatigue.

Gwen dreamt that she was in her bedroom, sluggish and wan. She stirred and looked to see Mavian perched beside her with a yellow rose. He placed the flower on her bedside, then took her hand. "How are you feeling?" he asked.

"Terrible," Gwen whispered.

"I did warn you," he said without hurt or anger. "Here, I've brought you something sweet as well."

"I'm not thirsty..."

"This is just to warm your belly and help you dream good dreams."

"Isn't this a dream?"

"Of course," he said. "Soon you shall fly across the city. Drink this." Assured, Gwen sipped from the vial he handed her.

It tasted of mulberries and crushed herbs. Almost instantly, Gwen felt her eyelids droop, her body relaxing. She smiled at Mavian. "Thank you."

"Tell me what you saw when you followed Druam," Mavian said, his tone coaxing.

Gwen murmured, nearly in a doze, "He went to a tavern...Bertha's Bosun. He fought another man for coin and won. They took him to back rooms with poppin powders and...and..." She trailed off, her thoughts muddled.

Before she fell asleep, Mavian asked, "What was Druam's father's name that he invoked at your wedding?"

A name floated up, out of her subconscious, something her waking mind had blocked from memory. Gwen slurred, "His father's name was Ephraine."

"Good. Now rest, dear friend. We have much work ahead of us."

Gwen slipped into sleep. When she woke the following morning to see Druam snoring in a chair at her bedside, she did not recall her dream with Mavian, and thought nothing of the yellow rose on her bedside table.

CHAPTER THIRTY-TWO
Seanna

"TELL ME of Rask," Seanna said. Ralston stood just over her shoulder, his peaked brow reflected in her mirror as she styled her hair.

"He is difficult to grasp, Your Grace. All of his servants were brought with him from D'Clet, and they are unwilling to disclose his affairs to strangers. None outside his household are allowed into his chambers. However," he said quickly when Seanna glared at him, "I have nonetheless obtained some useful information. One of his maids has an addiction to poppin powders, and said quite a bit when under their influence. She told me that Rask has been writing and receiving letters from an unknown source. He has also corresponded with the Lord Rivers, apparently to broker a deal to bring a third candidate to the fore as Exalt. The pair has skimmed their owed taxes and used the money to pay multiple predicants to support their candidate. This money has also gone toward paying the king's advisers to support a new law that would grant more sovereignty to the earls."

"Hm," Seanna mused. She smeared her lips with a thin red paste and admired the effect. She asked, "What of Druam Strilu and his wife? Any news?"

"The earl and his wife have made amends despite the accusations against her. However, the lady has become quite ill, but no curates have given her treatments. There has been some talk of her going often to the abandoned wing, but no one knows what she does there. I will do everything in my power to learn it, Your Grace."

"Good. And my allies...how many have turned to me?"

"You have pledges from two-score lords and ladies, and the attention of more. But your husband the king still has the backing of the majority of courtiers."

"Damn him." Seanna's fingers longed to grasp her idiot husband's neck. "Why? Haven't they seen my generosity and love for those who support me?"

"Your alliance with Earl Seastone is a concern, as his marriage to a foreign girl offended many of the courtiers. The nobles not yet allied with you or the king have abandoned Strilu's camp, but they hesitate to come to you when you still dine so easily with him."

"Enough." Seanna dismissed him with a wave of her hand.

After he departed, Seanna contemplated her reflection. Druam Strilu had been good to her, but, as Ralston said, he was becoming unpopular. After the Masque, how many courtiers would remain loyal to him?

Seanna startled at a knock on the door before Henrik swept into the room. He paused a few feet from her and said gruffly, "We were to breakfast together this morning, wife. Or did you forget?"

Seanna had, indeed, forgotten, but Henrik wasn't to know that. Rising as gracefully as she could, she said, "I was simply engrossed by the presents left in my drawing room from the party last night. We did so miss your stern presence."

Henrik grunted, but said nothing as she led him to her private dining room. After they both settled and filled their plates, Seanna said, "I have been making quite the mark on society here. Lady Petrica has invited me to spend my confinement at her castle in Fanmir, and the Restas have offered their summer manor for a tourney in my honor."

Metal scraped against porcelain as Henrik chopped his pastry with a bit too much vigor. He stuffed it in his mouth and chewed loudly, staring anywhere but at Seanna. *He's annoyed,* Seanna thought with glee. She pushed him further. "I am sorry to hear that you have had to cancel your festivities so often while we are here in Riverfen. Your friends have reached out to me instead, and I have quite enjoyed getting to know them."

"Hold your tongue, woman," Henrik muttered. He sat stiffly in his chair.

Seanna ignored him. "Lady Meirtown has expressed to me how much she misses your company. It is a shame, but what can one do? Her soirees have become the highlight of my evenings, and she has told me frequently how much she appreciates me."

"Is that so."

Seanna should have noticed Henrik's dangerous tone, but she prattled on, "If you're not careful, you may find that nearly all the elite social circles have begun excluding you. Really, I wouldn't be surprised if by next season, even Rask himself will have taken to me."

Henrik slammed his fist on the table. Cups spilled and plates jumped, sending their contents spilling over the pristine cloth. Seanna flinched despite herself. His face turning red, Henrik growled, "You reach too far, *wife*. How long until your 'friends' abandon you for the next brainless noblewoman? Your ambitions will bring you to ruin. You have no idea of the powerful people you might offend with your bragging and your gossip."

He's furious, Seanna thought. At first, she trembled, but then she realized, *He is threatened by me.* Straightening herself in her seat once more, she nonchalantly picked up her goblet, drank, and popped a sliver of fruit into her mouth. She chewed slowly.

"Lord Rivers is a dear friend of yours, is he not?" Seanna asked. Henrik blinked in surprise, his whole frame tightening.

"He is," he gritted out.

"Friends sometimes hide harsh truths from each other. They wish not to hurt one another, and so in the end hurt them more. It is a shameful fact of life."

"What are you insinuating?"

"Lord Rivers is working with Rask. Together they've been

taking from the taxes owed to you and putting their money and support behind a third candidate for Exalt. Of course, you must have been informed of all this and found it perfectly acceptable; the king has greater spies than anyone."

Henrik's face grew redder and redder as she spoke. He stood abruptly and threw his napkin onto the table. Without a word, he stormed away. Selecting a small sweet from a platter, Seanna treasured his reaction.

Before Seanna left for her visitations, her steward arrived with two notes on a platter. One was a crisp white envelope with a blood-red seal, and the other a thick, creamy parchment that had been folded elaborately and sealed with an embroidered ribbon under gold-colored wax. Intrigued, Seanna selected the fancier of the two and slid her thumb under the wax to open it. The penmanship was light and flowing, clearly from an elf's hand. She listened as the steward read:

"To the esteemed Queen Seanna of Con Salur - Our countries have long been stalwart allies, but our rulers barely friends. It would be an honor to have your attendance tonight for a small dinner of the most favored courtiers. Fondest tidings, *Kair* Aremo Teru of Dedaria."

The steward paused, then asked, "Shall I read the second, Your Grace?"

Seanna nodded, though she didn't much care who else had written to her. *Kair Aremo Teru...having such a man as an ally would shame Henrik to no end.* Henrik had always loathed his elven neighbors, both Dedarian and Rengu, for betraying his forefathers and seceding from the great D'Ehsi kingdom in ancient times. Though they were currently at peace, Henrik refused to entertain either elven prince in Con Salur.

The steward cleared his throat, then read, "To my dear friend Seanna - Since the revelations you brought to my attention, we have not had a chance to dine together. I would like us, and Gwen, to eat in privacy tonight. Perhaps we may come to a better understanding of each other. Your loyal servant, Druam Strilu, Earl of Seastone."

Seanna mused for a moment, considering her options. On

the one hand, Druam had been her closest ally until she met Maeria. But, if what Ralston had said was true...then dinner with Druam could ruin all her work. *And Henrik would hate my becoming friendly with the elven prince.* "Send my regrets to Druam and an eager acceptance to *Kair* Aremo," Seanna said to the steward.

Elves were not uncommon in Dotschar, though they mostly stayed in their own kingdoms. Rengu and Dedaria were the domains of the elves; in the dark days, the Dedarians' ancestors, the Lofalin elves, were brought over to serve as slaves to the D'Ehsi peoples before winning their freedom centuries later. Most elves lived longer than men, if only by twenty or thirty years. That, and the elves' pointed ears and extra finger on each hand, led to many men distrusting them. Though Seanna had not met many elves, she didn't much care about the racial divides.

Pride filled her lungs the remainder of that day; Seanna could not help but brag to the courtiers about the *kair's* invitation and "fond tidings." By suppertime, nearly everyone knew of the queen's plans for the evening, and envy-laden notes came by the dozen. Everyone wanted to meet with her the next day to hear of the exclusive dinner.

Seanna dressed in her loveliest silks and pinned her finest jewels to her hair and breast. She shimmered from every angle, an angel descended to walk among mere mortals. Though the outfit weighed heavily, she walked with her head held high and her back straighter than the king's scepter. Jealous eyes followed her through the corridors to the prince's private dining room.

As was Dedarian custom, tables encircled a wide space in the center of the room. A band of troubadours played foreign songs as courtiers mingled in the open area, and a set of bay windows had been opened to let in the cool autumn breeze. *Kair* Aremo had yet to arrive. His guests drank their wine nervously, glancing often to the carved double-doors leading to his personal chambers. Seanna glided among them, greeting each warmly.

Ten minutes passed before a steward announced the *kair's*

arrival. The troubadours struck up a regal melody as the double doors opened and a tall, handsome elf stepped into the room. He carried himself with inherited grace. Jet-black hair barely touched his shoulders, and his skin had a coppery tone. A black, sleeveless robe embroidered with golden dragons draped over his shoulders and left his shaved chest exposed for all to see. A beautiful elven woman accompanied him, her flowing gown nearly as revealing as his.

Seanna was the first to offer her hand to the *kair*. He took it and pressed moist lips to her palm. His dark eyes flicked up to meet hers, and he gave her a small, private smile. She returned it, her chest swelling.

Seated in the place of honor to the prince's right, Seanna focused all her attention on *Kair* Aremo. He languished in his cushioned chair like a contented cat. He never stared for long at any one person; rather, his eyes flitted between all the guests and the troubadours, resting for just a moment on each as if he were choosing a target on which to pounce.

"Your wife is lovely," Seanna said. The beautiful elven woman sat on the opposite side of the room, and Seanna saw that her eyes often drifted to rest on Aremo.

Aremo laughed in a warbling, birdlike tenor. "She is enchanting, isn't she? Though I'm afraid to say she is not my wife."

"No? Your betrothed, then?"

Again, his high laughter lifted to the chandelier. "My dear queen, we Dedarian have different ways of doing things. While I am currently betrothed to Ulalia Etrila, the daughter of the Rengu prince, I feel no social pressures to halt my current trysts with my paramour. Edlyn is a wild woman with wild tastes, and I am loath to abandon her for the sake of propriety."

Aremo lifted his glass in a toast to the woman across the room. Edlyn returned it, her jewelry shimmering in the candlelight. Fascinated, Seanna asked, "Is it proper in Dedaria for love affairs to be open for all to see?"

"Proper? Hardly. But they are so common that we might as well tear apart all our marriage papers. *Ameer* Voclain was hesitant to give his daughter to me, as I am – what did he say? – ah, that I am a vile, repulsive man with no sense of decency, and that I bring shame and dishonor to our entire race." *Kair* Aremo smiled fondly, as if recalling a day in the gardens rather than insults from another prince. "But, he did acquiesce when I showed him the gold and trade routes I was willing to offer for her hand."

"What are you getting out of the bargain? Other than a prestigious wife?"

"Princess Ulalia is Voclain's eldest child and heir to the Rengu province. With our union, and plentiful children to prove our consummation, I will have control over both Rengu and Dedaria, and unite the elven nations of D'Ehsen as they were in the old days."

"It would be quite difficult to have a united kingdom with seas dividing them."

"Ah, yes, a great obstacle. How ever shall I overcome such horrid boundaries?" Aremo again smiled a secret smile, but this one unnerved Seanna. Goosepimples shivered over her arms, and she forced a grin to hide her sudden chill.

"I have heard," Seanna said in an attempt to lighten the atmosphere, "that there have been more and more immigrants from Lofaliri to Dedaria. Have your small territories become overrun with refugees?"

Aremo drawled, "More ships have sailed there, but carrying armies."

"Armies?"

The prince laughed at her shock. "A joke, Your Grace. How ever could the barren Isles support armies of any size? We can hardly feed our own people with our scarce farms and wet moors."

"True," Seanna said, flushing at her paranoia. He was right, of course; everyone knew that the trio of cliffed islands supported only the hardiest of vegetables and sheep. The elves living there depended on trade from their kin across the sea in Lofaliri.

Bolstered by wine, Seanna redirected the conversation.

They spoke for a long time – well over a candle – of religion, trade, the Exalt, anything Seanna could think to interest the elf. All the while, Edlyn sat across from them sending sultry looks to the prince.

After their conversation, Aremo rose suddenly and extended his hand to his lady. Edlyn practically leapt to her feet and latched onto his arm. With a small bow and a wink at Seanna, Aremo said, "I thank you for coming to this dinner. I have appreciated coming to know all of you, especially Her Grace the queen. I have needs that must be attended, if you will forgive such a blunt remark. Farewell, and good night."

As soon as she left the private dining room, Seanna sent a message to Maeria. It said simply, *Come as soon as you can*. Seanna hurried to her chambers while replaying the evening in her mind. Henrik would be furious at her burgeoning friendship with the prince, and she envisioned trips to Dedaria once her confinement ended. Nobles poured to her like wine from a bottle, and she would make their cups overflow with wealth and grandeur. Henrik was wrong; Seanna would succeed in this.

Around midnight, a knock came at her door. Seanna called softly to enter, and Maeria's beautiful face peeked around the door, desire and anxiety warring in her features. She wore only a simple white shift. Suddenly, Seanna was aware of her own body. In the deshes since leaving Con Salur, her belly had grown more, and no one besides her maids had seen her naked. Unconsciously, she started to cover herself, turning away from Maeria.

A soft hand pulled Seanna back around. Maeria's white fingers ran over Seanna's body, from her shoulders to her breasts and then down to her belly. Seanna's breath caught, her heart pounding with a nervous beat. *Will she reject me, as Larka did?* Then Maeria leaned down and kissed her bellybutton.

"There's no need to be ashamed," Maeria murmured. "You're beautiful."

Something released in Seanna, a tide of guilt and self-hatred that had haunted her since the day she left Con Salur. She hadn't even realized she had harbored it.Taking Maeria's chin, Seanna pulled her down and kissed her deeply. She tasted of apples and salt, of cool water and hot lust. With a sudden urgency, Seanna pulled the girl to the bed. They stared at each other, cleanly naked, nothing but warmth between their smoldering skin.

"Onto the pillows," Seanna said. Maeria obeyed. Though her pregnancy made her feel heavy, and she moved slowly, her confidence grew as Maeria squirmed and panted with her touches. She kept going until Maeria screamed and kicked in confused delight. While Maeria recovered, Seanna pulled herself up to meet the girl's mouth, letting her taste herself.

"Whatever you want," Maeria gasped at last, running her hands through Seanna's thick hair, "Everything you want and more. Just do – *that* – to me as often as you can."

"Oh sweet maid," Seanna breathed. "I shall teach you everything about your body and mine. I'll–"

She was cut off as Maeria pulled her into another kiss.

CHAPTER THIRTY-THREE
Cara

"SANDU!" Cara shouted until her voice was hoarse. Her leg hurt after Jagger had hauled her to her feet, and she couldn't move from her blankets. Alex roamed the forest outside the camp. Cara watched him, sure that she'd see a flash of a knife, but Jagger didn't reappear. Neither did Sandu. Eventually, Alex returned to her in defeat.

"I can't track them," he said. "It appears that – Jagger, was his name? – knows how to shake someone following him." Alex slumped beside her and ran his fingers through his dirty blonde hair. "We can try again in the morning."

Cara leaned against him and stared into the darkness. "Should we?"

"What do you mean? We can't just abandon him to that madman."

"Sandu said it himself: I was his next bounty. I can't trust him–"

"Yes, you can," Alex interrupted her. "He told me about his bounty. When it was clear his master wouldn't let him give up the job, he tried to leave you. To protect you. I made him stay, and I know he wanted to tell you."

"You knew?" Cara drew back. Her heart had already been broken that night by Sandu's words, and now Alex had betrayed her, too? Was there no one in this world she could trust?

"I did," Alex said, giving her a level look. "But it wasn't my truth to tell. Wouldn't you have rather heard it from Sandu himself? And if you could have, you would have kept the beast a secret from both of us."

Cara grappled with his blunt statements. Yes, she would have kept her beast close if she could have. She wished she could keep it from Renna, too. He was also right about Sandu; she would have wanted to hear it from him. But even so, had Sandu only sought her out in the first place as a bounty? How long had it taken him to decide not to sell her? Before Merick's death? After their first encounter with Jagger? If Sandu were there, he could have answered all her questions. He was gone, though, and his truths with him.

Eventually, Cara leaned back into Alex. "I understand why you kept it from me. I don't know if I can forgive Sandu, though."

"If he even comes back."

Maybe it's for the best that Sandu dies out in the swamp, thought Cara, though she immediately felt guilty for it. The beast pushed against her mercy, and she wondered if she would have tried to kill Sandu herself if Jagger hadn't taken him.

Her thoughts, and the pain of her leg, made it difficult to sleep. She lay beside the jumble of blankets that was Alex and recalled all her conversations with Sandu. She had always believed him to be genuine, but now she knew what he had really been: a con man from the start.

After a candle of tossing and turning, Cara pulled Alex's blanket up and snuggled against him. He snuffled in his sleep, then opened one eye.

"Is something wrong?"

"I can't sleep," she whispered. "Can I stay close to you?"

"Oh...yes, of course." Putting one arm around her, Alex's breathing soon returned to its slow cadence. With him beside her, Cara finally embraced her own dreams.

In the cold light of morning, Cara woke to find Alex missing. She sat up, heart pounding, and stared wildly around. Their horse was still there, as were all their packs. Sandu's blankets were rumpled and cold.

After a few minutes, Alex stepped from the swamp and held up a rabbit. At Cara's questioning look, he shook his head. "Still no sign of him."

While Alex prepared their horse for travel, Cara went through Sandu's pack. Tears dotted the worn fabric as she found his Valadi spices and spare shirt which still carried his scent. Deep at the bottom she found a rolled up parchment. Her hands shook as she undid the string and smoothed it open.

She saw Jagger's name crossed out, and many more names or requests with locations and prices. Her own name, she noted, had many hunters after it – including Sandu. And her price? Five marks. A weighty sum. It was no wonder Sandu had wanted to find her.

"Alex," Cara said, "Have you heard of a Laris Stanthorpe?" That was the man who wanted her. She would find out all she could about him before she confronted him. The beast trembled at the thought of spilling the bastard's blood.

"Stanthorpe?" Alex came beside her and looked at the list. "He's the master of the Peddler's Guild. Stubborn and shrewd, but fairly harmless to my knowledge. I can't say I've met him more than once, though."

"What would a man like him want with me?"

"Who knows? Once the Hooded Man is taken care of, we can seek him out and demand answers. We should be careful, though; Sandu says he has magic, and he clearly knows more about you than most do. He might even know that you're *sulpari*."

Cara shivered and stuffed the parchment back into Sandu's bag.

As Alex lifted Cara onto the horse's back – her leg, splinted and wrapped as it was, limited her movement – he asked, "You're sure about leaving? We can wait longer, see if Sandu–"

"I'm sure," Cara said. His bounty list had only cemented her resolve. "He had many chances to tell me. I hope his soul finds peace."

Alex hesitated, then nodded. He kicked dirt over their pitiful fire, then took the horse's reins.

They left the swamp by late morning, then traveled through beautiful countryside of rolling green hills and copses of trees decorated with crowns of orange and red. Farmlands spotted the landscape, laborers working to bring in the early harvest while shepherds brought their flocks down from the higher hills. Each town had a smithy and well-tended market, and most had inns or public houses. The people looked to be healthy and in good humor, and children played carefree in the streets wearing grass-stained smocks.

Though the pain of Sandu's betrayal and likely death flared often within her, each day it grew less and less. Her grief had turned into numb acceptance. Alex could not make her laugh as Sandu had, but she clung to him anyway, often pushing her blanket against his at night. Without Merick's fatherly touches, or Sandu's carefree joy...all she had left were Alex's scholarly comforts.

"This seems a prosperous region," Cara commented as they rode through yet another peaceful village.

Alex nodded. "Earl Seastone has spent years making sure all of his rustics are provided for. There are great warehouses of grain for times of famine, but we've been blessed with good rains and warm summers for many years now."

"Aren't the people afraid of the prowlers?"

"Of course. But there are patrols of both Realm's Protectors and the earl's hired men constantly making rounds of the region. The people are as safe as they could be. That being said, a plague has spread in the northern hills; not here yet, but it will. And then, tides of refugees fleeing the disease will come to Riverfen's gates."

"What will happen to them then?"

"From what I've heard, Earl Seastone has built simple wooden homes outside the city. Each should fit ten to fifteen people, and there will be a hospital for the sick. The city itself is too crowded to let in everyone, and with so many people pressing in together, the plague would spread that much faster."

Cara nodded. She had heard of Earl Seastone in the past, but never paid him much heed. After all, he wasn't her lord. She asked, "How will we find Renna once we reach Riverfen?"

Alex hesitated, but after a minute said cheerfully, "We'll try to get you into the Cascade Palace; the earl can help us root out the Hooded Man and find Renna."

It all sounded so distant and impossible. Why would the earl care about them? She and Alex were nobodies: she was a rustic, barely more than a slave, and he the son of some lowly noble. She doubted they'd even be allowed into the palace, let alone given an audience with the most important people of the land.

Rather than confessing her doubts to Alex, though, she stayed quiet. If the gods intended her to rescue Renna, then they would find a way for her. *They have already taken Merick, Ulton, and Sandu for Renna's sake. Surely they would let us find her.*

In her musings, Cara thought often of the battle in the swamp. Alex hadn't known anything of how she could make time slow, and she almost wished for another opportunity to test the ability. As soon as her leg healed, she was determined to practice using the beast and its strange powers. She knew now that that was the only way to defeat the Hooded Man.

During an unusually hot afternoon, Alex told her, "We should reach the city in a couple of candles." As the evening clouds rolled over the horizon, tinted with shades of pink and orange, they crested a hill and looked down on Riverfen. A tremendous lake, formed by a dam, lay to their left, and they stood at the top of a series of white stone cliffs. The road wound in a serpentine pattern down the chalky cliff on the other side of the dam. Waning sunlight shone on the ocean beyond the city, while hundreds of thousands of colored lights danced and sparkled in the streets. Stretching between a multitude of rivers were miles and miles of white-washed buildings and blue-stoned roofs.

Cara stared and stared. She had never imagined such a place to exist, and now she looked upon it. It seemed unreal, a mirage that would shimmer and fade the closer she drew to it.

Alex led them down the road and to the top of the dam. There, they waited their turn to pass across the architectural wonder. The dam was massive, over two hundred feet tall and a hundred from bank to bank. Its surface was large enough to accommodate two streams of people going each direction, with wagons passing side-by-side four at a time. Cara gaped over the edge, looking down the smooth grey wall to the river far below.

It took another half candle to descend the white cliffs to the delta. They passed rice paddies and cultivated fields, the road now congested with traffic. Alex clung to the horse's reins, and Cara winced as her leg was jostled again and again by the surging crowd.

At last they reached the city gates. The wall surrounding that part of the city was only thirty feet tall, the gates thrown open with a small patrol of four guards watching the crowd. As Cara and Alex drew closer, one guard elbowed his companion. The companion looked at them, then rushed away. Cara's hands sweated on the reins. As she and Alex came alongside the guards, a captain with a blue feather in his helmet strode outside. He shouted an order and more guards trotted out. They had not drawn their weapons, but they surrounded Cara's horse in two straight lines. The captain, who bowed to them, took up the lead position and blew a horn. The crowd parted before them.

"What's going on?" Cara asked. "Are we under arrest?"

Alex stood on his tiptoes and whispered, "Just play along."

Despite Cara's fears, the soldiers were not aggressive. They merely walked alongside her and Alex, their armor clinking with each step. The crowd flowed around their small entourage as people threw disgruntled looks at Cara atop her road-weary horse.

They passed over arched bridges and underneath aqueducts. Small boats thrummed along the waterways as the rowers sang merry tunes. Overhead, the glass and paper lanterns shone brightly, coloring the faces of the people in the streets. Merchants in stalls shouted their wares, and people free from the day's labor drank openly in outdoor courtyards. If Cara could plug her nose against the smell of the sewers and stench of thousands of people, she would believe she had walked into a faerie song.

The guards escorted them to a wide thoroughfare paved with white stones which led straight to the plateau. It was lined with houses of increasing size and splendor; each home could fit all of Kell's residents within it. The houses had gardens and courtyards circling them, all protected by high walls and stewards at the gates. Some even had personal guards patrolling the ramparts.

By this time, Cara felt her nerves unravelling. All the people, the smells – freshly baked bread, perfumes, body odor, fish – and the sheer vastness of the city overwhelmed her. She craned her neck to see the top of the plateau and the marble palace gleaming in the last rays of sunlight.

Nobles and courtiers, most riding or carried in sedans or palanquins, gradually replaced the commoners in the crowd. They too made way for Alex and Cara, most looking at them curiously.

At last, they reached the marble gates into the palace complex. Cara didn't know what to expect, but as she, Alex, and their entourage approached, the gates opened and guards bowed to them. Suspicion knotted itself in Cara's gut.

The road now was almost clear save for servants and pages bustling about on their master's business. Cara could no longer smell the rank city below her, and save for the wind and the clanking of the guards' armor and weapons, she heard only the strains of sweet music from somewhere nearby. Night had nearly completely fallen, and the sky overhead was dusky blue painted with streaks of purple and dark orange. Lanterns and torches illuminated the palace nearly as brightly as the day.

Cara's arse hurt from being in the saddle all day, and she shifted to try and relieve the ache. A flare of pain burst from her calf, and she winced. Alex noticed and took her hand, squeezing it. "It'll all be fine," he said. "Trust me."

A steward waited for them on the grand staircase. The escorting guards lined the steps to either side, leaving a path clear between the horse and the steward.

The steward – a small, wiry man dressed in a brocade tunic – bowed and said, "Welcome home, my lord. Your brother is waiting for you in his study, but he expects you to wash and rest from the road." His eyes turned to Cara. "May I have the pleasure of your companion's name so that I may inform the earl?"

Alex smiled. "It's nice to see you, Master Eigbrett. This is Caralyn Gellder, who fought bravely when the Mott caravan was attacked."

Eigbrett's brows flew into his hairline. "Attacked, my lord?"

Nodding, Alex said, "I'll inform my brother as soon as I'm rested. Tell him I'm bringing Cara with me." Leaning in closer, he whispered, almost too low for Cara to hear, "Tell him she's *sulpari*." Straightening, he said louder, "My companion needs a curate's services for her injuries, and the palace tailor to find her fitting clothes. I also would like baths drawn for us; give her the Lilac Room."

The steward bowed low. "All will be ready for you after you have supped, my lord."

As Master Eigbrett led Cara and Alex up the steps, he snapped his fingers and gave out Alex's orders. Cara leaned on Alex as they walked, murmuring, "'My lord'?"

Alex ran his hands through his hair. "I'm sorry for hiding it from you."

"Who are you really?"

"Alexandro Strilu, Lord of the River Valley. My brother is the Earl of Seastone." His tone showed his remorse, but Cara drew back from him. Here she had believed him to be a minor lord, sent to Mott to study since he wouldn't inherit any estates, but instead she had been traveling with one of the most influential men in the land.

Stammering, Cara tried to find words to express her dismay. None came. Alex laughed a little and said, "Come now,

Cara, it's a surprise, but not nearly as large as the one you've brought here. You're something completely different, whereas I'm just the brother of an earl."

"I suppose..." Cara said weakly.

Cara was immensely grateful when the steward led them to a private dining room and pulled a chair for her. She occupied herself with the immense spread before her – some were foods she had never seen in her life – and tried not to think back to everything Alex had said, and change the meaning of his words based on her newfound knowledge.

They were quiet at dinner. Alex looked perfectly at home in these sumptuous surroundings...and why shouldn't he? This was his home. Lord Alexandro Strilu.

It was quite unbelievable.

After dinner they went to their rooms. Cara's suite had an entryway, a drawing room, a bedroom, and a washroom, each decorated with rugs, tapestries, chairs, sofas, paintings, silver candlesticks, flowers, and all sorts of expensive things. She was afraid to touch or sit on anything.

Alex took his leave of her then, promising that he'd return after a bath. As soon as he'd left, the tailor arrived. He swiftly took Cara's measurements before scurrying away. Soon behind him came a curate carrying salves and powder. He inspected Cara's wounded leg, poking and prodding at the inflamed skin as she gritted her teeth.

"A break in at least one place," he said. "And bruising all around." With vigorous professionalism he rubbed a sweet-smelling ointment from her ankle to her knee. In moments, her leg went mercifully numb. Cara started to thank him, but he then sprinkled a powder and spoke a spell. The numbness helped at first, but then her skin began to itch. Her bone creaked painfully back into place, the skin around it repairing itself. Cara tried not to scream, but the agony grew too much to bear. She whimpered and cried out until, at last, her leg was whole and unmarred once more. Tears pricked her eyes and she took great gulps of air. After a few minutes, the numbness returned, and the curate nodded in satisfaction. "The bone powder helps the spell, which makes you heal the same way you would naturally, but all at once. This, of course, is far more painful."

"Can...can I walk on it?" Cara asked. She had never been healed by a curate before, and even Madame Freebane's ministrations had little magic in them. *Little wonder curates are so expensive.*

The curate said, "Your leg is healed. It may be sore for a few days, but is perfectly usable." Once again, he bowed and left before Cara could properly give him her thanks. *Is it this way for every noble?* Cara wondered. *People coming and going just to take care of you, and not even giving gratitude for it?*

A maid swept in and efficiently disrobed Cara despite her protests, then helped her into a copper tub filled with steaming water. Cara bathed, or was washed, really, since the maid didn't let her do any work at all. The bath didn't last long. After the maid dried her, the tailor returned with a lovely dress that slipped against Cara's skin. Once she had been dressed in proper undergarments (who knew a lady's dress required so many layers?), the tailor slipped the gown over her head and tightened the laces at the front.

When Cara looked in the mirror, she couldn't quite believe her own reflection. She had never thought that she could be as pretty as Renna, but dressed in a fine gown with newly-washed hair, she thought she looked rather lovely.

Cara did not have to wait long before Alex returned. He, too, wore fine clothes: a clean white shirt with a long tunic over it, well-tailored wool breeches, and leather boots with brass buttons. The tunic was embroidered with the Strilu crest and bordered with a Gallic pattern. He now looked a proper lord, and Cara felt very small beside him despite her own beautiful clothes. He said, "Druam is waiting for us in his study."

Earl Seastone's study was even more luxurious than Cara's rooms. The walls were made of blue- and green-veined marble, as was a towering fireplace. Thin silk curtains fluttered in the breeze from an open terrace door, and beyond, Cara could see the multi-hued lanterns of the city glowing in the night. On the third wall was a floor-length bookshelf creaking with gold-embossed tomes. A blue rug covered the floor from door to door. A large desk sat in front of the fireplace, and the earl himself perched in a high-backed chair behind it. He indicated for Cara and Alex to sit in comfortable chairs across from him.

Cara obeyed, darting glances at the most powerful man she'd ever met. The earl had worry lines written across his brow, his dark hair smoothed back. It was his lips, though, that fascinated Cara. They were carefully controlled, without a betraying twitch, barely moving even when he spoke. Outwardly, his face was a neutral mask, but when Cara briefly met his startling blue eyes, she saw a flicker of some inner emotion.

Cara gratefully accepted a cup of wine. She sipped the warm liquid and felt it settle in her stomach. When offered to Alex, he shook his head and went to stand behind Cara, gripping the back of her chair.

Earl Seastone tipped his own cup, drinking the entirety of its contents before placing it back on the tray. Dabbing at his lips with an oft-stained handkerchief, he asked, "Is it true, then, Maid Gellder?"

Cara's cup shook in her hand. She quickly swallowed a gulp, suddenly afraid. What was she to say? Luckily, Alex spoke for her, "It is."

The earl contemplated Cara curiously. She could almost feel the weight of his gaze pass over her; it made her feel naked. His posture changed almost imperceptibly: what had been tired relaxation became intent and commanding. Cara gripped her cup with both hands to keep them from shaking.

Some unspoken agreement passed between Alex and the earl. Alex took a seat while the earl rubbed his temples. Cara shivered at a breeze from the window, and the flames in the candelabras flickered. She tried to ignore the itching in her leg. The smell of candle wax irritated her nose, and she sniffed as quietly as she could. Resisting the urge to begin braiding her hair, she instead played with her fingers in her lap.

The men had not spoken again. Cara shifted in her seat, then noticed that both men avoided the other's gaze, their fingers twitching rapidly on the table. *Are they communicating through gestures?* Cara wondered, watching the complicated movements. Whatever they meant, Alex stood again and began pacing behind her.

The silence stretched on. Earl Seastone stared levelly at Cara. She squirmed and took a deep breath. Before she could speak, he said, "If what Xandro says is true, then you are a person of high interest to the court. With the growing threat of the prowlers, the king and other earls have convened often to discuss what we can and should do. You are an anomaly, and therefore, to many, you will be seen as a threat. But I believe that we can help each other."

"I don't know how," Cara said, her voice squeaking. She swallowed and said, "I haven't mastered the beast yet."

"There are those who could help you: court wizards, scholars, and the like. Much knowledge is already to be found, if one knows where to look for it. The loss of Xandro's years of research is a crushing blow, but not an irreversible one."

Cara felt more than a little foolish. She had no place in this palace sitting before this powerful man. "I just want to find Renna," she blurted. "I'm not a great hero or someone who can defeat the prowlers. I'm a servant girl hired to guard her mistress, and I failed at that."

Earl Seastone's eyes bored into her. "Some men are pawns, and some emperors, but oftentimes we do not know which we truly are. Your destiny, Maid Gellder, is not written plainly."

Cara had no idea what to say to that. She glanced up at Alex, but he still paced and stared at the floor with a faint frown. Licking her lips, Cara chose not to respond at all. This didn't seem to unduly bother the earl. He stood, stretched his arms, and walked to the open windows. Hands behind his back, he stared out into the night.

Softly, the earl said, "I fear that this peace of a hundred years has come to an end. We are on the brink of war, and the prowlers are but one of our enemies. The nobility hide behind their parties and their politics, ignoring the growing threats within our kingdom. Threats from the prowlers, from traitorous nobles, from this 'Hooded Man.' Who knows the harm that will come to Dotschar: the men killed, the women raped, the children captured and enslaved, our libraries and statues destroyed. War does not just end our lives: it invades the hearts and souls of our people." He reached out and closed each window, shutting out the sea winds, then turned back to Cara with a somber expression. "I hope that we may be allies in the coming war. You may think yourself a mere servant girl, but the gods have granted you gifts not seen for hundreds of years. If you hide yourself away and ignore all around you, you may win a peaceful life. But, somehow, I doubt that you can evade your fate for long."

Cara looked at the floor and said, "I wouldn't even know where to begin. Everything has changed so quickly; I'm barely holding on."

"Such is the way of life." Regaining his seat, Earl Seastone continued, "While you are here, you will be a lady of the palace. My personal guest. I would advise you to keep your gift secret. I will do all I can to help you find your mistress, though this Hooded Man is unfamiliar to me. Perhaps others here have fallen victim to his attacks."

"Am I free to go into the city?"

The earl nodded. "Though I would advise against it. There are many dangerous people lurking about. I would advise you to start your search with my wizard, Avallune Martill. He may know something about the Hooded Man's dark magic."

Cara felt a swell of hope. Perhaps, with the earl's help, she would find Renna. She asked, "What about Stanthorpe?"

A brief look of amusement crossed the earl's face. "He would not dare defy me and take you from the palace. If it would make you feel safer, I could assign a guard–"

Alex coughed. Cara twisted to look at him as he spoke for the first time since they'd entered. "It's been a long day, Druam. You've met her and seen me safely returned. May I escort her back to her rooms, to allow her time to think over everything you've said?"

It seemed as if the earl wanted Cara to stay, for his eyes

flicked back and forth between her and Alex, but he acquiesced. "Very well. I am sure we will have many more talks, Maid Gellder. My apologies for keeping you from your rest. Good night."

Cara held Alex's arm, her thoughts whirling as he walked her back to her rooms. Her mind had still not quieted as they stood outside her door, and without questioning her need, she said, "Alex, can you come sit with me awhile?"

"Of course." They curled up on a well-cushioned couch, his knee brushing hers. Cara's head felt light from the wine. And, perhaps, Alex's closeness. He smelled of soap and musky sweat, and his hair drifted into his eyes no matter how often he brushed it away.

"If you're such a great lord," Cara asked, "why did you go to Mott?"

"My elder brother, Verdon, studied there. After his disappearance, I visited the library, hoping he might have just...fallen asleep among the tomes. I began to read the scrolls and books, and now I spend as much time there as I can. After the prowlers became more than a pest, I spent my days researching them and translating ancient texts that might have some hints as to their origin. That's how I learned about *fampir*, too."

"Oh. I didn't know you had another brother."

"Verdon was kind, and fair." Alex settled deeper into the cushion beside her. He spoke wistfully, "Whenever Druam and I fought – which was nearly constantly – Verdon would intervene and find a compromise, or just tell us both to shut it. He was the only one who could make us stop. Since he's been gone, Druam and I have done our best to avoid quarrels.

"But beyond that, he was a gentle soul who hated palace politics. He wanted to help people, but never knew how. He eventually chose the scholarly life. His trips home were infrequent enough that Druam and I didn't even know he'd gone missing until over a month after it happened.

"Verdon never took a wife, but he would have been happy with one. He and Druam used to talk about how they'd name their children and where they'd want them raised. Druam often went to him for advice." Alex paused, and Cara shifted closer to him. He said quietly, "I always imagined us growing into old men together, watching our grandchildren play in the gardens while we talked aimlessly about the weather. It's impossible, but it's such a peaceful dream that I can't let go of it."

"Then don't," Cara said, taking his hand. Heat grew in the space between them. They leaned together into the couch.

"We're going to find Renna, you know," Alex said, his light touch sending thrills up Cara's arms.

"How can you be so sure?" she asked.

His head fell into the nook of her shoulder and neck. "Because you're here now, and there's nothing you can't do."

Cara smiled. "I hope you're right."

For a time, they simply stayed quiet, enjoying the other's presence. When the candles guttered, Alex mumbled, "Are you tired?"

"Yes," Cara said, feeling every ache of the journey.

"Then come to bed." Slowly getting to his feet, Alex offered her his hand. Taking it, Cara followed him into the bedchamber, his skin warm against hers. Though she knew it to be wrong, that she was a lowly rustic and he a high lord, she didn't stop him, didn't hesitate when he kissed her and drew her into the sheets. All the pains of the journey, the losses and the hardships, were forgotten for a time, and all she knew was the taste of his lips, the smoothness of his skin, and the intense need to be with him as they moved together.

CHAPTER THIRTY-FOUR
Sandu

DAWN BROKE, cold and harsh in the mist-folks' swamp. Sandu stretched, his arms and legs aching. Looking around, he saw nothing but pale green-and-grey trees with fog curling around their trunks. Jagger had drowned, and his friends were back in their camp...wherever their camp was.

In the hazy light, Sandu couldn't quite tell the sun's position. It all looked the same. Plugging his ears against the mist-folks' cries, he trudged through the mire, his boots squelching with each step. His stomach rumbled in hunger, his throat clenched against thirst. All that pushed him forward was the thought of finding Cara and Alex.

Around midday, Sandu reached a farmer's track cutting through the swamp. Looking to his right and left, he knew that he was utterly lost. Going right might lead him back to the village, but it could also lead him farther away.

I was a gambler once, he thought, taking out a shem and flipping it. It landed printed-side-up, and so he went right. The track was old and worn, and he stumbled and scrambled over rocks, tree roots, and small streams, his hands and knees scratched and his clothing torn. At least he could quench his thirst with the streams, and knew enough of botany to pick a few non-poisonous berries to eat. His stomach rumbled around the meagre food.

As the sun began its descent, Sandu realized that he was heading vaguely west. *Away from the town.* Darkness closed around him, but he saw firelight gleaming through the trees. Bashing through shrubs, he ran as fast as his lungs would let him until he crashed down a hillside and into a circle of torchlight. Large sconces ringed a good-sized camp, which was filled with carts, a smelter, lumps of stone, and ten or fifteen well-muscled men. One of them shouted something as Sandu flopped to his feet, and he found himself surrounded by a ring of axes and picks.

"He don' look like a prowler," one man said.

"Or a misty," said another.

"I'm a vecking man," Sandu said, raising his hands. "A traveler. I was separated from my companions; I mean no harm."

"You look like shit," said one man, brawnier than all the rest. "I'm Mason, foreman of this mine. Who're you?"

"Sandu Crin. Can I share bread and ale with you tonight? I'll be on my way come morning, as long as I'm shown the road to Riverfen."

"Aye, we can grant you that. Stand down, fellows. We've got ourselves a right purty little man dining with us tonight."

With a meal and ale in his belly, Sandu relaxed. These were good, simple folk. All of them were friendly enough, swapping stories around the fire. A small group sat a little ways off, throwing dice and alternately laughing or cursing.

"Care to join?" one of the gamblers shouted to Sandu, waving the dice enticingly. "Only a copper penning to start you off."

Sandu hadn't gambled in deshes; surely one night wouldn't hurt? He could recoup some losses, maybe pay off his debts, maybe even go home to Tambrey and the twins someday...

...The stench of mead clung to his tongue and spilled out onto his breath. He hadn't bathed in a deshe, and old vomit stained his filthy shirt. Bartholomew scrabbled at the door until he found the worn metal handle. He lifted it and tripped over the threshold on his way in.

"Veck!" he swore, louder than he intended. He couldn't see any

shapes moving in the dark room. The door to the only bedroom was closed. Tambrey was asleep, then, cuddling with the children.

Bartholomew Barrow – for he had yet to change his name to Sandu Crin – shuffled to the fireplace with its cast iron cauldron hanging above smoldering embers. The cauldron still had stew left over from that day. Making more noise than he thought he was, he found a bowl and spoon and proceeded to feast on the cold food.

"You're drunk again." Tambrey sounded as if she hadn't slept at all that night. Slurping down the last dregs in his bowl, Bartholomew said, "Your stew's as good as always." His words were more slurred than he had hoped.

"You're lucky you didn't wake the twins." Suppressed venom layered Tambrey's voice, as if she wished to rant and shout at him but resisted. "How much did you lose tonight?"

"It's not–"

"The pot on the hearth is empty, I know you took the last of our silver."

"I'll win it back."

"Horseshit."

"I promise, I've just had a string of bad luck..."

Tambrey didn't wait for him to finish. She stalked into the bedroom, and when Bartholomew tried to follow, she shoved him back and lodged a chair against the door. Tired and with a pounding headache, Bartholomew slept in front of the fire.

Every night for months, Bartholomew came home drunk with an empty purse. Always, he had an excuse. Tambrey grew more and more angry with him, but it was only after his father was dragged to debtors' prison in his place that Bartholomew found his house empty. All their belongings had been taken to the property of Tambrey's new husband. When he'd tried to beg her forgiveness, Tambrey told him coldly that he was dead to her and everyone else in town. She'd already told the twins he had drowned in a river. So he changed his name, left Dunfrey, and took with him the few things he had left in the world...

...Declining the miners' invitation, Sandu turned back to the fire. He couldn't start all over again. His father was in jail, but not Cara. He would make her see how much he regretted his betrayal, yet how happy he was to have met her. *I won't gamble again. I won't do that to myself.*

But as the night drew on, and the gamblers' talk grew more boisterous, Sandu found it harder and harder to resist. His fingers tugged at the purse on his hip, his mind straying to the many good times he'd had playing cards or dice. *But those good times didn't last.*

One of the miners sat down beside him and offered a drink. Sandu accepted it, taking the excuse not to speak. The miner said quietly, "You can join 'em if you like. They don' mind dealing to strangers."

Sandu hunched his shoulders. It appeared the miner had misinterpreted Sandu's glances at the gamblers. For a moment, Sandu didn't know what to say. After a minute's awkward silence, he mumbled, "I really shouldn't."

"What's to lose? A penning or two? A game won' hurt, and you'll feel better for the company."

The words beat against Sandu's resolve. His fingers danced with a coin in his pocket. *He's right, one game can't hurt. I need some fun after the last few days.* Sandu lurched to his feet and stepped toward the gamblers before he realized what he was doing. He stopped short, halfway between the fire and the table, and stared at the ground.

"Alright there?" the miner asked. "Come on, let's join the next throw."

"No," Sandu forced out. "I...I think I should just go to bed." He could have said that he needed all his money to reach Riverfen, but he knew these sorts. They'd merely say that he had a chance of winning far more than he lost.

The miner shrugged as Sandu turned away. Quivery steps took Sandu to a tent, and he crawled into the blankets with no small relief. As he shut his eyes, he tried to stifle the sounds of the gamblers outdoors. *If Cara turns me away, then I can gamble everything I have,* Sandu told himself. *I just have to hold on another day.*

In the morning, Sandu hitched a ride on the miners' cart which deposited him in a town on the western edge of the swamp. The only people he saw were strangers. Sandu half-wondered if he shouldn't just go join the miners and live out his days doing menial labor and gambling away his earnings.

Then he sighed, hefted the pack a kindly miner had given him, and headed into the town's bunkhouse. The man at the bar gave him a small nod and said, "Bit early for a bunk, isn't it?"

"I'm not staying," Sandu said. His eyes drifted over the empty tables where he had hoped to find Alex and Cara. "I'm looking for someone."

"Mayhaps I can help."

"A man and a woman, about my age. The man is well-dressed, with light hair. The woman has dark hair and a sword."

"Aye, I saw them both last night. They left early this morning. Though the woman was fairly hurt by the looks of her." The innkeep held out a mug. "Friends of yours?"

"Yes." Sandu took the mug, slapped a coin on the counter, then gulped down the bitter ale. He handed it back and gave another coin. "Thank you, sir."

Though his body still ached and his feet were sore, Sandu set off once more for Riverfen. His lightened heart gave him strength to push on. They would all meet in Riverfen. Everything would be right again. *And Cara will forgive you. You just have to keep believing that.*

CHAPTER THIRTY-FIVE
Seanna

SEANNA WOKE first and gently rolled to her side so as not to wake Maeria. The young woman slept on, heedless of the sunshine pouring across her cheeks and golden hair. Maeria snuffled a little bit, one hand cupped against her chin. Reaching over to stroke the girl's hair, Seanna smiled. If only this simple moment could last a lifetime...

Leaning down, Seanna kissed Maeria deeply, savoring the taste of the girl's morning lips. When she drew back, Maeria's eyes flitted open. The girl yawned and stretched out her arms, then pressed herself against Seanna, entwining their legs. Her fingers traced across Seanna's skin, pale white against light brown, and ran down to Seanna's belly.

"How did you sleep?" Seanna mumbled.

"Like a babe. I had the sweetest dreams of being with my lover."

"Mm. Sounds exquisite." *If only Dotschar could have two queens...*

"And you?"

"I slept perfectly."

"The child? Did he kick at all?" With a longing look, Maeria cupped her hand against the largest part of Seanna's pregnancy.

Seanna said, "Oh yes. But I loved each one."

"Good." For a second, neither spoke, merely enjoying the

other's presence.

Maeria said softly, "I wish I could be with child. To feel it moving within me, to know that soon I'd be the mother to a new life. I'm terrified that I will live to old age having never experienced such profound joy."

"I do feel so blessed. To feel him grow and wonder what his life will become. All I want is to shape him into the finest, kindest king D'Ehsen has known. But it's not all joy," Seanna said, remembering her miscarriages. "There is pain, and discomfort, and sometimes loss. Children die so often before their parents."

Maeria sighed. "Yes, but that is a risk we must take. And think of the times when the parents get to see their child ride a horse for the first time, win tourneys, marry. I want so badly to have the chance to rear a child born of my own flesh and blood."

"I'm sure you will someday, dear one. Then we can raise our children together and watch them grow up side by side. Who knows...perhaps you will produce a daughter that marries my son and becomes queen."

"To be the queen's mother..." Maeria sighed again, though wistfully this time. "To see that fulfilled would be the greatest achievement of my life."

Seanna kissed her forehead. "If the gods are good, they will see it done."

They rested together for a few minutes more before Maeria rose and slipped away through a servant's passage. Seanna lay among the disheveled sheets, thinking of Maeria as the baby moved inside her.

The day passed the same as many now did, with tea and small gatherings to talk and embroider with other noble ladies. That evening, though, was yet another dinner with an exclusive guest list.

A guest list, fortunately so, which included Egil Rask's favorite nephew, Sir Chadron Elliot of Goblinshield.

Sir Chadron was in his early thirties and a prime target for Seanna's wiles. He had not yet arrived, so she practiced her craft among the nobles. Druam was her target this time, as his constant notes and invitations had started to annoy her.

"Poor Earl Seastone; his young wife is still carrying on in a most disgraceful manner with Lord Far-Eyes."

"Have you heard that Earl Seastone's health is fading? Accounts by those closest have reported his failing humors."

"The upcoming Masque is the earl's last effort to make a place for himself among my husband's closest supporters. If it has any disturbances or issues, who knows what the results may be?"

Seanna's words caused ripples of murmurs to spread across the room. Buoyed by the effects, she plunged into her agenda regarding Predicant Manderly. Speaking to a group of lords, she said, "From what I've gathered, there are three undecided predicants; they are the ones who will choose between Manderly and Ropaz. Lord Rockhaven, I believe one of those predicants to be within your province...is there *anything* you can do to sway him toward the more righteous path?"

Lord Rockhaven tapped the side of his nose. "I hear Predicant Krinnow has a taste for fine wines. Perhaps I can send him a few bottles as an offering for his vote?"

"That would be most appreciated, my lord."

At last, Sir Chadron arrived. He had the stern, chiseled look that Egil must have possessed in his youth. Seanna waited for him to ask her to dance – it would not do to seem desperate – and during a Dotsch *cantinella*, her desire was fulfilled. He took her to the dance floor, leading her stiffly through the stately steps.

"Is it true," Chadron asked as they danced, "that you dined with *Kair* Aremo? I have heard such tall tales of the Dedarian prince that I question their veracity."

"I did dine with him, though in mixed company. Which tales intrigue you?"

"That he flaunts his paramour as if she were a creature of noble birth, and that he is overly lewd in his speech. Most importantly, that he is outright dismissive of any concerns that his kin are gathering on Dedaria."

"All true," Seanna said. "I asked him myself, and he believes his lands to be too small for a sizable host. And his paramour, while beautiful, is so obviously of low means that I cringe to think of a prince consorting with such a woman."

"Really? That is refreshing to hear. So often, all these rumors fly about with nothing to verify them."

"Absolutely. The gossiping in these courts is astounding, and to be frank, too much for one to keep up with."

Drawing Seanna as closely as her protruding stomach would allow, Chadron said, "Astonishing, the lengths one will go to in order to dangle rumors in front of the mindless cattle. I certainly would never associate myself with such base pastimes. Why, just the other day I left a lady alone in the middle of the dance floor for filling my ears with nonsense."

Though his words were harsh, his tone was playful, his eyes glinting. Taking the risk to please him, Seanna said in a low voice, "I do abhor such trifling things. But one cannot be too careful these days; even when I made efforts to associate myself with men of integrity, I found myself overhearing matters of the worst kind."

"Such as?"

"Well," Seanna drawled, forcing him to slow his dancing to hear her better, "I took great pains to spend time with Earl Seastone, but I discovered that his actions are seemingly altruistic, yet hide a nefarious agenda." Seanna made up the lie as she spoke. "For years the earl has been sheltering Valadi criminals and allowing them free reign in his lands. But, his compassion has extended to those far beneath dignity. He is close with his cousin Mavian Strilu, who has been known to experiment with prowlers. There are some who say that Earl Seastone has been harboring the wretched creatures for his cousin's sake."

Sir Chadron's eyes widened. "Could it be? The earl has been given much leeway; my uncle has often bemoaned the freedoms allowed to Seastone and his family."

Seanna shrugged. "There is a grain of truth to everything, is there not? There are more prowlers reported in the River Valley than anywhere else, but Seastone seems uninterested in sending men to hunt them down and destroy them."

"I have heard that indeed," Chadron mused. Before he could continue, the music slowed to a stop and they halted their dance. Chadron bowed to her, clearly preoccupied with his thoughts, and hurried over to a small group of lords and knights. They all leaned toward him, and without needing to hear the conversation, Seanna knew that she had succeeded in ensnaring him. He would spread her rumors for her, then come pleading for more.

Sudden nausea overcame Seanna. She gagged and held it down, but nobles around her had noticed. Patting her belly, she said ruefully, "The baby is acting up, I'm afraid. He's as obnoxious as his father."

Laughter followed and Seanna made her excuses. She couldn't vomit in front of Sir Chadron. Just outside the door, Sir Eric waited patiently for her. Seanna moved slowly and carefully so as not to further upset her humors.

"You're leaving early," Sir Eric commented.

"Damn pregnancy," Seanna muttered. Waves of queasiness washed over her; it must have been the pickled herring. "I'm going to take a walk in the gardens. Some fresh air might help. Lend me your arm."

He obeyed, and she leaned heavily on him as they made their slow way outside to the vast gardens. Seanna had not had much interest in exploring the graveled paths or viewing the exotic animals; such things were what lovesick couples and pink-cheeked girls partook in.

Still, it was a cool evening with a chipper autumn wind, and Seanna found herself much rejuvenated after a brief sojourn of vomiting into the bushes. She wasn't cold, so decided to wander the gardens for a time and take pleasure in her recent victories. In a low voice, she said to the baby, "Your mother will not only give you a crown, but a kingdom of loyal vassals. I'll raise you away from Henrik's backwards politics, and you'll be the greatest king ever known." As she spoke, her imagination ran wild. "Will you have my eyes and skin? How handsome you'll look on a grey charger. You'll start swordsmanship as soon as you can, and make your Grandfather Ulmer proud of your talent. And I'll be at your side when you take the crown, ready to give advice whenever you need it." She sighed happily at the thought.

The sun's last rays turned to blue dusk, and as the lanterns lit in the city below, Seanna turned to head back to her rooms. Despite eating just a couple of hours before, she was hungry again. She took the shortest route through a series of hedges and overhanging trees meant for seclusion and privacy.

Giggles and the smacking sound of kissing caught Seanna's attention. Normally, she would pay it no heed, but a mischievous part of her wanted to spy on the lovers. *Fodder for gossip*, she thought happily, gesturing Sir Eric to be quiet. Seanna made as little noise as she could as she crept forward. She peered around a hedge, and, in the moonlight, saw the two young lovers. They stood pressed against the hedge, their hands creeping all over each other's bodies.

The man, she saw, was none other than Mavian Strilu. His head was turned her way, though his eyes were closed as the woman nibbled at his neck. He moaned, brushing the woman's hair aside to kiss her.

Seanna stifled a gasp. Mavian didn't notice as he kissed Maeria. He stroked her long blonde hair, whispering sweet things that Seanna couldn't hear. She didn't want to hear it. Just that morning, Maeria had lain in *her* bed, giggled at *her* sweet words, and promised *her* the world.

Pulling back so they wouldn't see her, Seanna seethed. Sir Eric reached out a comforting hand, thought better of it, and pulled back. He rattled his sword in its sheathe a little, a wordless question: *Shall I take care of the problem for you?* Seanna shook her head and pushed past him. She meandered through the trees and hedges until she found a small bench. As she sank down, she straightened her back and did her best to halt her quivering lip.

She betrayed me, Seanna thought. *She doesn't deserve my tears.* Maeria was a schemer and a liar, just like every other noble. But Seanna couldn't help but think of the smoothness of Maeria's skin, her laughter, the wonderful nights they had spent together. If the law had allowed it, Seanna would have left Henrik forever and taken up Maeria as her partner.

The anger broke down into gross sobs. Sir Eric stood a short distance away, keeping his eyes averted. Each time Seanna's tears dried, they came anew and stronger. Her face grew red, her eyes swollen, her throat hurting from the harsh sounds she made.

Eventually, though, her crying ceased, replaced by a deep, burning, roiling need for revenge.

"I'll destroy them both," Seanna mumbled, her voice raw. "I'll make her pay for the hurt she caused me." The light in her eyes transformed from grief to fire.

Chapter Thirty-Six
Sandu

AH, RIVERFEN: the bustle, the splendor, the shit in the street, just as I remembered it. After thanking the merchant who had given him a ride in the back of his wagon, Sandu set off along the busy cobbled road. Compared to the fashionable people around him, he looked like a beggar with his travel-stained trousers and sweaty shirt. He wished he had Galen so he could ride through the crowd.

Snippets of conversation showed the concerns of the people around him. Some lamented the waste of their taxes on the exorbitant Masque, while others complained about the price of eggs nowadays. Many feared that prowlers or the plague would reach the city soon.

As he took a shortcut through a small alley, Sandu remembered his first time in Riverfen. He had recently been turned out by Tambrey, and with no money in his pocket, he sought his fortune in the famed city. For days he had slept in the streets, dodging piss tossed from windows and fighting with stray dogs for scraps of meat behind a butchery. Half-starved, he found his way to the Peddler's Guild, and there begged for a job – any job – so he could fill his stomach. The boss had taken a liking to him and offered him the peddler's pack.

I had no clue what that really meant, Sandu reflected. *I thought it was an easier position than it turned out to be. Peddlers that are really bounty hunters...it is clever, I have to admit.*

Sandu turned his feet away from the Guild and headed down Faller Road. He knew of a decent inn by one of the major waterways. The inn, Kote's Rest, was still there, its clean windows shining with a beckoning light. He had always heard gossip there; it was as good a place as any to start his search for Cara.

But Sandu hadn't any money to speak of. The moment he entered, the bartender squeezed out from behind his counter and cornered him. "Do you have the coin, up front, for our services?" the barkeep demanded.

Sandu raised his hands defensively. "Hold, friend. I used to drink here back when Kote still ran the place. He used to offer an ale and crust of bread in exchange for cleaning the floors."

The bartender hesitated. "Kote was a trusting man. Got him killed doing favors like that."

"I'm sorry to hear it. If you're not willing to make the exchange, I'll leave. I don't want any trouble, just something to drink and a bite to eat. I'll do honest work for honest pay."

Scratching his beard, the bartender said, "I've got about a candle, mebbe two, worth of work in the kitchen. If you can peel the potatoes, work the stew, and help with the bread before the supper crowd, you'll have earned a drink and a meal in my eyes."

Sandu shook the man's meaty hand. "Agreed. Perhaps you have a washbasin where I could clean up before I start?"

After dousing his hands in cool water and cleaning off his grimy face, Sandu felt a tad better about himself. He settled into the simple task of peeling potatoes while he thought about his plan. *It'll take too long to find Cara by working at taverns for each meal. I have to establish myself somehow, find a place to stay and make some coin while I search for her. Surely there'll be rumors floating around, too, about the warrior woman and the scholar recently arrived.*

Once all the vegetables were chopped up, Sandu heated a cauldron over the large cooking fire at the edge of the room. While it warmed, he slid a pan of bread into the oven.

A little over a candle later, the barkeep came to check on

Sandu's progress. The bread sat cooling on the table, jams and butter already laid beside it ready to serve, and the stew gave off a merry steam.

"Put some flavor into it, did you?" the bartender asked, taking a whiff of the cauldron.

"I took some liberties, hopefully ones your customers enjoy." Sandu offered the man a taste. "It's my mother's old recipe. Valadi caravanner food, hearty and delicious."

"Hm. I like it. Well, looks like you've certainly earned your supper. Fill a bowl for yourself and take a chunk of bread. What's your name, lad?"

"Sandu Crin."

"Call me Master Frest. It's not often I get a hardworking young man in here to help out; these days it's just my daughter, when she's not occupied with her husband and new babe. I can't pay much coin, but you can have a cot by the fire and two meals a day if you help me with the food until you find better accommodations."

"Thank you kindly. I'm actually in Riverfen looking for a friend, a woman about twenty with dark curly hair. She traveled with a scholar from Mott. Heard anything?" Sandu asked as he took a tray and prepared his dinner.

"Can't say as I have. Don't have much time to listen to gossip, to speak truthfully. I'll point out old Winster in the common room, though. He's a bit of a friendly layabout, as it were. People don't usually notice him, so he hears more than most would think."

"Thank you again." Sandu followed Master Frest back out into the main area, which had become crowded while Sandu worked in the kitchen. Frest pointed toward a small table in the far corner where an old man sipped a large mug of ale. The man had frizzy white hair that spiked around his head and wore patched trousers with a sackcloth for a shirt. As Sandu approached him, however, he noticed that the fellow had a suspiciously large money purse tied to his string belt.

"May I sit with you?" Sandu asked. The old man nodded, and Sandu took the seat opposite him. Tearing into his loaf,

Sandu said, "You look like you've been around the streets a few times. Tell me, what's the news?"

Winster took a slow sip from his mug. "Oh, lots o' things. There's a Masque that's driving everyone mad. The low districts are waiting for their new glass lantern to be finished. The earl's new wife is a foreigner. All the courtiers are playing their political games while the rustics fight for scraps in the streets."

Sandu tried not to let his impatience show. "Anything about a young woman accompanied by a scholar, newly come here? The woman carries a sword."

"Ah, fishing for information. You could've just asked straight off, you know. I'm old, not stupid." Winster looked out over the crowd, half-mumbling, "Men are always raring to get to the next place. Always looking for the fast way, not the right one." To Sandu he asked, "Do you fancy a hand at cards?" He took out a worn deck from his purse. "Maybe gamble some information?"

Sandu bit the inside of his cheek and declined. Winster looked disappointed, but deftly slid the deck from the table. "I'm old, you see, and need something to justify spending my time talking to wayward lads. How do you propose we go about this?"

"Well," Sandu said, "we could always swap stories. I've got a few that might entertain you."

"Stories about what?"

"Betrayal, lost love, revenge, regret."

"I've lived all those, boy. Something better than that."

Sandu raised an eyebrow. "How about clandestine deals with good men to kill bad ones? Desperate escapes from murderers and prowlers?"

The old man scratched his chin. "Aye, I could stand to hear a few of those."

For the next candle, Sandu told him about working with Fauste's Shiv and the attack on Daggenhelm, of his and Cara's encounters with Jagger and prowlers, and the Hooded Man. All the while, Winster leaned back in his chair with his arms crossed over his chest. His eyes betrayed his interest.

At last, Sandu wrapped up his tale. "And now, I seek my companions in this fabled city, and have come to a wise beggar man for help. Have I gained the beggar man's confidence?"

"I dare say you've given me a good amount of entertainment," Winster chuckled, "though I think it's all folly. I have heard of your friends. They paraded through the city up to the palace. Servants have come out describing the girl in all manners of ridiculous ways: that she can speak to prowlers, make gold from straw, bring the dead back to life. Lord Strilu himself brought her here."

"Earl Seastone brought her? That doesn't make sense."

"Don't mistake my words, boy. I said Lord Strilu, the earl's younger brother."

Sandu sat stunned for a minute, piecing the information together in his head. After pondering a moment, though, it all made sense. Alex couldn't possibly have trusted two strangers enough to reveal his identity, but had to once they reached Riverfen. *Cara must have been furious with him.*

So, Alex and Cara were at the Cascade Palace.

"How does a rustic find his way into the palace?" Sandu mused out loud.

"Ha." Winster gave a short laugh. "Easier to find your way onto the moon. No one in or out without express permission from the stewards. And you have to know someone on the inside to have any hope of finding any jobs there."

"Hm." Sandu realized that he'd let his stew go cold. He shoveled it into his mouth as he thought. He said through a mouthful of potato, "But merchants with deliveries go in, right?"

"Have to have a marked parchment with entry permissions. Those are only given to trusted suppliers."

"What about entertainers? Troopers and the like?"

"Again, you need to be a part of those chosen troops. Fat chance you'd weasel your way in without them suspecting something. Face it, lad, you're not going in there unless you somehow find out your true father was a landed lord, with seal and writ and everything."

Sandu didn't want to give up that easily. He thanked

Winster for his time and returned to the kitchens. There was a pileup of bowls, plates, and trays. Sandu set to washing.

"I was going to ask you to help with that," Frest said, bringing in a tray. "You look preoccupied. What's on your mind?"

"My friend is in the palace," Sandu said, scrubbing at a particularly hard spot on a tray. "And I have no way to get in to find her. I'd be lucky for her to come out again, but I can't stay at the gates waiting for her."

"Then join the Protectors," Frest said.

Sandu looked up at him in surprise. "The Realm's Protectors? You can't be serious. Do I look like a soldier to you?"

Frest shrugged. "My cousin was with them, but he's taken ill in the last deshe. Plague, so his wife tells me. They need more good men, what with the Masque and all the nobles flouncing around up there. The Protectors have doubled their patrols on the plateau, but they don't have enough recruits. Sure, you're scrawny, but they aren't in the position to be picky. If you go in tomorrow, I'd wager you'd be given a set of armor and steel and sent out the same day."

Sandu paused, his arms wet and soapy up to his elbows. He stared at the filthy water. "It's the best chance I have, really. I don't want to offend your hospitality by leaving so quickly after I'd agreed to stay and help, but I have to find my friends."

"I understand, lad. In the morning, you can fetch the bread from the baker and prepare the day's food before you leave. Fair?"

"Fair." Sandu dried his hand on his tunic and offered it to Frest.

Once his chores for the evening were done, Sandu laid down on a straw mat in front of the kitchen fire, drawing up the quilt Frest had lent him. He slept peacefully, despite the mice skittering in the walls and the errant ember stinging his cheek.

In the morning, Sandu dithered about his chores. He wasn't quite sure why he moved so slowly, and didn't feel like pausing to contemplate his own thinking. Frest didn't make any comments, and Sandu stayed quiet. In two candles, he had done everything the barkeep had asked of him, and had no further excuses not to go to the barracks.

"Best of luck to you," Frest said, handing a small sack to Sandu as he gathered his things. "I've packed you some cheese, bread, and apples. The Protectors may seem daunting, but they're just men like us."

"Thank you, Master Frest," Sandu said, putting a hand on the older man's shoulder. "You've been kinder to me than I deserve. I hope to return here often and share stories with you by the fire." It was an old Valadi saying, one the caravanners used to say to those who had given them hospitality along the road.

Frest beamed. "Call me Lod. You're a good lad; we'll see each other again soon."

The streets of Riverfen teemed with people: merchants hawking their wares, street urchins darting between wagons, knights on horseback, rustic servants laden with packages, and all sorts of other people cramming shoulder to shoulder on the cobbles in front of colorful storefronts.

Sandu, long experienced in melting into crowds, allowed himself to be swept up along Ogden's Crest all the way to High Road, and then to the gates at the bottom of the plateau.

Near the gates was a low, simple building with the sign of the Realm's Protectors hanging from the gutter. Inside was as dreary as the outside. Torches lined the walls of a small room, doing nothing to dispel the air of gloominess. A Protector sat at a small table, a red badge pinned to his tunic. Quills, ink, and parchment filled the table's surface. The Protector glanced up from his work, looked Sandu up and down, and said, "Bottoms Tavern is next door."

"I'm here to join the Protectors," Sandu said, trying not to shift from foot to foot like a child in trouble.

"Is that so? Have you any pedigree or experience in the field?"

"I have some arms training, sir, though no pedigree. My father was a brewer." Sandu licked his lips nervously. The Protector's stern mouth betrayed no hint of a smile.

"What makes you think that we'd be in want or need of a scrawny thing like you?"

Sandu shrugged in what he hoped was a nonchalant way. "With so many nobles in one place – including the king and queen – the Protectors need all the men they can arm. I may not look much, sir, but I have fought against prowlers and lived." That was a stretched truth at best, but Sandu was not above small falsehoods.

"Why do you want to join, Master...?"

"Crin, sir. Sandu Crin. I want to make coin, sir, and earn an honest living. My father is in debtor's prison and I mean to earn his freedom." With these soldierly types, blunt honesty could sometimes be the best tactic.

The Protector deliberately placed his quill on the table, then leaned back in his chair. "Not the most honorable of answers."

"If all men claimed to be of the highest honor, there'd be no criminals in this world. I've met plenty a Protector who values coin and loose women over any sort of glory." Immediately after he spoke, Sandu winced. He'd let his mouth run away from him, and the Protector did not look amused.

"Look, sir," Sandu said, "I've spent the last few quinns traveling with a scholar, an expert on the prowlers. He taught me much on what they are and how to defeat them. They'll be in the city soon enough. I can teach your men how to fight them. In return, I want to be one of you."

"Why should I believe you?"

This is hopeless, Sandu thought. His shoulders sagged ever so slightly. He hesitated, unsure what to say.

"Crin...why do I feel I've heard your name before?" The Protector leaned forward, his eyes intense in the torchlight.

Sandu bit the inside of his lip. *Might as well tell him.* He said, "I'm the peddler who gave the location of Fauste's Shiv to your company. I'm sure you received a report about the attack on Daggenhelm."

"Hm. I have heard those reports." The Protector dipped his quill in ink, moved a few papers around on his desk, then looked expectantly at Sandu. "Our rate of pay is five copper pennings per quinn. You'll be given full livery and a standard weapon, and a bunk if you need one, though that'll be four iron pennings deducted from your pay. All meals are your own responsibility."

"So...you'll accept me?" Sandu didn't dare believe it.

"Hmph. I will, but you still need one of our captains to take you on. If none of them want you, you're shit out of luck. Captain Dirgard is off his patrol; I'll see if he's interested in you."

"Where does he patrol, if I may ask?" It would be worthless to join only to be assigned to a district far from the palace walls.

"In the palace. Night shift." The Protector rose as Sandu took a silent sigh of relief. When the Protector came back, he was accompanied by a tall, lithe man of Skallish descent.

Captain Dirgard was only about as old as Sandu, though he was a good bit taller. He had a carefully trimmed golden beard and strangely soft grey eyes.

"So, Kenning here tells me you're the man responsible for the Daggenhelm incident," Dirgard said. He had a melodious tenor, not unlike a singer's. "And that you've experience with the prowlers. Thank you, sir," he said to Kenning, "I'll take it from here. Follow me, Master Crin."

Sandu followed him past the table and into a long, low hallway. They entered the first room on the right, which had a small bed, a table, a washbasin, and a bookshelf, all very utilitarian. Dirgard sat on the edge of the bed, waving at the only chair in the room for Sandu. Feeling self-conscious, Sandu sat down and placed his pack on the floor.

After a moment's silence, Dirgard said, "Is it true that you know about the prowlers?"

"Yes," Sandu replied. "My companion fought against them, and then she and I met a scholar who had studied them."

"Tell me what you know."

Though much had happened in the intervening days, Sandu did his best to recollect everything Alex had told them. When he finished, the captain gave him an appraising look and asked, "Is that all?"

"Yes. I might be forgetting more, but I wasn't always

listening to the lessons Alex gave to Cara."

"Your companions, I assume."

Sandu hesitated, but Dirgard appeared a good, honest man. He said, "Yes, sir. To tell the truth, I'm here in Riverfen because we became separated. I hope to find them in the palace. When I do, I can bring them to you to give you more information on the prowlers."

Dirgard laughed. "So you need a way in. Well, we're as good as any, I suppose. If you serve me well, I'll allow you some time before and after each shift to roam and find your friends. I might even use some of my contacts, if I'm really pleased with you." Dirgard offered his hand. Sandu shook it; the captain had a strong grip.

"Thank you, Captain. I can't express how much this means to me."

"We'll make a soldier of you, and if you're true to your word, your friends will make us better fighters against those foul creatures. Now come on; we'd best get you armored."

"I've always wanted to wear the Protector's red cloak. Thought I'd look rather dashing," Sandu said as he followed Dirgard to the livery.

CHAPTER THIRTY-SEVEN
Seanna

THOUGH SURROUNDED by gay laughter and the clinking of metal goblets, Seanna was unhappy. Her food lay mostly untouched and her eyes had dark circles under them. She slumped in her seat feeling none of the merriment. All the while she dwelled on the thought of Maeria cavorting in the gardens with Mavian like a bitch in heat. All that talk of affection, of loyalty...it meant nothing to the girl. *And she has turned her friends against me now, too, I know it.* The cohort of young ladies had stopped coming to Seanna's soirees and ignored her notes.

Henrik thumped his hand on the table, catching Seanna's attention. He growled, "She's just a common whelp! Why are you entertaining your brother's latest tumble in the palace?"

Druam shook his head. "Your Grace, I've told you that she's not a simple peasant. My brother–"

"Your brother is love-addled." Henrik waved his hand dismissively. "I want no more time wasted on this rustic girl. Throw her out and be done with it."

"With all due respect, this is my palace and my lands. If I choose to keep her here, there is little you can do to stop me."

Intrigued, Seanna asked, "Are you speaking of the peasant girl paraded to the palace?"

Henrik's eyes flicked to her, then back to Druam. "Yes, wife. We speak of this whore that Lord Strilu dragged out of the wilderness. Earl Seastone, I advise you, I *implore* you, rid yourself of her. Imagine the scandal if she convinces Alexandro to marry her."

Druam chuckled. "I'm not worried in that regard, Your Grace."

"Perhaps you should be," Seanna said, surprised to find herself siding with Henrik. "Alexandro is your heir, and if Gwen should not give you a child...then the line would pass to him, and subsequently, the girl should she marry into your family. There is precedent of low women doing so, and once the vows are made, there is no turning back for Alexandro."

"Seanna is right," Henrik said, though grudgingly. "I will hear no more talk of it. Do what you want with the girl, Seastone, but do not expect any help from the crown when it goes wrong. And it will go wrong, I promise you that."

"When did you become so cynical?" Druam asked in a low voice. "You never had such pessimism when you were younger."

Seanna grew bored with their conversation. She didn't really care about the rustic girl nor what would happen to her. She rose from her seat, curtseyed to the king and earls, then made her way to the lower tables. There, she chatted amiably with her supporters and friends. She was delighted to eavesdrop on neighboring conversations and hear talk of Rask and Druam spreading among them.

Seanna paused, though, when she heard two lords speaking quietly together. One said, "I find it incredulous that these earls that we've known for so long are behaving so erratically. I don't believe what the queen says."

"Neither do I," replied the other, but before he continued, his companion hushed him and pointed to Seanna standing nearby.

Seanna strode away. *It does not matter what those oafs believe,* she thought as confidently as she could. Then a small worry surfaced: *They're not the only ones. I've gone too far, and now I will be shunned again.* She shook that thought away and beamed at a passing noblewoman. *I am the queen. They* will *respect me.*

Near the back of the hall, she came to a halt. Maeria and

Mavian sat together, whispering and giggling. Seanna's throat tightened. Feeling a flush rising on her cheeks, she turned swiftly and left the hall.

"Is everything well, Your Grace?" Sir Chadron stood a little beyond the hall door, holding a long pipe and blowing smoke into the air.

"Yes," Seanna muttered. "The baby is moving around too much for comfort. A bath, I think, would be apt now."

Chadron inclined his head and returned to his pipe. Still sickened from seeing Maeria, Seanna walked as quickly as her pregnancy allowed. Sir Eric emerged from the shadows of a column and joined her, her silent companion.

What's so wonderful about a man, anyway? Seanna thought miserably as she walked. *The member is nothing special, and a man's whiskers are nowhere near as pleasant as a woman's lips. What does she get from Mavian that I could not provide her?* She recalled Maeria's wish for children. *But she doesn't have to grope at him at every turn to achieve that.*

Rounding a corner, Seanna saw a young man of the Realm's Protectors wandering around. He snapped to attention when he saw her. *Maybe I just need to try a man other than Henrik,* Seanna thought as she paused in front of him. He was not bad-looking at all; in fact, he had a rather handsome, rustic look about him, with sandy hair and soft brown eyes.

"What's your name, soldier?" Seanna asked.

"Sandu Crin, Your Grace."

"How long have you served with the Protectors?"

"Less than a quinn."

"Hm." For a second, Seanna debated with herself, but the idea of Maeria in Mavian's bed pushed her to say, "Escort me to my chambers, Master Crin."

"Yes, Your Grace." He offered his arm to her, and she leaned on it gratefully. Sir Eric trailed behind, and Seanna could sense the questioning in his eyes. *No answers for you, my knight.*

As they walked, Seanna asked the Protector, "Where do you hail from?"

"Dunfrey."

"Ah, Sir Vlasimir's lands! My sister lives there now, did you know?"

"No, I've not been there for many years. Sir Vlasimir was a kind lord; I am sure Your Grace's sister is most pleased living there."

"Oh, she is, according to my father. Why did you join the Protectors?"

"For coin."

Seanna laughed. "An honest answer, if not a noble one. Not for the honor, or the women, or even the tournaments? Surely a man like you had other opportunities to make coin."

"I was a peddler once."

"Peddlers get to wander, see new places, trade with all sorts of people. A far more exciting life than spending days at a time cooped up in a palace with silly ladies and blockheaded lords. Are you married, Master Crin?" Seanna took a deep breath; he smelled like apples and fresh hay. A rustic smell, though not a bad one. She tried to imagine laying beneath him, and was not wholly disgusted by the idea.

"I was. A long time ago."

Good. Then he knows a little of how a woman is in bed. "Have you been with anyone since?"

"I...no. I have not found another woman like her."

"Tell me of her." By this time they had arrived at Seanna's chambers. The soldier opened the door, and Seanna beckoned him to follow. Sir Eric stayed in the hall, shutting the door behind them.

Seanna led the Protector to a couch and motioned for him to sit. He did, and she looked at him expectantly. He blinked, then said, "Her name was Tambrey. She was a sweet girl from the next village over, the baker's daughter. I wooed her for half a year before she agreed to marry me."

There was a bittersweet longing to his tone. *This won't do. I need him to be raring and eager.* Seanna poured them each a glass of wine. "She sounds absolutely lovely. I can see why you would not want to replace her."

Seanna allowed the heady feeling from the wine to

overcome her, and prodded the soldier to drink of his own cup. He did so, though somewhat reluctantly. When both their cups were nearly empty, Seanna put hers down. The soldier followed her lead, then rose. Seanna grabbed his tunic and pulled him back down onto the couch. Without thinking, without second-guessing herself, she kissed him deeply. His lips tasted of wine, a scent of lotion on his cheeks. He did not move.

Seanna awkwardly pushed him down into the cushions and straddled him. Her hands explored his neck and hair, reaching inside his tunic to feel the hard metal of his mail. He gasped when she bent to kiss his throat. His hands gripped the cushions as if afraid to touch her. She kissed him again, her tongue darting inside his mouth, her teeth biting at his lips.

As quickly as she'd started, Seanna sat up and adjusted her diadem on her hair. Though she had kissed him as passionately as she had Maeria, she felt nothing. She had no attraction to this man, no desire to feel him moving inside of her.

"Sir Eric will send you back to your post," Seanna said, failing to notice the soldier's horrified expression. She did not wait to see him leave her chambers before she went to her washroom. The maids had already brought hot water for the copper tub, and the room had grown steamy with it. Seanna slipped off her clothes and stepped into the warm water. She sat down and stretched out her legs, feeling her normally heavy belly float, taking some of the pressure off her spine. Closing her eyes, Seanna tried to relax.

Heavy footsteps came from behind her. Her eyes still closed, Seanna said, "I have called for no one. Leave at once."

The footsteps came closer. They were a man's, heavy with a long stride. Likely just Sir Eric. Before Seanna could twist around and tell him to go, large hands grabbed her bare shoulders and pushed her into the water. She let out a short, high scream before her head submerged.

Seanna's mouth gaped, her hands struggling fruitlessly to find purchase, to lift her back to the surface. The hands on her shoulders kept her down. Flowery soap stung her eyes, water flowed past her tongue and filled her ears. The baby kicked once, twice, a third time. Water crept into her throat, forcing itself down. She couldn't breathe, soap blurred her eyes, the world swirled.

The hands were gone for a moment, then returned. Seanna fought against them, though the hands scrabbled at her arms instead of her shoulders. The pressure released again, and gloved hands gripped her now, strong hands that pulled her from the water, back into the precious air. Seanna coughed and retched, throwing up water and shaking the drops from her eyes. She heaved water until her head no longer spun and her vision cleared.

Sir Eric was there, holding the Realm's Protector's arms behind his back. Both were sopping wet.

"I didn't do it, I swear, there was–" Sandu Crin shouted, but Sir Eric punched his stomach, causing him to fold over in pain.

"Your Grace," Sir Eric said, somewhat breathless, "I heard your scream, but feared I came too late. I found him kneeling over you."

Seanna shivered; the water did not warm her now. "Get me a robe, then take this scum to the dungeons. Do what you please with him until he confesses."

"As you will it, Your Grace."

Alone in her washroom, Seanna realized how close she had come to death. Tears came to her eyes as she held her belly. *You would have died before you'd ever seen the world.* She shivered. Nausea threatened to empty her stomach as blind terror scraped up her throat.

Would anyone have mourned me if I had died? Somehow, she didn't think so, and that frightened her even more.

CHAPTER THIRTY-EIGHT
Cara

WHEN CARA woke, Alex had gone. Her bedchamber was lit with beautiful morning light. The whole room was nearly as large as her and Merick's whole cabin at the Nellestere Manor, and that was just one of the few in her suite.

And this is all just for me? It seemed horribly wasteful, and the abundant comforts didn't help her sense of not belonging. A warm bath waited for her, as did a tray of breakfast. As she ate, she looked at a note the earl had sent to her. It described when and where she could meet the wizard.

Two days, Cara thought. *He'll see me in two days.* She hardly thought she could wait, but she had to admit to herself that she was excited to have time to explore. When they were young, she and Renna had been told many stories about Riverfen and its beautiful marble palace. Never had she imagined she would ever come here, much less be dressed in finery and given leave to go wherever she pleased.

She wished that Alex had stayed, though. He'd left a note that, as Lord of the River Valley, he must attend duties while at the palace. Apparently, these duties started quite early in the morning. While maids helped her to dress, Cara wondered how long it would take to find Alex in the vast palace complex.

Letting her steps carry her wherever she pleased, Cara wandered the stately halls and marveled at the architecture, the tapestries, the mosaics, the finely carved furniture. She cast her gaze demurely down whenever someone approached, and found that no attention was paid to her.

Sounds of laughter drifted through the corridor accompanied by the tinkling of goblets. Cara followed the merriment until she came to a terrace. It was alive with nobles in their silk and jewels, none of them seeming the least concerned about food tread on the ground or wine spilling from their cups. Backing away, Cara left behind the careless people. Any rustic would give a hand to eat any of the assorted foods on those tables, yet the nobles cared not for their waste.

During the evening, Cara passed two more gatherings of courtiers, each full of drunken laughter, music, wandering hands, and pounds of food. Though her mouth watered, Cara didn't intrude on the parties. She didn't want any questions or suspicion, and hated the wanton disregard.

Eventually, Cara made it back to her rooms. She had to stop and ask directions more than once from a passing servant or steward, and they all looked down their noses at her once they heard her rustic accent. Cara flushed under their condescension, but thanked them regardless.

Alex visited her that night looking worn and stressed. He stayed still for a long time in Cara's arms, then said, "I hate politics."

The next day passed in much the same way, with Cara exploring and Alex spending the evening and night with her. At last, the time came for Cara's meeting with the wizard.

Cara dressed in her most sensible gown – she didn't understand why the tailor had given her so many lovely yet constraining outfits – and tried not to rush through the halls to her appointment. She had found her way to Avallune's tower the previous day, and retraced her steps back to her room so that she wouldn't be late or get lost.

Not soon enough, she knocked on his door. A curt "Enter!" sounded, and Cara pushed open the heavy wood.

The wizard's tower was clean and well-swept, its bare stone floor cold under her slippers. Bookshelves lined the walls on one side, and a desk laden with organized papers stood near a window. One corner held a small table with a mortar and pestle. Neatly labelled bottles of liquids and ingredients stood on the shelves above it.

To her surprise, the wizard sat cross-legged in the center of the floor, an open book on one knee and a vial in his opposite hand. He mumbled to himself as he swirled the vial around, his attention fixed on the liquid inside. Cara thought she saw a red glow come from his fingers, and realized that he must heat his potions with magic.

"Shut the door," the wizard said without looking at her. Cara complied, then stood before him, waiting patiently.

"Avallune Martill," he said, holding out his free hand. His eyes never left his book. Cara shook his hand, then let it go quickly.

"Cara Gellder," she replied.

"The so-called *sulpari*," he said.

"Yes."

"And you need what from me, exactly?"

"I need to know about dark magic. A man in a cloak has attacked me twice now using some sort of black power. He—"

"Yes, yes, the 'Hooded Man.' The earl was so kind as to inform me of that earlier." Avallune turned the page and huffed with impatience. "This blasted thing will take far too long." He flung the potion up over his shoulder. Cara gasped, expecting it to hit the floor and shatter. The wizard uttered a few strange words and the vial instead floated to the table and came to rest beside the mortar.

He looked at her for the first time. "I have never dealt in dark magic, and neither has any mage I've encountered. It's forbidden."

"That didn't stop the Hooded Man," Cara said.

"No." Avallune snapped the book shut and stood. "I suppose it didn't. I would need to experience his magic firsthand to know what arts he practices. I cannot help you."

Cara's fragile hopes began to slip away. She asked desperately, "Surely there's *something* you've heard?"

"Dark magic goes hand-in-hand with any power from Autorus. Lord Alexandro would be the firsthand expert on the latter. Though...I suppose his cousin, Mavian, might know something more. He studies undeath, too."

"Where can I find him?" Cara pressed.

"Do I look like I have the time to keep track of every petty noble?" Avallune snapped. "Ask Strilu." He waved his hand, dismissing her. Cara fought to keep herself calm as the beast roiled in her. *Nothing that helps me find Renna,* she thought, gritting her teeth. She turned to go, then thought of another question.

"My...my friend knows a man, Laris Stanthorpe, who can do magic. Have you heard of him?"

Avallune paused, his inquisitive eyes resting on her for a moment. "I've heard of him. Peddler's Guild, correct?" At Cara's nod, he cocked his head. "He's not registered with me as a mage."

"He put a spell on my friend." With a pang, Cara realized that she did still think of Sandu as a friend. *I hope he survived, that he's out there somewhere.*

"That may be so, but still...I should investigate..." Once more he turned away from her and waved his hand. Cara didn't dare push him farther, so she departed in a gloomy mood. If Avallune, the earl's best mage, knew nothing of the Hooded Man, how was she ever to find him?

I suppose my only hope lies in this Mavian fellow, she thought. That night, she spoke to Alex about meeting his cousin. He promised to speak with Mavian, and the next morning she found an invitation for the following day.

Once more Cara spent her free time exploring, but now she saw that nobles skirted around her or gave her sneering looks. *It seems some rumors have spread about me,* she thought. Cara carried her head high and ignored them. Still, she hoped that Alex hadn't found himself too embroiled in scandal by bringing her here.

As she wandered, Cara constantly looked for Renna. Her heart leapt with every blonde woman she saw, but none of them were her lady. She found herself despairing, and clung to the hope that Mavian could help her.

With the help of a servant, Cara found her way to Mavian's chambers the day of their appointment. Too full of anticipation and frazzled by worry, she knocked a little too hard. A pleasant voice called her to enter, and she went down a spiral staircase to the main chamber.

Mavian's large central room held a fireplace along with the various furniture Cara had grown used to seeing in the palace. A young man greeted her, his long dark hair pulled back and tied at the nape of his neck. His sharp green eyes took her in. He stepped aside, bowed, and offered her a seat.

"I am intrigued," he drawled, carelessly holding a goblet in one hand. "My cousin brings a rustic to the palace, and she wants to see *me*, of all people."

"Avallune believes you know something of dark magic," Cara said.

"I'm no mage," he said immediately. "I can barely cast a cantrip."

Cara had no idea what that was, and didn't think it prudent to show off the gaps in her knowledge. She said, "I don't want you to cast a spell or anything like that. But I had hoped you might have heard about someone using dark magic."

"There are whispers here and there. Have you seen this magic performed?"

Cara nodded and described it to him: Renna's kidnapping, the black tentacles, the attack on the caravan. She finished by saying, "If I find the Hooded Man, I can find my lady. That's why I need help; I have no idea where to start."

Mavian played with his goblet, his brow furrowed. After a moment, he said, "I hear the queen has a fondness for a young noblewoman with blonde hair. You could ask her."

"The queen would never see someone like me."

"She would if the earl demanded it." A small smile played about his lips. "The noblewoman in question had been thought dead in a fire, and miraculously appeared in full vigor around the time your lady went missing. There could be a connection there."

"Renna would never impersonate someone else." Cara found the very idea insulting.

"She would if she were spelled to do so. Remember, no one knows what this dark magic can do."

Cara was about to argue, but thought better of it. *Don't make a lord angry with you*, she reminded herself. She said instead, "Thank you for your information. I'll be sure to speak with the earl about an audience with the queen."

Mavian tilted his cup back and took a long drink. He wiped his mouth and said, "I've heard, too, that there have been unusual happenings at a certain tavern by the docks. Men turning up with lost memories and strange injuries, things like that. Your Hooded Man could be involved somehow."

It was only a thread, barely a hint, but Cara had no choice but to pursue it. She asked, "What's the tavern called?"

"Bertha's Bosun, down on Fester's Wharves."

Cara nodded and stood to leave. Before she could, Mavian asked, "Why did Alexandro bring you here? I've never known him to be a love-besotted fool, especially not one who would bring a rustic into the palace. There must be another reason he wanted *you*, above all others."

His green eyes held hers. Cara swallowed, unsure how much to tell him. Earl Seastone had advised her to keep her powers secret, but she had never lied to a lord before. She tried to find the right words, and eventually said, "I'm sure Alex could tell you better than I can."

"Of course." Mavian bowed his head in farewell and Cara left him.

She now had gained two more clues, neither substantial, but more than she had started the day with.

I'll find you, Renna, Cara promised. *I'm close.*

A full quinn later, Cara finally gained an audience with the queen. She shifted from foot to foot in the antechamber, feeling horribly overwhelmed. Her maids had made her hair into an elaborate pile, then painted her skin with various cosmetics. Alex had given her a "humble" necklace and bracelet to wear, though their cost could have fed one of Kell's villagers for half a year. Her dress was the most elegant from her wardrobe and weighed heavily on her shoulders. Her legs felt encumbered by the skirts that swirled around them.

When the queen admitted her, Cara held tightly to her skirt, her hands shaking. She had been told to wait to speak until spoken to, and to curtsey immediately. As soon as she saw the queen, she dropped into the lowest bow she could manage in her tight slippers. When she looked up, she saw the queen give her an appraising look, like she was a horse for auction. A knight stood in the corner, his hand on his sword as he, too, watched Cara.

Queen Seanna waved Cara forward and said, "Earl Seastone was most insistent I meet with you. I cannot fathom why, unless he wants my status brought low by such an encounter."

Cara's mouth went dry. Her eyes fell to her shoes, and she said, "I...I had hoped to ask you a question, Your Grace."

"Oh? My brother won't tumble with you. Only the Strilus would look to a peasant for such entertainment." The queen popped a grape in her mouth, one hand resting on her swollen stomach.

Cara's eyes flicked up, her mouth dropping open before she remembered to shut it. *Is this how she speaks to everyone? Or just rustics like me?* Before her nerve fled her, Cara said, "I wanted to ask about a noblewomen you're said to be great friends with."

The queen paused. "I have many courtiers in my company."

"I serve this woman, and I just want to find her," Cara pressed on, horribly aware of Queen Seanna's judging eyes. "Renna Nellestere, who went missing a month ago. She is taller than me, with golden hair and blue eyes."

At that, a look of pain and anger flashed across the queen's face. She pushed slowly to her feet, and Cara nearly went to help her. She held back, and after some cursing, the queen stood.

"You're describing Maeria Westerburg," the queen said, "who is no longer in my favor."

Cara licked her lips, hoping she didn't betray her disappointment. "I...I had simply hoped–"

"Even if this Lady Nellestere was here, I would have no reason to entertain her. Kell is a small fief, barely worth anyone's time. Sir Eric, escort this peasant from my sight."

The queen's assessment of Kell stung, and Cara didn't object as the knight came forward and took her arm. Her shoulders slumped as he led her through the antechamber to the door. *One clue wasted.*

Just as her fingers brushed the doorknob, the queen screamed.

Cara and Sir Eric both whirled. The queen shouted again, and the knight ran back. Cara followed him, her skirts blossoming around her legs. Her heart made a staccato rhythm. She heard the scraping of something sharp against wood, and harsh, rattling breaths. She and the knight stopped at the threshold, arrested by the sight before them.

There were prowlers in the palace. Three of them advanced on the queen, trapping her against the far wall. They stayed away from the sun streaming through the windows, but still crept forward, jaws slathering.

Cara had no time to get her sword, no time to free herself of her entrapping skirts. Her hands sweating, she turned to Sir Eric.

"Give me a weapon!" she hissed. Sir Eric drew his sword and dagger. He tossed the smaller blade to her, his eyes fixed the whole time on their enemies.

Cara walked slowly into the room as the knight circled away from her. The prowlers looked between them and the queen, their red eyes full of hunger. Without a thought for the hours of work some tailor had put into her gown, Cara slashed the front laces, shrugged off the sleeves, and stepped out of the large skirts. Dressed now only in a shift and bodice, she drew the dagger across the back of her hand, letting a few drops of blood fall to the ground.

The prowlers sniffed the air, turning toward her. They panted at the sight of the ruby droplets.

"Get the queen and get out," Cara said. She circled closer to the prowlers, her dagger a feeble weapon against the monsters. "If they attack, go for their heads and hearts. Try not to get cornered."

Sir Eric grunted, coming closer to the prowlers from the other side. The queen held her belly, her eyes wide. As the prowlers came to Cara, she felt the beast within her howling for blood. She acquiesced to it.

Cara's thoughts turned only to death. The prowlers moved slowly, their claws digging into the rug. Each drop of spit from their jaws, each blink of their red-rimmed eyes, lasted a candle. Cara's breath moved up through her chest and down into her powerful arms. All other sounds grew muffled in her ears, the din of prowler cries no more than the murmur of wind through trees.

She had all the time she needed as the creatures moved through tar to get to her.

Cara drove her dagger into the first prowler that reached her. She watched in fascination as the creature gasped and gargled, its black blood cascading onto her hand. The spark behind its eyes vanished.

With a dancer's grace, Cara threw off the dead prowler. She moved as water through a sieve, her dagger an extension of her hand. One foot behind the other, she turned to half-face the next prowler. Her arm jarred as her blade met its neck, too small to quite get through. She pulled back, readying the next swing, when a sharp pain pierced her back.

The third prowler clung to her shoulders, its talons biting into her. The injured one backed away. As quickly as the room had gone quiet, the crashing noises returned. Cara heard once more the queen's whimpers, shouts of alarm from the hall, and the prowlers' shrieks. Her breath drew ragged in her throat and her limbs shook. She stumbled under the prowler's weight, slashing her dagger over her shoulder with one hand and trying to hold back its head with the other.

Don't let it bite you, she thought. *Don't become more of a monster.*

Suddenly, the weight lifted, the talons scraping her skin as they pulled off her. Cara whirled to see Sir Eric, his armored arms encircling the prowler. She plunged her dagger into the beast's chest, and it collapsed in his arms.

"Get down!" Sir Eric shouted. Cara dropped to the floor as his sword swung over her head, decapitating the monster behind her.

Cara looked around her, sure that more prowlers would appear. All three lay dead as the queen sobbed in the corner. Suddenly exhausted, Cara rocked back on her heels and wiped her eyes. Her white shift was spattered with black, its back nearly torn to pieces. The beast slunk down into her belly, satiated for now, and she felt her features melt back into her normal, human face.

The beast saved the queen's life, Cara thought. *It helped me kill the prowlers.* She doubted she could have fought them all and won, even with the knight's help, had she not been strengthened by the beast. *Perhaps its evil truly can be used against worse things.*

And Cara couldn't lie to herself: she had enjoyed the power that flowed through her veins, delighted in the violence wrought at her hand. In that moment, she craved more of what the beast could offer her. What greater powers could it unleash?

The knight loomed above her, and Cara pushed back her thoughts. His expression was hard and stern, reminding her of those days when she'd failed to live up to Merick's expectations. She almost smiled at him, but he leveled his sword at her.

"You're a prowler," he said, his tone merciless. Behind him, Cara could see the queen's frightened tears.

"If I were, then I would have joined them," Cara said, pointing to the bodies on the floor. "But I'm not, so I didn't."

He didn't back down. Queen Seanna stepped forward. "Stand down, Sir Eric. She just saved my life."

Sir Eric hesitated, then sheathed his sword. He said, "The king will want to know of this."

The queen sighed. "I suppose you're right."

By this time, a crowd had gathered at the queen's doors. Guards kept them from entering, but a steward ducked past them and went to the queen. She murmured to him, and he bowed and left.

"Bring her," the queen commanded. She wiped her face with a kerchief, then strode sedately to the door. The knight bent and took Cara's elbow, pulling her to her feet. He held out his hand, and she returned the dagger. He didn't release her, and she let him lead her after the queen.

The crowd backed away, whispering among themselves. Sir Eric held Cara tightly, his gloved hand rough on her skin. They went down the stairs to a large gathering hall. Its windows were shut against the sunlight, and sheets covered the furniture and chandeliers. Queen Seanna carefully seated herself on a cushioned couch.

The king sat next to her, proud yet tired-looking. His grey eyes took in Cara's appearance and the blood that covered her and Sir Eric. The knight closed the door behind them, sending a loud *boom* through the empty hall.

Cara felt small in that large space, with the two most powerful people in the kingdom staring at her. She curtseyed again, and nearly stumbled to her knees. She hadn't realized how tired the beast's efforts had made her.

"Who are you?" the king asked in short, clipped words.

"Caralyn Gellder, Your Grace. From Kell."

The king scratched his full beard. "Your parentage?"

"My mother is Sura Gellder. I don't know my father's name."

King Henrik looked at her as if she were a game piece he had yet to decide where to place on the board. The queen had fear in her gaze. Cara shifted from foot to foot, wishing that Alex were with her, or even the earl.

"What are you?" the queen asked. "I saw your face: you looked like a prowler."

Cara hesitated, a mouse caught between a cat and a fox. The earl had told her to keep her powers a secret, yet it was treason to lie to royalty. She had no choice but to tell the truth. "I'm not a prowler. I...I am born of a mortal mother and undead father. Lord Alexandro called me a *sulpari*. When the beast rises, I turn into something similar to a prowler. But I'm human, and would never harm the innocent." *I hope.*

The king's eyes blazed. "So the Strilus knew what you are?"

Cara nodded. He rubbed his temple and said, "Sir Eric, send for Jacobi. I want to see Earl Seastone and his brother before the day is done."

The knight bowed and left. Alone now in front of the king and queen, Cara swallowed back her fear. *Would they have me imprisoned? Executed?*

"Are you trained in combat?" asked the king.

"Yes, Your Grace. My mother paid a mercenary to train me."

"How did a woman gain the wealth for such a thing?"

Cara shrugged. "I don't know. I haven't seen her in years. She also had me learn reading, writing, arithmetic, and history."

The king's eyes narrowed. "A woman who fights and reads...even if you were not akin to the prowlers, I would find you suspicious. Why are you here in Riverfen? What business have you with the Strilus?"

"I need their help," Cara said, shifting her weight and flexing her hands. She told them about Renna's disappearance and the Hooded Man's attacks.

The queen rubbed her stomach, then said, "So you sought an audience with me on the earl's orders? To find these people?"

Cara affirmed this, and the king leaned forward. "Does the earl believe this Hooded Man to be a threat?"

"He does."

"Dark magic was banned in Dotschar by my father," King Henrik said. "I will lend my weight to these investigations. They may be tied to today's events; prowlers appearing in the palace can only be the work of dark powers." He straightened, and spoke with a king's commanding voice. "While we are grateful for the queen's life, we have not determined your place in this court. You are to remain in Riverfen until we have spoken to Earl Seastone and our advisors and come to a decision about you. You are dismissed."

Cara bowed and left the room, glad to escape the royals. They were vultures, circling above her, ready to swoop once she showed usefulness. A pair of guards escorted her to her rooms. Everyone looked at her as she passed, at the blood on her underclothes and the cut on her hand, and they murmured behind their hands.

This time, Cara found it much more difficult to ignore them. She felt naked and unsure, as if the loss of her secret had weakened her.

Alex waited for her. He gave a soft exclamation at her appearance and embraced her. She melted into his arms.

"You're hurt," he said, his hands feeling at the scratches on her back.

"They know," Cara said, her voice muffled as she buried her face in his chest. "The king and queen know. They'll want to speak with you and the earl, and I'm so sorry, I couldn't lie, I didn't know–"

"Shh, Cara. It will be alright. Druam knows how to handle the king. But word will spread; we can't help that." Alex pulled her into the washroom. "Worry about Renna and the Hooded Man. We'll take care of everything else."

Cara slumped in the bath as the cuts on her back protested. She held Alex's hand. "I'm no closer to finding her, Alex. I'm lost, and everyone is looking at me now."

"Rest now. You'll feel better soon." His comforting words burned through the upheaval in her head, and she closed her eyes. The suspicious faces of the king and queen danced behind her eyelids. As Alex kept soothing her, the images eventually disappeared.

"Don't leave me," Cara mumbled, her body finally relaxing in the peaceful water.

"Never," he said.

CHAPTER THIRTY-NINE
Gwen

DAY BY DAY drudged past, each candle longer than the last, each night an eternity of aimless sleep interspersed with restless waking. The draughts Avallune gave to Gwen made her both restless and tired, alert and half-awake, all in shifting bursts. Though her Gaiar no longer troubled her, she wasn't herself; her humors felt as awful as if she had a fever.

Then there were the thoughts that someone had done this to her, someone who knew of her magic and wanted to bring her harm. When those dark musings intruded, Gwen found it difficult to make them go away. She spent candles imagining the queen, or Ambassador Daghorn, or even an unknown enemy tipping poison into her glass.

Eventually – Gwen lost track of the days – her humors came back into balance. With Avallune's blessing, she eased back into her magic, casting a small cantrip each morning. But no more, according to his orders. Despite her growing strength, she did not want to return to the feasts or parties, nor did she wish to even think of the Masque. She feared the whispers and askance looks of the courtiers, and hadn't the fortitude to bear their scorn. Books had lost their charm, and she didn't want to drudge through yet another history of the kingdom. Without parties, reading, or constant magical practice to distract her, Gwen became irritably bored.

Druam, though he had been constantly comforting, had grown frustrated with her. One day, as she paced her chambers, he said, "I do wish you would find something to occupy yourself. Embroidery, or singing, or the like."

"I have embroidered half the candles of my life, and sung for most of that. I'm tired of both."

"Then what if I gave you something to care for?"

Gwen paused. "What do you mean?"

"I meant it to be a surprise after the Masque, but where's the harm in an early gift? Come, my love. I have something to show you. Are you well enough for a long walk?"

Druam led her from the palace into the gardens where they'd first met. Soon, she realized that their destination was the conservatory, a vast glass complex at least two acres wide and three long with translucent blue and green windows on its sides and roof. Even so, she couldn't see inside it, as trees and shrubbery lined it both inside and out. She knew that none but Druam, his gardeners, and the extremely rare guest were ever allowed inside. Druam told her it was his sanctuary, a place to escape the worries of the kingdom and immerse himself in the beauty of the natural world.

Inside, an overwhelmingly sweet smell assaulted her: tulips and roses, lavender and herbs; every flower she could imagine, sweeping the walls and climbing trellises, carpeting the floor between stone paths and gurgling streams. Trees grew here, too, massive things that had been carefully trimmed to provide a leafy roof overhead. Here, they were still green, only just turning to their autumn colors. Manmade rivers and streams ran throughout, an imitation of the city below, with bridges over them built in an architectural style reminiscent of old Gallic designs.

Druam and Gwen meandered the path. Once Gwen adjusted to the smell, she noticed the trill of birds and calls of small animals. A fox darted across the stones in front of them, only pausing long enough to sniff at the intruders. Gwen wondered aloud how many animals lived there.

"Hundreds, I suppose," Druam said. "I've collected birds

from all over D'Ehsen and from across the sea. Lizards, turtles, wild cats and foxes, even a nightcat once. At night the lantern faeries come out, as do the dragons."

"Dragons? How could they even fit?"

Druam laughed. "No, not the large wyrms and wyverns people often call 'dragons.' These are small creatures, some the size of cats, others as large as a sheep. They eat fruit and plants, and while some of them eat fish, most prefer plants. But they're much rarer now than in years before," he said sadly. "I fear some species are only found here, hunted to scarcity in the broader world. They live an extraordinarily long time, you know. And breed infrequently."

Though Gwen strained to catch a glimpse of one of the wondrous creatures, she saw only the gently swaying branches and shrubs.

They came to a section of the conservatory which was walled off by wooden partitions and creeping vines, with an exquisite metal gate wrought in the shape of a pair of peacocks. Druam unlocked the gate and opened it, gesturing for Gwen to enter. She stepped into the hidden world and gasped.

A huge hanging willow dominated the landscape, its branches trailing through a set of circular concentric pools. In the green space between each pool, thousands of exotic flowers in all colors climbed over and between shrubs, small trees, and green-veined marble boulders. The water in the pools held brightly blooming lilies and croaking frogs that hopped from pad to pad. Chirruping birds sang from above. A mosaic path wound through the whole scene, connected by stepping stones across the water and leading to a stone bench strewn with cushions that lay next to the willow's trunk. A cat uncurled itself from a sunny spot, gave Gwen a lazy look, then yawned and stretched itself over the tiles.

"It's beautiful," Gwen said. She hadn't the words to express more. She looked to Druam, and saw, for perhaps the first time, true happiness spreading across his normally reserved features.

"It's yours."

Too amazed to speak, Gwen wandered into her own

pristine garden, stooping to sniff the flowers that caught her eye and marveling at the fish swimming in the pools. Any bad humors melted away in the humid air. Taking a deep, clean breath, she suddenly wished she were not wearing a tight-laced bodice so she could completely fill her lungs.

Druam followed her across the stepping stones. "I've scoured plants and flowers from the known world: Demar lilies, Dedarian orchids, Rengu trees, Lofalin tulips; anything I could think of and cultivate these last few deshe. The animals, too, came from all over: ten different bird species, three types of frog, lizards, fish, ferrets, possums..." He trailed off, and Gwen saw a hint of uncertainty creep into his expression. She rushed back to him.

"It's wonderful," she murmured, her head buried in his chest. "It's the most...it's...no one has ever gifted me anything as incredible as this. Thank you."

"Come here whenever you like. The gardeners will tend it for you, but if you wish, I can show you how to care for the plants and animals." Kissing the top of her head, he said, "I cannot express how glad I am that this pleases you."

"It's perfect, beyond anything I could have dreamed. I wonder...since no one else comes here...perhaps, when I am well again, Mavian and I could practice magic here?"

"I hadn't thought of it, but I suppose, if it would help you, then it cannot hurt."

They sat on the bench and spoke more, mostly of lighthearted affairs. Druam pointed out plants or birds and explained them. At midday, he stood and told her he had councils to attend. He promised to send Mavian later on. Content, Gwen relaxed on the bench, watching the cat chase a frog.

Some time later, a guard opened the gate to let Mavian in. Mavian took a moment to marvel, then stepped over the pools with a heavy tome she hadn't seen before. Gwen said, "I have missed you so! These days have been so dull without you. How have you occupied yourself?"

"Oh, with this and that," he said with a sly grin. "I have won the hand of a charming lady, and finally been given her father's blessing."

"How wonderful!" Gwen kissed his cheek. "I wish you both great happiness, though I hadn't known you were courting. You must tell me more about her."

"In time," he laughed. Then his expression grew serious. "I heard about your illness."

The memory of her boiling Gaiar and the agony of purifying it made Gwen shudder. "It was awful."

"Do you know what caused it?"

"Avallune isn't sure, though Druam tells me that he's spent a lot of time trying to find the contaminant."

Mavian regarded her with a dark look. "You attended many parties. Someone could have poisoned you during them."

"I know." The thought had plagued her throughout her confinement.

"I told you it was too dangerous."

"I'm sorry," Gwen said. "But I promised Druam–"

"Druam knows *nothing* of magic and Gaiar. Did you ever think that he could be the one who caused this impurity, or that he wanted you to see the wickedness of your Gaiar?"

"Stop it," Gwen said even as doubt made tendrils through her mind. *But Druam was so afraid for me; he would never...*

"I know that you love him, but he is cunning. He can guide people to his way of thinking in the most subtle of ways. This could all have been a ruse to force you away from your magic."

"What book did you bring?" Gwen said abruptly. She couldn't bear the thought of Druam doing anything against her, and Mavian's words distressed her.

"This is *A Gathering for Baldthera*," Mavian said impatiently. "There's a spell in it that I think would help you see more clearly: a scrying spell. It allows for the caster to project themselves somewhere else, a great distance away. They can see and hear everything going on."

"Wullum..." Gwen murmured. She fingered the gold-filigree title on the ancient tome. "I could see him. Could I speak to him?" *He can help me see what I'm missing, help me find the truth.*

She smiled at the idea of seeing her brother again.

"Perhaps. It doesn't say one way or another. The spell is quite complex, so I asked the gardener to fetch its materials; they may help you cast it."

"I don't know if Druam would approve of me doing something so large so soon..."

"You don't need his permission, nor his approval. Would you let him ruin your ability to reunite with your brother?"

"I do wish you wouldn't speak of him so. Why hold such disdain now?"

Mavian muttered, "If you won't allow me to disparage him, allow me to convince you to cast this working. Would you try it?"

After a moment's hesitation, Gwen said, "Yes."

The spell took up an entire page, the words written in a small hand. As she read it, she mouthed the words, feeling their rhythm. They had a similar cadence to the melody Wullum would sing to her after their mother's death: a warm, simple song that held a litany of memories.

A gardener came into Gwen's sanctuary with a bowl in each hand. The sweet smell of incense rose from one, while the other held water with rose petals floating in it. He bowed, then departed.

After a deep breath, Gwen splashed her face with the water. Then she placed a petal on her tongue while she breathed in the incense. Her mind felt cleared. As she chewed the foul-tasting petal, she concentrated on her Gaiar. It rose up to her throat, fluid and cool, awaiting her working.

Gwen closed her eyes, swallowed the petal, and began her song. The magic buoyed her limbs, and she felt weightless even though she still rested on cushions. Gaiar flowed over her skin as she sang. It tickled and pricked, but did not overpower her. Once she finished the working, she opened her eyes.

Gwen lay on a smooth tiled floor, and saw not the bright garden with its birds and flowers, but Wullum's throne room. Tall pillars lined each side, carved with vines and scenes of battle. At the head of the room was the high throne, polished wood inlaid with ivory. Gwen stood half-behind one of the pillars, and two men were in the center of the room. One was Wullum, the tattoos on his bald pate shining in the torchlight, and the other Isten Angi, his adviser.

"Ebarren is dead, Wullum," Isten said. He had a hunched back and seemed to cower before the liegelord, though Gwen knew that he was unafraid of Wullum. "Hanged yesterday morning."

"Damn," Wullum muttered. He ran his hands over his head, his rings flashing. "Damn, damn, damn. What of our security? Have the reinforcements made it past the siege?"

"No. They were heavily rebuffed; we have no recourse but to surrender."

"Horseshit! I will not allow my kingdom to fall into Rolf's hands. Send a messenger to my commanders on the walls, tell them to do whatever they can to boost the mens' morale. If we make it through the night–"

"The men are nervous, Wullum. They've heard the rumors of Gwen, and now there are accusations against you, too. Rinar, the handmaid who disappeared after Gwen escaped, has come forward with evidence of magic from Gwen's chambers." Isten put a hand to Wullum's shoulder, and Gwen crept closer. Neither man noticed her. Isten said, "You must flee the city while you still can. The battle is already lost, the Inquisition too strong. They will kill you, your wives, and your sons and daughters."

"The Liegelord does not flee."

"Wullum, *think*–"

"I said, the Liegelord. Does. Not. Flee." Wullum strode to his throne, sat down and grasped its arms. As he did, the grand double doors at the end of the hall burst open and a lone soldier collapsed to the floor.

"Enemies!" the soldier gasped. "Enemies have breached the walls!"

"Go!" Wullum shouted to Isten. "Don't let them into the castle!"

Isten hurried away, past the dying soldier, as Wullum paced in front of the throne. He ran his hands over his head again, muttering to himself. Creeping out from her hiding place, Gwen approached him. He looked up, his hand going to the dagger at his side. Then he gaped, frozen, as Gwen came closer.

"Gwen...?" Wullum said weakly. His commanding demeanor collapsed into a boyish joy, and he ran to her. When he tried to touch her, though, his hands passed through her as if she were a ghost. "What is this?" he said, stepping back. "Is it really you?"

"It's me, Wullum," Gwen said. She cupped his cheek, though could not actually touch it. "I'm here. I had to see you again."

"But...how? Whose magic is this?"

"Mine."

"You should not–"

"It is not evil, Wullum. I have so desperately wanted to write to you, to tell you how much I miss you. I'm married now to Earl Seastone, and it is with his blessing that I am growing in my magic. Please, Wullum, forgive me, but I could not live without it."

For a moment, she thought that he would not accept her, but he said, "I'm just glad you are alive. Demarren has grown far worse in your absence, and every moment I've regretted sending you away."

Before Gwen could say anything more, a troop of soldiers in red tabards poured into the room, wielding pikes, swords, and crossbows. Their faces were masked by silver helms, and they rushed toward Wullum, their weapons seeking him.

"Wullum!" Gwen cried.

"Witchcraft!" shouted one of the soldiers. "Kill them!"

A volley of bolts shot over the advancing soldiers. They clattered through Gwen to the floor, but Wullum fell to his knees. Four bolts pierced him in different places, and he stared desperately at them. "Go, Gwen."

"Wullum!" she screamed, but the soldiers' pikes were upon them, slashing through her magical form and bloodying the floor with Wullum's ruined corpse.

Gwen's magic pulled at her, and though she screamed, tried

to stay with Wullum and hold him, she felt a wave of dizziness overcome her. Shutting her eyes, she let the working dissipate. Her Gaiar returned to its resting place. When she opened her eyes, she saw the garden again, and Mavian, still beside her, looking excited.

"'Did it work?" he asked. "You looked like you were asleep."

"He's dead," Gwen said numbly. "They killed him."

"What?"

"The Inquisition came, and they killed him. He's gone." Gwen's final memory of Wullum was not his laughter, or his joy in seeing her, but of his blank eyes staring up at her and his red blood tinging the ivory throne. She had watched him die, and did nothing to stop it from happening.

Mavian and Gwen rushed back to her chambers. Gwen felt in a haze, confused why the world moved so normally around her when she felt so distant and tired. Wullum's death lingered before her eyes, white bone showing through dark skin and red blood.

Druam ushered Gwen inside her rooms, concern etched in his body language.

"What happened? Are you well?"

"Wullum is dead," Mavian said when he saw that Gwen hadn't the strength to speak. "She saw him through a scrying spell. The Inquisition has taken control of Demarren."

"You're sure?" Druam asked. Gwen nodded as she sank to a couch. Druam frowned. "I must confirm it. Gwen, my love, rest and do not think on it. Mavian, come with me."

The men hurried away, conferring quietly between themselves. Gwen didn't care much. She didn't need confirmation to know that what she saw was real.

Gwen curled up on a chair, trying to remember the Wullum from her youth. But each memory came tainted with blood: the recollection of their first horseback ride ended with an image of him dangling from the stirrups, eyes glassy; instead of joy and pride the day he was crowned Liegelord, she only saw him dead on the throne; his last hug, so strong and comforting before, yet his arms grew slack around her.

She couldn't think of him without thinking of his death.

His final moments pelted her mind. She could see each bolt that struck him, a tear falling for every one. The phantom pikes slashed him into the pool of red.

I should have stopped it.

It was all her fault. Her magic, and that of those like her, had brought the Trials upon Demarren. Her escape no doubt spurred his enemies into a frenzy. It was even possible that Ambassador Daghorn had sent word of her.

Grief and self-loathing assaulted her. If she were more powerful, she could have stopped it. She could have called lightning from the skies or summoned monsters to take down the soldiers. Perhaps she could even have altered time. She could bring Wullum's soul back from the dead.

Such wishes were futile. She hadn't the power to change the past.

But, Gwen thought, feeling anger rising in her, *perhaps I have the power to end those who destroyed my country.* She sprang to her feet and rushed to her shelf of spell books. There, she found the one Mavian had warned her away from: *Dunalan's Compendium.* Her thoughts mired in anger and grief, Gwen clutched the book and ran from her rooms, her skirts swishing around her ankles. She sprinted through the long corridors, heedless of other nobles' shocked expressions. Running, running, she returned to the conservatory, pushing past a gardener who cried out for her to slow down.

When she came to her sanctuary, she finally stopped. She sank to her knees and opened the book. In its pages, she found a curse of vengeance and destruction.

This time, she did not sing a Demar lullaby or a Dotsch tune. From the very roots of Earda, a dreadful chanting song came to Gwen's lips. Her rage fed into her Gaiar, consuming her, all her limbs shaking from the force of it. As she sang, the hot fury built and built within her.

Waves of invisible heat shuddered out from her, the air shimmering as red runes wrote themselves above Gwen's head. The runes were ancient, drawn from the power of beings as ancient as the Cythra. Plants nearby burst into flame, birds' calls turned into panicked shrieks.

For a moment, Gwen reveled in her power. Soon, the Skals that did this would feel her righteous fury.

Fire flowed around her, and her tender heart suddenly knew that this spell was wrong. It spoke to cruelty and pain, with no regard to the things it destroyed. Darkness surged through her, and she had to stop.

But Gwen found she could not halt the spell. The working flowed from her lips, uncaring of her sudden desire to stop. It snatched her Gaiar from her without her consent. She tried to pull back, but the song ripped at her throat.

Hot Gaiar rolled off her in all directions. The water in the pools bubbled as floating lilies withered into ash and frogs leapt in panic to meet their deaths in the air. Gwen tried to scream, but the awful song overpowered her. Her vision turned hazy and distorted.

Remembering her first failed working, Gwen took all her strength and repeated the last phrase, over and over, holding the Gaiar within as best she could. She drew her magic back into herself as she chanted the singular phrase. The runes slowly stopped writing, simply hanging in the air. The heat pulled back into her, but now she felt as if she had a high fever all over. Her skin crackled and popped with sudden blisters.

A cool hand descended on her shoulder, and, still chanting, she turned to see Druam. They stared at each other, the runes above them glowing hot as molten steel. Then he scooped her into his arms and carried her away. Gwen's magic boiled inside of her, desperate to be released, but she held on. Each moment threatened to lose her the battle with her own Gaiar.

As Druam ran, he murmured comforting words that Gwen couldn't catch. Before they reached the doorway, Avallune appeared. He shouted an order at Druam, and Druam knelt, setting Gwen onto the cool floor. She panted, the repeated phrase like a drumbeat in her head. If she released it now, the working would take her and the entire conservatory with it.

"She's tangled in her working," Avallune said. "Stand back."

Though Druam obeyed, Gwen longed for his cool touch. She shuddered when Avallune laid his hands to her chest and head. He chanted the spell Mavian had used to help undo her working, but his was more powerful, more controlled. As he spoke, Gwen felt a chill shiver pass through her, seeking out her Gaiar and freezing it. Her chant now barely whispered, Gwen sought out the frozen pieces of Gaiar within her and gathered them back to herself. With each one, she could sense the curse's hold on her fading. At last, after what seemed to be candles since she had started the working, she released it.

The heat in her dissipated, leaving only emptiness. She knew the runes had vanished, but the plants and animals which had perished by her curse could not so easily be mended. Gwen looked to Druam. "I'm so sorry. Are you hurt? Did it burn you?"

"It didn't touch me," he said. "But you're covered in blisters. We must take you to a curate at once. Avallune, how did you know to come here?"

"I could feel a vast, evil working, like a swarm of locusts spreading throughout the palace. I simply followed the Gaiar here; I'm glad I came in time. Any longer, and your lady would have completely lost the spell. It would have torn her apart and set half your palace aflame."

"Why did you try to cast it?" Druam asked as he lifted Gwen once more. "What were you trying to do?"

"I had to do something," Gwen murmured, her whole body aching as if a wyrm had fallen on top of her, her skin burning. "I couldn't let Wullum's death go unpunished."

"Take her to rest," Avallune said. "My lady, your Gaiar is tender and volatile. You should not attempt to use it for at least two deshe, if not a month or longer. Your whole body is wracked with bad humors; you must rest to heal."

"I will make sure she does," Druam said. "Avallune, tell no one what you saw here. Not even Mavian. We cannot let this spread farther."

"As you wish it."

As Druam carried Gwen back to her rooms, she said softly, "I have displeased you."

"Shh, my love. Just rest."

Though she was now safe from the working, Gwen hadn't any strength. Her heart slowed to a whisper, and her Gaiar shifted, as if it were draining from her like water from a dam. Before she fainted, she saw the glimmer of a silhouette in the corner of her eye. It had the form of an old woman. It beckoned to her, whispering, "Let the Sisters Three teach you, child. Come to the witches, for we know your true calling. We will help you have your vengeance."

CHAPTER FORTY
Sandu

OF ALL THE dungeons Sandu had ever seen, this one was certainly the nicest. An echo of the airy splendor above, the cell was large and clean with a sturdy oak door. Sandu's hands were tied to a beam nailed to the wall, his shoulders aching from the uncomfortable position. He had been stripped of everything but his breeches.

They had let Sandu sleep on a mat of straw on the floor for a few days, though Sandu had lost track of how many had passed. The gaolers were kind enough, giving him bread and clean water twice a day, though none of them spoke to him. That morning, however, soldiers had come and tied him with rough rope to the well-worn beam. He'd been there for almost two candles now, alone and waiting. The longer he waited, the more difficult it became to breathe.

A key scraped in the door's lock and the knight who had arrested Sandu stepped into the cell. One hand rested on the hilt of his sword as if Sandu, tied as he was, had any prayer in fighting him.

"I saved the queen," Sandu said quickly. "There was someone else, a man, he–"

"I'm not here to listen to your lies. We shall see how long you cling to falsehoods." The knight closed the door behind him.

"What's your name? I like to know the names of those who

unjustly torture me," Sandu said.

"Silence." The knight strode over to Sandu and slapped him. Sandu's head jerked into the beam, bright lights flickering in his vision.

"I think I've heard of you," Sandu said once the knight had backed away. He couldn't resist the verbal jabs; his mother had always told him his tongue would get him into trouble. "Sir Bearic, or Sir Eric, something like that. That's it, Sir Eric. Good, strong name. Suits the queen's dog."

"Shut up, swine."

"Slurs are unbecoming of a knight such as yourself." Sandu's rational side screamed at him to stop now before his sharp tongue led him to an early grave.

"I said *shut it*, assassin." The knight's tone was dangerously soft.

"I can honestly say I've never been called that before. Bastard, twat, ass, but never assassin. I'm far too kind for that sort of work."

The knight raised his fist, and, with a sharp jab, punched Sandu's nose. It broke with a loud *crack*, and Sandu tasted blood as it squirted from his nostrils.

"Let that serve as a lesson, you bastard," Sir Eric growled. "I don't want to hear another word from you that's not 'I confess.' Understood?"

Sandu nodded, and resisted spitting blood at Sir Eric's face.

"Lucky for you, I brought my tools with me," Sir Eric said. "I would have preferred the rack or the scavenger's daughter, but those are specialty pieces." Sir Eric carried an ominous-looking leather case. "Before I joined the royal guard, I was one of the Bloody Dwarves; the bloodiest, you might say. Had a knack for torture." The Bloody Dwarves were a mercenary company that had been forcefully disbanded years ago for its cruder methods.

"Is Queen Seanna alright?" Sandu blurted.

"She lives."

"Good. I just wanted to make sure I wasn't getting tortured in vain for saving her life."

"The queen herself requested this be done. Most lords

361

dislike it, but she and I think it an excellent practice when done properly." Sir Eric opened the case and began arranging its contents on a table. Sandu couldn't see the table, though he heard the clinking of metal. "Yes, this shall do for now. Your official trial will be held after the Masque, and I am free to do what I like with you until then. Farewell."

Sir Eric left his implements of torture lying out for Sandu to see. Sandu waited, expecting him to come back any moment, but he didn't. The tools caught his eye, and though Sandu tried to look away, he found he couldn't for long. He tried not to imagine what each one did, but his mind wandered there anyway. As time passed, he fought to keep his panic from rising. *Remember Cara*, he told himself. *She'll find out you're here, she'll help you.*

Hanging there in the dungeon, Sandu wondered if Cara would even want him back. Last he had seen her, he had confessed to betraying her. Would she forgive him? Would she do as Tambrey had done and turn him away? Sandu choked back a sob, then laughed at himself. *If there's any time to weep, it's this.* He gave into the grief and fright, and cried openly. He mourned for the life he could have had with his wife had he not been so stupid. He wept for Cara and her hardships, and that he had made her life worse. *If I'm freed, maybe I should just leave. She probably already thinks I'm dead. I shouldn't burden her again.* Then Alex's words came to him, reminding him of how much Cara needed both of them. In the chill dungeon, though, Sandu found them hard to believe.

A candle passed, then another, until evening came and went. Sandu's eyelids grew tired, and he shut them to catch just a bit of sleep...

A bucket of water was upended on his head just as he was starting to drift off. The guard who held it grinned, then retreated back to the hallway. Every so often during the night, guards would come in, and if Sandu was sleeping, they would wake him with water, clashing their swords on their shields, or slapping him with the flat of their blades. After the sun had risen, Sir Eric returned. Sandu had had no rest, his shoulders felt as if they would tear from their sockets, his nose still hurt, dried blood caked his chin and chest, and he had driven himself mad looking at the metal tools on the table.

Sir Eric wore only a pair of breeches and boots, his chest and arms bare. "I had a wonderful day yesterday, with three splendid meals. Sweet pasties with sugared fruit, cordial from the earl's personal store, meat dripping with grease. It was so very relaxing. How did you fare, Master Crin?"

Sandu spat onto the floor. He had no energy for anything else.

"That poorly? Well, the next few candles will be even worse for you."

"What do you want from me?" Sandu asked, his voice hoarse. He had just noticed that Sir Eric carried a cat o' nine tails, a vicious whip with cut glass and stones tied to leather straps. It would tear his skin to shreds.

Sir Eric lifted the whip, studying it. "I want a confession, Master Crin."

"Wait," Sandu croaked. *I don't want to be tortured, oh gods, I don't want it.*

"Tell me everything," the knight commanded.

"Fine," Sandu said, his head hanging. "I was a member of the Peddler's Guild. I was sent to find Caralyn Gellder and bring her to my guild leader. I found her, and then we met up with a scholar named Alex. We traveled, we got separated, and I came here looking for them. I joined the Protectors because this was the only way into the palace.

"The queen requested I go with her. You saw that. In her chambers, she kissed me. Then she just...left to take her bath. I wasn't sure what to do, so I was about to leave when I saw a shadow on the floor. I went to investigate, then I heard her scream. I rushed into her washroom. There was a man standing over her, drowning her. I pulled at him, then he ran into a servant's passage. I was trying to help the queen get up without violating her when you entered. Please, *please*, you must believe me. I don't know who the man was, but I'll help you find him. Ask Alexandro Strilu, bring him to me, he'll tell you the truth of my story."

The knight pondered a moment, his hand twitching the whip back and forth. At last he nodded. "I will bring Lord Strilu here, and he will determine what is to be done with you."

Leaving his tools and whip, Sir Eric departed. Sandu let his head sink to his bloodied chest and bit back tears. He prayed that Alex was the Lord Strilu, or else he would certainly be headed to the gallows.

Before he could close his eyes, Sandu felt an oddly familiar headache overwhelm his temples. It built up behind his eyes in spasms of dull pain, but he could do nothing to stop it. Just as his eyelids drooped, the old man appeared before him.

Sandu glared, but hadn't the strength to do anything else.

"Master Crin," said the blurred form of Laris Stanthorpe, "I know you're in the city. Why haven't you brought the girl yet?"

The apparition paused, looking down at Sandu's restrained body. "Ah. Well, find a way to free yourself, then report to me."

"Veck off," Sandu mumbled over a dry tongue.

Laris shook his head. "Don't make this worse for yourself. Caralyn Gellder belongs to me, by all rights, and I will have her. Her conception was no easy feat, that I can tell you, and I refuse to allow a disobedient man to keep me from her. Either you send me a letter once you're freed, or I will personally have you killed as slowly as possible."

Sandu licked his lips to retort, but the vision shimmered and vanished, leaving bright dots dancing across the cell walls.

He had been dozing off and on when the door slammed open. Sir Eric strode in wearing full armor and looking extremely dissatisfied. Sandu recoiled from the knight's sour look. But then another man entered, his dirty blonde hair tousled.

"Alex!" Sandu cried, straining against the ropes. "Alex, oh thank the gods, I promise I'll go to novum three times a quinn. Alex, I'm innocent, I was just trying to find you and Cara. Please, Alex, make them believe me."

Sandu paused for breath as Alex motioned to Sir Eric. The knight undid Sandu's restraints. As Sandu fell, his limbs too weak to hold him upright, Alex caught him and eased him to the floor.

"Shh, Sandu, it's all well," Alex murmured. To Sir Eric, he said, "That is all we need from you today. Have the servants fetch a clean robe for my friend."

"He's not proven innocent," Sir Eric protested.

Alex twisted to glare up at him and said, "Sandu was not here to kill the queen; he has traveled with me. I know his mind and heart. Do you doubt the word of a Strilu?"

"The queen herself has ordered him be sent before the justiciars."

With a sigh, Alex carefully let Sandu to the ground. He then stood and guided Sir Eric to an opposite corner of the room. He spoke quietly and calmly, though Sandu couldn't hear what was said. To his tired mind, though, Alex's tone brooked no argument.

Sir Eric hesitated, then gave a stiff bow. "I leave him in your charge, Lord Alexandro. I apologize for this man's false imprisonment. Before I go, though, I request a full description of the suspected killer."

Alex looked over, and Sandu, still collapsed on the floor, said, "He was tall, with dark hair. No beard or mustache. There was a house crest on his tunic, but I didn't see what it was."

After Sir Eric was gone, Alex helped Sandu sit and lean against the wall. "I'm sorry they did this to you. I should've told you both who I am, then you could've just asked for me instead of trying a ridiculous ruse. You would never have been brought to the queen's rooms had I been honest with you. I'm so sorry."

"Not your fault," Sandu muttered. His chest hurt as he took a deep breath. "Not *any* lord's third son, though, are you? Son of the previous Earl Seastone. I can't vecking believe it."

"Neither can I, sometimes. I've never been comfortable with the title." As Alex spoke, a servant bustled in with a soft robe. With Alex's aid, Sandu stood and draped the robe about his shaking shoulders. Alex put an arm around him, and said as they left the dungeon, "Cara is safe. She's here in the palace, but she was away when Sir Eric came for me. I didn't waste time finding her."

"Thanks for that." Sandu stumbled over his own feet, which buzzed with the effort to hold him.

For a time, neither spoke. They made their slow way up through the dungeons and into wide marble halls. Courtiers stopped to stare at the odd sight: Lord Alexandro, dressed in a fine tunic, supporting a barefoot man in a robe. At last, up several flights of stairs and down a long corridor, they arrived in a sumptuous set of chambers.

"I've sent for a bath for you," Alex said. "These are my personal rooms, but you're free to use them. I'll stay with you until I'm needed in council."

Sandu's sigh of relief showed his gratitude as he slipped into the steaming hot tub. Alex left while a servant helped clean the blood and grime from Sandu's bedraggled body. Sandu dried himself off and took a closer look at the clothing Alex offered.

"I can't accept this," he blurted, fingering the edge of the shirt. "This is all expensive stuff. I'm not nearly worth as much as any of this."

"It's a gift," Alex said, lifting the trousers and holding them up. "From my own closet. You're my guest here."

Sandu didn't need much convincing. Once he was decent, Alex led him to another room, this one filled with cushioned chairs, couches, small tables, and bookshelves on the walls.

"This is fancy," Sandu commented, sipping at a cup of wine. It was far better quality than anything he'd be able to afford.

Alex shrugged. "You get used to it, after awhile. I'm sorry for lying to you. I was an ass."

"A rich ass, though. That counts for something. If you pay me gold for each lie, I'll consider the debt settled." Sandu grinned, feeling like his old self again. His aching shoulders reminded him of his ordeal in the dungeon, and he shuddered at the fate he escaped.

"Take what you want!" Alex threw his arms wide. "There's books, jewels, all manner of things in here that I've never even glanced at. A new horse, too, if you want."

"Well, that seems a bit much. Galen was probably about as costly as one of the palace horse's shoes. Though I wouldn't mind looking at your library, when I have a chance. It's the largest one I've ever seen. Have you even read all of these books?"

"At least once. You should see the library at Mott, it puts mine to shame. Are you feeling better?"

"Much."

"Then stay here as long as you need, but Druam's expecting me. Sandu, please go find Cara. We both thought you were dead...she needs to see you. It would mean everything to her. Hers is the door carved with a lilac flower. Go see her."

Sandu averted his eyes from Alex's. "I...I will. But not yet. I don't think I'm ready yet." Despite his longing to see her, his desperate attempts to find her, she was so close now that he found he was afraid. He'd seen the hurt in her eyes when she learned the truth about him. "Don't tell her that I'm here. I'll go to her soon, I promise."

Alex frowned. "I'll do as you wish, but...Sandu...don't lose us again. Here, take this seal. The guards will let you in and out of the palace, though I don't think you should leave. You should find Cara. Please."

"I'll go to her when I'm ready."

"Don't let that take too long." Alex pressed the hard metal seal and a small pouch of coins into Sandu's hand, then left the room.

A good amount of time passed before Sandu pushed himself off the couch and out into the hallway. He ambled slowly toward Cara's room, but when he reached the intersection of corridors, he paused. As he stared at her door, he pictured his and Tambrey's hut in Dunfrey, the door forever closed to him. The longer he avoided Cara, the longer he could pretend that all was still the same between them.

His cowardice won out, fueled by his fatigue from his days in the dungeon. His hands shook as he hurried away from the lilac room.

For another candle, he wandered the huge palace, ducking

into alcoves or against a wall whenever someone passed him. He pretended not to understand why he couldn't see Cara just yet, but deep down, he knew: he had abandoned his family and betrayed Jagger. Could he trust himself *not* to do the same to Cara? She thought him dead...it would be so, so very easy to disappear and let her continue thinking it. He had already done it once before, even changing his name. Who was to say he couldn't do it again?

Laughter and raised voices caught his attention. Following the sounds, Sandu found a group of palace guards taking a rest in a cozy room far off the main corridor. They passed mead around and bet on a card game, jostling each other in a good-natured way. Sandu paused at the threshold, his hands tapping at his thighs.

Don't do this, he told himself. *Nothing good comes from drinking and gambling.*

After days wrongfully imprisoned, he wanted so much to do something fun. He felt, ever since losing Galen, that he'd been haunted by his past. He'd tried so hard to rid himself of the man Tambrey hated, but he knew that that man was still there, deep inside him. *No man can deny himself forever. Just one game to make myself feel better. Then I'll find Cara.*

One of the guards saw him. "What do you want?"

"Can I join?" Sandu asked, giving in to the weakness. He flashed Alex's seal at them. "I'm a guest here, but I don't belong with the noble folk."

They exchanged looks, then made room for him.

Candles passed, and Sandu grew more and more loose as the drink flowed and luck shifted hands. Rather than face himself and his past mistakes, Sandu bet almost all of Alex's coin and drank far more than he should as the night grew longer.

I'm going to have a hell of a headache tomorrow.

CHAPTER FORTY-ONE
Seanna

SEANNA DID her best to ignore the ladies' staring and focus on her embroidery. The thread caught and tangled with itself, and with nimble fingers she undid the snare before pulling it taut. She could feel their eyes on the top of her head, and resisted glancing up; she would only see them look away so quickly they might snap their necks.

Ralston had reported to her that, after two assassination attempts, nobles feared to be seen too close to her. They would rather their queen be shunned than to feel the bite of a prowler's fangs.

"Has anyone expressed any sympathy?" Seanna had demanded.

"Of course, Your Grace. They all do. But they fear falling into similar disfavor. Some say the king himself tried to have you killed." Ralston paused, then continued, "There are also rumors that you have consorted with dark powers and are now reaping the consequences. Others that you have been carrying on affairs so scandalous that the king would rather you be killed now than go through the ordeals of a trial and proper execution. Even those that have ardently supported you are questioning your innocence."

Seanna cut the thread irritably. She should be surrounded by well-wishers, not treated like some sort of pariah. What point was there remaining at the soiree? Although every lady stood as she did and curtseyed as she left, they all avoided her eyes. *Treacherous minxes.*

Even her handmaids, one by one, had left her service, and so only Sir Eric was there to escort her down the corridors to her chambers. He looked tired, as if he hadn't slept in a long time.

"Did you get a confession from the Protector?" Seanna asked. She had already forgotten the soldier's name.

Eric's frown nearly imperceptibly tightened. "He was ordered free by Lord Strilu, but claimed innocence before that."

"And you just let him go?"

"Lord Strilu was...rather convincing as a witness."

"If he didn't do it, then who did?" *Dammit, the culprit needs to hang for this treason.*

"I don't know though my men are searching tirelessly for one who matches the description. I have also sent a scout to tail Master Crin, just to be sure."

"Good." Seanna wanted to ask more, but *Kair* Aremo Teru rounded a corner. Strangely, he was completely alone. He appeared lost in pensive thought before Seanna coughed politely.

"Ah, Your Grace. My apologies for my lack of respect." Aremo's tone conveyed no such remorse.

"How are you, *kair*? It has been too long since our last dinner together. We must dine again soon."

The smile that stretched his lips was wholly unpleasant. "I think not, Seanna."

The impudence! "You are to address me formally, *Kair* Aremo. Or had you forgotten that you are no longer in Dedaria?" Seanna stopped, glaring up into the *kair*'s smug face.

The *kair* only smiled. "While you were amusing enough during dinner, I have no interest in aligning myself with a doomed woman."

Sir Eric loosened his sword in its sheath and took a step forward. Holding out her hand to halt her knight, Seanna said in a low voice, "Are you threatening me? I am no more doomed than the heir I carry, and once I have given birth to the king's son, I will be untouchable."

Aremo chuckled. "My dear queen, I am not threatening you. I am simply stating a fact: by the end of next year, you will no longer be queen. I rather imagine your pretty head will adorn a spike."

"How *dare* you speak to me so! Sir Eric, arrest this elf. I hear a cell has recently been vacated."

The prince held up a finger and tutted. "Tsk, tsk, Seanna, surely you know the laws by now? I am a foreign ruler who came here on goodwill. If your man were to attack me, my country would be forced to declare war upon yours."

"Hold, Sir Eric." Seanna's breath came faster now, as if she had run a short distance. "Let him pass."

"A wise choice, Your Grace." Aremo sailed past her with his smug look. Seanna took a deep breath, furled and unfurled her fingers a couple of times, then proceeded forward as if nothing had happened, her head high and her shoulders straight. Her mind roiled with the prince's implications. *Does he mean to replace me as queen with a Dedarian? Would he convince Henrik to execute me for my affairs?*

Nervousness filled Seanna's lungs with each breath, coming to a head as she arrived back at her rooms. Sir Eric remained outside, as always. Seanna sank onto a couch and tried not to panic. What had these last few quinns been for, if not to assure herself of her own power and status? And now she felt it all slipping through her fingertips. Each breath was too light, not enough air to give her oxygen. She breathed faster and faster, her heart pumping in her chest. The baby kicked, sensing her stress. With shaking hands she poured herself a glass of wine – some of it spilled onto the oak table – and gulped it down, cool liquid cascading over her cheeks and down her throat, forcing her to breathe normally again or choke.

When she had regained herself, Seanna wiped her face clean then stroked her belly. The baby had calmed once she had, and she whispered to it, "Shh, little one. Mumma's fine now. Don't you worry, my sweet. They'll see how strong of a queen I am, they'll see you grow into a magnificent king." But she didn't quite believe her own words.

The door opened and Henrik entered. His face looked worn, his forehead holding new creases and his beard having more grey than brown now. His crown still shone with a faint gold luster, but the robes on his shoulders, though once perfectly tailored, hung more loosely about him.

"Henrik," Seanna said stupidly. "I wasn't expecting you." *Surely he is here to bestow me with pity and love for all that I've endured.* "Sit and have a cup of wine."

"No, thank you, Seanna," Henrik said. He stood stiffly in front of Seanna. For a moment, he regarded her silently, and she could not read his expression. With everything that had happened since that horrible night in the tub, Seanna wanted him to be concerned. She *needed* him to be the doting husband so many other ladies had, to soothe her and wipe away her tears.

"You're a filthy whore," Henrik said softly. Seanna blinked, her eyes welling. *No, don't show him your emotions.* She tried to force back her sudden grief, but it poured out instead. Seanna cried silently, her body heaving ever so gently, as Henrik continued, "You thought you could fool me, that I wouldn't notice as you took women to your bed."

"Henrik, I–"

"Don't try to lie to me!" Henrik spat. "For years you've disgraced me. Did you think I'd never find out? That none of the rumors would ever reach my ear?"

"Who told you?" Seanna whispered through her tears.

"Does it matter? You make a mockery of me by sleeping with others while you carry my child. You don't deserve the jewels around your neck." He shouted, his face turning red with anger, "I brought you to this status, I made you everything you are! I should have wed Rask's other daughter or even the court bard before I accepted you. You mock me every day, yet feel nothing. I tried to love you, Seanna, I did. I loved Fleta with my whole soul, and I thought it unfair that you should never feel that from me. But you made it so difficult, with your gossiping and your pettiness. Put that cup down and listen to me!"

Seanna flinched as if he had actually hit her. Henrik loomed over her, his shadow cast over her tear-stricken face. "You've spent marks and marks of gold from *my* coffers, and for what? To bribe nobles to pretend to love you? You tried to turn my friends against me, and my enemies against each other, and you failed. You failed so miserably that you angered one of them enough to try and have you killed. They hated you so much they would rather you be dead than listen to another screeching rant from your horrible lips. If it were purely political, then I would be the target. But no, you drew so much unwarranted attention to yourself and made yourself into such a foolish spectacle that someone couldn't even stand to let you birth a creature that may turn out like you."

"You have no proof–" Seanna started, but he cut her off.

"*Proof?* You think you're so clever, don't you? Did you never suspect your little spy? I ordered Ralston to serve you, I told him to watch you and report to me. You truly believe you *ever* had his loyalty?" Henrik's chest heaved, his hands raised as if he wanted to strangle her himself. Seanna stared at him, half in disbelief, half in rage at herself. *Why did I ever trust Ralston?* she wondered miserably.

Henrik pulled back, and Seanna thought, *Surely he must be done, surely he will leave me to my misery now*, though much of what he said was true.

But he merely took a deep breath and said, "You are *nothing* compared to the earls and lords of this land whom you attempted to slander. You acted like a jealous, spoiled child who didn't get the toy she wanted, and now I must make amends with the powerful men you offended. You meddled in affairs beyond your understanding, and now you reap the consequences of your ill-thought actions.

"I was proud of you," Henrik said, more gently now, "for forging friendships with Earl and Lady Seastone. Druam is a good man. But you betrayed them the first chance you had: you accused Lady Seastone of crimes you yourself committed, drove a wedge between a loving couple, and then dared to spread false rumors of the earl. It is one thing to speak poorly of me, for petty wives often rail against their husbands, but it is another entirely to defame those who offered you affection and hospitality. I watched you burn any chance you had of their love, and for what? For the attentions of lesser men and silly women."

Seanna did not try to speak over him. She sat, crying, each word stinging her flesh. Resentment flowered anew in her heart, that her husband dared punish her for being what he had made her to be. The tears streaming down her cheeks were tainted not by remorse, but fury.

Henrik's hands clenched at his sides. Without looking at her, he said, "I am ordering you back to Con Salur. A ship will be made ready for you. It will leave the morning of the Masque.

"Once you are at the Silver Keep, you will be forbidden from writing or receiving notes, letters, and other messages. You will be confined to your quarters unless I give specific permission otherwise. You are to have no visitors and no companions save for Sir Eric and two ladies-in-waiting of my choice. You will only attend banquets or festivities when I allow it, and then you will not leave my side. You will form yourself into the image of the perfect, obedient queen.

"When our child is born, it will be removed from you and given to a wetmaid to nurse. The child will go to live with my kin to be raised without your influence."

"No!" Seanna cried, standing and grasping at his robes. "Please, Henrik, all your punishments I will take, and gladly, but please, leave me my child. I have carried him these months, I am his mother, you cannot take him from me!"

Henrik's eyes softened ever so slightly. "*If* you obey me," he said, gently removing her hands from his tunic, "then, in a year's time, I may allow you to visit our child. I am sorry, Seanna, I am, but be grateful I am not ordering your execution."

Henrik turned abruptly on his heel and left. Seanna sank onto the couch and rubbed her belly, letting herself be overcome by heaving sobs. Her babe. Her only child, taken from her. And for what? For seeking love the only place she could find it?

Yet even that love had abandoned her. *First Larka, then Maeria. Even for my sins, could the gods not have granted me some mercy?* Her child should have been the one person she could rely on for unconditional affection, and now she would lose him, too.

In the mirror across the room, Seanna saw not a noble queen with a royal bearing, but a small woman with red eyes and a shuddering lip.

Chapter Forty-Two

Cara

PROWLERS PLAGUED Cara's dreams. Sometimes they chased her, and no matter how she tried, the beast would not answer her call. In other dreams, her friends became prowlers, their faces distorted by monstrous features. In the worst ones, Cara herself was a prowler, hunting down those she loved.

In the darkest hours before dawn, the Hooded Man and his large monster crept into her sleep. The Hooded Man's chill laughter seeped into her bones as the monster beat her, its large fists swatting her as if she were no larger than a mouse. She felt helpless, her beast unresponsive, her muscles small and weak.

For once, Alex had stayed with her until morning, his bright eyes full of worry when she woke.

"You tossed and turned all night," he said, one hand cupping her cheek. "Bad dreams?"

"Awful." Cara cuddled up against him, shivering despite the warm sheets. "I don't think I can face the Hooded Man."

"You can, and you will," he said. His soothing voice reached past her fears and wrapped around her heart, and she relaxed in his arms. He continued, "You're stronger than you know, and you have mastery over the beast. Twice now you've used it in battle against enemies and brought no harm to innocents."

"But what if it doesn't answer my call? What if—"

"Shh." He ended her protests with a kiss. "You won't be

alone. Druam and I are with you, and the Realm's Protectors are sworn to help us."

Slowly, as his words penetrated her, she let her fears fade away. Though they lingered in the back of her mind, she felt more like she could face the morning.

As Alex dressed, he said, "Try to rest today. I've sent for tailors to make you a dress for the Masque; enjoy it, and imagine dancing the night away soon." He bent down and gave her a slow, lingering kiss. "With me."

"I only know rustic reels," Cara said teasingly. "You'd be ashamed of having me as a partner."

"Never." He grinned, then departed, leaving behind his clean scent of soap and pine.

Though Cara tried to rest, her thoughts drifted again and again to the prowlers. How had they gained entry to the palace? It was no coincidence that those monsters had found their way to the queen's chambers. *Someone can control them,* Cara realized with a jolt. *And the only person I know who has such dark powers is the Hooded Man.* That meant that he was there, in Riverfen!

Cara's nerves thrilled with anticipation. She would start at Bertha's Bosun, the tavern by the docks that Mavian had told her about. From there, she would hunt him as she would any dangerous predator.

She tolerated the tailor's visit, and even cooed over his fine clothing choices. He presented her with an array of beautiful dresses, but the one she kept returning to had light skirts that split at the sides, under which she could wear breeches. It was far simpler than the others, but she felt more comfortable in it. *I am a country girl no matter the jewels they drape on me.*

By the time the tailor left, the sun had begun its slow descent. Cara ate her supper quickly, then left a note for Alex: *I'll be back late tonight; following a hint into the city. Don't wait up for me.* She paused, considering how to sign it, before she finally just put her name. They had yet to express love, and she didn't feel right using that word. *He's a lord, and you're a rustic. This fairytale can only last so long.*

With that, Cara dressed in her old traveling clothes,

strapped a dagger to her hip, pocketed a letter from the earl proving her identity, and left. Stewards and nobles gave her odd looks as she left the palace, but she didn't care. For the first time since her arrival, she felt herself.

Once she made it down from the plateau and into the streets, Cara reveled in her regained anonymity. No one here cared who she was. She stopped at the shop stalls and peered into window displays. She had never seen such a wide array of goods for sale: exotic pets, seeds, fashionable hats, walking canes, fruit pastries, vegetables, meats, wooden toys, jewelry, clothes, magic totems, all presented as if the merchant had scoured the earth for his wares.

Cara continued to the slums. Though most lanterns here were made of paper, every so often one was crafted from blown glass molded into fantastic shapes. Cara paused at each one, craning her neck to see the details.

One caught her eye and she gazed at it for a few minutes. It was a red dragon, its eyes lit and its tail curling around its body. The maker was clever, designing it so that the candle smoke was let out from the dragon's nose, making the thing seem alive. Cara circled it, looking from all sides, before moving on.

Cara followed the smell of fish to the docks. There, she found a crate to perch on to watch the working sailors. A large caravel had just come in, and men scurried up and down the gangplanks unloading its cargo. In the berth next to it, a series of small fishing boats had been tied up. Even at this late hour, laborers shouted to each other, dock handlers checked each berth, and prostitutes materialized at alley entrances, their faces painted with white cosmetics and their dresses pulled down to show the tops of their breasts.

Not wanting to be perceived as a harlot, Cara left the docks and began to look for Bertha's Bosun. In this part of town, even the beauty of the lanterns could not disguise the smell of shit.

It didn't take her long to find the tavern. It hummed with activity, patrons coming and going as the street echoed with laughter and shouting. Cara squeezed her way inside, paid the man attending the door, and took her bearings. A brawl took place in the center of the tavern as the crowd threw out bets and called encouragement to their fighters. Some tables had gamblers, and the bar was full of men throwing back drinks.

Cara edged around the room, her senses assailed from every direction. Sweat and spilled ale filled her nostrils, her ears thrummed with the noise, and people bumped into her from every direction. Her heart beat rapidly, and the beast clamored for her to join in the tumult. She quelled it uneasily and went to the bar.

As she stepped up to the counter, the barkeep eyed her.

"You the new girl?" he asked.

"What?" Cara said.

"You're supposed to be working the back rooms," he said. "Get there and make the customers happy."

Cara drew herself up. "I'm no harlot, sir, I'm—"

"I didn't say whore yourself out, just make sure that the poppin keeps flowing." The barkeep shoved a pouch at her and led her to a set of doors at the back of the establishment. She tried to protest, but he ignored her. Through the doors, Cara saw a long hallway.

The barkeep left her abruptly. Cara thought a moment about dumping the pouch and leaving, but then stepped forward. This hall was far quieter than the rowdy tavern room; if the Hooded Man conducted business in this establishment, wouldn't he do it where no one could see him? Cara went to the first door, knocked, and opened it. She found a room filled with cushions and rugs, with an elaborate water pipe in the center. Men lounged around, inhaling the smoke from their individual tubes. They grinned lazily at her as she refilled the bowl and backed away.

As Cara went along the hallway, she noticed tendrils of smoke creeping under the doors. None of the people in the lounges spoke to each other. Music players sometimes serenaded them, but otherwise she detected nothing out of the ordinary.

Near the end of the hall, Cara noticed a door with very little smoke drifting out. She paused, her heart galloping in her chest.

If he is here, he wouldn't be imbibing. Too dangerous. With one hand on her dagger, Cara opened the door.

This room was darker than the others, with only one lantern in the far corner throwing shadows across the room. The water pipe still smoked, but very little, as if it hadn't been refilled in some time.

Two dark figures lay on the couch opposite her, one leaning over the other, close enough to kiss. At first Cara thought she had intruded on an intimate moment, but the beast stirred within her belly. Then she smelled it, at first imperceptible, then stronger once she noticed it: blood. Her neck tingled, jolting shivers traveling down her spine.

The door creaked as Cara pushed it farther open. The figure on top snapped its head up and turned toward her.

Cara gasped and dropped the pouch, poppin powder flying out into the room. She stumbled back, hardly daring to trust her own eyes.

Alex.

His face was contorted by a ridged brow and heightened cheekbones, his eyes glowing red in the dim light. Blood dotted his chin and coated the long fangs that curled over his lips.

"No," Cara whispered. Her fingers dangled limply at her sides. She fell against the door, sure she must be hallucinating. *It's the poppin powder*, she thought. *I accidentally inhaled it, and now I'm seeing visions.*

Alex quickly wiped his mouth. His face shifted and transformed back to human. But he still had a red glimmer in his eyes and blood droplets on his chin. He pushed off the couch, but Cara backed away.

"You're a prowler," she managed to say. Her whole body buzzed, all other thoughts swept from her mind. *This isn't a vision. This is real, and he's a monster.*

Alex shook his head. "No, I'm–"

Instinct overcame all of Cara's other senses. She ran away from his pleading hands and begging shouts, up the hallway and into the crowded tavern. Men shouted at her, but she bulled through them without care. Her numb fingers found the door latch, and she ran out into the street. She panted, her legs burning, as she sprinted from the dockside districts, through the stately merchants' streets, and all the way to the palace gates. There she stopped and bent over to regain her breath. The guards looked at her apprehensively.

"Maid?" One of the guards stepped forward. "Are you well?"

Cara nodded. What could she say? *Your lord is a monster. No one is safe.* She felt sick, as if all the fine food she'd eaten that day had turned rotten in her stomach.

"Maid?" The guard asked again. Cara fumbled for the parchment in her pocket and held it out. He scanned it, then offered his arm. "Let me escort you back to your rooms."

Cara gratefully accepted his arm. She leaned on him as he took her back to her room. He bowed, then left her outside her door. Now that she was there, though, Cara didn't want to go back inside. Inside was where she and Alex had shared a bed, where he'd comforted her and spoken to her as if he had no secrets from her.

No wonder he knew so much about prowlers. Away from the shock, Cara reviewed what she'd seen. *He's not a prowler, he can turn back into a man. Is he like me? No, I don't drink blood.* She shuddered, remembering the beast's thirst. *At least, I don't yet.* Then she remembered Alex's lessons about the *fampir. He's not a prowler, and he's not like me. He's* fampir.

Her first thought was to run away. She could find a small village, start anew; no one would stop her. *But that would be cowardice. I'm not a simple rustic anymore.*

Alex was one of the enemy. Who knew what treasons he could work, what horrors he could bring to the innocent folk of the city? All this time, he'd pretended to care for her, but it was all a lie.

I have to tell someone, Cara thought. The earl would want to know about his brother, but what proof did Cara have? He wouldn't believe a country girl over his own blood. *The king.* Yet without the earl's help, Cara couldn't get an audience with the king, and certainly not that day. *Someone needs to be told tonight.*

She remembered Mavian and his interest in the prowlers. He'd been the one who told her about Bertha's Bosun. Could it be he suspected something, and so sent her to investigate? Did he know of a connection between *fampir* and the Hooded Man?

Despite the late hour, Cara went straight to Mavian's chambers. If he was the only one who might listen to her, she had no choice but to tell him.

And if I stay alone too long, I'll have to listen to my broken heart. Every kiss, every small moment, had been brought into question. Just like with Sandu. But this betrayal hurt her far more, because she felt like she had finally found a true kindred spirit in Alex. As a rustic girl, she hadn't ever thought she would meet a man who wasn't afraid of her strength. *Did he ever care for me?* she wondered. The truth could be too painful, and so she pushed it away.

When she reached Mavian's door, she knocked briefly and entered without waiting for an answer. Rude, certainly, but she couldn't wait. She descended the staircase, then halted at the bottom.

The lord wasn't there. Cara halted, her fevered mind unsure what to do. *Should I wait for his return?* Then movement from a side room distracted her, and she turned, ready to tell Mavian what she'd seen. The words died on her lips, and her fractured heart nearly broke again.

"Renna," Cara breathed. After so long, her lady stood before her, beautiful as the day Cara had last seen her. Renna wore midnight blue with clear jewels, her golden hair curled perfectly around her lovely face.

Renna stopped, too, her mouth hanging in a little 'o' as she stared at Cara. After a moment, she recovered herself and asked, "What are you doing here?"

"Renna!" Cara said again, rushing forward to embrace her lady. So many long nights, so much loss and betrayal, and now Renna was here. She wasn't a dream, but flesh and blood. Cara laughed as she hugged her old friend. "I thought I'd lost you forever!"

Renna didn't return the embrace. She stood stock-still in

Cara's arms for a moment before gently removing herself and stepping back. Her cool blue eyes swept over Cara's disheveled appearance, and a slight frown puckered her lips.

"Come inside," Renna whispered, taking Cara's arm. Her eyes darted past Cara, but there was nothing there. Cara followed her old friend into the side room, her joy quickly turning to confusion. Renna shut the door behind them and whirled.

"What are you doing here?" Renna hissed.

"I...I came to rescue you," Cara said, wounded at Renna's fury. *Why isn't she happy to see me?*

Renna pinched the bridge of her nose and sighed. "I don't need rescuing, Cara. As you can see, I'm perfectly safe. Now you should go, before–"

"But the Hooded Man!" Cara exclaimed. "He kidnapped you, he *murdered* Ulton and Merick!"

"I went with him willingly!" Renna shouted. Cara stepped back, her heart stinging, her flesh tingling as if she'd just been slapped.

"I don't understand," she said.

"Sit down before you hurt yourself." Renna poured them each a glass of wine and took a long drink. "If I had told you what I'd planned, you would have tried to stop me. It's better this way, though I am sorry for Ulton and Merick. They were good men."

The sincerity of Renna's words floundered under the lightness of her tone. Cara stared at her mistress in disbelief. "Those men served you faithfully for years! They're *dead* because of the Hooded Man. And I've had no easy journey to find you. All this time searching, and you *wanted* this?"

"Yes," Renna said simply. "Mavian and I met–"

"Mavian?" The truth crashed down on Cara: Mavian's smile at the mention of Renna, his hints of the tavern and the queen. *Did he set me up?*

Renna smiled. "Yes, Mavian. He was traveling through the fief when we met. Father had already betrothed me to that loathsome man, and Mavian gave me a way to escape that. He brought me here and spelled everyone to think that I was Maeria Westerburg, an heiress of a powerful family. His magic is incredible, Cara. You wouldn't believe–"

"Oh, I've seen it," Cara said, anger burning out her incredulousness. How *dare* Renna sit there smiling after all Cara had been through? The beast rumbled inside her, and Cara was sorely tempted to give into it. "He attacked innocent scholars from Mott, he poisoned Merick with dark magic and made him suffer a cruel death. You call *that* incredible?"

"You poor country girl," Renna simpered, her pink lips twisting in a false smile. "You wouldn't understand. With his power and my new wealth, we can change the world. He wants so many things, things that will help people like you. Libraries and councils for the rustics, a new system that would bring down the corrupt aristocracy."

"Can he control prowlers?" Cara asked bluntly.

"His dark power can do many things; that's one of them."

"So he tried to kill myself and the queen?" Cara shouted. "Did you know that he tried to murder me?"

"I did," Renna said coldly. "You both were becoming too meddlesome."

Cara stood up, the beast burning inside her. She built her mental walls around it, urging it to stay down. She asked, "And you didn't mind that I would be killed?"

"I was absolutely distraught, but I knew it was necessary. If you would just *listen* to me, you'd understand why it all has to be done."

"And why should I listen to you?" Cara demanded. "You abandoned us, you don't care if we were killed! Was there ever a day you loved me as I loved you?"

Real hurt showed in Renna's eyes. She stood, drew close to Cara, and took her hands. "Of course I loved you. I still do. But things have changed now. My loyalty is to Mavian above all others. I've heard what you can do; you can help us make the world better."

"I want nothing to do with him!" Cara shouted, pulling back.

Before Renna could respond, Cara felt a call, a magical tug on her heart that came from nearby: *Help!* She waited, but it didn't come again. Renna stared at her.

"Did you feel that?" Renna asked. Cara nodded.

Renna cursed and ran out the door. Still reeling from all she'd learned, Cara stood still. Even after all Renna had said, she wanted to believe that her lady felt some remorse for her actions. She couldn't believe that all the death and pain from the last month was intentional, that Renna didn't care for the harm done to her faithful followers.

In that moment, Cara knew how terribly, absolutely alone she was with Merick dead, Sandu murdered, and Alex a lying monster. Her only solace had been the hope – no, the certainty – that she would find Renna, bring her home, and make all the tribulations worth it. Now even that dream had been torn into bits, and she didn't know where else to turn.

The beast growled inside her, and she welcomed its anger. *I still have you*, she thought.

A crash sounded from the next room, someone shouted, and a woman cried out in pain. Cara dashed to the door, the beast already in her veins. *I'm ready*, she thought.

She could never have prepared for what she saw when she entered Mavian's sitting room.

CHAPTER FORTY-THREE
Gwen

GWEN DID NOT know she had lain, unmoving and unresponsive, for over a quinn after her failed curse. She did not know that Druam had barely left her side, his face gaunt with worry, lack of sleep, and malnourishment; she did not even feel herself being spoon-fed or given water in sips through a glass vial, her throat massaged to force it down.

All she knew was that, one moment, she had been in Druam's arms, her skin blistering, and the next she felt as if a ten-horse carriage had run her over, her heart had been compressed and squeezed of all its blood, her head stung by a hundred bees.

Gwen groaned, and immediately felt someone come to hold her hand. When she opened her eyes and blinked away her blurred vision, she saw – of course – Druam. With his help, she sat up and leaned against the pillows he stacked behind her.

"Uh," was all Gwen managed to say. Still, relief shown through Druam's worry. He took a cup of water from the table and offered it to her. She sipped it, her throat burning as if she had done nothing but yell for days straight.

"How do you feel?" Druam asked.

"Hurt," Gwen whispered, her throat raw. She remembered him carrying her out of the flames. Guiltily, she rasped, "Are you injured?"

He shook his head. "No." His eyes ran over her as if unsure that she had really woken. "I thought I'd lost you. That I'd never see you smile again, or hear you singing as you embroider."

"I'm sorry," she whispered. "I want us to be happy, but I only thought of myself when I did the working." Even as she said it, though, Gwen felt that anger, that desire for vengeance, welling within her. She still wanted to make the Skals pay for her brother's death.

"I am simply glad that you're alive." Druam's pale cheeks reddened and his eyes grew brighter. He kissed her forehead, then rose to leave. "I have ignored my duties for days now, but I can confidently return knowing that you are regaining your health. Rest now, my love, and I will see you tonight."

After he had gone, Gwen noticed the gifts and notes piled on a table beside the bed. She rose shakily to her feet and picked a lavender-colored envelope from the top of the pile. It had been sent by some lord she had never met before, and expressed a sentiment she highly doubted was true. Note after note and gift after gift all said the same: *We are sending these to gain your husband's favor, not yours.*

But there, near the bottom and hidden beneath a bouquet of blue wildflowers, was a letter from Mavian. Despite his recent comments about Druam, Gwen felt a twinge of delight in seeing his handwriting. Curling back into her bed, Gwen read:

Dearest Gwen,

I hope this letter finds you in good humor, and not the worse for wear for your exertions. Your lord husband has told the court that you suffered a weakening of the heart, but I felt the ripple of magic. I know you cast an enchantment beyond your abilities, but have survived it. We can still work together, to hone your magic and bring justice for your brother. Seek me out when you are ready.

Ever your friend, Mavian

Gwen contemplated the letter, her mind a tumultuous wind that blew apart any thought before it fully formed. Pain gathered at her temples, pounding with a beat that echoed the curse she had spoken days before. She closed her eyes until the ache dissipated.

Gwen wanted to see Mavian, to ask what had happened with the working and why it had gone so wrong. Without thinking beyond that simple idea, Gwen pulled a dressing gown over her shift and clad her feet in silk slippers. Concentrating the shreds of magic that darted around inside her, she projected one thought: *I am a mouse, nothing more. I am a mouse traveling the halls*, and whispered the words that had allowed her to follow Druam to the tavern so many quinns ago. Her Gaiar trembled within her, and she doubted she could keep it for long.

As she slipped past the two guards stationed outside her bedroom, Gwen felt a freedom comparable to that of anonymity: she was a mouse, a mouse that skittered past Realm's Protectors and nobles, page boys and servants, through the wide halls until she reached the high wooden doors to the lesser nobles' corridors. Though she had only passed through these once before, her instinct told her that Mavian's would be the farthest set of chambers that bordered the old wing.

Gwen found the heavy oak door to be unlocked. Behind it lay a spiral staircase that descended for some ways before emerging into a small room. A dead fireplace lay on the other side, and antique couches and rugs occupied the cold granite floors. Four other doors led to the rest of Mavian's chambers.

A shiver jolted her whole body as she stepped into the room and saw a heavy door in an alcove beyond the fireplace. An old, musty smell reminded her of the abandoned wing. She tiptoed past the other closed doors to stand at the heavy one. The alcove was built of older materials, its arch jagged and rough-hewn as if someone had once sealed it and another had later broken through the stone.

Every nerve in her screamed not to open the door, but she could not resist. The metal handle felt cold in her hand, and the hinges creaked slightly as she pushed the door inwards.

The back of Gwen's neck tingled. Mavian watched her, a goblet of wine in one hand, his hair unkempt and his tunic hanging open.

"What were you hoping to find beyond that door?" Mavian asked as he raised his goblet. His eyes never left her.

"I don't know," Gwen said. "Answers, perhaps."

"Answers to what questions?"

"I don't know. I thought maybe someday things would return to normal, but now they never can. My brother is dead." That horrible, stark fact made a hollow inside her.

"I know. I am sorry."

"What am I to do now? I can never go home. This place isn't home. I can't walk one step without being judged or attacked." Gwen clutched at her dress, the soft silk warm in her fingers. "I thought my magic could help me, but it's caused so much trouble. I know Druam fears it, and maybe rightfully so. I don't know what to do, Mavian."

Mavian placed his goblet on a table, then took three steps to stand in front of her. He stared down at her as he took her hands. Gwen's eyes darted between his, searching for something, though what she did not know. Truth and simplicity, perhaps.

"Your magic is a boon, Gwen," Mavian said. "You can use it to change things in our world, to bring about a new era. An era which Druam, I'm afraid, cannot be a part of."

"I don't understand..."

"I want to help you," Mavian said. "But you must realize Druam's falsity, and recognize that the court is filled with fools and liars. They are selfish. I want to give the rustics what they deserve, to bring in an era of knowledge and prosperity. The court shuns me for my values, for my earnestness." His voice gained fervor. "With your Gaiar, Gwen, we can overturn the elite and create a new society. We can share our wealth with all."

Gwen stammered stupidly, overwhelmed by his sudden passion. *How has he never spoken of this to me before?*

"I can teach you. With me, you can unlock so much more than you ever realized, than you ever dreamed. We are not alone, Gwen. Powerful men and women believe in me; every day I gain support from those who wish to see a new world."

"But Druam–"

"Veck Druam!" Mavian's grip on her hands grew tighter, and he held her firm when she tried to pull away. "He has failed to create his utopia! He is the epitome of the old world, and he will ruin you. Druam will be the first to be destroyed. Can't you see? He has made you succumb to his banal wishes. He has you convinced that this world is as good as it can be. Will you fall with him, or join me in my quest for justice?"

His manic words frightened Gwen. She tried again to escape, but he held on, his nails digging into her wrists. He was raving mad. Gwen wished she had never left her chambers, that she had waited until Druam was with her again. She tried to summon her magic, but felt only a small stirring in her belly. The attempted curse and her earlier working had drained her.

As she tried to pull away, Gwen said, "Druam is a wiser man than you. He wants what is best for his people, just like you. Work with him! Don't create a chasm where there is none. Surely–"

"See, he has you under his spell! He is not what he seems, Gwen! He is a monster, and his lies will bring this valley to ruin. I don't want to see you perish with him. Please, Gwen, find your inner strength and free yourself from his bonds."

Gwen struggled to find her inner strength to free herself from this madman, but it would not come. She was too weak, too fragile; she would not win against him without her magic.

"You're frightening me!" she shouted at him. "You were my friend! How could you say such terrible things?"

"Because it's the truth, Gwen. Can't you see that? I'm trying to free you from him. I'm trying to free everyone from him. Our society is dying. I can save us all, if you just help me."

Gwen stilled as a terrible realization dawned on her. "You poisoned me. That wine you sent..."

"I had to make you see that Druam would cause the dam to burst," he said, as carelessly as if he were admitting to a late night stroll. "It was the only way."

"And the scrying spell?" *Was it all a dream? Please, if it was false...*

"My allies in Demarren told me that the Liegelord would soon fall. I made sure you were there to see it." His voice was cold. *Who is this man I thought was my friend?*

Mavian grew quiet, though his hands did not loosen. He pushed through the ancient oak door. Gwen was overpowered by the dreadful smell: mustiness, blood, decay, excrement...she gagged.

Gwen resisted, but Mavian dragged her down the stairs into darkness, turning and turning until the light above faded and she couldn't see past her nose. Her feet slipped on the worn stone, but she couldn't reach out to steady herself. Before she fell into Mavian, he stopped, jerking her upright. He proceeded more slowly, his hand hot around her wrists.

At last, the stairs ended, but Gwen could not see what lay before them. Another door? A hall? The stench was overpowering now. Bile rose in her throat.

Mavian whispered something, too low for her to catch, and a mellow red light blossomed from his palm. He held what looked like a glass lantern lit by some magical source. He lifted it and said the command word once more, louder this time, and a hundred more of the lanterns glowed all at once, illuminating a large natural cavern.

Gwen squeaked, too terrified to scream properly.

Human silhouettes crawled out of nooks and from behind rocks, the light reflecting in their scarlet eyes. Their apelike foreheads crinkled, drool pouring from their mouths and over their fangs as they advanced. The prowlers grunted and growled to each other in some guttural language. Gwen realized that she recognized some: a stable boy, a minor steward, a kitchen girl who had once brought her supper, her sweet smile now taken over by a feral grin.

They drew closer. Gwen tried to flee. She kicked and scratched at Mavian, but he stood firm. He watched the prowlers calmly, as if they posed no threat to him.

"Don't try to run," he said to Gwen. "They will chase you."

Gwen froze, her heart pounding, sweat dripping down her arms. Again she tried to summon her magic, to bring forth any spell that could help her. It would not come. Desperately, Gwen reached out beyond herself, a wave of fear pouring from her with only one word in it: *Help!* Mavian shook her, though he still focused on the prowlers.

"None of that now, Gwen. Look at what I've created."

She did. The prowlers had all stopped some distance away, their eyes darting between Mavian and Gwen as they licked their lips and scratched at open sores. Mavian's eyes narrowed, his lips thinning as he glared them down. He uttered a series of harsh, horrible sounds that Gwen could feel were laced with magic. A dark magic, though, like the curse she had wrought: vengeful, angry, drawn up from the deepest parts of the world.

The prowlers scraped and bowed, then retreated, their cries to each other eventually fading in the darkness. Gwen's mouth had gone dry, and she shivered suddenly in the cold, musky air.

"I can control them," Mavian said. "Ever since I saw them, I knew that they retained part of their human intelligence. I knew that, if I could learn about them, I could make them mine. I spent years researching and studying them, and only now have I unlocked the secret."

"You let prowlers into the palace," Gwen whispered. "You sent them after the queen."

Mavian shrugged. "I had to see what they would do for me, and my ally wanted her dead. Can you see now, Gwen? I've turned this creature into a tool for the betterment of man! Druam and the king would refuse, they would call it dangerous necromancy, but with the prowlers and my noble allies beside me, no one can stand in the way of progress."

"You're mad. They're monsters, you can't trust them."

"What do you think men are? We are no better than them, animals driven by instinct. Don't you think that these prowlers, if once they were men, could be turned back into men? Only someone like me can try. And someone like you. Understand that, Gwen, please. Together we can bring man to his full glory."

In his fervor, Mavian released her, his hands gesticulating wildly. Gwen edged away from him, back toward the staircase. *He has gone insane*, she thought. Before he realized he had let her go, she darted up the steps, back up into the pitch black. She heard him curse, and then the slap of leather against stone as he pursued her. Keeping one hand on the wall, Gwen raced as fast as she dared. She slipped once, her leg colliding with the unyielding stone, but she could not stop. Her breath came ragged in her lungs, her palms scraped by the stone.

Light! Gwen ran from the stairs, past the couches and tables, not daring to look back to see if Mavian had caught up.

A woman stepped in front of her. Gwen crashed into her and they both tumbled onto the hard floor. Spasms of pain shocked Gwen's body and she lay stunned for a breath. Mavian shouted something. The woman, Maeria, clutched her head in her hands.

The way out was clear. Gwen sprang for it. Her breath came hard in her throat. Shadows descended the stairwell in front of her.

Mavian's iron hand closed around Gwen's upper arm, dragging her back toward that horrible, prowler-filled place. The blonde woman regained herself and stood at last, her cold blue eyes turning on Gwen.

"Stop whoever's coming!" Mavian shouted. Gwen struggled against him, tore at his hand with her long nails, drew blood, but he did not care.

Maeria drew the dagger at her side. Gwen screamed, hoping that someone would hear. Mavian slapped the back of her head, sending stars reeling in her vision.

Through a teary haze, Gwen watched Druam emerge from the stairwell, a naked sword in his hand, and others behind him. Maeria rushed at him, her dagger raised. Another woman cried out as Gwen shouted to Druam.

It happened too fast to see. Maeria's dagger slipped from her hand as Druam's sword pushed through her chest and out her back. Druam wore an expression Gwen had never imagined on him: unbridled hatred. He pulled his sword back, letting Maeria slide gasping to the ground, and turned his fury to Mavian.

Gwen pulled, and found herself released. She stumbled into Druam. Mavian stared at the dying woman, mouth agape.

"Maeria..." Mavian half-whispered. He took a step forward, then stopped as Druam moved in front of Gwen, sword raised.

"I have tolerated your misdeeds for far too long," Druam said, his voice like steel. "Come with me, and–"

Behind them, the other woman cried out. Druam and Gwen whirled to see the *sulpari* collapse beside Maeria's corpse and sob. She took the dead woman's hand and caressed her cheek.

Mavian raised his arms, a silver amulet with clear gems held in one hand, and muttered some ancient tongue. Once more Gwen caught a whiff of terrible, dark magic. A void in the air, purple and black, erupted from nothing, as tall and wide as a man. Black shapes crept out of it, along the walls, dancing on the ceiling; evil things from places no man should ever walk. They sprang into being, demonic shadows that surrounded Druam and Gwen, separating them. The shadows wrapped around Gwen, trapping her and sinking their incorporeal teeth into her skin. She screamed and writhed in a hundred thousand pinpricks of sharp pain.

"*Ettrili marin, corav alon,*" Gwen whispered, pulling from the very depths of her magic. Warmth crept from Gwen's bones, seeking out the shadows and prizing them from her in a wash of golden light. The effort of this reserve of magic drained her already-exhausted body. The shadows shrieked and fled from her.

Gwen released the magic, feeling as if her very soul would crumble.

But Mavian yelled something in that deathlike language, and a black tendril, a tentacle of fear and loathing, emerged from the darkness. It moved fast, snaking across the floor. Gwen stumbled from its path, but it moved beyond her.

The tendril coiled around Maeria, immune to the *sulpari's* efforts to strike at it. Then, just as quickly, it transported the dead woman to Mavian's side.

Gwen met Mavian's eyes, and though all around her was chaos, she saw in him a deep, dark pool of freezing hatred. He took Maeria's hand, then stepped backwards into the void. It closed in around him, then was gone.

Druam gasped, and Gwen rushed to him as the shadows dissipated. His skin was covered in hundreds of red burns, and when Gwen looked at her own arms, she saw the same shadow-marks all over herself. With everyone looking on, she narrowed her eyes, pointed a finger at a large burn on the back of his hand, and uttered the healing words Ebarren had taught her so long ago. A small spark of magic sputtered out and zipped around the burn. When it vanished, it left that part of Druam's skin unmarred and unscarred. She smiled, pleased despite the horrors in that chamber. But her gaze returned to that ancient door, and she shuddered, knowing what lay below. *I thought Mavian to be different than them...and he only wanted to use me, too.*

Chapter Forty-Four

Cara

MAVIAN'S SITTING ROOM was filled with chaos. The Lady Seastone screamed as Renna drew a dagger and ran at the stairwell. Druam raced into the room with a drawn sword. Mavian stood with his hands spread, ready to use his dark magic.

It happened too quickly for Cara to stop it. She shouted at Renna, but her lady didn't listen. Renna ran at Druam, and his sword slammed into her. Cara watched, time rushing past despite her agony.

Renna fell prone to the ground, and Cara raced to her, her scream lost in the confusion. She cradled her lady, barely aware of everything else around her. Stroking Renna's face, Cara whispered, "I'm sorry for everything I said, I should have listened."

A rattling breath came from Renna's bleeding mouth. Her blue eyes stared past Cara. Still Cara cuddled her, praying to all the gods that her lady might live. She couldn't have said which breath was Renna's last, for each came slower and softer. Cara keened over her lady's body.

"Not now, not when I've just found you," she mumbled. She didn't care anymore that Renna had abandoned her fief, nor that she wanted to go with the Hooded Man. As long as Renna was alive, they had a chance of becoming friends again. Death was too final to allow for forgiveness.

From the corner of her eye, Cara saw the battle between Mavian, Druam, and Gwen. She didn't try to intervene or help either side. Suddenly, a black tentacle erupted from the void behind Mavian. It moved too rapidly, and curled around Renna. Cara cried out and tried to stab at it with her feeble dagger, but it didn't even cringe from her blade.

Before Cara could blink, the tendril took Renna from her. She knelt in blood and watched as her lady was brought into the blackness for the second time.

I failed her, Cara thought. *All my friends died for nothing.*

Cara stood before Earl Seastone and the king in the earl's study that night, her head clouded with grief. Lady Seastone was safe, and she was thankful for that, but her melancholy allowed for no more thought.

"Why were you in Mavian's chambers?" the king asked without preamble. Even in his dressing robes, his presence spoke of well-earned command.

"I needed his advice," Cara said dully. The events in the tavern felt like a lifetime ago. "And then I saw Renna."

"Your lady?"

Cara nodded. "She told me that Mavian was the Hooded Man, and that she went with him willingly. They used a spell to disguise her as another noblewoman."

"Maeria Westerburg," said Earl Seastone. He stood by the windows. "We were all fooled."

"And you claim to know nothing of this, Seastone?" demanded King Henrik.

The earl glared at his king. "I have known Mavian from when he was a boy, yet I never could have imagined this. He tried to hurt my wife, Henrik. You think I would condone such a thing? He wanted her to betray me."

"Easy, Druam," said Henrik. He rubbed at his temples. "I

meant no offense."

Cara stared at the desk, her eyes aching from tears. She wished only to go to bed. *But if I go to bed, I'll sleep where Alex has been.* It was all too much to bear.

"You killed her," she said softly, her eyes meeting Druam's before flicking away.

The earl nodded gravely. "She threatened my wife; I had no choice. But I am sorry."

Beneath his blank exterior, Cara saw a hint of remorse. She would reckon with him someday, but not that night. She nodded and went back to staring at the table.

"Mavian has shown his hand now," said Druam. "He intends to overthrow us with the prowlers at his command, and whatever other dark magic he possesses. If his claim of allies in the court is true, then we must find these traitors before it's too late."

The king let out a long, low sigh. "Conspiracies within conspiracies, lies within lies. Will it ever end, Druam?"

"I dearly hope so." Druam turned to Cara. "We will need you before this is done. You are *sulpari*, one of the few capable of matching the prowlers' strength."

"I can't help you." Cara didn't meet his eyes. "I'm not strong enough."

The earl knelt beside her chair. "Look at me." She obeyed. "Listen to me. There are many forces at work here which we don't understand. But we will need you, and you will be strong enough."

"How do you know?"

Druam smiled at her. "Because heroes always find a way."

The king lumbered to his feet. He yawned, and said, "Let's convene in the morning. We have much to discuss."

"Indeed we do," said Druam. He and the king began to walk away.

Even in the depths of her despair, Cara knew that she had to tell them about Alex. She turned and said, "Before I went to Mavian, I went to the dockside taverns. I saw–"

Druam spoke over her, "Whatever it is can wait until

morning. Rest now, Cara. I'll send for you once you've had time to rest."

The two powerful men left her. *They didn't listen,* Cara thought. *Why wouldn't they listen?*

Someone must have remembered that she was still in the study, for a steward showed up some time later and offered to walk her to her rooms. Though she wanted to be anywhere else, Cara followed him. She was too tired to protest.

As she entered, she wished she had been strong enough to request something else. Fresh flowers in vases decorated the whole sitting room, but those weren't what she regretted.

Alex waited for her. He had washed and dressed in simple cotton clothes. Cara thought about turning and running, yet she knew she'd have to talk to him at some point. *Might as well be now, when I'm too tired to censor myself.*

Cara looked away from Alex and went to pour herself a glass of wine. Mercifully, he remained quiet until she turned to face him again.

"You lied to me," she said.

He shrugged, a hint of his carefree smile playing about his lips. "I did."

"Did you ever think about telling me?"

"Every minute we spent together, and even the ones apart." Alex walked to her then, but stopped an arms-length away. "I'm sorry, Cara. I wanted to tell you, but I never could find the words. And I couldn't forget how you spoke about the *fampir* as evil things."

"Are you evil?"

"Who knows?" He gave her a bittersweet smile. "I lust for blood. I need it to survive. It's horrible, but when it comes over me...I can't stop it. You can understand that, can't you? But you're still mortal, you can live without killing. Not that I kill every time; we do try not to if we can help it."

Cara clutched at the goblet in her hand, though the liquid inside sloshed as her hands trembled. Every time she looked at Alex, her heart fluttered. She wanted so, so badly for everything to be as it was.

"Who is 'we'?" she asked.

"The *fampir* of Riverfen. Myself, Master Eigbrett, Shepherd Marin...and my brothers."

"Surely not the earl," Cara said. He had seemed so wise, so caring, so...so old, now that she thought about it.

"Druam created me," Alex said. "A hundred and seventy years ago. But he and Verdon were brothers before they became *fampir*, many more centuries before that. He built Riverfen and the Cascade Palace, he made the traditions of the lanterns."

Cara's throat constricted. She stared at her wine, unable to look at Alex for fear of breaking. "Someone would have noticed an immortal earl."

"Some did. They were bought or silenced. But Druam has a gift for mental manipulation, just as I have a gift for persuasion. He always goes into seclusion to 'die,' then returns as his own son. Most people believed it with his *fampir* talents. Sometimes Verdon would take his place, or myself. But Druam has always been the better ruler."

Cara merely nodded, not particularly caring about the earl's tricks. It wasn't him that had seduced her and lied to her. She glanced at Alex, and her heart stirred. She had held him against her, comforted by his presence. He had taught her, laughed with her, saved her from her darkest moments.

"When I found you, I thought I was dreaming," Alex said. "For the longest time, you were only a concept in my head, a word in my journals. The real you was incredible: strong and brave, but also gentle and compassionate. And you had the beast inside, like me. Can you blame me for falling for you?"

Cara's eyes brimmed, and she wiped them angrily. She had thought the same things about him.

Alex said, "The *sulpari* were first created to stop creatures like me. But you don't have to be like that. You don't have to kill us."

Cara laughed bitterly. "I couldn't do it even if I wanted to." She knew it to be true the moment the words left her lips. She couldn't kill him after all he had done for her.

Silence built between them. After a minute, Alex took a step toward her, hands held out, pleading. She stepped back, still trying not to look at him.

"Are we so different?" Alex asked. His green eyes held decades of loneliness. "I have never met anyone like you. Autorus' gift beats in both our hearts. Can't we enjoy it together?"

Unconsciously, Cara drifted toward him. *It wouldn't be so bad*, she thought. Then she stopped herself. "Don't use your *fampir* gifts on me."

"I'm not. I'm speaking honestly as a man who loves a woman."

There it was: love. That morning, she thought she loved him. Her skin ached for his touch, her heart yearned to be near him. But could she trust him after such a tremendous lie?

"Is it even possible for the undead to love?" Cara asked, playing for time. If she didn't send him away soon, she knew she would give in. *Just a few more moments, then he'll be gone*, she promised herself.

"Beneath this monster, I am still a man. Please, Cara. I promised never to leave you; please don't abandon me. I can't change what I am, but–"

"But what? What will happen when I grow old and die, and you continue into eternity? Will you find another gullible girl to tumble?"

"It's not like that and you know it." Alex closed the gap and took hold of her arm. She finally looked at him, and her heart trembled at his sorrow.

"I don't know anything anymore," Cara said. "Everyone I ever loved betrayed me. You could do it again, so easily. You'll make a plaything of me."

He flinched away, his green eyes wounded. Cara pressed him, "How many mortals have you taken to your bed? How many that thought you loved them?"

"Would you expect me to be abstinent for all my long years?" Alex snapped back. "Yes, I took mortal and *fampir* girls to bed. Men, too, when the mood took me. And I did love some of them. I mourned for many years after they passed. But never have I known what I feel for you. You complete me, as none of the others ever have. I didn't understand Druam's letters when he spoke of Gwen, and his depth of emotion for her, but I do now."

Cara stared up at him, her cheek flushing where his breath touched it. It would be so, so easy to give in now.

But I can't forgive him, she realized. Even as she stared into those passionate eyes, she knew that his was a sin she could never forget. For all his proclamations of love, he had never trusted her with his secret. *He may never have told me.*

Cara pulled herself from his grasp. "Go, Alex."

"But–"

"Just go." She turned away from him.

He didn't move, and she brushed past him. He asked softly, "Will you at least stay for the Masque?"

Cara paused, for the question had also been on her mind. What could she do now? Mavian was still out there, and she had seen the light of vengeance in his eyes. The Masque would be the perfect place to hurt as many people as he could.

"I will," she said, "but not for you, or for Druam. I'll stay to defeat Mavian. Once he's gone, I'm leaving this hellish city."

She thought he might argue, but he only sighed. His muffled footsteps sounded on the carpet, then the door opened and shut. When she looked over her shoulder, he was gone.

Cara retreated to her bedroom, where she locked all the doors before perching in the center of the bed. She stared into nothing.

I should have killed him, she thought, though she knew she couldn't bring herself to do it. *And if what he said is true, then the* fampir *are everywhere. I can't trust anyone.*

If only Sandu were there. He'd help her find a way out of this. Cara laughed at herself; she had thought Sandu's betrayal to be so awful, then she'd experienced the truths about Alex and Renna. *At least Sandu tried to do the right thing.* Cara cried then for his loss as she hadn't cried before.

With a knot in her stomach, Cara knew what must be done. *The king must be told everything.* But even with this realization, she felt resigned instead of empowered. She was but a woman with a sword and no friends.

The hardest part was the earl. He had seemed so determined, earnest, full of hope, and she had thought him the greatest lord one could ask for. Was it possible he truly wanted the best for the people? What if he and Alex were *not* sinister?

After all, Cara herself was somehow kin to the prowlers. Her own morals were questionable, for she'd killed a child, even if that child was a prowler. She had reveled in slaughtering her enemies, and felt the draw of greater power. If only everything was clear instead of muddled. Prowlers were horrid beasts and must be destroyed. But were she and the *fampir* similarly bound to darkness, with no chance of redemption?

You were created to destroy creatures like me, Alex had said. Cara thought, *Maybe I still will. Just not today.*

She had never felt such intense loneliness than in that moment. No one remained to comfort her or give her advice. She remembered the earl calling her a hero. *Perhaps this is what being a hero is: being alone.*

CHAPTER FORTY-FIVE
Gwen

"...AND WITH all of the courtiers gathered in the same ballroom, we must ensure proper security..." the speaker droned on. He was one of many stewards the lords had called upon to speak during morning council. Though Druam sat forward, listening attentively to every word that had been spoken in the last two candles, Gwen could not bring herself to care. All the other earls, and the king, were distracted as well: they stirred in their seats, inspected their fingernails, or played with quills and bits of paper. Each earl was seated with his advisors and vassal lords behind him while King Henrik occupied the center table, his crown removed for the time being and placed on a cushion in front of him. Gwen was the only woman in attendance.

When the steward finished, Druam said, "Thank you, Master Eldon. We will fully consider what you have said and deliver instructions for the Masque as soon as we are able. You are dismissed."

The steward bowed and waddled from the room. As soon as he had departed, the earls and king sat forward, focusing their attention on Druam. King Henrik asked, "Is there a possibility that your cousin will attempt something tomorrow night, Earl Seastone?" The king looked pointedly at Gwen. "He has already attempted assassinations on our wives."

Murmurs followed as the earls turned to speak with their

men. Druam sighed and sat back, taking Gwen's hand as he did. "I cannot say with certainty that Mavian will not do something rash. From what I understand, Maeria Westerburg – or Renna Nellestere, as the *sulpari* has claimed her to be – was a woman of great importance to him. In his grief, he may try to inflict the same pain upon the rest of us."

"We see." King Henrik's eyes again turned to Gwen. "Can the Lady Seastone tell us anything about his machinations? You told us he spoke with her; we want to know what he said."

"My wife–" Druam started, but the king cut him off abruptly.

"From the lady herself, please. We want as much clarity in this as possible."

The memory of that dungeon's horrid smell and Mavian's cruel smile leapt forward in Gwen's mind. Her throat tightened and her hands shook as she straightened. She took a deep breath, swallowing the terror stuck in her mouth, and said as calmly as she could, "He wanted me to...to help him. He said that the lords of this land were corrupt and would bring the people to ruin. All he wanted, he said, was to bring knowledge and peace to the rustics, a new era of enlightenment and prosperity. He...he said that Earl Seastone, and King Henrik, and all the other earls and lords, would need to be brought down, and that he himself would rise as a benevolent ruler." Mavian's exact words twisted in her memory, but she did her best to recall them. "And then he brought me below the palace to a cavern filled with prowlers. He spoke to them, and they obeyed him."

Gwen stopped suddenly, for her breath came faster, and she spoke quicker than was proper. She knew that she must look wide-eyed and scared. Druam squeezed her hand, then said to the king, "My wife does not have the constitution to re-live such horrors now, Your Grace. I have kept her beside me as often as I can since such events, and the terror she experienced has quieted her bright humors and brought her soul to a dark place."

"That may well be," the king said, his tone flat, "but we have an enemy in our midst who plans murder. You said, our dear lady, that Mavian Strilu wanted you to help him. Why? How could *you* aid him in his coup?"

Gwen hesitated. Druam nodded, though his eyes betrayed his nerves. Her eyes focused at a spot on the wall behind the king, Gwen said, "I...I possess magic, Your Grace. Mavian believes there to be a cure for the affliction of the prowlers, and that I can help him."

"We see." Though his expression did not change, the king's eyes grew colder. Murmurs had once again come up at Gwen's words, and she felt so small surrounded by Dotschar's powerful men.

"Your Grace!" Lord Daghorn, the Skallish ambassador, strode to the front of the room to face the assembly. "Would you allow this woman – this foul creature – to go free?"

"What is *your* complaint against her?"

"She is a witch! And, far worse, she has evaded the righteous arm of the Inquisition for too long. She fled Demarren knowing her own guilt and treachery. My kin, the rightful heirs of that kingdom, demand her head."

"Or what?" Druam said.

Daghorn smiled cruelly. "Or the allied kingdoms of Demarren and Skålland shall have no choice but to declare war against Dotschar for harboring a traitor and a witch."

"You go too far, ambassador," Druam said, his soft voice carrying to every corner. "You dare threaten my wife in my own palace? Get out."

"Seastone, be careful," Henrik warned Druam. He turned to the ambassador. "We have our own laws and customs, Lord Daghorn. You must give us time to consider this issue."

"You would give in to his threats?" Druam demanded.

"We would not have us go to war – after a hundred years of peace – for the sake of one woman!" Henrik shouted. "Leave, Lord Daghorn. Our answer has not yet been given."

Gwen shied away from the ambassador's taunting look as Daghorn swept from the room. The earls and lords bent their heads together, whispering urgently.

"Well," Henrik said after the murmurs had died down, "We think it time for the earls and ourself to convene privately. We have much to discuss."

King Henrik took his crown and seated it on his greying hair. His chair scraped against the stone floor as he stood. Druam kissed Gwen's forehead and whispered, "I won't let anything happen to you," then went with the other earls and the king to the adjoining private council chamber. Though fear made her shiver, Gwen took a deep breath, straightened her neck and shoulders, and strode purposefully for the exit. The vassal lords and advisors parted around her like water around a stone, watching her as if she might set any one of them on fire.

In the past two days, Druam had barely left her side – or, more accurately, barely allowed *her* to leave *his* side – but now, he would be in council for gods knew how long, and Gwen could spend some time alone to think.

Well, as alone as she could be with handmaids and assigned guards dogging her every step.

Gwen returned to her chambers and there tried to content herself with embroidery. She pricked her thumb a dozen times before she stopped. Lord Daghorn was now her declared enemy. What lengths would he go to in order to see her executed? Would he even wait for King Henrik to decide her fate? He could just as easily take her while the lords sat in their council and drag her screaming back to Demarren. But he wasn't the only danger to her: Mavian knew the ins and outs of the servants' passages; would he try to kill her while Druam was otherwise preoccupied? Or perhaps Mavian himself wouldn't come, but his prowlers, their jaws slathered with spit and blood.

Gwen thrust the embroidery into its basket and moved restlessly about the room. Her maids and guards watched her, as still and silent as statues. Pausing at a bookshelf, Gwen ran her fingers over the leather-bound covers and gilt titles, remembering sadly that Mavian had shown her how to use her magic to read.

Sometime after luncheon, a knock came at the door. Druam entered, followed by a servant carrying a wooden chest. Something in Druam's expression made her pause, and Gwen slowed as she drew nearer to him. Surely the council had come to a good decision?

"I have a gift for you," Druam said, his voice low and tired. He gestured the servant to step forward. Curious, Gwen opened the chest and drew out a long, silky dress embroidered from neck to foot with trees and flowers, birds and animals that cavorted around and around in a wearable tapestry. Shaking it out, Gwen examined the needlework and cut of the dress. It was as beautiful a thing as she had ever worn.

"It's gorgeous," she said. "What is it for?"

"The Masque. I wanted you to wear something utterly unique, for that is what you are. The tailors and embroiderers have spent a month working all night and day to finish it in time. Are you pleased with it?"

"Oh yes." Gwen took Druam's hand and led him to a couch. "What did the king decide?"

Druam licked his lips and glanced toward the silent guards as if itching to dismiss them. His hands lay utterly still in his lap, and though his shoulders were not hunched, there was a tightness about them. He ran his fingers through his hair, looked to her, then up to the ceiling. He wrinkled his nose, like there was a bad smell in the air, and brushed underneath his eyes with his fingertips. Gwen watched him, her concern growing. He did not seem himself.

After a minute of fidgeting, Druam finally met her worried eyes. He took a deep breath and said, "You will not be sent to the Inquisition...but the king wanted to bring you to Con Salur to serve as his court mage. And so he could have you watched at all times."

The mere words pressed all thoughts from Gwen's mind and deflated her lungs. She stared at Druam, her violet eyes wide with shock. Remembering to breathe, she quickly sucked in air, though it tasted stale.

"But why?" Gwen gasped.

"Magic is not forbidden here as it is in your homeland, but King Henrik – and many kings before him – have questioned its use by those in the noble court. You have influence here, and if you use your Gift against the king...he would rather you be preoccupied with your duties to him."

Gwen imagined herself, trapped like Avallune in his tower, beholden to the king's whims. *It may not be so bad*, she thought, though her heart recoiled from the idea. "Couldn't you come with me?"

"My place is here," Druam said sadly. "We would be parted, only seeing each other when I visited Con Salur."

Forever trapped in the capital, with no opportunities apart from the king's will, and separated from the only person she still trusted...Gwen reeled at the implications. "I won't go! There must be some other way..."

"The king will allow you to stay here," Druam said. His voice betrayed his sorrow. "But only if you never practice magic again. He will assign a handmaid from his own household to watch you and report back to him."

"Did you know he would do this?"

Druam shook his head. "I feared his reaction, and so I said nothing. You were so happy, and I was a coward."

Gwen's heart fell to her slippers. *Are these my only choices? A life of servitude, or a life without magic?* She stared dully at the wall.

"Assume the mantle of a gentle lady, my Gwen, and leave your magic behind. It will cause us nothing but strife," Druam said, extending a hand to her shoulder. She shrugged it off.

"It's not fair!" she exclaimed. "This is who I am, Druam! Wullum sent me here so that I didn't have to hide myself. I don't want to go back to living a lie. And I can't leave you, not after everything. This is my home now."

Druam's strong arms encircled Gwen, holding her steady. "I'm so sorry, Gwen. Though your magic frightened me, I thought perhaps we could figure out a way together. I tried to hide it from the king as long as I could. But now we must move forward, forging a new path without your magic."

"I don't want to stop using it," Gwen said softly. "Even if Mavian was the one who taught me...I was happy practicing magic."

"I know, love. I know." Druam squeezed her, his musky

scent comforting. "But with the threat of war, I cannot see any other way. This is the only way to keep peace, both with Henrik and the Skals."

Gwen sank into her misery, her magic swilling uncomfortably inside her, as if it too knew the king's proclamation. She did not respond when Druam led her to her bed, or when he brought her supper that returned cold to the kitchens, or when he lay beside her in the growing night. A vast emptiness threatened to consume her. She lay quietly and stared up at the dark canopy as Druam fell asleep. Laying beside him, listening to him breathe, Gwen realized that she did truly love him.

But she loved magic, too. It had scared her, caused her pain, but it was a part of her as much as her eyes or fingers were. Even if she tried to suppress it, even if she succeeded for years on end, there would come a time when she could not resist magic's pull, and then she would be taken from the life she loved. Could she live here in Riverfen under that constant fear? But there was nowhere else to go, no one else who would take her...

At some point, Gwen must have fallen asleep, for she found herself in a dream. Not the dreams that one forgets immediately upon waking, but a dream that felt real save for the swirling red and grey dust motes in the air. Gwen marveled at the twisting tree trunks and grey foliage around her; this was an ancient, mysterious grove. Three women huddled beneath the trees.

"You seek us, child?" one woman said, her voice high and warbling.

"Or perhaps, you know that we seek you?" said another in a voice low as dirt.

The third woman hushed the others, her eyes bright. Her tones were motherly, inviting, warm: "Come to us in the Whispering Woods, sweet child. For years beyond measure have we waited, and watched, and listened, tasting the air for the signs that one has been born with the power of ancient times. Come to us, Gwendolyn Zaman of Demarren, princess of your people, but far more than that in the turning of Earda."

Gwen said nothing, but when the third woman reached for her, she held out her hand. The strange hag breathed on Gwen's palm, then smiled and said, "We the Witches Three are waiting. Open your magic and let our beacon guide you to us. Fulfill your potential – or waste away to nothing."

Gwen woke suddenly, her chest burning with desire. She glanced at Druam, but he slept as peacefully as a cat by the fire. Gwen saw no markings on her hand, but rather *felt* the presence of an old magic hidden in the folds of her skin. Closing her fingers around it, she lay back and wondered. That dream could not have been merely a dream.

Gwen hummed an ancient song and called her magic up. It flowed over her shoulder and through her arm, released from the tips of her fingers. Colors sprang above her, contorting into a tapestry grander than any ever sewn. The images moved around each other, creating pictures before her eyes: the last meeting with Wullum, his love shutting out the horrible world for just a moment; running down the green-singing path to meet Druam for the first time; Druam's earnestness as he offered marriage to her; on and on the images came. Gwen watched them, bittersweet tears staining the pillow against her cheek.

When the magic brought forth that night in the tavern with Druam, she held his hand, feeling that content emotion stirring within her breast. The magic faded, leaving spots behind her eyes in the dark room.

Gwen realized that she would have to choose between her husband – a life as the earl's lady in a grand palace – and magic, with all the adventures, mystery, and danger it offered her. If only the king had not made his proclamation, if only this dilemma were not set before her...

Druam murmured in his sleep, rolling to face her. Gwen folded her arms and legs around him, pressing his head to her chest. But still she lay awake.

Chapter Forty-Six
Seanna

SERVANTS HURRIED back and forth with Seanna's belongings. Already, maids had come to sweep the floors and change the sheets on the feather bed. By the time Seanna departed, there would be no trace of her left in these borrowed chambers. She could imagine the steward back in Con Salur ordering her rooms to be prepared unexpectedly early, and the whispers of the staff as they worked.

There were still over two candles until the ship must sail, and Seanna did not know how to fill that time. Her embroidery had been packed, she was already dressed for traveling, and no one had come to see her off. She stood alone in the center of the drawing room surrounded by bustling servants. Sir Eric waited next to the door, as stern as ever.

All the other courtiers in the palace would spend their day washing, applying cosmetics, and dressing for tonight's Masque while Seanna began her lonely journey back to the capital. It was almost preferable to leave, though, than to abide the scornful looks she would no doubt receive at the party. Her gold silk dress, still laid out on a chair, made her want to cry. That one would stay here in Riverfen.

A pile of letters and notes sat on her silver platter. None were from well-wishers or allies in the court. The stack represented the entirety of Mavian and Maeria's relationship, the letters found when Druam had ordered a search of Mavian's rooms. Almost as if he were taunting Seanna, Henrik had the letters sent to her. He must have delighted in knowing her reaction to the contents of each.

Seanna shed no tears at Maeria's death, but she wept at knowing how little Maeria had cared for her. The girl had used her, writing to Mavian: *I believe the queen to hold affection for me. Though I am repulsed, I will try to gain her favor and use it to our advantage. As her paramour, I could wield influence in our favor.*

The queen has asked me again to her bed. She does not rival you, my love, but if we are to please our allies, then I must discover her weaknesses. Perhaps I am one such weakness?

Oh, Mavian, if only we could wed sooner...I cannot stand another night in the queen's company. I must see you again and feel you in every way. Tonight, tonight, tonight!

There were the ones from Mavian, too: *You shall be the queen of my new world; nothing can stop us now that we are so close* and *Your father has succumbed to the potions you have given him. We shall be wed soon, my love.* Seanna regretted asking the steward to read each and every one to her.

When she could no longer stand the growing emptiness in her rooms, Seanna said, "I suppose I should go thank our host, shouldn't I?"

Sir Eric didn't say anything.

"Druam had been kind to me in the past. Maybe now he'll be kind again, now that I have no friends nor allies." Seanna bit her lip, thinking. "How am I to make amends for what I did when I feel no remorse?"

"Honestly, and with many apologies," Sir Eric said. He gave her the barest hint of a smile.

"Then send word that I wish to see him before I leave."

Barely twenty minutes passed before the messenger returned. "Your Grace, the earl is in the conservatory. He grants you leave to visit him there."

"Thank you." Seanna tipped the boy a silver shem and stood to go. She leaned on Sir Eric for support on the long walk down to the glass conservatory.

The soldier at the wrought iron gate bowed to her and allowed her inside a small antechamber, where a simple wooden door barred the way inside. A gardener opened this door and said, "Your Grace, your knight is to remain here. I will escort you to Earl Seastone."

Feeling some discomfort at leaving Sir Eric behind, Seanna stepped into the conservatory's humid air. She felt she had come into another world entirely, a world molded by the singing of birds and babble of brooks, that always smelled of sweet things; a world wholly apart from the one she'd left behind of petty squabbles and bickering gossip.

The gardener led her down a winding path lined with waterfalls – *It must be magic, how they continually flow* – and through differently cultivated sections. One grew roses of all types, another fir and pine trees, and others exotic trees and shrubs, until at last the gardener brought her to a trellis archway lined with orchid blooms of all colors. Beyond it was a garden with trees, shrubs, and flowers Seanna had never seen before. A gardener worked in one of the flower beds, a pile of weeds beside him on the otherwise clean walkway.

As they drew closer, Seanna realized that the gardener was not a servant. Druam knelt in the dirt, his embroidered tunic exchanged for a pair of worn trousers and a patched shirt. His boots were covered in mud, and he wore filthy gloves with holes in them. All his clothes were smudged with dirt and sweat, his normally slick hair hanging loose over his grimy face.

Druam did not look up as Seanna approached him. "You may leave us, Jerly," he said to the gardener. To Seanna: "I hadn't expected you this morning, Your Grace."

"I hadn't expected to come." Seanna sank onto a bench behind him. Druam kept on working, wiping the sweat from his brow and blowing his nose into a kerchief. Watching him, Seanna said, "This place is beautiful. Why don't you invite others to come here?"

Though she couldn't see his face, Druam's tone was friendly enough. "I built this conservatory as a sanctuary away from the politics of palace life. What good could it do me if I allow those same politics to enter and ruin the peace?"

"Ah." Seanna's heartbeat grew audible in her ears. *Now is the time to apologize, now or never. If you don't do this, you'll have no chance at regaining his alliance.*

As if sensing her thoughts, Druam asked, "Why have you come, Seanna?"

Seanna shifted uncomfortably on the bench and played with her hands beneath her belly. She couldn't see her feet unless she stretched out backwards and pushed them in front of her, but that might cause her to fall. Would that hurt the baby? She hadn't done anything wrong with the first two, yet she'd still lost those. Best be safe, and not try to look at her feet.

"Seanna? Do you have something you need to tell me?"

"Yes; no; I don't know...yes. Yes, Druam. I have betrayed your trust, and for that I am sorry. I am so sorry. You mustn't be angry at me, for I think it would be impossible to be angrier at me than I already am at myself."

Seanna paused for breath; Druam had not moved. He knelt, his head turned slightly over one shoulder. For a moment, it looked like he had even stopped breathing. He said nothing. Despite the dirt and greens on his hands and knees, Seanna felt a beggar next to him.

"You must believe me, Druam, I did not intend to hurt you," Seanna said, blabbering now. "Sometimes I do not think of the consequences of my actions. I was swept over by the promise of power. I was enticed to it by those conniving people; it was never *me* that did those things, it was an evil inside of me that I couldn't control."

"Gwen wore a cloak made of these orchids on our wedding day," Druam said in a soft, measured tone. "Purple, like her eyes. On that day, I had not imagined anything coming between us, least of all unfounded lies born of envy."

Seanna opened her mouth, but Druam spoke first. "You have said your piece. Listen to me now."

Seanna felt compelled to obey.

"In all that I do, I have done for my people. You came, and you did everything in your power to destroy the one selfish thing in my life. I am a man of my people, and all I had left over in my heart, I gave to Gwen.

"Your own marriage has left your soul empty yet your belly full with child, and you resent those of us who find joy in what the gods have granted us. I cannot forgive you for what you have done. All I can do is pity you."

As Druam knelt, covered in dirt, his head still twisted over one shoulder, Seanna thought he looked more kingly than Henrik. Some small part of her wished that he were king, so she could be his queen. But that was mere folly and fantasy, for they were only pawns of their births.

Turning away from her, Druam said, "I wish you fair weather and a short journey."

"But Druam, you *must* try in your heart to forgive me!" Seanna said. If she had a small belly, she would have thrown herself off the bench. Instead, she stood slowly and came to grasp his shoulder. "The gods would want you to find a way to forgive me."

He twisted to stare up at her with those sad, piercing blue eyes, but said nothing. He shrugged his shoulder from her hands and bent to pull a weed from underneath a flower.

"Please, Druam," Seanna pleaded. "You're my only chance at redemption. Without your forgiveness, how am I to recover the blows dealt to me?"

Druam sighed. "You planted sour grapes, and now complain that the wine made from them isn't sweet. Perhaps you should learn from your mistakes, and not beg for mercy from those who will not bestow it."

The rebuke was gentle, but firm, and final. Seanna recoiled as if physically burned. She blinked back tears and left him kneeling in the dirt, surrounded by beauty.

Sir Eric did not ask Seanna what had happened between her and the earl, and she did not tell him. She went to her carriage without complaint, and saw that no one waited for her on the palace steps to wish her farewell. *They must be at the docks,* she assured herself, but after the bumpy ride from the plateau and down through the city, she saw that the docks were empty save for sailors and whores.

As she boarded the ship, Seanna turned to look once more at the Cascade Palace on the hilltop, its white walls glowing in the sunlight. She had hoped to gain much while there, but the gods had planned a different fate.

No one had come to see her off.

CHAPTER FORTY-SEVEN
Sandu

A SPLASH of cold water shook Sandu from his drunken stupor. He sat up straight, a line of spit hanging from his cheek to the table he'd used as a pillow. Shaking his head, Sandu peered blearily around him. Where'd he ended up? Last he could remember, he'd been drinking and playing cards with the group of palace guards, but they must have taken him elsewhere, for he now found himself in a small tavern with the angry owner standing over him.

"Useless slob," the owner muttered, slamming a mug on the table. Sandu cringed at the loud noise; he had a horrible blooming headache. The owner said to someone behind Sandu, "He's all yours. Stupid Nessa, letting a drunk sleep here overnight."

Slowly, Sandu turned in his seat, blinking at the sunlight streaming in through a window. Once his eyes adjusted, he saw Captain Dirgard sitting at a table a few feet away. Groaning, Sandu said, "Oh, gods. I missed patrol, didn't I?"

"You've had more to worry about," Dirgard said, arching an eyebrow. "Took me ages to track down what had happened to you. Accused of high treason, freed by a lord, and now in bad humors from ale and gambling. I don't blame you for taking to drink."

"How'd you know I was here? Where is here, anyway?"

Dirgard chuckled. "The guards you gambled with told me. Said they left you in a bad state some nights ago at a different tavern. Men I met there told me where you'd ended up next, and so on and so forth until I came here. This is Red Ear Tavern, by the way. Off Cowley Street."

As Dirgard spoke, Sandu began to recall bits and pieces of the last few days. His dreams had been full of nightmares: prowlers and knights that whipped him, a queen that took something from him, though he couldn't give voice to what. He drank and gambled to stave off the ever-pressing horrors, yet they always returned in the place between sleep and dreams. As he grew sober, he would think about returning to Cara, who spoke with Tambrey's voice in his head. He couldn't go through such a rejection again, and so he had buried himself in yet more misdeeds.

Dirgard continued, "As I'm sure you can tell, the owner was not pleased with how he found the place this morning. I was prepared to be furious, too, until I saw that seal in your pocket. I'm not one to go against a lord like Strilu."

"So...you don't think I did it?" Sandu wasn't sure how much news had spread about his supposed guilt. There were bound to be people who believed him to have attempted treason.

"No. You've got an honest face, and you were too earnest about finding your friends. Did you find them? Are they well?"

Sandu had no idea why Dirgard had tracked him down if not to reprimand and imprison him for failing his duties, so he decided to trust the man's motives. "I found Alex. He's the lord, turns out. Cara's there, too, but...I couldn't face her. So..." He waved at the table and the mug. "The result of my cowardice."

"Then I suppose you haven't heard the news."

Sandu's heart plummeted to his shoes. Was he too late? Had something happened?

Dirgard continued, "Your companion – the *sulpari*, they call her – has quickly become involved with the dangers in the palace. She saved the queen from yet another assassination attempt, this one involving prowlers, and was there when Lord Mavian tried to take Lady Seastone. She is to attend the Masque tonight in case Lord Mavian tries something."

Sandu let out the breath he'd been holding. "I need to go to her. Before the Masque."

"I expected as much."

"But..." Sandu hesitated, unsure if Dirgard would agree to his idea. Dirgard leaned forward, his hand resting casually on the pommel of his sword. Taking this as a good sign, Sandu said, "But I don't think Cara can do it alone. Our enemies will be looking for Protectors and other soldiers, and make efforts to stop us first before they go for the courtiers."

"So what's your plan?"

Sandu quickly explained his rough scheme. Dirgard nodded thoughtfully, stroking his beard. "It's a possibility. From what I've heard, though, Mavian has dark magic. What do we have to combat that?"

A thought butted into Sandu's head, though at first he ignored it. But, as he and Dirgard talked back and forth about the details of their plan, he sighed. *Veck it.* Twisting his fingers together, Sandu said, "I know a man with magic."

"Who?" Dirgard brought his chair closer to Sandu's, their knees almost touching. "Does his power rival Mavian's?"

"I don't know," Sandu admitted, "but he's contacted me twice now through magical means. And he's seeking Cara. If I tell him she'll be there, he's sure to come; if she's in danger, he's sure to help. He needs her alive."

Another thought struck Sandu. Hadn't Laris mentioned Cara's difficult conception? *Maybe he's her father. Wouldn't I have a duty to bring them together?*

Dirgard spoke, "If this man has any semblance of power, we need him. Can you contact him?"

For a moment, Sandu said nothing. *I'd be betraying Cara, but for her own sake. Is that worse than doing nothing, possibly letting the enemy win, and keeping her from her father?* He knew that, were he in her place, he would want to know, would want to meet the man who had abandoned him for twenty years.

At last, Sandu said, "Yes. He gave me a way."

"Good. Then do it. I'll prepare everything for tonight."

Dirgard clapped Sandu's shoulder. "Thank you, Sandu. If this works, you'll be a hero."

That thought was more frightening than the cat o' nine tails.

Dirgard held out Sandu's tabard, armor, and axe, and said, "They confiscated this from you, but I managed to get it back. Easier than paying for a new set, eh?"

Sandu took them gratefully. Together with Captain Dirgard, he returned to the Protector's barracks, where he was greeted warmly by his fellows. *Seems like Sir Eric hasn't turned everyone against me.* While Dirgard explained the plan to the men and delegated duties, Sandu found his haversack. He scribbled a quick message on a small piece of parchment:

Laris Stanthorpe, I have found Cara. She is staying in the palace with our mutual friend, Lord Alexandro Strilu. We expect trouble at the Masque tonight, trouble Cara likely cannot handle on her own.

I want nothing of the reward money. Cara is my friend, and I will not sell her to you. I only give you this information out of conscience for her wellbeing. Whatever you do with her, wherever you take her after tonight, I ask that I may be allowed to stay her companion.

Sandu Crin

Sandu swallowed the guilty lump in his throat. He rolled the parchment tight and muttered the words Laris had burned into his brain: "*Exus marinel causin.*" As soon as the words left his mouth, the parchment shriveled and burned with an invisible fire, quickly turning to dust. Sandu coughed and waved his hand, but the letter was gone.

Dressed in his heavy chain armor, red cloak, and clean white tabard sewn with the Protector's sun crest, Sandu entered the Cascade Palace. No one had questioned him coming alone, and most nobles' eyes passed right over him as if he were a part of the scenery. He had squandered his morning at the barracks, chatting with his fellows and solidifying his part of the plan with Dirgard. In the pack on his back, he carried the gaudy mask and cheap robes that would be his costume that night.

Sandu showed Alex's seal to a steward and asked for directions. The steward led him up twisting staircases and down long, narrow passages that ran parallel to the sumptuous main corridors. By the time they came out a hidden door near Alex's rooms, Sandu had no idea which direction he could take to make his way out again.

Sandu took two steps toward Cara's chamber, but stopped. His hands sweated at his sides, and a drop of perspiration rolled down his forehead. *This armor's hot*, he thought, adjusting the forty-pound mail on his shoulders.

His mind filled with whirling images: Tambrey's fury, Cara's hurt, the queen's scorn as she kissed him, Sir Eric hitting him and breaking his nose. Sandu's breath hitched in his throat, and he turned away. *Maybe Alex will help me understand what's happening to me.*

Sandu knocked on Alex's door. A minute passed before Alex opened it, his eyes bleary. He looked as if he had drunk a keg of wine the night before: his eyes were red-rimmed and dark underneath, his face and lips pale, his hands trembling slightly. When he saw Sandu, he smiled, though not with the carefree grin Sandu knew.

"There you are," Alex said, opening the door wide and allowing Sandu to enter. "It feels like an eternity since you left. Where'd you go? Did you speak to Cara?"

Sandu let his pack drop to the floor. "I got drunk. I'm still gathering the courage to see her."

"You're back in your armor. It fits you nicely."

"What happened to *you*? You look as if you've been ill."

Alex's lips twitched. "I haven't had any sleep. And I've barely eaten. Bad humors are affecting me, I think."

"Clearly." Sandu stepped forward and embraced his friend. "I hope your good humors return soon. You're deserving of some decent luck after all the problems we've faced together."

"I doubt that."

Something in his tone made Sandu pause. He pulled back, his hand resting on Alex's shoulder. "Why would you say that?"

Alex sighed, running a hand through his hair. He drew away from Sandu, sitting shakily in a golden chair. "Renna's dead, Sandu. And when Cara needed my help, I betrayed her."

"You? *How?*"

"I lied to you both about who I am. What I am. She's only a hundred feet from me, but it might as well be a hundred miles for all the closure she would let me have."

Sandu was perplexed. He played awkwardly with his sheathed axe. "I don't know what you're talking about. Sure, you're the earl's brother, but that wouldn't cause her to hate you so much, would it?"

"I'm more than that," Alex said. "I'm *fampir*."

"You're having a laugh at me."

"I'm not." Taking a deep breath, Alex closed his eyes. Sandu watched, feeling both intrigued and horrified, as Alex's features contorted. When all was done, a prowler sat before him. With a voice that sounded like burning coal, Alex said, "I've been alive for the last one hundred and seventy-four years." His face returned to normal and he continued, "I was made to be a creature of darkness. At first I thought it would be wonderful: limitless lifetimes to pursue knowledge and gain mastery of our world. Then, I saw my family grow old and die, and my friends, and everyone I ever grew close to, the years stripping away their youth and vigor while I remained. I thought Cara, of all people, would understand me. But she doesn't."

Sandu stepped back, his fingers unconsciously loosening the axe in its sheath. *This is madness*, he thought. *Everything about this is madness.* Alex didn't stand or try to stop Sandu as he inched toward the door.

"I understand," Alex said softly. "I do."

Sandu didn't know how to respond. His mind had gone blank, his every instinct screaming at him to *Run, run as far as you can.* Sandu froze and asked, dreading the answer, "Who made you this?"

"Druam Strilu," came the reply. "He adopted me into his family, promised me the world. The three of us – me, Druam, and Verdon – were going to make this land into a utopia. Druam still believes it to be possible. But now I'm not so sure."

I have to leave this vile city and its undead masters, Sandu thought, his hand seeking the door handle behind him. *I have to bring Cara with me.*

Sandu said, "I'm sorry, my friend."

Then he quickly opened the door, backed out, and shut it, as if he could shut the newfound truths of the world inside. Before the latch clicked, he thought he heard Alex mumble, "As am I."

Sandu's breath came fast, his heart pumping within his chest to the beat of *run, run, run.* Stumbling to an alcove in the wall, he sank down and squeezed his head between his knees. He was in no danger from Alex – even his panicked mind knew that – but, oh gods, what had he gotten himself into? *I just wanted to pay off my debts and free Father,* he thought miserably. *And now I'm in a palace of monsters.* He saw the queen with a prowler's face, then Tambrey and Cara melding together and screaming at him for his gambling. No matter how he tried to halt the flood of images, they paraded through his head. His heart and breath both quickened, a tumult to match that within his head.

"Sir, are you well?" A young lady with dark skin stopped before him. She was dressed in a magnificent gown, her hair piled atop her head. But her violet eyes were kind as she stooped in front of Sandu.

"My lady," a servant said behind her, "we should return to your rooms to finish preparations."

"I know," the lady said, but she didn't move. She laid a hand to Sandu's wrist, and he shrank away from her touch. To his surprise, she hummed, too low for her servants to hear. A glow traveled from her fingertips to his arm, and then warmth filled his head.

She held a finger to her lips, then stood and drifted away.

The images faded away, and Sandu's breath slowly returned to normal. His hands stopped shaking as he regained his breath. He staggered down the hall. A passing steward looked at him suspiciously, but Sandu ignored him. He had to get to Cara.

The short walk down the corridor lasted for miles. By the time Sandu reached her door, each step was weighted with lead, and his hand, as he pulled it up to knock, was burdened with a hundred chains.

If this was the price of knowledge, Sandu would have gladly exchanged it for ignorance and a pint of ale.

Each thud of his fist against the polished wooden door sounded like a drum playing a death march. If Cara could not bring him the familiarity and warmth he so desperately craved in this moment, then he would have nowhere to go. Nothing to keep him grounded in reality.

A second passed. Sandu took a small step back. *Gods, I hope I do right by her.*

Before his inner demons could convince his feet to flee, Cara's voice called from within, "Master Hidley, is that you? Come in, please."

Without thinking, for if he thought too much he would turn and run, Sandu opened the door and stepped inside. Cara's rooms were not as nice as Alex's, though they were well-furnished and had tall windows that gave a view of the city stretching out to the sea.

Cara's back was to him as she faced a tall mirror. She wore a simple white gown with draping sleeves and full skirts, with a blood-red bodice over it. Her fingers scrambled with the laces; she cursed quietly. She hadn't yet looked up to see Sandu reflected behind her.

Sandu took a step forward, and the movement distracted her from the bodice strings. Cara glanced up into the mirror, then down, then up again, her eyes traveling slowly over Sandu's reflection. Her arms went still, her whole body tensing.

"I...I came back," Sandu said lamely. He stammered over his words, "I couldn't just leave you. I'm sorry, I–"

His tongue stilled as Cara turned to face him, the laces falling from her fingers. She stared at him, and Sandu couldn't decipher her look. Was it confusion or disdain? Welcoming or hating?

"I'm glad you're alright," Sandu managed to mutter. He stepped from foot to foot, very aware of the sweat gleaming on his forehead and the long red cloak swishing at his back.

Cara had seemingly forgotten the bodice. She rushed at him, and for a second Sandu thought she might attack him. Then she buried her cheek against his tabard, her arms squeezing around him. "I'm vecking glad to see you," she said through the fabric. "I thought Jagger had killed you."

"I was lucky."

Sandu wrapped his arms around her, feeling her warmth against his mail. Cara eventually pulled back, her smile slipping. "I'm scared, Sandu. This place...it's a shining city of color and light, and yet...all I've found here is darkness."

"I spoke to Alex...he told me everything. And...I heard about Renna. I'm so sorry, Cara. You spent so long trying to find her, and–"

"She wasn't who I thought she was. I came here to rescue her, but she *chose* Mavian over us. I don't understand it, but...what's done is done. We can only move forward."

"I think we should leave the city," Sandu said.

"And do what?"

"I don't know. We could form a rustic resistance against the nobles who are just letting the prowlers take control."

"They're fools, not villains. They do wish to get rid of the prowlers, if only for their own sakes. With no rustics to farm their lands or mill their grain, they'd be just as dead as if they were taken by the prowlers. I can help them, I think. In some way."

Sandu ran his fingers through his beard. It was growing longer and needed a good combing. "I don't know. They want you for your usefulness, not...not for who you really are. Once you've done what they want, they'll dispose of you."

Cara braided her hair. "I wish you were wrong, but after spending time with them, I can't help but believe you. What else could I do, though? I'm just one woman."

"One woman with a stalwart ally," Sandu said, gripping her hand between both of his. "And friends among the Protectors.

And..." Sandu hesitated, then said, "We may have a wizard of some sort helping us, too."

"Not–"

"Yes. The man who hired me to find you. Please, let me finish. He contacted me again, while I was in the dungeons – story for another time – and told me that your conception wasn't easy. Cara, I think he may be your father. Or he knows more about your family than anyone else you've met before. If he tries to hurt you, we can escape and find another way. I'm sorry, I *did* betray you, but I did it thinking of you. I think Laris is what we need now that we've lost Alex."

For a moment, Cara said nothing, and Sandu worried that he'd royally vecked it all up. He was nearly ready to leave when she said, "I trust you. I hope what you did was right, but it's too late now. I'm sure Laris would have found me sooner or later, and I'd rather have you at my side when he comes. Now," she said, "help me tie this damn bodice. The court may be full of *fampir*, but we'll be ready for them. And for Mavian. He took Renna from me, but I'll show him that I'm one to be reckoned with."

As Sandu helped her tie the strings, Cara murmured, "Alex was a close friend. I don't want him to be hurt. Earl Seastone wants me to help him make this world better. If he is as Alex says he is...I don't know if we can trust him."

"We don't know *how* he intends to create his utopia," Sandu pointed out. "But whatever path you choose, I'll walk it with you. I've made too many mistakes in life, and I don't intend to make another. My axe is yours."

Cara snorted. "Do you even know how to use it?"

"Just swing the sharp end at someone. Pretty simple."

"You're going to hurt yourself and I'll end up saving you."

"That's what heroes do for their companions, isn't it? What good would you be if you didn't engage in needless heroics now and then?"

They both laughed, and for a time, the impending Masque and its dangers seemed far removed. Every shredded nerve and bad humor that Sandu had harbored since he'd separated from her melted away, replaced by an unfamiliar confidence: wherever she was, he would be too. He had let down too many friends and family before; he would never leave her, not while she needed him.

CHAPTER FORTY-EIGHT
Gwen

HANDMAIDS LABORED over Gwen all day, bringing her from room to room: washing and brushing her thick hair, rubbing oils and lotions over her bare skin, dressing her and applying cosmetics to her eyes. During the Masque, all nobles would strive to hide their natural appearances. Of course, with Gwen's dark skin, she would stand out no matter how much powder coated her shoulders and cheeks.

When Gwen looked in the mirror, she saw a creature she wasn't wholly positive was her. Jewels and strands of beads strung through her piled-high hair, a silver filigree mask adorned with pearls and feathers covered her forehead and upper cheeks. Her eyes had been painted above and below with fantastic colors. Her tapestried dress flowed from her shoulders into long sleeves that tapered to the ground, with a train supported by a curved pillow placed carefully on her hips. Her neck and shoulders were bare, but painted to create a scene that continued off of the dress and onto her skin. Dark red lips, and cheeks contoured to give them a harsher shape, completed her foreign look.

Though she knew she was supposed to feel beautiful, Gwen only felt burdened. Ever since she had left behind the fashion of Demarren, she no longer felt comfortable in such styles. The Dotsch style suited her, and now that she tried to imitate her heritage...she looked like a child dressing in her mother's clothes.

This was no longer her, just as she could no longer be herself if she were to abandon her magic.

As she ran her fingers over the careful embroidery on her sleeve, Gwen thought, *Druam had this made just for me. He created a space in his conservatory just for me. Everything he has done for me, he has done out of love.* With a pang, she knew that, if she were to leave his life just as quickly as she'd entered it, he would be devastated. In the short time they had been together, their lives had become intertwined. *It would be selfish to choose magic over him.*

When Gwen reached the top of the grand staircase, she paused and marveled at the sight before her.

Five enormous chandeliers hung over the ballroom, their crystals and candles twinkling. A mezzanine filled with tables of food and wine lined three sides of the room. Below, the dancing floor was as large as some lords' entire manors. A series of floor-to-ceiling glass doors opened onto a terrace that overlooked the palace gardens. Candelabras lined each pillar along the bottom of the mezzanine, and windows on the upper floor let in a fall breeze. The ballroom's opulence was a cathedral to worship wealth and nobility.

The worshipping courtiers tried to out-peacock each other in masses of colorful silk. They moved around the space as fluidly as snow drifting over ice. A band of troupers performed traditional Dotsch melodies on a dais in the middle of the room. Below the music, a babble of voices rose and fell, ever-present but overwhelmed by the vastness of the room.

As she descended the stairs, Gwen felt eyes upon her, and knew that all who saw her knew her in spite of her mask: she was the Demarren princess. After her confession to the council, she wondered how many knew of her powers.

Gwen's palms sweated as her slippers hit the dancing floor, and in a thrill of terror, she thought that perhaps no one would dare to dance with her. But her fears lasted no more than a second, for out of the crowd came a lord, his features hidden by a lion mask, who bowed and offered his hand. She took it and was swept into the dance.

Whirls of sight twisted around her, the smells of perfume and sweat as strong as the stench of fish by the seashore; between dances, Gwen drank mouthfuls of wine before being pulled back into the throng, her tongue still tasting the sweetness of the drink. Her breath turned into a staccato rhythm that she never quite managed to catch. Each partner gripped her hand and held her firmly by the waist, and though she tried to see beyond their masks, she recognized no one.

The light outside dimmed until the only illumination came from the hundreds of candles above and around the dancers. Outside in the gardens, lanterns cast a soft glow on those smoking or dancing on the terrace flagstones. At last Gwen escaped from the throng and managed to eat some fresh fruit and bread on the mezzanine. But her desire for the thrill of movement superseded her hunger, and she descended once more to the dance floor.

This time, a tall man dressed in black and silver materialized from the crowd and took her arm. A black mask, the visage of Autorus, covered the top half of his face, and in the hint of his smile, Gwen knew that Druam had found her. She let him guide her near the dais, where he led her in a Dotsch four-step dance. They moved naturally together, uncaring of the dancers around them. Their eyes locked, and Gwen felt her heart pouring into every limb.

Her dress swirled around her legs, her sleeves drifting with each step. As they danced, the music gained speed and intensity. Druam moved closer to her, his breath on her hair. She looked up to him, holding his gaze. They moved with the music, their hearts beating with the drums. A strange sense of weightlessness came over Gwen, the feeling that of security, and passion, and certainty. She stood on the tips of her toes to kiss his cheek, her hot lips brushing against his cool skin, her hand resting on the line of his jaw.

Still they danced, as close as the pace of the music allowed, and Gwen felt that weightlessness drift all around her, encompassing Druam as well. But she dared not break away from him, for if she did, then this bubble of contentment would pop.

Gasps went out in a wave around them. Druam frowned, looking away from her. Gwen tore her eyes from him and saw with amazement that the two of them were floating, their feet at the level of the crowds' heads. A swirl of soft magic bent around them, carrying them aloft. But Gwen had cast this spell without words or intention, and as she marveled, the spell faded away. A space cleared around them as they came slowly back to the ground.

"Gwen, control yourself," Druam said softly as their feet landed on the marble tiles. "The king is watching."

"Let him watch," Gwen said with a rising anger. "How could he see that and not understand?"

"Come away, Gwen," Druam muttered, grabbing at her arm. "We should not discuss this here."

Gwen resisted, pulling out of his grasp. She glared at him. Love and anger warred in her.

Magic hummed in her fingertips. She pushed it out in a sphere around them, blocking the crowd. The music and murmurs of the crowd faded to silence within their little bubble. Though nobles pushed against the transparent sheen of magic, they could not get through.

"Mavian was right," Gwen said, satisfied at the effect her words produced. Druam's lips tightened, and she continued, "You *don't* understand my magic. It's not like your lanterns, to be lit or extinguished as you please. It's my heart and my fingers, my skin and my eyes. Take one of those from me, and see how well I fare."

"We don't have a choice!" Druam said. Behind his mask, his blue eyes were unreadable. "I cannot go against the king."

"What gives him the right?" Gwen demanded. "A crown, a birthright?"

"Your birthright protected you from the Trials," Druam said. He tore off his mask, but beneath his, his features were just as blank as they had been at their first meeting. Deep down, Gwen

432

knew that he was hiding the turmoil of emotions. Yet in that moment, she wanted him to rage or weep or tremble. To do anything but treat her to that inhuman blankness.

Druam pressed, "If not for your brother in his position of power, you would have been hanged with the rest of the witches."

"Maybe I should have been!" Renewed guilt surged in her breast as memories of her brother's final moments flashed in her head. "Am I so special that I should have been granted such a boon? Innocent women and men died, yet here I stand."

"The world has never been fair," Druam said. He reached for her again, and she let him take her hands. "So we must do everything in our power to find whatever hope we can. You brought me out of too many years of despair. Gwen, you cannot leave me."

His touch sent warmth through her. *If only we could go back*, she thought. She lifted a hand to his cheek. "You would have me cut off my feet and still try to dance."

"The king–"

Gwen shook her head. "I won't go to Con Salur. But neither will I stay here, wearing a mask for the rest of my life."

Before Druam could say anything, she kissed him as passionately as she had ever done, then stepped back.

"I love you, Druam, but I can't deny my Gaiar. It is me, and I am it. I'll come back to you, I promise. I love you." Even as she said it, Gwen knew that she meant it. She would return, once the secrets of the magical world had been revealed to her.

The sphere of magic fell around them. The increasing shouts of the crowd pressed on them, but Gwen had eyes only for her husband.

Druam grasped at her. "What are you doing? Gwen!"

She pulled gently away and opened the palm that the witch had touched in her dream. Words and promises spoke in her head. A pinprick of desire pushed itself to the fore of her mind, then spread throughout her entire body. That pinprick showed her the Whispering Woods. She let it consume her.

Gwen's body shook, her whole being threatening to tear

itself apart. Her heart stopped, her body froze, agony consumed every nerve. Then, in a flash of light, she vanished from the ballroom.

CHAPTER FORTY-NINE
Cara

WITH RELUCTANCE, Cara had given her sword to Sandu for safekeeping during the Masque. Even as she was swung around the dais by a string of masked gentlemen, she turned her head to Sandu. He stayed by a pillar, his own mask plainly cheap compared to the gold and silver ones around him. His weapon, along with hers, was concealed beneath his overly large player's robe. If the rest of the partygoers weren't so drunk, they may have questioned his appearance.

Cara, though, was dressed like a courtier in a white gown with a blood-red bodice. Her sleeves were tight around her upper arms, but trailed only a foot or so from her elbows, unlike the popular styles that draped to the floor. Her skirt, too, was unusual, for it was split down the sides, and she had been given comfortable breeches to wear underneath. The mask was crafted of supple, red-dyed leather, and covered the upper half of her face.

So far, the Masque had gone on without incident. Even as she rested her feet, Cara felt some doubt. Perhaps Mavian wouldn't dare to appear after his defeat and Renna's death. If he did, there were enough Realm's Protectors there to hold him off while the nobles escaped.

A tall man dressed in red and grey, his mask a wolf's head, approached Cara. He bowed and offered his arm for a dance.

Though she wanted nothing more than to sit down – or better yet, simply leave – Cara accepted. She let him take her hand and waist, doing her best to follow the complicated dance. Beneath her skirts, she knew that her feet stumbled and barely kept up, but no one else noticed. She put her head down, focusing on a complicated step.

"I'm glad we could have at least one dance," the man said.

Cara glanced up at him in surprise. Behind his vicious mask, she saw Alex's eyes. *Of course.* She hadn't spoken to him since that night. But, surrounded by laughing courtiers and socially obligated to finish the dance with him, she said, "Don't start, Alex."

"I'm not your enemy, Cara. We can help each other. Maybe with your help, I can convince Druam to leave aside his fantasies of a perfect world and instead focus on stopping the prowler scourge. No matter what you think of me, I hate the prowlers."

"Why should I trust you?" Cara hissed between her teeth.

"Haven't my actions shown my loyalties?"

"You–" Cara didn't finish her sentence. She halted, her dress swirling around her legs, and stared.

Earl and Lady Seastone rose above the crowd, borne aloft by some sort of magic. Slowly, they came back down. A magic bubble formed around them. Alex pushed toward it, his hand still entwined with Cara's. But no matter how he pressed against it, they couldn't pass through.

Suddenly the magic dissipated. The lady kissed the earl. Then there was a blinding flash of light.

Cara blinked the spots from her eyes. Lady Seastone had vanished. The earl seemed dazed, his fingers reaching for the spot his wife had stood only seconds before. The musicians on the dais stopped playing.

"Gwen!" the earl shouted, casting about as if she had merely gone into the crowd.

"She's not here. You drove her away."

Gasps and murmurs spread through the hall. Cara instinctively drew closer to Alex, familiar tingles sparking in every nerve. Without turning around to see the speaker, she knew who it was. She met Alex's eye, and together they faced Mavian.

Dressed in a swirling black cloak, his silver amulet glowing at his throat, Mavian stood at the top of the grand staircase. A space had been made around him by courtiers too nervous to draw close. The air hummed with energy, distorted by purple light, and, as everyone watched, a black rift opened behind him, large enough for the royal carriage to pass through. The ground shook. There were yelps and cries of confusion, and the nobles nearest him tried to back further away, pressing together to escape this new, unknown magic.

"He's blocked the door," Cara murmured to Alex.

"There's the terrace and servants' passages, but if he does anything besides talk, there'll be hysteria. We can't herd panicked people."

Mavian stepped forward. The crowd bent away from him, schools of fish evading a hungry shark. He raised his hand and a blanket of silence fell on the murmuring nobles. Ever hungry for melodramatics, they waited for him to speak.

"This man you call earl," Mavian said, pointing to Earl Seastone, "is a fraud!" He waited for the whispers to die down. "He is a liar, a villain, and, perhaps worst of all, inhuman. For years have I watched him, feeling my mind softening whenever I questioned his decisions or motives. He controls you all, and our feeble minds accept his false explanations as truth!" Again he paused.

Questions arose in the crowd. "What does he mean?" "Could it be true?" Cara craned her neck, looking for Sandu. He had straightened, his eyes fixed on Mavian. She squeezed Alex's hand and nodded toward Sandu. Together they wove around the entranced nobles.

In the center of the room, Druam stood tall. Even from a distance, Cara could sense the rage burning in his eyes.

Mavian shouted, "Druam Strilu is not human! How many of you clearly remember his father? How many of you can recall seeing him as a child? Look in the old, abandoned wing of this very palace, and you will find portraits of Druam's so-called forefathers, but each and every one resembles him beyond mere familial looks."

"I don't remember him as a child," someone muttered.

"I never saw the late Lady Seastone pregnant," another said.

Cara and Alex pushed past a few more nobles to Sandu's side. Sandu tore his gaze from the spectacle. He drew his weapon from beneath his robe before handing Cara's sword to her.

Holding his hands aloft, Mavian continued. "Now that the lie has been exposed, the truth is creeping up in your memories! The truth, which for so long has been hidden from you by Druam's vile magics. He has been ruler of this region for centuries, calling himself by different names, but always the same man."

"Is this true?" a man demanded. He tore his mask away, revealing himself as King Henrik. He stood with the circle of courtiers around the earl. Pointing at Mavian, he shouted, "Tell us, man, is what he says true? Shall we call a council to question you, Earl Seastone?"

Mavian didn't allow Druam to speak. His voice, now softer, carried to every corner. "I have studied the prowlers for years, ever since my father was murdered by them. In my research, I have found something different, and far more terrible: in the Gallic tongue, they are called *fampir*. They have the same bloodlust, the same disease as the prowlers, but they can dwell among us for years untold, hidden beneath a mortal mask. Druam Strilu is such a creature! He preys on the rustics, using poppin dens as his hunting grounds, and yet calls for action against his own feral kin."

"Answer me, Druam!" King Henrik roared. "Are these allegations true?"

The earl said nothing. Alex rose up onto his toes, his eyes anxiously searching for his brother. Cara said quietly, "Go to him. Get the king to safety. Sandu, find your fellow Protectors, have them open the servants' doors and direct the courtiers to safety. I'll face Mavian."

Before they could move, though, the hum in the air rose to a fevered whine, the floor shuddering underneath. More than one noble fell to the quaking ground or clapped their hands to their ears against the high-pitched noise. Mavian's voice rose again. "Let him reveal himself. The darkness will not let him hold back for long!"

The black rift behind Mavian widened farther, its edges frayed, blurring the space between dark and light. Black tendrils snuck out, reaching for prey. The nobles screamed and tried to run, but were pressed too tightly together. From within the blackness, shapes formed. Prowlers, their eyes red and teeth glistening, emerged one by one, spreading out behind Mavian. Though they drooled and whimpered, they did not attack.

Ladies screamed and lords shouted for help. Here and there in the crowd, Protectors threw off their masks and borrowed robes, running to place themselves between the prowlers and nobles. Alex dashed to the king and his brother, Sandu ran to his captain, and Cara pushed her way toward Mavian. All around her, nobles cried out and trampled each other to escape. Those on the dance floor fled to the terrace and out into the gardens.

Still more prowlers appeared. Mavian moved easily between them down the steps, his attention on Druam. Even as she ran, Cara could see the earl in her periphery. He knelt in the place his wife had vanished, his fingers brushing the floor. Protectors surrounded the king and pulled him to the terrace seconds before more black voids opened in front of the glass doors. Prowlers crept from those, too. They halted a few feet from their prey, waiting.

Cara skidded to a stop, still some ways from Mavian. All around her, nobles clutched at each other and called for help. The musicians had abandoned their instruments on the dais.

Mavian reached the hall's marble floor, his eyes sweeping the room disdainfully. "Pity some didn't wait to see the show." He stopped just before the Protectors, who raised their weapons against him, and laughed. "Clever Druam. Won't you at least fight, rather than let these brave souls die? Prowlers versus Protectors, all of them trained animals. Me against you and your scholarly brother, all men touched by death."

Her palms sweating on her hilt, Cara dared a glance at Alex. He stood in front of Druam. As she watched, the earl slowly lifted his head and said, "I raised you, Mavian. I cared for you."

Mavian's hands twitched. "You refused to share your secrets with me. You denied the knowledge which I craved. You have had centuries to craft your world, and still your people suffer. I tried to gain your favor, but you held it from me. So now I will take my birthright with the very magic you wished to hide from me."

"I wished only to protect you, Mavian. You are young, and in time...in time I would have trusted you. Xandro would tell you the price of knowledge gained too soon. Perhaps I wronged you, but I love you like my own son."

"Shh," Mavian held a finger to his lips. "Your lies and wheedling have served you long enough. The time for speeches is over. We both have our loyal men, we both have our gifts from Autorus, so let us dance with death and see who emerges victorious."

Then he uttered words in a harsh tongue, words that prickled Cara's skin and stirred the beast within her belly. His prowlers leapt forward, hungry and howling. The Protectors raised their weapons to meet them, some crying out in shock and pain as their blood spilled to the white marble floors. In the melee of red cloaks, sobbing nobles, shining swords, and yellow fangs, Cara lost sight of Sandu. She swung at the closest prowler that stood between her and Mavian. It fell, screeching, but two more took its place.

The prowlers lunged at her. Skipping back, Cara thrust her sword point at one. It yelped and jumped back with a new wound in its chest. Black droplets ran down the blade and pooled over Cara's fists. The other prowler clawed at Cara, its talons ripping through her dress and digging painfully into her skin. Cara shoved her weapon at it, driving it back. It slipped on the smooth floor and exposed its neck for just a moment. That moment was all Cara needed to shear its head from its body. The injured prowler hesitated a moment, then lunged again. Cara waited for the arc of its leap to reach her, then stepped aside and casually swept the blade into its throat. Its momentum tore the sword from her grasp. Cara retrieved it, then whirled to see where Mavian had gone.

Mavian retreated up the steps, a few Protectors advancing on him. Raising his hand, he called yet more prowlers from the rift. The Protectors fell back, set upon by the feral horde. Mavian smiled and directed his attention back to Alex and Druam. The brothers, like Cara, fought their way through the prowlers.

The way between Cara and the stairs suddenly opened. She sprinted forward, her feet slipping on the blood-soaked tiles. Somehow she kept her balance and gained the steps. She paused to catch her breath, glancing over the battle.

The hall, which only minutes before had been filled with music and laughter, now shook with screams and the clanging of metal. Protectors worked in pairs, standing back-to-back against the onslaught of prowlers. Defenseless courtiers either huddled by the walls or lay dead on the floor, while some lords joined the fray, their masks discarded. Despite the soldiers' efforts, for every prowler that lay dead on the floor, three more fought tooth and claw. It seemed that Mavian had a never-ending army of the undead.

Alex and Druam pushed forward, their blades soaked in blood. They made it to the bottom of the steps, then stopped. Cara returned her eyes to Mavian, feeling her resolve weaken.

A series of black tentacles crept from the void, surrounding Mavian like a writhing wall. He paid no heed to them. In his hands, he rolled and crafted some new dark magic in a ball of shimmering energy. Behind him, a man stepped from the rift, still dressed in Masque finery. The man held a long rapier in one hand and a curved dagger in the other. Mavian nodded his head in acknowledgement of the other, but did not raise his eyes from his work.

Edging over to Alex and Druam, Cara murmured, "Who's the newcomer?"

Alex's eyes narrowed. "Sir Chadron, Egil Rask's nephew.

Gods help us if Rask is in with Mavian."

"It may be just the nephew, not the uncle," Druam said. "I don't care to dwell–"

"Look out!" Cara yelled, grabbing Alex and pulling him aside.

The black ball of energy curved toward them, fizzing and letting forth flashes of electric heat. It hit the ground and exploded in dark magic. All three were flung apart, their bodies flying through the air before landing painfully on the hard floor. The steps where the magic had hit were gone, leaving a crater of jagged stone. For a moment, the world went silent, then Cara's ears buzzed.

Cara pushed herself back to her feet. She'd landed the closest to Mavian, but still he paid her no mind. He moved his hands around him, circling his body with strings of dark, crackling energy drawn from the rift. Sir Chadron advanced down the steps toward Alex, who lay prone on the ground. Cara could not see Druam; he must have been thrown back into the melee below.

Just as Cara moved to help Alex, she heard Sandu shouting, "Cara!" Whipping around, she tried to pick him out from the mass of Protectors and prowlers. There! He was backed against a pillar, three prowlers on him. Cara looked between him and Alex. Alex had regained his feet, but Chadron drove him back.

"Vecking hells," Cara muttered. She ran at Sandu, ducking Protectors' flailing blades and striking at any prowler in her path. One of the prowlers had jumped up on Sandu, its weight carrying him to the floor. Using her momentum, Cara swept past another, her blade easily beheading it. A prowler leapt at her, its claws digging into her back. She could feel its cold breath on her neck. Cara tried to thrust her weapon at it, but couldn't quite reach. From the corner of her eye, she saw a pillar. With all her strength, she slammed backwards, thrusting herself and the prowler that straddled her against the pillar. Its claws loosened for a second, then gripped her skin. Again Cara threw herself into the pillar. The creature's hold went slack, and with one hand, Cara dragged it over her shoulder and threw it onto the floor. It stared up at her, dazed. Cara lopped off its head.

Sandu was still trapped under a clawing, biting prowler. His movements were sluggish, his hands scraping feebly at the creature, his axe lying uselessly beside him. The beast rises within her. *About time.* Cara let it overwhelm her. Her nails turned to talons, her sight sharpened, and the smell of blood turned wonderfully sweet. She kicked the prowler from Sandu's chest. It scrabbled at the marble floor in confusion, trying to back away from this new threat. She killed it.

Sandu moaned. His red cloak was spattered with blood and gashes decorated his chest and arms. Sweat fell into open cuts on his cheeks and forehead. With gentle strength, Cara pulled him beyond the pillar to a dark alcove, away from the fighting. Leaving him there, she returned to the battle, the beast within her begging for blood.

Time slowed down. A Protector's sword arced gracefully toward a jumping prowler. Cara could see the red of the creature's eyes, the hairs on the Protector's arm. She, however, moved quickly, her own attacks untouched by the world's pace. To the rest, she must seem a blur, a whirlwind of death. The hall was muffled now, the noise that clamored within it no more than a fly in her ear. Death was her song, her blade her dance. Prowlers fell around her, too slow to realize what had killed them. Protectors straightened and looked around, bewildered, but she did not stop.

Mavian's eyes were finally drawn to her. Cara grinned. She would reach him, tear him limb from limb, before he could stop her. She took the steps two at a time, her path finally, thankfully clear, and–

"Argh!" Alex cried.

Cara turned her head to look. Alex fell to his knees, Sir Chadron's curved dagger sticking from his stomach. He met her gaze, then collapsed backwards.

"No!" Cara cried.

The dark lightning coiled around Mavian struck Cara. It moved faster even than she, though Cara could see its individual strands of blue, purple, and black as they raced at her heart. She could not stop her mad run, could not prevent it from hitting her, but she twisted from it. The pain that hit her felt like a cannonball charged with energy. It burned her ribs where it struck and sent jolts of electricity into each nerve in her body. Bright lights flashed in Cara's vision. She screamed, but no sound came out.

The beast retreated back inside her before she hit the floor. Her limp body rolled down the steps, white smoke drifting from her pores. The muffled world sprang back to loud life, each clang and screech invading her head with a noise ten times worse than normal.

For a moment, Cara was sure she was dead.

But black tentacles curled around her, their dreadful suckers gripping her skin. She opened her eyes, saw that she was being carried up and toward Mavian. Her head felt stuck in place, but she strained her periphery to see Alex.

He lay on the marble stairs, his eyes staring up, each breath harsher than the last. She watched in agony, unable to help, as Sir Chadron raised his rapier for the final blow.

Then Druam, his features twisted in his *fampir* form, came between predator and victim. He engaged Chadron in battle.

Cara's head twisted violently away from the fight. Still entrapped by the tentacles, she stared into Mavian's hard eyes. He regarded her with hatred.

"You tried to keep her from me," he said. Cara spat at him. He wiped the drop off. "You were so easy to toy with, blundering through the court like a child. No wonder Renna wanted to leave Kell behind her."

"She never would have left had you not spelled her."

Mavian's expression darkened. "Renna chose me, as I chose her. Your quest was thankless and worthless. But, perhaps, I can use you in some way to bring her back."

He drew a strange knife. Its blade had a channel formed into it leading to the handle, which was made of clear glass. Drawing near to her, Mavian raised it and made a small cut in her neck. Cara struggled in vain, but his magic held her tight. After a moment, he stepped back, the glass handle filled with her dark red blood.

"Now, I have a surprise for you. Do you remember him from that night in the swamp? I hope you haven't forgotten dear Merick." Mavian grinned cruelly.

The black tentacles grasped Cara's head, forcing her to look past Mavian. Her heart dropped into her boots. Merick stood there, but it was not truly Merick. His eyes were blank, his jaw slack. He held a dark blade in one hand and his shirt lay open, showing a rotting scar. His skin was pale and blue, but he was not a prowler. He was an entirely different horror.

"A happy reunion!" Mavian exclaimed. He uttered a harsh word, releasing Cara from the tentacles. Merick advanced on her, his black blade rising. Cara backed away. *I'm dreaming. This is all a bad dream. Merick wouldn't have beat me or broken my leg. It's not true!*

Merick spoke in a harsh, grating, horridly taunting voice. "Cari! Remember your lessons, Cari." He swung at her, his blade crashing onto the sword that had once been his. Cara's hands shook from the impact. She stumbled away, down the staircase toward Druam and Chadron's duel.

"Pull back!" she heard a Protector shout. "Reform our position!"

Daring a glance, Cara saw that many of the Protectors had fallen. They struggled to gather together as prowlers broke their ranks. She couldn't spare any more thoughts for them, though, for Merick growled again as she barely evaded his strong attack.

"Please, Merick, this isn't you!" she cried. "Come back to me, Merick!"

But the undead Merick didn't care for her pleas. He pushed her back, ruthless and cruel. This was not her Merick.

"Look out!" Druam shouted behind her. Cara whirled, dodging another of Merick's attacks as Chadron moved backwards into the space she had occupied. Chadron raised his rapier against Druam, but Merick's swing carried too far, slicing Chadron's hand from his wrist. He screamed, falling, but Merick did not falter. Cara scrambled away until she and Druam stood side by side. Chadron staggered up the steps, holding his bleeding stump to his chest. Behind him, Mavian's smug grin turned to a sneer.

"Destroy them!" he shouted to Merick.

"I'm with you," Druam said to Cara. He panted, his *fampir* features contorting in anger. "Stay with me. This man is not who you knew; he is only a mindless construction of underworld magics. Some foul new invention of Mavian's."

Merick's eyes flickered with darkness, his scarred smile twisting his cheeks. He raised his blade, lunging–

A tsunami of air crashed into them, sending them all stumbling. Cara picked herself up. Druam was dazed beside her, and their enemies reeled. Across the hall, an old man leaned on a cane. He was dressed in long robes, his arms raised as he chanted in a rumbling voice. With each syllable, a dart of white light flew from the man's hands, striking a prowler down.

"It's a vecking wizard!" Chadron shouted. "We have to retreat, Mavian!"

"The battle is ours! The Protectors and younger Strilu have fallen–"

"The tides have turned. We must leave while we still can."

For a second, it seemed as if Mavian would stay. Then he called out, "Return to me, my creature!" Without hesitating, with no emotion, Merick turned and raced back to the portal. Mavian and Chadron disappeared into the black void. As soon as they vanished, all the rifts in the hall popped shut. Cara blinked at the sudden brightness and shielded her eyes with a hand. Druam's face returned to human form. He panted, and Cara saw that he, too, had been injured during the fight: cuts and bruises decorated his cheeks and hands, and there was a large gash on his shoulder.

Throwing down his sword, Druam shouted, "Damn! Come back, coward! Vecking hells."

"Alex..." Cara said. She looked over the carnage, but didn't see him. "Is he alive?"

"Damn," Druam swore again. "We need to find him. He needs blood."

As they trudged down the steps, the few remaining

Protectors stood back in astonishment as the old man killed the last prowlers with his white magic. Nobles crept up the terrace, their terrified faces shining in the candlelight. The once-pure-white marble was stained red and brown, and the corpses of nobles, Protectors, and prowlers littered the dancing floor. The smell of coppery blood, sweat, and shit had replaced that of perfume. The air – once lifted with lilting music – was now filled by the clank of armor as Protectors looked through the desecration for survivors.

"Good. You're alive."

Cara and Druam both jumped and twisted to see the wizard standing behind them, frowning. His white hair and beard were immaculately trimmed. He glanced at Druam, then focused on Cara. "I was worried I might be too late. Come on, then, we've much to do."

"Who are you?" Cara asked. After all that had happened, she just wanted to find Alex. Find Alex, get Sandu, and rest.

The old man, however, had different ideas. He grabbed Cara's arm and dragged her up the steps. She pulled back, and Druam came between them. "The maid asked a question," Druam said.

Grumbling, the old man said, "Laris Stanthorpe. Head of the Peddler's Guild. I've business with the maid, and I'll be damned if a plain earl stops me."

One of the Protectors stepped forward. "Shall we deter him, Earl Seastone?"

Laris sighed and shoved his hands into opposite sleeves. "Go ahead, try and stop me. Want to end up like those prowlers?"

"Enough," Cara said. She looked at Druam. "Chadron's blade...will it do permanent harm to Alex?"

"I don't know. That blade was poisoned with garlic. Mavian knows more about us than we'd like."

"And gods know if Sandu made it through." Turning to Laris, Cara tried not to look so small and exhausted. "Look, Master Stanthorpe, I don't know why you want me. Frankly, I don't really care right now. But we're all vecking tired. I'm going to see if my friends are safe, and then, after I've rested...then we can talk. Fine? But if you try and take me now, I'm going to fight. One of us will probably die. Sure, you may be a wizard, but I'm *sulpari*, and I'm done."

The wizard opened his mouth to argue, then shut it. He nodded irritably. "I'll be back for you tomorrow. Now that I've seen you, you can't hide from me. Understood, lass?"

"I understand."

Mumbling to himself, Laris Stanthorpe disappeared into the air. After everything she'd seen that day, Cara was barely surprised. She said to Druam, "We need curates."

Druam nodded. Cara felt the weight of the battle finally settling on her shoulders. Good men had died, men who fought simply because they had been told to do so, and the blood of many innocent people had been spilled. Alex and Sandu might not live to see tomorrow, and Mavian was still out there.

He has my blood. Who knows what terrible things he could do with it? And he has Merick. At least, what used to be Merick. Still, with all the worries of death around her, Cara felt a small sense of relief. *Whatever happens, at least I'm alive. I survived, and I will fight again.*

CHAPTER FIFTY
Alex

ALEX LAY in a comfortable bed, white sheets tucked up under his chin and feather pillows cushioning his head. When he opened his eyes, he saw a small, dim room with curtains drawn over the narrow windows. Sandu was in the bed next to him, still sleeping. Cara was draped in a chair nearby. Her eyes were closed, her breathing deep. Standing next to the door was a Realm's Protector captain, his armor still bloodied from the battle.

As he sat up, Alex noticed that his torso was bandaged. Surprisingly, there was little pain; the curate's ointments did their jobs well. He grunted and threw off the sheets. As he did, Cara's eyes fluttered open.

"Don't move, Alex. You're still recovering from Chadron's blade."

"I feel fine," Alex muttered, though he let her help him back into the bed. He avoided meeting her eyes.

"That's the medicine talking. Without it, you'd be screaming loud enough to hear at the docks."

"No doubt." Alex glanced over at Sandu. "Will he recover?"

Cara chewed her lip. "We don't know if one of the prowlers bit him or not, but he's got scratches and marks all over him. We'll just have to wait for him to wake." She paused, then said, "Shepherd Marin didn't know what to do with you. He said the

449

healing magic didn't take, that Chadron's blade had some sort of magic in it to prevent the wound from closing. He sewed it up, but it still might bleed for a time."

"He dipped his dagger in garlic and onion extracts," Alex said. "I could feel it the moment it touched me. I'd have to drink a lot of blood before my wound fully heals, but I'll live if I don't. Uncomfortably, I'll admit, but better than the alternative."

Cara didn't reply. She stared at the bed. Wringing his hands in his lap, Alex said quietly, "I'm sorry for lying to you. None of it was right. I'm so used to hiding myself, lying to everyone around me...I should have trusted you."

"I do understand," Cara said softly. "I've hidden my beast for years, but this is still...somehow...different. I don't know if I can ever look at you the same again."

Alex sniffed and rubbed his nose. What had he expected? That she'd throw her arms around him, kiss him and forgive him? Those were the dreams of mortal men.

"What will you do now?" he asked.

Cara looked at a cut on her arm. "Mavian is still out there. Once Sandu awakens and is back in good humor, we'll find Laris. A wizard could be an incredibly useful ally."

"So you're leaving Riverfen."

She nodded. "Renna is gone and Mavian has fled. There's nothing left for me here."

"I'm here."

"Yes, I know." Cara gently took Alex's hand, her fingers rubbing the tendons in his palm. "I have to leave. My life as I knew it has ended, and you were a part of that old life. I can't unlearn what I know now."

"What if I weren't *fampir*? Would you still leave me then?"

"I don't know, Alex. 'What ifs' and wishes are mere fantasies. They can't change our reality. What is real is your condition and Mavian's threat. Just forget about me. Perhaps, in another world or another life, we could have been very happy together. But not in this one."

Cara gave his hand a final squeeze. "I'm going to go lay down for awhile. Dirgard, can you come get me if Sandu wakes?" She kissed Alex's forehead. "I'll say goodbye before I leave. I promise. You deserve that much."

Once she was gone, Alex discarded the sheets and stood. He took a quivering step to Sandu and laid his hand on his arm. "I'm sorry, friend, that you were caught up in all this. Take care of her." He turned to the captain. "Am I free to leave?"

Dirgard shrugged. "It's your palace, my lord. I'm here for Sandu, not you."

Each step easier than the last, Alex left the infirmary. His many years in the palace had taught him the fastest paths back to his rooms. He slipped shadow-like from doorway to alcove to hallway, careful not to tread on cracks between tiles. *Tread not on lines, lest you bend your mother's spine.* Well over a century ago, his mother would laugh and call the rhyme in a singsong voice as they walked on cobblestones. In his childhood, Alex stood on his tiptoes and tried to jump from cobble to cobble, all the while chattering to his mother. *She's gone to dust, as I shall too.* His memories of her had started slipping away, becoming no more than fragments of long-dead ghosts. *No one should live this long. And yet, Druam has lived centuries longer than I. Has he any memories left of his parents, his siblings, his first love?*

The chambers which Alex had adored years and years ago were now rich husks, tapestried cocoons that held not a butterfly, but an empty hole. Alex wandered each room, the once-beguiling paintings now lifeless, the tapestries representations of candles of meaningless toil rather than stories or tales. He rummaged through his wardrobe, each brocade tunic or silk shirt feeling cheap beneath his fingers. Any rustic would kill for even one of his embroidered vests, yet he found no joy in it.

How could he have mortal comforts, if he himself were not mortal? Alex longed for human touch, for the feel of Cara beneath him, her earthy smell overpowering him, no thoughts in his head but her and her alone. He had made love to many women in his time, but all were empty, devoid of real connection. *I had hoped that, since we were so similar...*But he had no one to blame but himself. *If only I had been honest with*

Cara...perhaps she would have seen past my condition.

There was a chance for a cure. An ancient manuscript, one of many taken by Mavian, had hinted at it. It spoke of *fampir* who traveled to far-off places and returned as mere men. Alex could become mortal again, he knew it deep in his tarnished soul. *And if I am mortal, then she may love me.*

Alex had no desire to set foot in his rooms ever again. He wavered a bit at the stairs, then decided to go up. Druam deserved a goodbye. *After all, he never had the chance with Verdon.*

Despite the early hour, Druam was awake. He still wore the battle-stained clothes from that night. When Alex entered, he gave a small, sad smile. "Xandro. I'm so glad to see you recovered. Have you drank enough to heal the wound?"

Alex shook his head. "I'm not going to drink, now or ever again. Let the wound fester and bite at me; I've had enough."

"What do you mean?" Druam's body tensed, his lips narrowing. "Why are you dressed for the road? Xandro, you will become a husk in a year, maybe less, with no blood. Why do this to yourself?"

"Because Cara knows me for what I am," Alex said bitterly.

"She would have found out sooner or later," Druam said gently. "Give her time; she'll realize that we are her kin."

"You don't know her like I do. She only sees us as evil."

"Then we must teach her otherwise."

Alex clenched his jaw. "She's not one of your gullible nobles; she's intelligent and resourceful, and..." He trailed off, his throat tightening.

For a moment, Druam was silent. Then, he said, "You really do care for her. So why would you leave? Surely you can speak with her–"

"There might be a cure," Alex said.

"What?"

"A cure. A way to stop being *fampir* and start living again. As men. You didn't see Cara's face, Druam. You didn't hear her words when she saw me for this...this monster!"

"So you'd let this woman drive you away from your home?" Pain filled Druam's eyes. "I've already lost Verdon. I can't lose you, too."

"What if Gwen were to scream at the sight of you? If she were to look at you with utter horror?" It was the cruelest thing Alex could have said. For a long time neither spoke.

"You were a bastard," Druam murmured, "and I offered you the Strilu heritage. I adopted you as my own brother. Do you forget so easily the bond that we have fastened together?"

"You will always be my brother, as will Verdon," Alex said softly. "I am going to become a man again. You do what you please. But I am leaving."

Druam's head fell into his hands. When he raised it, his expression was carefully blank. "I wish you had vanished and Verdon remained with me. My true brother would never abandon me."

If a *fampir* could cry, Alexandro would have felt salty tears trickle down his cheeks and drip to the floor as he fled from the palace. But *fampir* cannot cry. They are not as mortal men.

Epilogue

The Dead Man

THE DARKNESS terrified the dead man.

There were different darknesses, he knew. There was the darkness of night, when cool shadows enveloped the earth and the stars and moon gave a surreal brightness. Even when the stars were hidden behind steely clouds there was a normalcy to night's blackness. It was the same everywhere in the eight corners of Earda, an enveloping blanket that hides the earth from the gods' searing eyes. There was mystery and terror and a fear of the supernatural in the deepest dark of dawn, but that could be beaten back with torches and stories and the comfort of family.

This was not the darkness of a cave deep in the mountains, for that was rich and earthy, with embracing stone walls all around. No, for this darkness did not have the solid, unmoving air and musty smell, the sounds of hidden streams and echoing creatures that scorned light. The cave's darkness had a floor underneath and a ceiling above. The black of dark caves was a tangible feeling, of strength for some and fear for others, but it was there nonetheless.

This darkness was not even the darkness behind closed eyes. There was familiarity and thought to fill the blindness when eyes are closed, with spots of light flickering on the eyelids. Blindness could be overcome with touch and hearing, but this darkness was not blindness.

It was a truly terrifying darkness.

He could not move his hands in it, he could not even feel his fingers or his sweaty palm anymore. He knew they were there, for they had been there when he had fallen. At least, he thought they had been. Now he was not even sure if his waking life was a dream and this was the horrible reality.

He tried to recall where he was. He last remembered being outdoors, but the location eluded him. An even more worrying thought came to him: who was he?

Try as he might, he could not remember his name. It was right there, just beyond the darkness, but so elusive. Every time he felt the familiar words forming, they slipped away, wriggling like a rock eel out of his grasp. He wanted nothing more than to be wrapped again in his name.

The darkness toyed with him. He couldn't move, it controlled his thoughts, it was everywhere. When he opened his eyes there was nothing; it was worse when he shut them. The darkness allowed him – no – encouraged him to imagine horrible things behind his closed eyes, to see the horrors out of sight but not out of reach, tickling his spine and driving spikes of pain and fear into his naked flesh.

The dead man opened his mouth to scream.

"Hush, now. Everything's well." A soothing voice came from somewhere nearby. A warm light interrupted the black, growing and growing, until finally all the world was glowing golden light.

In the light, there was a figure, sitting down cross-legged. It gestured to the dead man. As he joined the figure, the dead man looked at his own arms and legs. He was naked as a newborn babe, his skin fresh and unmarked. He looked at his hands, two whole hands, pinkies and all.

The dead man found his voice at last. "I thought...I thought I had lost my fingers."

"You had, while you were living," the figure replied. He was a young man with dark hair and olive skin. He had a pointed face, but his eyes were cloudy and empty: blind. He continued, "You are in Autorus' domain, in the place meant for those who have done evil to repent before they can move on to Lyael. Do you remember your name?"

"It's..." The dead man tried to recall. He had had a name, he was sure of it. "Do you know it?"

"You were Jagger Cross," said the blind man. "An agent of Fauste's Shiv. You had a wife named Raven. She died before you did."

"Raven. I remember her." The memories came back, as vivid as the day he'd lived them. "She had beautiful hair and the sweetest smile. I loved her. I died for her. Is she here, too?"

"I'm afraid not. She has already moved on to Lyael, where not even Autorus can reach her. She has gone to the beyond, to the final death.

You cannot reach her, nor will you be able to for quite some time."

"I don't understand. We're both dead, why can't I see her?"

"She's in Lyael. You are not...you are in purgatory. You must earn your way to Lyael if you wish to see her again." The blind man paused, then patted Jagger's hand. "You could remain in purgatory, in this blackness. Or, you could come with me."

"Where would you take me?"

"Back to Earda. As my servant, you may earn back Autorus' favor – and the chance to gain Lyael – by doing good. There are always consequences to such resurrections, but they would be negligible. Loss of hearing, perhaps, or the inability to walk."

"How do you possess such power?"

The blind man smiled. "This, I do not know. I have worked all my life to find where I am most needed, and, apparently, the dead require my services more than the living. Now, you must decide. Shall you remain, or shall you return?"

Jagger Cross looked at his unmarred skin, his perfectly whole fingers, and then back to the blind man. "Will it hurt?"

"The journey from life to death, no matter which way you go, is always difficult."

"Good. It wouldn't be right otherwise."

The blind man's smile widened, and he held out his hand. Jagger took it and closed his eyes. *I'll find a way to you, Raven,* he promised. *I'll be with you again.*

Coming Soon

The stories of Cara, Gwen, Seanna, and Sandu will continue in:

The Fading Glow

Sovereigns of the Dead: Book Two

Join the monthly newsletter list for sneak peeks, extra scenes, and much more, at vistamcdowall.com.

Glossary

Places:

Con Salur - a cliff city home to King Henrik

D'Clet - a mountain city overseen by Earl Hjalder

Dedaria - an elven kingdom of D'Ehsen, ruled by *Kair* Aremo

D'Ehsen - the large island and surrounding isles on which multiple kingdoms are found

Demarren - a kingdom of D'Ehsen, ruled by Liegelord Wullum

Dotschar - the largest kingdom of D'Ehsen, ruled by King Henrik

Eadrion Empire - a large empire to the west which rules a small portion of D'Ehsen

Mott - a town which is home to the only university in Dotschar

Novum - a temple of worship for Dotschar's main religion. Typically has nine sides for the nine gods.

Rengu - an elven kingdom of D'Ehsen, ruled by *Ameer* Voclain

Riverfen - a coastal city overseen by Earl Seastone

Skålland - a kingdom of D'Ehsen ruled by a chieftain

Units of Time:

Candle - roughly equivalent to an hour

Quinn - five days

Deshe - ten days

Creatures:

Fampir - an undead which used to be a human or elf, and can disguise itself as a mortal

Mist-folk - swamp-dwelling creatures which lure their prey into the marshes

Prowler - an undead which used to be a human or elf, but is now feral and predatory

Sulpari - a woman with a *fampir* father and mortal mother

Positions:

Ameer - the Rengu (elven) word for prince; their equivalent of a king

Clothman - a low-level cleric of the Dotsch religion; usually practices in small novels

Curate - a mid-level cleric of the Dotsch religion; trained in healing, and employed in manors,   palaces, and large novums

Exalt - the highest position in the Dotsch religion, either chosen by his predecessor or voted in by his   fellow predicants

Kair - the Dedarian (elven) word for prince; their equivalent of a king

Liegelord - the sovereign ruler of Demarren

Predicant - the second-highest position in the Dotsch religion, there are three predicants for each of the four earls.

Acknowledgements

Mom, Dad, Michael, and Brandon, who would tell me they love it no matter what – thank you for always being there for me.

Wayne, Beth, and Kendra, whose brutal honesty led to many, many rewrites – thank you for pointing out all my "Disney men" and telling me how annoying you found Gwen.

Janet, Lauren, Ralph, Apryl, Bruce, and Wendy, who helped me polish up early chapters – thank you.

Rodney, for creating my beautiful map and bringing it to life – thank you.

Ysabelle and Forest, who helped me believe that strangers may enjoy this – thank you.

All my readers: May you have enjoyed this journey as much as I have. I hope you'll join me for the next one. Thank you.

About the Author

Vista McDowall lives and works in the rural mountains of Colorado, where she imagines great quests over the snow-covered peaks. She also teaches young adults the love of literature and writing, and hopes that they, too, find solace in fantastical places and magical beings.

She can be found on Facebook, Twitter, and Instagram. Her website is vistamcdowall.com.

www.ingramcontent.com/pod-product-compliance
Lightning Source LLC
Chambersburg PA
CBHW021119260626
47169CB00005B/1355